International number one bestselling author Melissa Hill lives in Dublin. Her page-turning contemporary stories are published worldwide, translated into twenty-five different languages and are regular chart-toppers in Ireland and abroad. One of her novels is currently in development with a major Hollywood studio.

Visit Melissa at www.melissahill.ie or find her on facebook at MelissaHillBooks and on Twitter @melissahillbks

THE HOTEL ON MULBERRY BAY

Melissa Hill

**SIMON &
SCHUSTER**

London · New York · Sydney · Toronto · New Delhi

A CBS COMPANY

First published in Great Britain by Simon & Schuster UK Ltd, 2015
A CBS COMPANY

1 3 5 7 9 10 8 6 4 2

Simon & Schuster UK Ltd
1st Floor
222 Gray's Inn Road
London WC1X 8HB

www.simonandschuster.co.uk

Simon & Schuster Australia, Sydney
Simon & Schuster India, New Delhi

A CIP catalogue record for this book
is available from the British Library

Trade Paperback ISBN: 978-1-47112-770-0
B Format Paperback ISBN: 978-1-47112-771-7
A Format Paperback: 978-1-47114-304-5
eBook ISBN: 978-1-47112-772-4

Typeset by M Rules
Printed and bound by CPI Group (UK) Ltd, Croydon, CR0 4YY

To my lovely Carrie

Prologue

'Penny, hurry up, you're going to miss it!' Elle Harte called out excitedly as she sprinted barefoot down the beach, her auburn hair swirling around her face in the breeze. Golden sand and ochre pebbles snaked alongside the deep blue of the Irish sea, little shaving foam breakers dimpling the surface.

Her ten-year-old sister; her junior by two years, strained to keep up. Penny's shorter legs weren't as fast and she was getting winded; Elle had always been much more athletic. Cool sand squished between her toes and she pumped her arms furiously, pushing herself to go faster. She didn't want to miss the ship before it headed down the coast.

'Elle stop, *please*,' Penny called out.

But Elle pushed on for another fifty yards until she stopped abruptly on the strand, one arm extended out

1

towards the horizon, the other shading her eyes. 'Look at that, it's just like the pirate ship in *The Goonies*,' she called back, referring to the swashbuckling adventure movie that they both loved.

A moment later, Penny finally caught up with her. She pushed her wispy fair hair out of her eyes and clasped a hand on her hip, working to knead a stitch out of her side from the exertion. 'Did we really have to run like that? I think I stepped on a jellyfish or something,' she complained, but Elle didn't answer. She was entranced by the sight unfolding in front of her.

Penny followed her sister's gaze towards the open water where an eighteenth century English Tall Ship, complete with three tall masts and billowing sails, was leisurely making its way south off the Wexford coast. The ship, a true original that had been saved, preserved and recently unveiled to the Irish public, had made a temporary home for itself in the water at their hometown Mulberry Bay, just down the beach from where Elle and Penny's family ran the local hotel.

Perched high on a hill above a sweeping bay, and overlooking the pretty little seaside town with a huge sugarloaf mountain as backdrop, the Bay Hotel's coastal location and seafront bedrooms were a perfect haven for tourists. For generations the popular hotel had housed visitors from all over the world, as well as weathered some of the worst of the storms the South East coast had seen.

Some of Elle's favourite memories growing up there were of dramatic lightning strikes at sea, while she, her family and entranced guests watched from the windows. She knew that the tourists took memories like that home with them, to be taken out and relived when life got too overwhelming.

The hotel was located just a short walk up the coast road from the centre of Mulberry Bay.

There was just one main street in the little coastal town, which led directly to the sandy beach. The street was cobbled with red sandstone and no cars were allowed to drive through, the space being reserved for walking and simply enjoying the pretty little shops and eateries. The lamp posts were old wrought iron style, brightly coloured flower pots hanging from them, in keeping with the town's tourist heritage status.

Elle knew all the shops in the main street: artisan bakeries boasting homemade bread, charming organic produce shops, little boutiques and craft stores with candles and jewellery made to order: tourist mementoes of time spent at the picturesque seaside town.

The local businesspeople were intensely proud of their produce and the homegrown/handcrafted nature of their wares. Elle loved walking on Main Street in the height of summer; eating ice-cream from Scoops, smells of baking from The Grain Store Bakery, fresh fruit from SunBurst Organics and ground coffee from Pebbles Café mingling in the bright air as tourists wandered down to the beach with buckets and spades and brightly coloured towels and inflatables.

In the winter, it was much quieter and considerably greyer in the absence of bright blue skies and the kaleidoscope of beach accoutrements, and populated solely by locals. The only thing she didn't like about Mulberry Bay was its size and the fact that you tended to meet just about everybody you had ever known.

The entire community had been buzzing about the tall ship for the past few days. Elle had already seen the vessel twice, and had used the fact that her sister had yet to see it as an excuse to get out of their hotel duties early and head down to the beach to watch it leave.

It was coming to the end of the heavy tourist season, and the Bay Hotel had held one of its famed ballroom dancing nights the evening before. Elle and Penny had been in the thick of the organising for days leading up to it. There was always so much to do at the hotel, but even more for any event in the ballroom; polishing the dance floor to a high shine, dusting the enormous glass chandelier, ironing the crisp white table linen, and arranging fresh flowers from the garden in the alcoves, and at reception. As well as a host of other boringly mundane tasks like replacing burnt-down candles in the candelabra, polishing the glassware, and tidying any rogue family-related paraphernalia away from the entrance or common areas.

Still, despite the annoying chores their mother, Anna, set them, Elle had to admit that there was a great buzz and energy about the hotel in the lead up to such an event, and indeed at the event itself. Her mother was in her element with all the preparations, though Elle couldn't understand all the fuss about the drinks or the food when ultimately people were coming to dance, and generally tried to hide out in the gardens with her dad, who she knew felt the same way. But inevitably Anna roped them all into participating, like it or not. And despite herself, Elle did enjoy the excitement and the fact that the bigger events always seemed to put a twinkle in her ever-busy mother's eye and an extra bounce in her step.

Elle and Penny weren't allowed to attend on the big night of course, but they routinely sat on the stairs and peeped out at the guests' arrival at reception below. Women in bright red lipstick and glittering jewellery, looking like peacocks in glorious dresses and shoes that exuded pure sophistication like those women in *Dynasty*, accompanied by handsome men in smart suits that on closer inspection were usually many of the locals surprisingly scrubbed up for the night.

Once the dancing got underway, the ballroom itself was a riot of colour and music, as the band – a group of part-time musicians from the town – played waltzes and lively jives well into the night.

Penny, who like her mother adored a celebration, had as a four-year old, nicknamed these events 'sparkle nights', and the name still stuck. Elle agreed that yes their hotel could indeed throw a sparkling party, but Mulberry Bay was just a small town, a tiny community, really. Imagine the likes of such an event in Wexford, or in Dublin even? She could only guess at how sophisticated a party – a *proper* event – in a big city would be, but one day she was determined to find out.

'Isn't it amazing?' breathed Elle now, as she watched the boat sail away, fascination thick in her voice.

Penny looked out toward the horizon and shrugged. 'It's just a big boat.'

Elle turned to her little sister, a look of amazement on her face. 'It isn't just a *big* boat, Penny. It's amazing. It's like a living thing. Can you imagine the places it's gone? The people who have sailed on it, the adventures it's been in?' She wrapped her arms around herself and proceeded to rub her elbows, warding off goose bumps. 'It just screams excitement.'

Penny considered her sister's words and turned around, squinting as the setting sun hit her in the face. She shrugged again. 'Like I said, it's just a boat.'

'I can't believe we're sisters. Where's your sense of adventure? You're just like Mum and Dad. Sometimes I wonder if I'm adopted,' Elle tisked. Not waiting for a response, she continued. 'Oh, I wish I was on that boat. I'm destined to see the world. To live a big adventurous life. To get out of *here*.'

Penny cocked her head, seemingly confused. 'What's wrong with here?' she enquired, genuinely curious.

This time Elle was the one who shrugged. 'It's fine I suppose. It's just ... I don't know. It's so *small*, isn't it? Like everyone who lives here has been here forever. It's as if none of them know that there is this big, huge world out there. Or if they do, they don't care. I just know that *I'm* not meant for this place. And as soon as I can, I'm leaving Mulberry Bay, you know.'

Penny's mouth dropped open, and she stared at her sister, shocked. 'You mean you're going to run away?'

Elle laughed. 'Don't be such a baby. No, I'm not going to run away. But when I'm seventeen, and finish school, I'm definitely leaving. Only five more years. And then I can go to college, somewhere that isn't here, somewhere glamorous and sophisticated and exciting.'

Her younger sister pondered this new information and sat quiet for a moment, as if trying to picture a world where Elle couldn't be found a couple of doors down the hallway from her own bedroom. 'Do you mean like Dublin?'

Elle looked out toward the horizon, where the ship was fading into the distance, going on to places and ports unknown.

'Maybe even further than Dublin,' she said wistfully.

Penny processed this and bit her lip, as if willing herself not to become upset by her beloved big sister's impending departure.

Noticing the silence, Elle smiled and placed an arm around her shoulder.

'Hey kid, don't worry,' she said (Elle always felt very grown-up and worldly when she referred to Penny as 'kid'), 'I'm not going anywhere yet. Besides, you might want to ski-daddle one of these days, too.'

But Penny was already shaking her head adamantly. 'No, I never want to leave Mum and Dad or the hotel. I love it here. Mulberry Bay is my home.'

Elle repressed the urge to roll her eyes – her mother was always telling her that it wasn't polite. 'All teenagers do it in the movies, Mum, it's what you are supposed to do. I'm simply expressing myself,' she had argued.

'I don't care if Molly Ringwald walks around with her eyes constantly in the top of her skull. It's not nice to have a perpetual look of disdain on your face,' scolded her mother, ending the discussion. Elle had rolled her eyes but Anna didn't catch it as she had been walking away.

'Well, OK,' Elle said, making an effort not to belittle her younger sister's (misguided) intentions to remain in their hometown forever. 'You can just come and visit me then. Wherever I'm living. In Dublin or London with my gorgeously handsome and insanely successful husband.'

Penny's eyes were as big as saucers. 'But where will you live? And where will you meet your husband?' she asked, wonder in her voice, as if Elle's words were law and the future was certain.

Her sister smiled and said flippantly, 'Who knows? I bet I'll meet him in college – and we will form a big company together, and make crazy money. And then we can live wherever it suits us. London. New York. Paris. Tokyo even. What with me being a high-powered career woman with a big business we might just live in multiple places. We'll … ah, split our time.' Elle hoped that she was using that phrase correctly – she had caught one of the characters from *Dallas* saying it on television the other night and thought it sounded very cool.

'But you'll come back here to visit won't you?' asked Penny. 'What about Mum and Dad? And me? We'll really miss you,' she added tentatively. 'The hotel will miss you.'

'Ha.' Elle laughed. Whatever about her family, she *definitely* wasn't going to miss the hotel and that endless parade of annoying visitors, ongoing chores and constant entreaties from their Mum to 'behave'. 'Well, of course I'll come to visit now and then.' She wasn't going to admit it, but she was pretty sure that regardless of where she was living or how rich, successful and worldly she might be, she would of course miss her family too. 'Or whenever you need me.'

'Promise?' questioned Penny, holding out her small finger.

'Promise,' Elle agreed, entwining it with her own, and the Harte sisters completed their usual ritual, forever sealing the vow.

Chapter 1

The Bay Hotel always seemed to mirror the mood of those who stayed there, temporarily or permanently, Penny mused.

For decades, its walls had been witness to some of the town's most memorable parties and occasions. In its prime, women in glistening dresses had made their way up its grand limestone front steps, show bands had shaken the ballroom walls with lively music, couples whirling in a kaleidoscope of colour on the dance floor below the stage.

Of course it had hosted quieter moments, too. The tea rooms overlooking the often turbulent Irish sea provided a dramatic outlook which contrasted with the interior's delicate Victorian décor. The cream lace tablecloths, dainty silver cake forks, eggshell tea cups and delicious morsels served there, all seemed to encourage words of affection and compassion, and that room had seen multiple proposals and romantic celebrations. Hands young and old joined over its tables, first and last birthdays were held there, and all were remembered.

Yes, any occasion in Mulberry Bay was deemed almost more special, more magical, for having been held at the Bay Hotel. It was as if there was a feeling about the hotel, an alchemy that had nothing to do with the supernatural; so much joy and so many memories had seeped into its walls over the years, adding to its allure.

Today though, the hotel was quiet, the sounds of normal routine muffled, as though a shroud had been laid over the whole building. Guests moved hesitantly about almost on tiptoe, and even those who hadn't known Anna Harte, or had only met her once, felt an unaccountable sense of nostalgia, of missing something they didn't quite know how to describe.

Penny could have told them what it was: if the hotel was the heart of Mulberry Bay, Anna had been its welcoming, wide-stretched arms.

She was in one of the back rooms of the property that served as the family quarters, looking out over the hotel's large gardens, still numbed by what had happened in the early hours of that morning.

Her beloved mother was gone. In the middle of the night, Anna had awoken with chest pains and collapsed. She had died before the ambulance arrived to take her to the hospital.

She didn't know where her father had got to. Following the shock of Anna's utterly unexpected collapse, Ned Harte had barely been sighted. He had been with Anna when she died, and all he'd said to Penny about it afterwards was: 'It was like she'd been hit by a bullet.' Penny winced at the description, though it detailed pretty much how she felt right then, as though she too had been shot through the heart, but by some cruel fate had gone on living. She suspected her dad felt exactly the same, but there was no point in asking, because Ned would never in a million years reveal anything of such a personal nature.

Penny guessed he was taking long walks on the beach, avoiding the well-meaning sympathies of the locals. And avoiding her. She knew that keeping his feelings to himself, locked away, until he hit on a phrase or a line from a song to express them was just Ned's way, but at a time like this she wished that there was some way they could comfort one another. She often wondered if Ned was quiet because he was afraid of saying too much, letting out some feeling that once spoken, could not be drawn back in. Her mother was the only one who seemed to instinctively know how to handle him, how to reach him, and now with Anna gone, Penny would be at more of a loss than ever. It was almost like losing both parents at once.

She was going through her mother's things in their bedroom, trying to obscure – for her father's sake – all immediate signs of his wife that would make the pain of her recent death all the more vivid: the half-read biography of Katharine Hepburn on the bedside table, the lemon lozenges she liked to chew in bed, the little scraps of notes Anna wrote to herself all day long and then promptly forgot about.

It was these intimate things she wanted to clear away, so her dad didn't have to feel like his wife was about to walk through the door again any moment. The rest – her mum's clothes, her make-up, her jewellery – that could all wait until Elle came home.

There would be the funeral to get through first, of course: sharing memories with all those in the community who knew Anna, and finding that all of them remembered her a little bit differently.

But then Ned, Elle and Penny would return to the hotel, which in some strange way would also be grieving Anna's loss. It might limp along without her for a few weeks, but there was no denying that she had truly been the soul of the place. If people came for the beautiful views and the faded splendour of the rooms, soaked in history, they also came for Anna and her slightly off-kilter sense of humour, her way of knowing what you wanted, what you *really* wanted, without having to ask for it.

Her mother had known people, understood that most of the time they simply wanted a little bit of a reprieve from their day-to-day lives. She strove to give them a break, to make them feel as though they'd almost gone back in time. The hotel was a beautiful stage, and Anna was the director, working to pull the whole experience together. People came for her famous roast chicken, her delicious old-style fairy cakes, the icing that dissolved on the tongue … They came for the fifty-three varieties of tea, traditional and exotic, and for her ready smile and easy chat over breakfast. When they came to the Bay Hotel, they were coming because of Anna, even if they didn't know it.

Of course, over the years, as these things go, local trade had dwindled, and more and more of those born in the little beach town had moved away to bigger Irish towns or cities. They said (much like her own sister had) things like: 'It's a great place to grow up in, but it's so small – there's no opportunity.'

And as tourist numbers to the town had also begun to falter, there was less money for the upkeep of the hotel. It was still beautiful, no doubt about it, but more like a memory of beauty at this point. Penny had heard more than one guest say: 'Oh, imagine what it must have been like in its heyday.' She knew that it was her mother's dearest wish to see the building restored to its old glory, but there was never enough money.

She couldn't imagine that Ned would have the heart or indeed the wherewithal for anything with Anna gone. Penny pushed the thought of the fate of the hotel out of her mind. It would have to wait. She couldn't deal with any of that just now; and it was something she and Elle would need to talk about together when the time was right.

Elle. She felt heart-sick at the thought of her sister. As bad as Penny was feeling, at least she still lived in Mulberry Bay and was just down the road when all of this happened. She helped out at the hotel and saw Anna every day, had only spoken to her mother yesterday, their last conversation a stupid and meaningless discussion about a linen change in the guest rooms.

But how must her sister feel right now, being away in London? She adored her mother more than anyone else in the world, Penny knew that. Elle was a very strong, stable person, and most of the time went around wearing armour, but Anna was the chink in that armour. Last night on the phone, Penny could only hear her sister's ragged breathing, the sound of something dropping as she broke the news. Elle had said: 'I'll get the next flight home.' And then nothing. She had hung up, and Penny hadn't had time to talk to her about anything more.

Elle had been one of those who moved away from Mulberry Bay. In fact, she'd seemed desperate to escape.

Penny was happy to stay behind, helping her parents out with the hotel, and working part time at the local tourist office, while Elle had gone for grand adventures in countries all over the world, testing her limits with bungee-jumping, trekking through jungles, eating wild locusts. Then she had become an architect, the hard edges of the buildings she designed seeming to match the edges of Elle herself. She had come home now and again for visits and holidays, treating the town she grew up in almost like a tourist would: admiring its beauty and the more relaxed pace of life, but in the end itching to get back to the city and her work there.

Last time she had visited, almost a year ago, Penny had enquired if there was anyone special in London.

'I don't have time for love,' her sister had replied easily.

'Don't you get lonely, though?'

She had seen Elle's green eyes flicker for a second, but then she shrugged. 'I don't really have time to be lonely either,' and that had been the end of it. Elle could shut a conversation off rather like closing a door; in that way she was more like Ned than she suspected. Perhaps for that reason alone, their father's withdrawn and sometimes aloof mannerisms never seemed to bother Elle in the slightest, whereas Penny would drive herself crazy trying to get her head around it, wondering why he always seemed so disconnected and distant. Although in truth, Ned always seemed to brighten when Elle was around; it was just Penny he seemed to stare straight through.

Her sister was due to arrive later this morning. But now with Anna gone and the family dynamic so utterly changed forever, Penny wondered how the Harte family would get through the next few days together.

Chapter 2

Elle was in shock. She knew it was true, but she refused to really believe it. She refused to really believe anything that had happened in the last twenty-four hours. Her sister *hadn't* rung her in the early hours of this morning to tell her that their mother had collapsed of a heart attack, she *hadn't* packed a suitcase of probably unsuitable clothes and booked a flight back to Dublin, she *hadn't* taken a sleeping pill to get through the flight, and she certainly *wasn't* in Dublin airport waiting in line for a taxi to take her home to Wexford.

If she wanted to wake up, if she wanted a dose of reality, all she had to do was look at her surroundings. There was a man in the queue behind her in a suit that smelt as though he'd been wearing it for days, in front of her a child held in its mother's arms was steadfastly picking his nose and rolling the results between his fingers. She'd seen dedicated draughtsmen work with less concentration. Elle stood straighter in line and told herself to face reality. This was happening, wasn't it? She took one deep breath after another and with each exhalation the news seemed to settle like dust over her heart. She was going home. For her mother's funeral. Her father, as usual, would be quiet and emotionally out of reach, and her sister would be still resentful of Elle for leaving, though pretending not to be.

Try as she might, Elle knew she would not be able to communicate honestly to either of them, especially without Anna's open and calming influence. Her mum could always make them all laugh when they were together at least. But Elle knew that the next week or so would be a mire of grief, things unsaid, memories left unshared, until she could go back to London and really let her feelings out in the privacy of her apartment.

It had easily been the worst week of her life. Barely a week before, Sebastian, her boyfriend of eighteen months, had told her that he was moving out, effectively calling time on their relationship.

'I'm tired of being second-best, Elle,' he'd told her wearily, after she'd yet again arrived home late to the Clapham flat they'd shared, after an exceptionally busy time at the office.

In truth, she wasn't sure how to feel about it. Sebastian was a musician and life with him had been fun at first, but lately he had become moody and demanding, expecting her to just leave everything at the drop of a hat to do things and go places with him. She guessed the writing had been on the wall for some time but she'd refused to see it, hadn't wanted to see it.

Sebastian wasn't the first guy to have given her such an ultimatum, but Elle didn't see why she had to be the one to compromise. She was who she was, take it or leave it. Though she did wish he was still around now to comfort her, help her through this unbearable grief.

She just had to get through this herself though, she knew. She just had to be strong.

Her bond with Anna had not been damaged by her moving away. Her mum understood her, just as she understood everyone, and knew that Elle had something to prove, if only to herself. She knew that her daughter hadn't disliked Mulberry Bay and its tiny charms, or that she hadn't resented the hotel, only that if she stayed, how would she ever truly know what she was capable of?

Anna understood this about her eldest as surely as she knew that her youngest would stay behind in the town, close to her parents and live as gently and unsurprisingly as she could. Penny was soft through and through, as light as a cloud, but Elle glinted like metal with concentration and purpose.

And that was how she'd lived her life: purposefully. She'd wanted adventure; she'd got it. She'd wanted a career, and now some of the buildings she'd designed might be famous one day. Elle didn't know how she'd get through her days in London now without Anna's regular emails, her little jokes about the townspeople and her gentle words of encouragement. She had always told herself she loved the city, loved its great bursts of energy, so many people struggling to fit into one small space all at once; the noise, the smells, the anonymity, but the truth was that sometimes she had to steel herself against it. Sometimes she longed for calm, and the only thing that could get her out the door was thinking of a message from Anna: '*So proud of my clever girl – go and build me a castle.*' She seemed to think Elle and Penny had each hung the moon, despite how different they both were.

She tried to remember the last conversation she'd had with her mother. They'd talked about all the usual things, laughed over some misunderstanding Anna had had with Ned. He'd spoken too quietly when he told her what he wanted for his dinner: she'd made him a cake, when he'd asked for hake.

'Oh, I knew what he wanted,' her mother had admitted mischievously. 'I always know what he wants. But I just thought it would teach him to speak up a bit. I think he enjoyed the cake.'

An avid music fan, Ned Harte was a deep thinker, and oftentimes silent above all else. An engineer by profession, but long retired, her father had always been cerebral, reserved, and analytical. Ultimately, he was the complete opposite of his buoyant, cheery wife who chatted happily with hotel guests, bubbled over in enthusiasm for making everyone comfortable at all times, and was always keen to know the life story of everyone who walked through the front doors.

Ned, however, had always appeared detached from the operations, despite it being the only source of income for his family. Elle wondered now what would happen to the place, which doubled as the family home and as Penny's place of work.

Penny and Ned both worked at the hotel, but it had always been Anna's passion. Her dad and sister had operated largely in the background, while it was her mum who'd kept on top of the day-to-day running of the place as well as the business side, keeping accounts, paying taxes etc. For as long as Elle could remember, her father's passion was his beloved Beatles music, not the The Bay Hotel, and with her mother gone, she wondered what exactly would happen next with her family's home and long-standing business.

Thinking again of that story about the cake, she certainly knew that there would be no such carefree joy in her family again.

Not without Anna.

As she moved to the front of the line, Elle put a fist up against her mouth, trying to stifle a sob, and push away the grief that was building afresh.

On approach from this vantage, Elle thought, as the taxi snaked its way along the coast road through Mulberry Bay and up the hill towards her childhood home, the hotel always suggested the splendour it once had been.

There was no sign of any obvious wear and tear: you couldn't see the paint peeling in flakes from the exterior window frames, the worn carpets at reception, the scuffed ballroom floor, or the hopelessly outdated wallpaper. You definitely couldn't see that the ballroom chandelier was lightly coated with dust, missing small jewels, or that the staircase creaked unmercifully when you took the wrong step.

Elle recognised that the 1800s architecture of the building was completely outdated, and guessed that her colleagues in London would no doubt chuckle at the high ceilings lined with dark wood, the large imposing doorways, and the turreted ceiling of the bar's sitting room, which she had so loved as a child. How glamorous, she had thought then, and although she knew she should dismiss it, the hotel hung off her heart like a fishhook, pulling painfully when she least wanted it to.

Her taxi pulled up to the entrance, and here was the moment she'd been dreading. She stepped onto the gravel and saw her sister waiting for her in the doorway. Penny came towards her, arms outstretched and Elle could tell that she was already crying. It struck her suddenly how much like their mother her sister was: slightly plump, blonde, easy in her body.

It was only when she saw Penny coming towards her that Elle finally broke down, letting out all the feeling that had built up over eight hours and six hundred kilometres.

Chapter 3

A few days later, for the first time in an age, the hotel was full of people, all talking and laughing with the kind of relief that comes after intense periods of feeling. It had seemed fitting to Elle and Penny that Anna's final farewell should be held here, after the church burial service.

The whole Mulberry Bay community had turned out, and they were moving in small, dark swathed circles, catching up on old times. It seemed to Elle almost like a duller reproduction of older celebrations the hotel had seen over the years.

She was glad to finally have a moment where she didn't need to keep bravely smiling and nodding as people gave their sympathies. Since coming home, she hadn't fallen apart again, and she had kept her composure through the hardest parts of the funeral arrangements and service. Her father, though, had showed surprising emotion (for him) when she arrived, and not for the first time she worried about how he would realistically cope once all of this was over and normal life, as such, resumed. She'd spoken a little to him about what had happened that first night of her arrival, when Penny had returned home to her little cottage in the town.

'I hate to ask, but what exactly happened?' she'd ventured. 'Mum was in good health – or so I thought. A heart attack seems a bit out of the blue.'

As always, Ned averted his eyes from his daughter's gaze. 'She was healthy enough as far as I know. There were little things of course. There always are as you get older. Just part of life.'

Elle narrowed her eyes as her father stopped talking. 'I'm sensing a *but* …'

'Well, yes. Your mother was dealing with some … anxiety.'

'Anxiety?' Elle frowned. She couldn't imagine Anna as an anxious, stressed person. These things were more Penny's domain. 'About what? What was she stressed about? Anxious about?'

'There were some money problems,' Ned said frankly without elaborating.

'With the hotel?' Elle hated to sound like she was pressing, but that was the way you had to be with Ned, and she needed some answers. And it seemed as if the state of the property was the big elephant in the room since her return. She'd noticed some things on arrival about the interior, over and above the usual wear and tear. The reception area was looking very tired – the wooden floors hadn't been polished in ages and really needed to be refinished, the moulding around the door frames was cracked in places, and the staircase leading to the second floor was sagging.

She'd noticed in particular the tea rooms, a once beautiful space that Elle and Penny had spent so much time in as children, having tea parties and acting out scenes from *Anne of Green Gables* – Penny had been Diana to her Anne of course. Now, the pale mint wallpaper was peeling from the walls, the fireplace lay dark and dusty, and all of the furniture looked worn and tatty. It was no longer the cosy inviting space that Elle had once known.

Ned shrugged; it was neither a yes nor a no. Elle could feel her frustration building. As an architect, she liked it when she had all of the information she needed in order to form an opinion, or a design strategy. She hated it when clients were evasive, especially when she was looking to help them and keep their best interests at heart.

As devastated as she felt over the death of her wonderful mother, the discovery that their family home and Anna's great passion seemed to also be suffering a horrible and painful death by deterioration, troubled Elle. And another part of her – the high performing business woman in her – wanted to know exactly why that was the case. And worse, if this 'stress' had contributed to her mother's demise.

She could see Ned now, sitting at a table nodding dumbly as the Italian owner of the fish and chip shop in town spoke to him. Fondly nicknamed 'Johnny Chips' by everyone in Mulberry Bay for as long as Elle could remember, she wasn't even sure what the man's real name was. His younger brother Luca, who ran the Bay's ice-cream parlour Scoops, had, fortunately for him, managed to keep his given Italian name.

Penny came up beside her. 'I can't wait for today to be over,' she sighed.

'Me neither,' Elle replied. 'It doesn't seem real. I feel like it's going to take so long to sink in. I keep thinking, Oh, I must tell Mum about this ... or she'd really enjoy hearing that.'

'I know ...' Penny's voice broke and she looked like she might cry again. 'She did love a big party though. It's the biggest crowd this place has seen in years.'

Elle bit her lip. It wasn't exactly the time or the place but she felt she needed to ask, if for no other reason than to keep her sister from breaking down again. 'Do you know anything?' she asked, indicating the tea room's worn wallpaper, 'about ... how this place is doing?'

Penny looked a bit taken aback. 'Not much about the financial stuff to be honest. We weren't doing well though, anyone can see that. The upkeep alone was crippling, and the dogs on the street know the place needs an overhaul.' She sniffed. 'Let's talk about all that later OK? Today is about Mum.'

She seemed annoyed and Elle felt duly chagrined for bringing the matter up but it was just how her brain worked, had always worked. In times of emotion, always try to look for equilibrium by seeking out the practical.

'Of course,' she said. 'It's just that so many people are

talking about Mum and the hotel, and what it means to them. All those life-defining moments, right here.' She shook her head. 'It's hard to believe it's not doing well.'

'Yes, this place – our home – means something to people,' Penny said proudly. 'It's beautiful and I know you might not think so, but it's also something even more than that. It represents something to this community, milestones in people's lives.'

'I do know that,' said Elle, annoyed at herself for raising hackles when it really wasn't her intention.

'Oh, there's Rob,' Penny said suddenly, perhaps to change the subject or just to needle her. She couldn't tell. Either way, simply the sound of the name had an unnerving effect. Even after all this time.

All those years ago she'd tearfully said goodbye to Rob Callahan at the bus stop outside Pebbles Café on Main Street, promising to return for good when she'd finished college in Dublin. But she hadn't. She'd written him a letter instead, begging him to leave and move to the city too.

But Rob wouldn't go. He had told Elle that he wouldn't be the same man if he left the small town where his heart and family belonged. And this sense of loyalty appeared to have worked for him, Elle realised, studying him now. He did look much the same man as he had all those years ago; broader across the shoulders, creased around the eyes, skin darkened from time spent outdoors, but the same Rob. Same dark twinkling eyes, same dimple on his left cheek. She wondered if her teenage self was also still visible, if despite the years he could look at her now and see the girl he had once loved.

Elle mentally slapped herself. It was the whole weight of the day making her think such maudlin thoughts. It had been a teenage fling: that was all. Rob Callahan probably had a wife now and a tribe of kids. She had stubbornly refused to ask after him after they broke up, and over the years had purposely tuned out if her mother ever mentioned him.

'He's coming over,' said Penny.

Elle flushed despite herself. 'Yes, I can see that, thank you.'

Rob didn't bother with platitudes, but moved in smoothly to kiss Elle's cheek. She got a second of his sharp, woody smell, before he stepped back and turned to Penny.

'Holding up?' he asked softly, squeezing her arm.

Her sister nodded wordlessly, overcome by fresh emotion.

'Your mother was a legend,' he said. 'My Friday nights won't be the same without her.'

'What Friday nights?' asked Elle, surprised.

'Oh, I always came up on a Friday night, for Anna's famous roast chicken and mash spuds. Kept up with all the news,' he added, and looked at Elle in a way that let her know that she had been part of this 'news' now and again.

'We've had some great times over dinner, haven't we?' whispered Penny, her eyes shining. 'I know Mum loved seeing you too, enjoyed you teasing her.'

Rob gave a wistful smile and as he and Penny continued to reminisce, Elle felt suddenly that she had missed out on something precious, something that wasn't replaceable. She felt bereft, at the whole day, but also at how everyone was treating her like a stranger, almost. At the graveyard, old school friends and past acquaintances had come up to give their condolences, and while they all hugged and exchanged memories with Penny, they simply nodded and formally shook hands with Elle, as if she was an outsider. Then again, she supposed she was.

'... repairs,' Penny was saying and Elle guessed she must be talking to Rob about something concerning the hotel. His family's construction business had been one of the reasons he'd decided to remain in town, and as far as she knew he was still in the same line of work. 'Would be great to get your opinion.'

'Don't worry about that, Penny,' a miffed Elle found herself saying, 'I know someone eminently qualified to drag this place into the right century.'

Though she'd intended for this to sound reassuring, she realised that it actually sounded patronising, and feeling again like a fish out of water, Elle turned and left Penny and Rob to their silly chat about times they'd had in this small little town, while she was off doing something that was actually important.

The next morning, Elle badly needed coffee. It was the only thing that would truly ready her for the trials of the day. She'd had a terrible sleep, kept awake by the creaks of the building and the old rickety bed, not to mention thoughts of what she'd said to Rob and Penny. She kept seeing her sister's crushed expression and Rob's coldly amused one as she'd tumbled into a dream-ridden, restless sleep.

Coffee was one of Elle's long-held grumbles about the hotel: there was no modern Italian coffee machine, just an old sputtering coffee urn on the end of the breakfast buffet table. What few guests there were today sat by the windows overlooking the sea, which the wind was whipping into a fury. Despite being springtime in Mulberry Bay, it definitely wasn't yet beach or swimming weather.

Elle despaired of the breakfast options, too. Good, hearty Irish fried fare of bacon, eggs and black pudding, fine in its own way, and locally sourced, but no vegetarian options, no dairy or gluten free, nothing at all for the health conscious.

Honestly, it was like perusing a menu from the seventies. An artefact. She slapped together a quick bacon sandwich and took it with her coffee outside, in spite of the threatening weather. She didn't want to sit in there like a guest. There was no sign of Penny or her father. She had barely seen Ned since the funeral. He was holing away somewhere, listening to his precious music, no doubt, and hiding from his feelings.

But Penny was outside, pinning sheets to the washing line that stretched along the residential side of the building, close to the family's quarters. Another sore point for Elle: Anna had insisted on line-drying laundry, where possible, to 'give it that sun-kissed, fresh smell'. All well and good, thought Elle, when there was actually sun. Not to mention the extra labour.

The sheets were blinding in the pre-storm glare and Penny

31

was struggling against the wind to hang them. Elle put her coffee down and went to help her.

'Sleep OK?' her sister asked.

'Not too well, actually. You know yourself.'

'Yes, I was up half the night too, worrying. Mostly about how I'd do the morning routine without Mum.'

'What about Linda and Clive?' Elle asked, referring to the long-time staff. 'Didn't they help?'

Penny looked at her strangely. 'We had to let them go a couple of years back, Elle. There's only really Molly left in the kitchen now, and only part-time. Dad does the gardens, when he remembers, and Mum did the cleaning, manned the bar, made the lunches and afternoon-teas, welcomed people at reception ... I actually don't know how she did it, when I list it out like that. Of course, I helped with all the behind the scenes stuff ... but I just don't have the same way with people that she had.'

Elle was too shocked to contradict her and make her feel better. 'But Mum never said, she never told me that things were that bad. So she was basically running this place single-handedly?'

Penny's cheeks reddened. 'Mum loved the hotel, Elle. She knew that you'd just tell her to give it up if it wasn't making money. But this place was her whole world. It wasn't really about money.'

'Oh come on, everything's about money, in the end,' Elle retorted drily and then added almost to herself, 'It's no wonder she had a heart attack, carrying that load.'

'Well, I didn't see you here offering a hand,' Penny shot back, flinging down a sheet.

'I didn't know she was under that kind of pressure, did I?'

Suddenly they heard a sound from behind. 'When you're finished ...' Ned muttered. 'Family business inside.'

It was the most they'd heard their father say since the funeral, and the sisters stared at each other for a second, both still flushed with anger before they hurriedly hung the rest of the sheets and followed him inside.

The three sat at one of the now-deserted dining-room tables.

Guests typically left the hotel after breakfast to scour the shops down town, walk the beach, or drive out to hike the sugarloaf. Although none of those activities seemed very attractive today, thought Elle, looking out again at the sky, which had darkened to an ominous deep grey.

The dining room seemed like the right place for this kind of conversation, which Elle guessed would be about what needed to happen to the hotel from here on. This room was superbly impressive, even in its decline. The cream walls contrasted with the dark wood furnishings and the carpet was red and gold, the ceilings high and mouldings still intact. A bar ran the length of the room, bottles glistening behind it, and champagne glasses that had toasted so many occasions hung gleaming like icicles. The circular and turreted room that Elle had always loved was off to the side: originally it had been built as a reading room from when the hotel was still a private residence, in

33

the late 1800s. All in all, it was a beautiful room, even Elle could admit that.

She cleared her throat again and decided to just be out with it.

'I think we all need to talk about the state of things around here,' she said bluntly. There was a silence. To speak, to suggest any changes to the way things were done would be to ignore the memory of Anna, which was still so fresh that it seemed she was sitting at the table with them. But Elle decided she might as well be brave and get to the point. Someone had to, and her mum would have understood.

'I'm not blind. I can see that things aren't great with the business. And I also have a good idea why.' Her gaze settled upon her father. 'Dad, I'm sorry, but after you mentioned that Mum had been stressed, I wanted to find out what was going on.'

Penny looked confused, she shifted her attention from one family member at the table to another. 'What is going on? Elle, what are you talking about?'

Elle sighed and got up from the table. She left the room and walked into her mother's old 'office', a tiny area behind reception. A moment later she returned with a stack of documents. She set them on the table in front of Penny as if displaying evidence in a courtroom.

'This is what's going on. See this file? All arrears notices. Dad, again, I'm sorry for airing dirty laundry, so to speak, but you two aren't going to be able to solve this on your own.' Elle felt guilty as she saw the colour rise in Ned's face.

It was clear this was a terribly embarrassing moment for him. 'I've been looking at the finances. And I'm honestly surprised that the bank hasn't tried to come in and claim the place.'

Penny was looking at each individual arrears notice, her face pale. 'Why wouldn't Mum have said anything about this? I mean ...'

Elle sighed. 'Penny, come on. You can't honestly say that you didn't know something was awry. You said yourself that most of the staff had to be let go.'

'But I thought that was because we were quiet, and tourism is down in general in the area and—'

'And when was the last time this place had steady business? When was the last time it was profitable?'

Penny was flustered. 'Well, I'm sorry not to have all the answers for you at the drop of a hat, Elle, but I didn't pry into Mum and Dad's business because it isn't *my* business.'

Elle exhaled. 'Funny you should put it that way. Actually, this document,' she placed an envelope on the table, 'says that it's all of our business now. Mum left her share of the place to us, Penny. This is her will. Obviously Dad automatically keeps half but ...' She pushed the envelope across the table. Penny seemed afraid to touch it.

Elle swallowed hard, hating how pale and withdrawn her dad looked. She opened her mouth to speak, but Penny interrupted her. She had the document open on the table in front of her.

'Twenty-five per cent a piece to us.'

Elle already knew what the document said. 'She made me executor a long time ago.'

Penny made no effort to disguise her dismay. 'But why? You're never here.'

Elle shrugged. 'Because that's what you do when you have a professional businesswoman in the family.'

Penny nodded, but she still seemed hurt by it. 'So what does it mean? For the hotel?'

Running her hands through her hair, Elle decided to call a spade a spade. 'It means we have inherited not only the hotel, but quite a bit of debt too. I think ...' she ventured, trying to sound reasonable, 'all things considered, that it might be time to think about selling. It's falling down around our ears and based on what you've already said, Penny, Mum was about the only thing keeping the place together. Now that she's gone, it's ... it'll be impossible.'

'What? But we can't just give up on the hotel,' retorted Penny. 'This is our family home, the house we grew up in. It meant so much to Mum, to all of us. Can't we just do a few quick repairs, as much as we can afford for now, and keep things going as they are for the moment?'

'But think about the cost of maintaining an old property like this. Are you truly aware of the man-power you would need to keep things running smoothly day to day? I know that Mum was a powerhouse, but some aspects of the hotel leave a lot to be desired, Penny. Modern guests expect a lot.'

Ned sat, listening to the exchange but saying nothing. Elle had guessed that these decisions would be left up to them in the end. When had their father shown any real interest in anything except his Beatles music?

'I can't,' said Penny, swallowing back tears. 'I don't want to let things go just like that. I don't want anything to change, but maybe you're right, it's going to have to eventually, isn't it? You'll go back to London, and there's no way Dad and I can keep this place going by ourselves. I can't just give up my job either. Oh, maybe we should just sell before we turn it into a wreck altogether.'

She looked distraught and Elle felt like a complete heel now. She reached over to pat her sister's hand. 'It is the right decision, honey. It might not feel like it now, but it is.'

There was a moment of silence, then the sharp noise of Ned's hand slapping against the hard dark wood of the table. It sent a shock through the room.

'No,' he said. 'No, this can't happen. It isn't what your mother would want. It's out of the question that we sell it. For all your talk, Elle, you don't really know what goes into a place like this either. You've got no idea what it means to love it like a third child. That's how your mother felt about this hotel. I won't give it up. Not with the sacrifices we already made to keep it.'

Elle looked like she had been slapped, she was so shocked. She didn't say anything and neither did Penny. It was clear that their father was readying himself to say more, but they were also too taken aback to speak. It was possibly the most Ned had said in years and certainly the first time they'd ever heard him assert himself in this way. And what did he mean by the sacrifices they'd already made to keep it? Was the hotel in more trouble than they thought? Had it *ever* made a good living for her parents? Elle never really thought about the ins and outs of it before, assuming that it must have been holding its own.

Ned looked at his youngest daughter. 'Penny, your heart is in the right place but you, also, have no idea of the love and work your mother put into this place. It is the only legacy she has. And I will not see it sold it away like nothing.' As always Penny looked wounded. Elle wished her sister didn't take his ways to heart so much, take everything Ned said as some kind of personal rejection. But it had always been that way.

Elle and Penny let his words sink in and after a moment they looked at each other and nodded.

'OK Dad, I'll take a look at the finances again and see what we can do,' Elle suggested.

Penny bit her lip, tears in her eyes. 'We'll do our best by Mum, I promise.'

'That's all I ask,' said Ned. He left then, evidently tired out by so much conversation. Elle heard him hum a few bars from a song, (no doubt a Beatles number) which indicated exactly how he was feeling, but she couldn't pinpoint which one it was. While playing 'guess the song' used to be fun growing up, it had got old over the years and unlike her mother, Elle had long given up trying.

'Well,' Penny said, turning to her sister. 'Looks like you and I have become hoteliers.'

'Seems that way, yes.' Elle got up and stood at the windows, looking out at the grey, roiling sea below. She sighed.

Keeping the hotel, or trying to whip it into shape wasn't something she'd envisioned during her short leave of absence for the funeral. She would have to ring her boss, tell the architects firm that she would be off the grid for a little while longer, at least until she and Penny could get some kind of basic plan of action going for the hotel in the medium term. They would arrange some basic repairs, come up with some kind of marketing plan to try and bring in some more business, examine the staffing situation ...

This was going to be a challenge. She couldn't even begin to fathom how utterly unrealistic it was.

Her father was right, Elle might know what kind of standards a place like this should run to, but she didn't have the foggiest about how to actually make those things happen.

Chapter 4

She and Penny decided to go into town to talk things over later that evening. Elle felt like they needed to get away from the hotel to discuss it clearly, without emotion or nostalgia getting in the way.

Ned didn't seem to care what they did, as long as they didn't sell or tear the place apart completely so he was happy to leave them to it.

In the meantime, Elle officially signed in to one of the empty guest rooms (only about a third of the hotel's twelve rooms were booked).

For a start, she'd advised Penny to get someone else in to do the cleaning and general duties as she certainly wasn't volunteering to take up that mantle. She imagined her mother laughing at this. It was a long-held joke in the family that Elle had a distaste for getting into the thick of things.

That's what she loved about being an architect. She was able

40

to attend to the most minute detail as well as the grandest, sweeping, most impossible plans, all without getting her hands dirty. She didn't want to deal with the nagging realities, the hold-ups and the messiness. She guessed this was also what made her so bad at relationships. She never wanted to deal with the day-to-day humdrum and at the first sight of trouble, she fled like a startled cat.

In the room, she ran herself a deep bath. Well, that was one good thing about this place. Huge luxurious bath tubs. A lot of modern hotels had stopped putting in baths these days because they took up so much space. In fact, the bathrooms in the majority were positively tiny. Elle remembered bumping her elbows on the walls of the stingy shower at one place she had stayed at for work.

She could certainly admit that there was a charm to the Bay Hotel that most new builds could never achieve. Is that what visitors wanted though – charm?

Didn't they want to be swept off their feet by funky décor, shiny modern surfaces, Wi-Fi and fast elevators? Didn't people value convenience and a good deal over charm these days? Elle didn't know.

She sunk into the warm bathwater with great relief.

The stress of the last few days had built up. Elle wished again that she had someone to sound off to, someone who would be on her side even when she was being a bit prickly (and she could admit that she sometimes could be). Sebastian hadn't been great at that; they frustrated one another very easily. Much of their relationship had been based mainly on the physical, Elle realised now, and the emotional side had been sorely lacking. But she couldn't identify which of them exactly was to blame for that either. She knew that she didn't let people in too easily, found it difficult to drop the mask of the in-control independent woman. Unlike Penny, she hated showing her more vulnerable side, always felt it made her seem weak. She wriggled in the water, frustrated with herself for the way she was thinking lately. All these thoughts of emotions and feelings since her mother died. Almost like her grief for Anna had opened up a floodgate.

For one, she had thought a lot about Rob since seeing him at the funeral. What had gone on in his life in the intervening years? Did he think of her at all? Elle made a face and shook her head. All these soft, nostalgic feelings.

Though she guessed that if she was going to stick around here for a little longer, she would have to steel herself, as no doubt she would see him around town. Best to be civil, but not overly familiar. After all, they were pretty much strangers now. His attitude at the funeral had taught her as much.

As Elle lay there thinking about her feelings, she began to actually feel something on her arm, something unpleasant. Dripping, cold, constant dripping.

Alarmed, she opened her eyes and looked up at the ceiling. There was a light brown stain forming, growing bigger with every second. This bedroom was on the top floor, and rain was leaking through the roof.

'Bloody hell,' she muttered as she got out of the bath, 'All we need now is for the whole roof to collapse.'

This was going to be a bigger job than she thought.

While Elle was getting ready, Penny had gone back to her own little cottage nearby to feed her cats and change her clothes. She was looking forward to this outing more than she should really, given the seriousness of the topic at hand, but it was lovely to have an opportunity to spend time with Elle. Over the years that closeness they'd had growing up had all but completely dissipated, and Penny had often longed for her sister's strength and wise counsel, particularly when it came to affairs of the heart.

She was useless at love, had had her heart broken multiple times over the years and most recently by Paul, a tourist from Scotland, who'd been in Mulberry Bay for an extended stay a few months back. He'd sought out Penny's advice in the tourist office not long after his arrival, and she'd practically fallen for the handsome jovial Scotsman there and then. They'd had a brief tumultuous affair, and Penny was fully convinced they were heading for happy ever after when Paul promptly told her his time in the Bay was up and he was heading home to Glasgow. Not a word about what would happen to them afterwards or whether they'd even keep in touch. She gave herself up to love too easily, she knew. Her mother was always telling her that. Whereas Elle was always just so together, and seemed to have a handle on life in ways that Penny couldn't ever envision.

She knew that she and her sister would have vastly different ideas on how to handle the hotel from now on, and she just hoped that she'd be able to get across to Elle her own ideas and intentions for the place, instead of being steam-rolled. Though on that front, she had a secret weapon.

In more ways than one.

As she put a little mascara on, in the mirror she could see a brief smile playing on her lips. She tried to ignore it, but she couldn't forget the thought that had just occurred to her. She could imagine what her mother would have said, if Anna were here.

'Don't be such a *meddler*,' she mimicked out loud to herself. Her cats, Boo and Lou, watched patiently from the bed.

'Well, it can't do any harm, can it?' she told them, as if they could read her thoughts. *And who knows, Mum ... it might just persuade her to stick around for a while.*

She brushed her hair into a blonde halo, and wrapped a pink silk scarf from the local accessories boutique, The Wonder Room, around her neck.

Penny smiled at the mirror again, feeling pleased with herself on all fronts.

Penny drove Ned's battered old Ford Cortina down to the centre of town, and they had to run from the car to the restaurant.

Rain was coming down in buckets; it was awful to be outside in this weather, but Penny had been adamant they should still head for a bite in the SugarTree Restaurant, despite Elle's suggestion that they wait till the following night. What with her job in the tourist office and helping out at the hotel, Penny didn't get out all that much, Elle supposed, and wondered idly if she had anyone special in her life.

She knew her little sister hadn't had much luck in love over the years, giving too much of herself too easily as always, though in truth she and Penny hadn't talked about that kind of thing for a while. By rights men should be tripping up over her little sister, but chances were, her unashamed openness scared them away.

The inside of the SugarTree had been modernised since Elle was there last. A Mulberry Bay institution, it had been in business for as long as she could remember and was popular with tourists and locals alike. The food, good hearty Irish fare, was delicious, which made up for the restaurant's surly proprietor, Anthony. Elle still couldn't work out how someone so lacking in basic cheer got away with running such a successful business, but luckily his friendlier staff and reliable food more than made up for it.

The interior was clean and modern. Blonde wood, simple furnishings. Dim lights sat in brackets in the walls, and for a rainy week-night the place looked busy. Elle couldn't help but contrast this to the empty dining room at the hotel.

She was confused for a moment when she saw Penny head directly to a table at which sat none other than Rob Callahan. She felt a flush of uncharacteristic embarrassment.

'I invited him,' her sister was saying, 'so he could give us

45

a bit more insight in terms of the renovation side. I hope you don't mind.'

'No,' Elle replied, swallowing the thing in her throat that felt a little like joy. 'No, that's fine.'

But all through dinner she felt like she was an insect stuck in amber. Gamely she struggled to act and speak like a normal person, the kind of person she was at client dinners in London. Sparkling, sharp, quick to wit, yet ever so slightly unattainable.

But try as she might, she couldn't get away with that here. Rob and Penny knew her too well, knew the skinny, unsure teenager she once was. Penny knew about her awful fear of spiders, the way she had run crying to their father when they had spotted an enormous one in the ballroom when they were children. And she had confided all of her hopes and dreams to Rob when they camped out on the beach as teenagers.

Here were the two people left in the world who knew Elle to her core, and yet somehow they had become strangers. What did she really know about Penny's life these days? She had never asked her sister about how she really felt about having lived her whole life in Mulberry Bay. She had been afraid that it might bring up any old resentment and disappointment that Elle herself had left and never come back.

Now she stared randomly at a large painting of a bull on the wall, while Penny and Rob chatted easily. It was an ugly, violent picture. Nothing was actually happening in the scene, it was just the bull lowering its head against an unseen threat, the coming bloodshed foreshadowed by the dark sky in the background. Obviously chosen by Anthony.

'What do you think, Elle?' Rob asked suddenly.

She started, unsure of what they had been talking about. 'Well, I'm not so certain actually,' she said, hoping that this was some kind of appropriate answer.

'Oh, Elle would just like to see the whole thing gutted,' Penny laughed, not altogether indulgently. 'She'd love to see the hotel as a gleaming homage to contemporary architecture.'

'Seriously?' Rob looked impassively at Elle, waiting for her to speak.

'That's not true,' she retorted. 'I think that there are some unique features that should be preserved. But I don't think there's any reason not to rid it of some of the heavier, more Victorian aspects. It feels slightly oppressive at times doesn't it?'

Rob took a sip of his wine.

'Well, I'm not sure that oppressive is the exact word I'd use,' he said, looking at the light passing through his wine glass, rather than at her. 'I wonder if it's just that the place is a little bit worn down now, and doesn't get the same number of guests that it used to. You didn't feel that way about it in the old days. It's supposed to be full of people. That's when any hotel is at its best.'

'True, but what can we do?' Penny sighed. 'There wouldn't be enough money for a complete renovation, to say nothing of the bare essentials. A lick of paint, new carpets, repairs ... we definitely couldn't do any more than that.' She looked pointedly at Elle.

'Well, let's just wait and see what happens when we talk to the bank. I'd really like to do something with the entrance if we could,' Elle offered, musing a little.

It was the hotel's biggest design flaw, in her opinion, a dark area at the side of the property which had once been a hat and cloak room. 'People's first impression straight away should be: "I've arrived at the perfect place to relax and unwind." It should give people some idea of what to expect from the rest of the hotel.'

'Well, who knows – we might be able to do both,' said Rob. 'Both the necessary and something a little snazzier, I mean. I'm not going to charge you the earth. I've known you both and your family for a long time. I had a soft spot for your mother, and I'd love to do something in her memory. So why don't I come up tomorrow, go through the place and see exactly what we can do?'

Elle and Penny looked at each other. 'Sounds good,' said Penny. 'Ah, you're so good for doing this, Rob.' Her voice was slightly husky, and Elle figured that she was overwhelmed by his generosity.

She couldn't muster quite the same gratitude. She said: 'Yes, thanks Rob, very kind,' but couldn't stop herself from sounding stiff and a little sulky.

She couldn't escape a thought that had crept into her head like a worm over the last hour: was there something between

Rob and Penny? Is that why her sister had hardly mentioned him all these years, even when apparently, she had seen him regularly and had 'good times' as she had put it, back home at the hotel?

Perhaps Rob wasn't upset at all after Elle left, but had just moved on to the other Harte sister, maybe the one he had always wanted, secretly? She tried to keep the thoughts out of her head but they grew stronger and stronger, until every moment of the dinner was poisoned with it. When Penny gave Rob the salmon she couldn't finish, was that a sign of their intimacy? When he urged them to have dessert, was that because he wanted to spend longer in Penny's company?

Elle sunk further and further into herself, unable to speak in case she accused them right out of being lovers, of going behind her back and making a fool of her. It was all she could do to eat her meal of locally caught mussels that she had so looked forward to.

But then again, why should she care? She had no right to care. If there was something between Rob and Penny, it was perfectly right and natural and no business of hers. She told herself this very sternly, and pulled herself back together. The last thing she wanted was for them to think that she cared. For the rest of the meal she was her usual self, witty, but slightly acerbic and completely impersonal, almost as if the other two at the table were just vague acquaintances.

Rob paid the bill and walked them to the car. He kissed Penny briefly on the cheek in farewell, but Elle held herself so rigid and aloof that he looked afraid to go near her. He watched them drive away and back up the hill into the stormy night, his face unreadable for the few seconds that Elle allowed herself to watch in the passenger side-mirror.

Back in her room, she undressed with her usual care, separating clothes, folding them and putting them away in the big old dresser. The furniture in the guest rooms was mainly vintage and antique, and had been there since before her parents bought the place. Probably worth quite a bit though, Elle noted. But time had taken its toll, and various guests over the years had left scratches and dents. Wardrobe doors creaked, dresser draws stuck maddeningly. Her parents didn't know a thing about the maintenance of fine furniture. They'd just thought that you could put things in a room and they would take care of themselves.

Elle smiled fondly. Anna had applied many of those same principles to their upbringing really. She and Penny had been left to run quite wild around the hotel and on the beach. It had been a joyous childhood in that way, almost unthinkable in this day of over-safety-conscious child-rearing. Elle and Penny, separated by only a couple of years in age, had been completely inseparable. They roamed from morning till dusk, Elle in the lead, informally responsible for her sister. They formed gangs with guests' children and made up great sweeping fantasy games in the gardens. Shipwrecks, wars, hospitals, the garden could be made into anything. Penny often wanted to play the domestic, serene part in these make-believes: mother, nurse or wife; but Elle was always in the thick of things, directing the action, making sure everyone had a part to play.

There had been rainy days too, when they made the hotel itself their castle, much to their mother's chagrin and the indulgence of the guests. They had delivered tasty treats in the tea rooms, helping Mary the chef and hoping to be rewarded with a slice of the hotel's infamous chocolate and vanilla cheesecake. Elle sighed, remembering the delicious creamy texture with chocolate buttons on top of the perfectly crumbling base. She'd sampled cheesecake all over the world, and nothing could ever hold a candle to that one. Mary had been dead and gone for many years now so it was unlikely she'd ever taste anything like it again.

Most of all, Elle remembered she and Penny always going to bed happy and exhausted, sometimes still slightly dusty with sand or salt if bath-time had skipped Anna's notice. Their mother really had given them the best childhood possible, Elle thought, without appearing to meddle much in their tiny affairs.

She got into the shower and stood under the jets, as hot as she could stand them, and closed her eyes. When had things changed between her and Penny? When had that closeness begun to strain and stretch, until they told each other less and less? She guessed when they were teenagers, as is normal. Elle had started to yearn towards something bigger, and even though Penny pretended, it wasn't what she wanted.

And then there was Rob, handsome, slightly shy, but who

felt to Elle like cool, still water on a hot day. All she could think about was Rob, Rob, Rob, and she had been protective of her feelings, of their conversations and promises, not wanting to tell Penny anything when she came knocking at her bedroom door.

Elle thought now that that was the thing about teenage love. Part of you knew it could never last, so you built up little walls around it, grew defensive and slightly embarrassed about the intensity of it. But it didn't matter how you tried to shield it in the end, it would be lost anyway.

After her shower she fell into bed, suddenly exhausted. All night long, the wind howled in the eaves of the hotel, and the drip above the bath entered her dreams as she tossed and turned. In her dreams she saw Penny, but a mean-faced Penny, not really her sister, who didn't say anything to her at all, just smiled cruelly and shook her head, as though there was something Elle had missed, something she couldn't see.

Chapter 5

When Elle woke the next morning, two things were different. There was a gap in her ears where the wind had been howling the night before, and a weight at the end of her bed. She sat up to find Penny sitting there, as patient and imperturbable as a yogi.

'What are you doing?' she asked 'How long have you been there?' She felt irritated and self-conscious. Had she been talking in her sleep? Snoring maybe?

'Not long. Just enough to catch the last few minutes of your sleep and to see that you're not *quite* as attractive in slumber.'

'Shut up,' said Elle and threw a pillow, which missed by miles. She didn't know why Penny was playing the annoying little sister today, but she didn't altogether mind it.

'You were certainly in a bad mood last night,' Penny ventured.

Elle was surprised that her sister would even mention it.

Usually, she preferred to ignore awkward situations and conflict. It was perhaps why she'd always found Ned so difficult to handle. While Elle accepted his gruff mannerisms and silence for what they were – simply their father's nature – Penny internalised them and turned them into something greater, something hurtful.

'I wasn't exactly in a bad mood ...' she argued. She eyed her sister. 'Maybe I just resented being the third wheel ...'

'Is that how you felt?' said Penny, her face impassive. 'Well, I think that you might be misreading things, but I'm sorry that you felt that way.'

'What exactly do you think I'm misreading?' Elle pressed. She was becoming annoyed afresh. Was Penny taunting her?

Her sister laughed and shook her head, which made Elle even angrier. For a moment, it was almost a replica of the dreams she'd had during the night and she wondered if over the last few years Penny had somehow changed into a completely different person.

'I think,' Penny wheedled, 'that you think that something is going on with me and Rob, because we're comfortable together, because he comes here a lot, because he loved Mum. You think that we've got something going on, and we've been hiding it from you.'

Elle didn't deny or confirm it. She just didn't say anything.

'Am I right?'

Elle got out of bed and began getting dressed. 'Look, I'm actually not too bothered, either way. I really have to get up and get going on those financials—'

'Oh, for goodness' sake, Elle. Get off your high horse for one minute and let's just talk the way we used to.'

'OK,' said Elle. She didn't know how to feel about this newer more direct Penny. She almost felt like the younger sibling under her sister's stern gaze.

'Rob and I are good friends,' her sister continued. 'He knows what it's like to have stayed in town when the rest of your circle went away, and wonder at times if you've done the right thing, if you might not have been happier somewhere else.'

'You could still go, Penny. You know that you don't have to stay here ...'

'No, it's not like that. I love it here. But of course you do wonder about these things occasionally.'

Elle nodded. She understood. She was, in fact, going through an extended and rather unnerving period of 'wondering about things', particularly since she had arrived back in Mulberry Bay.

'But Rob understood, whenever I had doubts. He went through the same thing and it helped to talk it out. And you know that he and Mum always got on like a house on fire. Truly Elle, you might not understand it, but he was like a son to her. Always willing to help with fixing things up or send some of his crew when he was too busy. Or if ever they needed to lift furniture or something and Dad couldn't do it on his own.'

Elle nodded again. She felt a bit like a puppet. Why was Penny drawing this out? Elle wished she would just get it over with. She and Rob had 'connected', fallen in love, whatever ... she got it.

'So yes, we've seen lots of Rob around here over the years. He's been a good friend to our family. But that's all.'

Elle rolled her eyes. 'Oh come on, Penny,' she said, refusing to believe this for a second. 'You and I both know I'll be sticking around here a little longer than we thought, thanks to the hotel. You and Rob might have trouble hiding things for that long.'

Penny stood up. 'I don't know when you got so bitter, Elle. How could you think I would do that to you? I know how you felt about him.' She shook her head. 'Apart from that, I really do see him as a brother. It's laughable to think of anything else.'

'Really?' said Elle, her heart lightening a little.

Penny sighed. 'Mum was expecting Rob to be her son-in-law one day. When you never returned from college, and we realised that would never happen, we couldn't all just pretend we didn't know each other any more. He's been like a brother to me, and a son to Mum and Dad. It just didn't happen the way we all expected.'

Elle believed her, but this almost felt worse somehow. All of them, through the years, forming a little family, loving each other and having good times, without her. As though she wasn't really essential to any of their happiness.

When she didn't say anything, Penny shrugged and got up. 'Well, that's how it is, anyway.'

'OK. Thanks for telling me. I mean, it's not so much that

I cared either way; it's just I didn't like the thought of it being a secret.'

'Right,' said Penny. 'Of course. It's not like you would have feelings for Rob after all these years.'

As her sister left, Elle thought she caught a glimpse of her rolling her eyes as she said this. But that couldn't be right. Penny was never sarcastic.

After breakfast, Elle followed Penny through the house with a notepad and pen. They were intent on going room by room, inspecting the premises, and making a log of the repairs and renovations that were needed. This would allow them to help Rob price the project out so that they could approach the bank for finance with a realistic number in mind.

Penny was eager – but Elle already felt tired by the entire endeavour, as she believed they were still looking at this situation non-objectively and through rose-coloured glasses.

'So I think that we should start in the ballroom,' smiled Penny. 'After all, that's the focal point for weddings and parties. It should sparkle, don't you think?'

'Sparkle requires money, Penny. Don't forget that.' She looked down at her pad of paper and scribbled, 'Sparkle = do' at the top of the first sheet.

'OK, let's get started,' said Penny, as she swung the ballroom doors wide. She flipped on a set of lights and the wood panelling of the ornate and regal space seemed to glow in appreciation of its residents' attention. 'God, I love this room,' she crooned.

Elle stepped forward and crossed the threshold – even she couldn't deny feeling impressed. Yes, it was a bit dusty right now – the wood floors needed a good sanding and some of the gold leaf trim around the top of the high-ceilinged space needed some tender loving care – but this room had never failed to impress Elle. She had always felt like a princess growing up – knowing that she lived in a house that had an honest-to-goodness ballroom in it. How many kids could say that?

'When was the last time it was used?' she asked, running a finger along a ridge in the panelling, finding it in need of some wood polish.

Penny shrugged. 'I don't know, last summer?' Then she nodded. 'Yes, it was a wedding. About two hundred guests as far as I can remember.'

Elle nodded and made a note. Two hundred guests and a full ballroom – that was the kind of event they needed. Her mind spun into marketing mode – she wondered if anyone had taken pictures? Did anything get posted to social media? Did the hotel even have a Facebook page? She knew the website was boring, basic and sorely in need of updating as well as some drama and pizazz.

She returned her attention to the room and looked up at the ceiling. 'I've always loved the chandelier. I think much of the glass needs replacing, though.' Penny nodded her assent and Elle made another note. 'What about those curtains? Don't they date the space a bit? We could make everything look a lot more open and get some better natural light in

58

here if we got rid of them altogether.' Elle felt her mind whirring to life with new possibilities.

'But Mum loved those curtains,' Penny stated simply. Elle briefly felt irritation rising in her chest, but it abated when her sister spoke again. 'I don't know, maybe you're right. They do get very dusty – maybe sorting out something different will make the room even more appealing.'

The two continued, making notes regarding a cracked mirror, some slight wood damage in a corner of the ballroom's floor, scratches that really needed to be buffed out of the wood panelling on the walls, and the missing pieces of glass in the chandelier.

After leaving the ballroom, they made their way through the more formal sitting room and library, the 'smoking' room where no one would dare smoke any more, then the kitchen, and the pantry. Elle continued to make notes – the kitchen equipment really needed to be modernised, and new shelving was badly needed in the pantry. They agreed that new carpeting was needed to freshen up the sitting room, and that the antique Louis XVI chair also needed careful reupholstering. Elle personally believed that new furniture outright was necessary there, but they certainly didn't have the budget for that. The fireplace could probably use a new mantel and it went without saying that all interior walls needed to be repainted or re-wallpapered.

'So where to next?' Penny asked.

'How about the dining room?' Elle offered.

Elle walked down the hallway, heading for the space

where her own family dined on festive occasions such as Christmas dinner or in celebration of a birthday. For guests, the space was used for formal dinners and smaller parties – for which all the stops were pulled out – silver platters, tall candlesticks. She wondered, with all the recent interest in TV shows like Downton Abbey, if there was a real marketing opportunity there. She recalled the time when her mother allowed Elle and her best friends Hazel and Paula and their respective partners to use the formal dining room to meet up before their debs dinner. Smiling at the memory, she opened the doors and allowed herself to be taken back to that night, so many years ago.

She remembered feeling so sophisticated in her full-skirted ball dress made of pink tulle and a satin corset bodice and Rob looked so handsome in his rented tuxedo. Though thinking back, she realised now that she and her friends looked just like any other group of debutantes – teenagers playing dressing-up in formal wear that either had too many sequins, was too revealing, or borderline silly.

'This room is still in good shape,' she said to Penny, 'we just have to make it great again. The bones are already here – we just need to ...'

'Make it sparkle,' finished Penny, smiling.

Following the storm, the day was as beautiful as Mulberry Bay had ever seen. Birds swooped in graceful arcs over the sea, and everything was glistening and shining where the sun touched it. People walked along the beach and ran in and out of the shallows. There was almost a feeling of celebration in the air, a sense of relief that the frightening fury of the weather the day before had abated.

When Rob pulled up to the hotel, he thought that the building itself looked strangely changed, as though it too, was affected by the mood of the day. The windows were all flung open, curtains flapping in and out of the frames. In the bright sun you couldn't see where the exterior needed painting, or the worn wood of the timber. As he often did, Rob tried to imagine it restored to glory, filled to the brim with satisfied guests.

He drove around the back and parked the van, and as he did so, Elle came around the corner, arms full with laundry. Looked like she really was giving this a go then. It surprised him. He thought she'd be off like a shot back to London when the funeral was over and the associated familial necessities attended to. But maybe things were that bad here that she needed to stick around and see what needed to be done, for the sake of her mother's memory.

He studied her as she hung freshly washed sheets on the line. In the sun, her hair shone like a struck match. He remembered how she had worried about freckles when they were younger, always asking him to smother her in sunscreen. He pushed that thought away, the vision of him caressing the creamy skin on her back. He had mixed feelings about her staying longer. A part of him wanted her to go back to London so he couldn't be reminded of what they had lost. When she was here in town, it felt a little at odds seeing this sophisticated, shinier Elle from years before, turning up in familiar places, like the restaurant last night. Though he'd forgotten how she could slice you open like an orange, just with one of her looks.

Well, they'd just have to get used to being around one another again. He would do everything he could to help her and Penny get the hotel back on its feet, then Elle would go back to London and things could get back to normal.

Chapter 6

When Elle, Penny and Rob sat down in the kitchen to discuss plans, they were surprised to see Ned come in and join them. He set a carafe of coffee on the table, and a plate of biscuits and sat down with them.

'Don't worry, I'm not here to interfere,' he said to them. 'I just want to see how things are coming along.'

Over the next two hours, they wrangled over a list of what needed to be done.

Mostly Elle and Penny argued from their different viewpoints, Penny firmly in the corner for leaving everything much the same, Elle arguing for parts of the building to be torn down and completely rebuilt.

Rob acted as a voice of reason, though Elle noted that he seemed more inclined to take Penny's view. Ned interjected here and there, but mainly seemed to enjoy the strenuous discussion. Elle supposed that it was a good distraction for him.

'Well, here's what we've definitely decided on,' said Penny, reading from a neat list she'd made. 'Painting the exterior and interior; re-carpeting the entire place, replacing some of the wallpaper and repairing cornices and moulding. Repair the chandelier and re-sand the ballroom floor. Refurbish the entrance hall, including ripping out the wall to expose the entrance to the staircase. Which will be the most expensive thing by far.'

'And the most impressive,' finished Elle with some satisfaction.

'*And,*' Penny went on, 'there's the landscaping of the gardens, including the installation of a what did you call it again ...?

'A pagoda,' Elle said. 'If you're going to attract weddings in.'

'Plus we have to get someone to repair the antique furniture. Is that about it?'

'Don't forget sparkle,' Penny added laughing.

'Sparkle. Of course,' Rob chuckled. 'Well, sparkle is my speciality.' He focused his gaze on Elle. 'Anything to add?'

She met his gaze and a burst of some kind of energy passed between them. She wasn't sure what it was, but at that moment Elle knew that he truly would be the best person for this job. 'There might be a few other bits and pieces as you go along,' she mumbled, looking away, 'but those are the major things.'

'It'll be a big job,' Rob said, nodding. 'You'll have to close for a couple of weeks, and we'll have to work around the clock if you want to be back open for the summer trade.'

'Which we absolutely do,' said Penny.

'OK then. We'll go to the bank, talk to this new guy, and then we can get started,' said Elle.

'New guy?' said Ned. 'Who's that? What happened to Maurice?'

'Retired end of last year,' Penny told him. 'We got an appointment with his replacement, Doug Grant.'

'But we've always dealt with Maurice,' said Ned, looking troubled.

'It will be fine, Dad,' Penny assured him. 'Everyone here knows us.' Though she didn't add that she'd asked Elle to meet with the new manager, arguing that she'd be much more professional. 'And formidable,' she added teasingly, but Elle didn't mind. In fact, she welcomed the opportunity for getting a full overview of the hotel's finances, and agreed that it was best for them to present a professional front to the new guy from the outset.

'I have to warn you, though,' Rob said, looking through the list. 'Even with me doing much of this at cost, it will all still add up to a fair amount. We're talking ...' He wrote down a figure on the bottom of Penny's list.

Even though it was no surprise to Elle (actually more reasonable than she'd anticipated) her sister's eyes widened and she nodded gravely. 'Well, it has to be done,' she said. 'Before the whole place falls down.'

'Oh, that reminds me,' Elle said. 'Can you take a look at the room I'm in? There's a leak above the bath.'

Elle and Rob went up the stairs to her room while Penny and Ned stayed behind and cleared things away.

'Why aren't you staying in your old room?' he asked.

She shrugged lightly. 'I don't know. It felt too familiar, like Mum might walk in at any second. I worried I'd feel suffocated by memories there, I suppose.'

Rob nodded. He felt that this was the first honest thing that she had said to him since she had been home.

'How's your family?' she asked.

He grinned. Elle had never got on with his mother and sister. He himself had always felt closer to the Harte family, as his mother was a hard woman with high standards and she had brought up his sister in her mirror. 'I'm sure you'll be delighted to hear that they are in fine fettle,' he replied, with no small trace of amusement.

She smiled and it changed her face entirely, bringing him right back to those teenage years together. They went into the room she was staying in and Rob took note of the laptop sitting on the dressing table, and scattered papers and tubes containing, he supposed, important plans for important buildings in London. 'Working on anything big?' he asked.

She nodded. 'It never stops.'

'Well, how you will be able to handle all this and the hotel too?'

Elle sighed. 'I'll be honest, Rob. This has me worried. I've discovered some ... stuff ... about my parents' finances and the state of this business – and well this is just a huge project – there are a lot of variables and moving parts – and not all of them automatically guarantee or lead to success ...'

'You never were a gambler,' he said simply.

'What does that mean?' she said quickly, narrowing her eyes.

'Hey, don't be offended, I'm just stating the honest-to-God truth. You hedge your bets – and you like certainty.'

'No, I like security,' she clarified. 'I don't like making bad choices.'

Her words echoed through the room and were met with silence.

'Have you made many? Bad choices that is,' he asked then.

Rob guessed that they both knew were no longer talking about the hotel and the renovation project – and he felt momentarily worried that they had crossed over into dangerous territory.

'I haven't made any bad choices in a long time,' she said assertively.

His voice was quiet. 'The person I remember simply lived in the moment.'

'And that's how mistakes get made,' Elle replied, certainty thick in her voice, and right away he knew their brief moment of intimacy was over.

'Let's have a look at this leak then,' he said, all business once again.

'Here,' she pointed at the ceiling over the bath. 'It started dripping on me while I was in the bath tub last night.'

Rob looked at the ceiling for a long time, not speaking.

'Well?' she asked eventually. 'What's the verdict?'

'I'd have to get into the attic to make sure,' he said with a sinking feeling, 'but, I'm sorry Elle, it looks to be pretty major. I'd say that the whole roof needs doing. Forgive the pun but it'll send your costs through the roof.'

She looked at him, horrified.

'Sorry, I don't mean to make light of things. But a job like this, it could quadruple the budget.'

Elle sighed and they both looked back up at the ceiling at the offending mark, as though willing it to disappear, solving their problems for them.

Chapter 7

Penny was just as crushed over the news about the roof as Elle, but she tried to take it in her stride. 'You'll just have to ask the bank for more money,' she reasoned.

'But we'll be completely ruined if we take out a loan that big and business doesn't pick up,' said Elle. Though 'picking up' wasn't enough; in truth they would need the hotel to take off altogether.

'It will. It will pick up. Why shouldn't it? It was popular before, and it can be again. People still flock to this town, to the beach and Main Street. You're right, we just need some modernisation.'

'You seem so sure,' Elle said, not feeling quite the same optimism.

'I *am* sure. But I think it's probably best not to say anything to Dad about this latest little set-back for the moment. God knows, he doesn't need to feel any worse than he already does.'

'That's true. I know that he's barely sleeping or eating.' To say nothing of talking.

'We just have to give him some time,' said Penny. 'Mum's death is hard for all of us but it's worse for him. We just forget about that because he never says anything.'

Elle wondered when Penny had become so wise. She felt like a complete novice at life compared to her sister. 'Well,' she said, 'we'll know more tomorrow anyway. Are you sure you don't want to come to the bank with me? At this stage, we might need to gang up on the guy.'

'No,' said Penny, 'I'll have to stay here and do breakfasts. You'll be a million times better at that sort of stuff, anyway. But can you do me a favour and pop in to my place afterwards? I'm going to move back here while we do this, and I need you to bring the cats over.'

'Sure,' said Elle, but secretly dreaded the thought of manhandling those creepy animals.

Penny stayed in the kitchen while Elle went for a walk along the beach. Of course, she had helped her mother a thousand times, but she had never truly realised how much work went into making the hotel what it was. There was all the cleaning and linen, and food of course; greeting people and tending to their every need, all of those things took time.

But guests here, having been so well looked after by Anna over the years, had certain expectations. There was a couple booked in for dinner that evening who had celebrated their first wedding anniversary at the hotel. It was now their tenth, and they wanted the exact same dessert they had all those years ago. The husband, whom Penny had dealt with over the phone, couldn't exactly remember what that dessert was, though. 'It had chocolate. And berries in it,' he said uncertainly. 'Sauce maybe?' Which wasn't much for Penny to go on as she searched her mother's daunting stack of recipe books. Possibly something that Anna had created on the spot, now lost forever.

She scanned all the recipes containing chocolate. Fudge cakes, souffles, meringues ... 'Ah, this could be it. Maybe,' she said, pulling out a loose page. Light, fluffy meringues, sandwiched with a chocolate cream, drizzled with berry sauce. 'Well, let's give it a go then,' she said out loud to the empty kitchen.

Elle loved the beach. It had been such a long time since she had gone for a proper walk on the golden sands.

Locals still made bonfires on the shore now and then and let off fireworks in the height of summer and at New Year's. She could still see in her mind the old hut she and Penny had made out of driftwood and filled with scavenged items from the hotel.

Further up was where she and Rob had first kissed, where he said to her: 'I've always had my eye on you, Harte,' and she had laughed and felt thrilled at how daring he was, how cheeky.

'Elle! Elle Harte?'

Someone was crashing down the dunes and waving madly

at her, a child in tow. They came over, the woman laughing and puffing with exertion.

'I knew it was you,' she grinned. 'I'd recognise that hair anywhere.'

'Hazel!'

They had been partners in crime in secondary school, but had lost touch when Elle left for college in Dublin. Just like everyone else.

Elle had seen her from a distance at the funeral a few days ago, but somehow hadn't had the chance to talk to her. And how strange that she'd been thinking about her and their debs night in the dining room only that morning.

'You look amazing,' her old friend cried, and Elle sensed that behind the effusive welcome was the tiniest hint of hurt, or regret.

'So do you,' said Elle, meaning it. Her old friend had finally grown into her tall awkward limbs and her dark hair fell in soft waves around her face. 'And who is this?'

'This,' said Hazel proudly, 'is Alex. Say "hello", Alex.'

The child, who looked about six, dutifully said hello and then moved closer to the water's edge, running away from the little waves, much like she and Penny had done as children.

'I'm so sorry about your mum,' said Hazel. 'She was so much a part of this place.'

Elle nodded. 'Thank you. I saw you at the funeral but didn't get a chance to chat ... how have you been?' she asked, not wanting to dwell on sad times.

'Well, as you can see ...' said Hazel, indicating Alex. 'Busy!

But I only have the one child so far. I run a garden centre out on the Dublin Road with my husband. Specialist plants and so on and we hope to open a café and a food market soon. You know how these lifestyle places are all the rage now.'

'Really? Not in the old orchard?' She spotted a garden centre on the way in to town and had idly wondered who had bothered to fix up the abandoned stone farmhouse set in the old apple orchard.

'Exactly,' said Hazel. 'The house is a bit more respectable these days though.'

Elle laughed. It had been where Hazel and Elle had gone to smoke cigarettes and talk about dreams when they were sixteen. Back then Hazel had wanted to be a set designer, Elle remembered.

'I hear you're going to do up the hotel?' Hazel continued conversationally.

Elle was surprised. 'How did you hear that?'

'Oh, Rob pops in and out sometimes. And you know yourself, small town ... news travels fast.'

'Of course,' said Elle, slightly annoyed that Rob was blabbing their business around town. 'Yes, we thought we would see what we could do. It needs a lot of work.'

'You know I was married there?'

'Yes. Yes, I remember,' said Elle. With a flush of shame she remembered that she had been invited to the wedding but hadn't replied, had forgotten all about it, until it was too late.

'It was a wonderful day,' said Hazel, perhaps remembering the same thing. 'We had the ceremony in the garden and

73

your mother made the most beautiful cake. She remembered how I loved the roaring 20s and did a big Gatsby theme with the food and in the ballroom. Everyone danced there until dawn almost.'

Elle smiled. Trust her mother to remember her old friend's likes and dislikes. 'There probably hasn't been a party quite like that there in a while . . .'

'No,' said Hazel. 'It's a shame, but I'm afraid that's the way things are going around here now. Everyone looking for bigger, fancier places in the city. That's why we're planning the garden café and a gift shop and hoping it'll bring day-trippers in. Oh Alex! Listen, I'd better be going,' she said, moving towards her son who had got his trousers all wet. 'Let's catch up properly soon?'

'Of course,' said Elle. 'It was great to see you. Maybe I'll pop into the garden centre one day, take a look.'

'Do that. We'd love to show you around.'

But Elle wasn't sure that either of them really meant what they were saying. And she waited until she was sure she wouldn't catch up with Hazel and Alex before she started her own walk back to the hotel.

She came in from the beach to find Penny staring dejectedly at a pile of failed meringues. 'I think they're supposed to be . . . not quite so flat,' she said, unhelpfully.

'Well, obviously,' her sister moaned. 'These are a complete disaster.'

'Well, the dinner guests won't be here for a few more hours anyway. Let's just try again.'

But the next batch was hardly better, and in fact ended up a strange grey colour.

'It's no use!' Penny cried, 'I'm just no good at this kind of thing.' She put her head down on the shiny metal bench and Elle realised that she was actually crying.

'It's just a dessert, Penny,' she said. 'It's no big deal. Hardly the end of the world.'

'It *is* important!' her sister sobbed. 'People come to this hotel for something special. It means something to them, and it should mean something to us.'

'Well, where's Molly today?'

'Off till tomorrow. There's only one table tonight so I thought it would be OK. But they want this special ... *thing* they had last time they were here.' Each word was cracked by sobs and Elle realised that Penny was probably exhausted from the strain of holding herself, and everyone else together.

Ned walked in, looking for a snack. He was only eating in dribs and drabs these days, a morsel here and there. 'What's the matter?' he asked, looking uncomfortable.

'Penny's been trying to make a special dessert that some guests have requested for tonight. Apparently Mum made it for them years ago and they want it again. Meringue something.'

'Well, these aren't right,' said Ned, holding up a meringue.

'We *know* that, Dad,' Elle glared at him, patting Penny's back.

'I might have a go at it.'

'You?' Penny gasped, in between sobs.

'Yes, well, I've learnt a thing or two over the years. And I don't think you're up to another go.'

'He's right,' Elle said. 'Let's go off and do something else, Penny. Dad can hardly make a bigger mess of it than we did.'

In the end, Penny was too exhausted for more chores and Elle felt they'd done enough for one day, so the two of them curled up on the couch in the family sitting room and watched an old black and white film on TV.

They must have seen it a thousand times when they were children. They had loved the slapstick, the valiant efforts of the hero to get the object of his affection to notice him. Watching it made them both feel calm and safe. And closer.

When it was over, they decided to check on Ned.

'You know he won't have been able to do it. With the way things are going, we'll be lucky if he doesn't burn the kitchen down.'

'I know.' At this point it seemed everything without Anna was just impossible.

But to their surprise they found him in the kitchen gently sandwiching together perfect meringues. So perfect they were like plump, fluffy little brides.

'See,' he told them, while Penny stared, mouth agape. 'It's surprising what I've picked up from watching your mother. I've actually quite enjoyed myself.'

In the end, the evening went off reasonably well. Ned took over the kitchen duties, immersed in his new found-role of stand-in chef. 'I'm actually afraid he might throw a tea towel at me if I make one more mistake,' Penny told Elle, only half joking.

Elle waited the tables: the husband and wife on their anniversary and another young couple who had just come up from the town for dinner.

'It's our first weekend away together,' said the girl to Elle, who had to force a smile at her enthusiasm. And it will probably make you or break you, she though silently.

Elle had been to enough restaurants to know how things were done. She poured wine and carried plates perfectly. She knew when to ask if there was anything else and when to stay away.

The older couple ate in a pleasant routine, sometimes saying something to make the other smile, as if carrying on a conversation they had been having for years. The young couple were obviously more excited, more nervous, more pre-occupied with making conversation. Had she and Rob been like that back then, Elle wondered. Most likely. That nervousness had all been a part of it, the shaking of her hands and fluttering of her stomach letting her know she felt something.

All in all, she thought, she preferred the easy companionship of the older couple. It was no less real for being a bit more comfortable, she mused.

And when Penny brought out *the* dessert and set it proudly on the table between them, Elle and the husband both looked at the woman expectantly.

'Don't you remember, Donna?' he asked. 'This is what we had for dessert the last time we were here. You loved it.'

'Did I? You know, I barely remember what we ate that night,' said Donna. 'I was too busy trying to think of how to tell you about the new baby.'

Elle and Penny left them to it. They were laughing away to themselves. Elle supposed you would have quite a bit to laugh over after ten years together, things to cry over too.

She didn't know why, but the whole night had made her miss her mother even more.

'Yay,' said Penny afterwards. 'We did it! This might work after all.'

She and Elle were sitting at a table in the now empty dining room, sharing a bottle of wine and eating the left-overs of the meringue dessert.

'Let's not get too excited,' she warned. 'There were only two tables here tonight. If the place was full things might have been a bit different.'

'Don't be so negative,' Penny replied. 'The point is: we *can* do it. I mean, I don't want to speak in clichés here ...'

Elle laughed. 'I know, I know. If we all work together ...'

'We can do it, I know we can.'

'It's promising, at least,' Elle admitted. 'I suppose we all feel a bit better, knowing that we can continue Mum's work and not make a complete mess of it. But let's wait and see what happens tomorrow at the bank,' she said, feeling she needed to be the voice of reason. 'Then we'll really know the meaning of hard work.'

Chapter 8

The following day dawned as brightly as the last. In her room, Elle stood in a patch of sun streaming through from the window as she surveyed the clothes she had brought with her. She didn't think Penny would have anything suitable amongst her wardrobe of floaty skirts and floral tops and cardies.

If only she had her array of work suits, she could really look like she meant business, fierce and determined. But how was she to know she would be going to the bank to discuss the hotel's financial affairs and ask for a loan? She put on a grey, high-necked dress and tied her hair up in a high bun. It was the best no-nonsense look she could manage, considering. It would have to do.

She went down to the dining room for a quick bite before she left. To her surprise, there was a platter of fresh fruits on the buffet table, and she piled her plate with fruit and yogurt and took a couple of pieces of wholegrain toast.

Penny came out of the kitchen and broke into a smile when she saw Elle.

'Rob brought some fruit over first thing this morning. He must have been listening when you were going on the other night about the dearth of healthy breakfast options.'

'Was I? I don't even remember,' Elle lied.

'Well, *he* certainly did. He was here at six a.m. with a pile of fresh fruit from SunBurst,' she said referring to the popular organic produce store on Main Street.

'How thoughtful.'

'Exactly what I said,' Penny's grin widened.

'So how did it all go with breakfast this morning?'

'Not too bad,' her sister said. 'Apart from the dreaded early morning. I was here at four making muffins. Did you know Dad's quite the dab hand at making pancakes?'

'I wouldn't have guessed that,' said Elle.

'Me neither. But they're delicious. Not too far off Mum's, either.'

There were a few guests dotted round the tables and they all looked reasonably satisfied, if you could tell such a thing, Elle thought.

'I sent emails this morning cancelling existing bookings for the next month,' Penny went on.

'What? That's jumping the gun a bit,' Elle said, frowning.

'Not really. There were only one or two, and I gave them vouchers to come back when we're renovated. It'll be fine. Absolutely fine.'

'I hope so,' said Elle, thinking it possibly wasn't the finest idea to start cutting off existing revenue just yet. Not when she still had the bank to face. Suddenly, in the face of Penny's new-found confidence, it had become a bigger hurdle to overcome.

Elle didn't like asking for things, especially not for as much money as this.

She had briefly been in debt when she graduated from university, but she had worked hard, paid her bills, made a good living for herself, and compared to the rest of her family was able to live in great comfort. She owned her London flat outright and she quickly thought of her investment and savings accounts – she was by no means wealthy – but she wasn't a pauper either. The thought occurred to her then that she might be able to invest some of her own money in the project.

But will I ever get it back? she asked herself. The idea of putting her own financial future at risk to pay off the hotel's debt frightened her, especially when there was no guarantee for success.

As she drove Ned's sputtering Cortina down the hill along the coast towards Main Street, she turned up the radio extra loud to try and chase the worries out of her head.

She took a quick glance at the financial reports that she had compiled last night, along with Rob's estimate – which sat on the seat next to her. They weren't anything to be proud of; that was for sure. Still, Elle hoped that the short business plan she had hammered together would be enough to present a compelling case as to why the Bay Hotel needed an extension of credit and a brand new loan. And how the planned renovations would eventually put their arrears back into the black.

The town was bustling. Locals were picking up coffee and pastries on their way to work, and others – tourists, no doubt – were completely at leisure, reading the newspaper over breakfast on the outside tables in front of Pebbles Café.

Elle had fond memories of that cosy little space, she remembered gossiping with her friends as a teenager over hot chocolates there; she, Hazel and Paula spending hours on end watching passers-by and sizing up the tourists for any good-looking boys. Vera, the owner, had been close to Elle's mother but despite this she never told any tales. What happened in Pebbles stayed in Pebbles.

Peering in the windows was like glancing backwards into her youth, and she saw that the space was just as inviting and buzzing with energy. Maybe she would pop back there for a bit after the meeting before going to Penny's to collect the cats.

The shops on Main Street were all open and Elle stopped to take a closer look at a few of them. There was a lovely leather bag she spotted in a new place that she hadn't seen before; it seemed to specialise in accessories and was filled with colour and ... *sparkle*, Elle thought, thinking of her sister. She guessed a magpie like Penny loved it here. Taking a closer look at the bag, she sized it up, deciding it would be perfect for carrying building plans. If she ever got back to her real life, that was. Elle had called her boss at the firm the night before and he hadn't been too impressed with her request for an extended leave of absence. Well, if things went her way this morning, it wouldn't be extended for much longer.

'That one's handmade,' said a younger woman from behind the counter. 'They're all a little bit different.'

'I might come back for it later,' said Elle. 'Though I'm not sure that I'll be needing it.'

'Ah, you can never have too many bags,' the woman grinned. She looked speculatively at Elle for a few moments and she wondered if she'd said something wrong. 'You don't remember me do you?' she continued to Elle, who was now even more wrong-footed. 'Karen Casey – I'm Paula's sister.'

Elle couldn't believe it. Annoying little Karen who used to run after Elle and her old friend Paula back in their primary school days. Wow, talk about the time flying by …

'Of course I do, it's great to see you again.' She put on her most winning smile, the one she used with clients. 'Hope Paula's keeping well?'

'Didn't you know? She emigrated to Australia about ten years ago. Married an Aussie and has two kids now.'

Elle swallowed. She didn't know. In fact, she knew very little about what had become of her old friends these days. Her meeting with Hazel yesterday had underlined that.

After a few minutes of idle chit-chat with Karen, Elle smiled and left the shop, promising to call back and have a proper look around some other time, although she was really only being polite. But she was too distracted (and dare she say it nervous?) to go anywhere else for the ten minutes or so till her appointment. She might as well go to the bank early and wait.

The bank was one of the oldest buildings in town. Set at the very top of the pedestrian walkway, it was built from sandstone blocks, and lay gleaming under the sun, as bright and imposing as the day it had first stood there. It was a lovely building and Elle had always liked it, though she had long since moved on from thinking of that style as sophisticated.

She arrived at ten minutes to ten. As soon as she entered, she immediately spied several familiar faces.

There was Joanie Sawyer, who left secondary school a year before her, she thought, as she took in the appearance of one of the bank tellers. She also saw an old friend's mother whose name she couldn't remember, and Elle was pretty sure that her old Maths teacher was waiting in line. Crikey, she knew practically everyone in here. Elle had no doubt that news of her visit to the bank would soon spread, along with speculation about what was going on. After all, this truly was a really small town, and if Elle remembered correctly, Joanie was a hopeless gossip.

A staff member at reception (who for a change didn't seem to recognise Elle) informed Mr Grant that she had arrived, but ten o'clock came and went with no sign of him. At 10:15 the girl smiled anxiously and went to check again.

'It won't be long,' she said when she came back out. 'Mr Grant can be very busy in the mornings.'

Elle smiled tightly. The long wait wasn't really improving her mood, and poor time-keeping was one of her pet hates.

At 10:30, Doug Grant finally appeared. Elle felt like giving him a round of applause. He swept into the room and looked around as though expecting someone else, even though she was the only one in the waiting area. He was a small man, given slightly to thickness around his middle. His face was bland and unremarkable and his hair a mousey brown, restrained by copious amounts of gel.

He took Elle's hand. 'Hello,' he said. 'I was immersed in some paperwork.'

'That's fine,' Elle replied pleasantly, though inside she was seething that he hadn't had the good manners to offer an apology. Still she knew she had to turn on the charm. 'How was your holiday?'

He looked surprised at the question. 'What's that? Oh yes, I have been away. Italy. Had to take the wife; she gets bored out of her tree here. But I tell you, I just can't stand to be away from work too long. I was thinking about numbers the whole time we were looking at Roman ruins.'

Elle chuckled politely, not altogether convinced he had made a joke.

They sat in his cubicle and Grant looked at her expectantly over his desk. There was a file in front of him; she assumed it was the hotel finances.

'Well,' she said, deciding to take the reins since he seemed to expect her to. 'Our mother died recently and my sister and I need to make repairs and renovations to the hotel.'

As soon as Elle began to speak, Doug started to nod impatiently, as though he knew what she had come to say and just wished she would get to the point.

'Obviously we need finance to carry out these repairs, as it seems there isn't enough cash on hand in the business account at present.'

'I see,' said Grant at last, looking down at the paperwork. 'And how much do you need to make these ... repairs.'

Elle said the amount out loud for the first time and the tiny space seemed to echo with it. Grant flicked again through the file in front of him, and a small smile began to quiver around his lips.

'My family has a longstanding history with this bank,' Elle felt the need to say, as this man clearly hadn't the slightest knowledge or indeed interest in the business, 'particularly with your predecessor. Maurice was a great friend of the hotel.'

'The thing is,' Grant said, as if Elle hadn't spoken. 'That's a huge amount. I can't see how a company with these finances could support such a substantial amount of additional borrowing. To say nothing of existing outstanding liabilities ...'

'Well, there's a substantial amount of repairs,' said Elle, trying not to sound curt.

'Yes, I gather that. So I approve further finance, or rather, the bank approves finance, you make these repairs, and then what?' He waited and seemed to genuinely expect an answer to his question.

'Well, business will improve of course,' Elle replied, wondering how on earth a guy with such a poor sense of commercial vision ended up managing a bank.

'Ah, I see. Business will improve. You truly believe that making rudimentary repairs to this ramshackle hotel, this decrepit eye-sore on the waterfront, will make tourists come flocking?'

Decrepit eye-sore ... This was her family's business – their *home* – that he was talking about. For a moment, Elle didn't say anything, because she knew that if she opened her mouth, she just might bite his head off.

'Look, I'm not trying to insult you, or your mother's ... establishment.' Doug Grant knew the value of a well-timed pause, and how to make the word following it sound questionable in itself. It seemed to cast doubt on whether The Bay Hotel really was an establishment of any kind, whether it should even be allowed to exist. 'What I am trying to do, Ms Harte, is to show you how this would sound when I try to justify any decision to give you money to my superiors. This does not present a sound investment for the bank. In fact, this spells disaster from beginning to end. The hotel finances are already in disarray. There is no sign of the Bay Hotel being able to break even in the foreseeable future. It would be a bad decision. And I don't make bad decisions.'

'My family is very well-known and respected here,' said Elle, her voice shaking. Her blood was boiling but she knew she had to do her best. If she lost her temper, everything would be over and they wouldn't get a cent.

'Ah but you see, *I* don't know your family. And even if I did, I don't go around giving loans out like sweets, like little favours. Perhaps you don't realise, being from a small town like this, but in the real world, in the city, it's quite different.'

'I know how things work in the real world, you patronising git,' she snapped. The dam holding her temper back had been well and truly burst, and now it was unstoppable. 'I've never seen such an unprofessional display. They must have been mad when they employed you to replace Maurice. I wouldn't employ you to sweep a barn.'

Elle stood up, and her chair went clattering to the floor behind her. 'My family and the hotel will cease all business with this bank, you can be sure of that much,' she said, knowing that this would of course be impossible while they were still in debt to it. 'I hope this keeps you awake at night, you sorry excuse for a professional.'

It was then that the receptionist arrived, no doubt alerted by the sound of a kerfuffle coming from inside the cubicle.

Elle ended up being escorted from the building like some kind of threat, Doug Grant behind her saying: 'You're just overwrought. Completely understandable, being recently bereaved,' while Elle's former schoolfriend, teacher and acquaintances, mouths agape, looked on.

Outside in the hard light of day, she didn't know what to do. She barely remembered where she had left the car. She stumbled down the bright limestone steps, which were now sickening to her. She didn't want to remember a time when she had admired them, or anything about this bank.

She moved unseeingly through the smattering of tourists on Main Street, thinking of other, more intelligent things she should have said, and rebuttals she might have offered. Suddenly, she turned on her heel. She would tell Mr Doug Grant a few more things, actually. Why not, when everything was ruined anyway?

Elle turned, and with a blunt thump, crashed right into the hard solid chest of a man.

Rob had enjoyed a peaceful morning. He'd delivered fresh fruit to the Bay Hotel, taken his dogs for a walk along the beach, and then come into Pebbles Café for a cup of coffee and a pleasant chat with a few of the locals. He was just about to head onto site, when he looked out the window of the café and saw Elle walking along Main Street, looking like she was about to go into a boxing ring. He paid for his coffee and walked out onto the street, hoping he hadn't missed her, when she came crashing into his chest, nose first.

'Elle. Are you all right?'

As she pulled back from him, he could see that no, she wasn't all right. Blood had already begun to flow from her nose, startlingly vivid against her pale skin.

'Oh shit, sorry. We'd better get that looked at. It might be broken.'

For once she had nothing to say, so Rob brought her to his truck, where he kept a first aid kid. After performing some rudimentary first aid on her nose, the biggest challenge was getting her to breathe normally: she was taking huge gulping breaths, like a fish landed in the dry. It was the shock, he supposed, feeling guilty.

'Let's get you home,' he said. 'Give me your keys and I'll get one of my lads to come and drop back your car.'

Elle looked at him with her wide green eyes, and spoke for the first time since the incident. 'No. Don't take me home, please. I can't face them just yet.'

Chapter 9

Having finished breakfast duties, Penny decided, upon Rob's advice, to tackle emptying out her mother's old office in preparation for the roof repairs. Though she wasn't relishing the thought of sorting through all the paperwork and hotel-related flotsam, she figured she might as well do something worthwhile to pass the time while waiting for Elle to report back from the bank.

Catching an all-too familiar scent as she entered the tiny cramped room, she gave a bittersweet smile. Elizabeth Arden White Door, Anna's signature fragrance, the perfume her mother had worn for as long as she could remember. It was because of this familiarity that she felt herself relax. If anything, her mum existed still in this space more than anywhere else, and it was with that comforting thought in mind that Penny sat down at the desk and stared out of the window towards the sea.

'I hope you don't mind me organising your things,' she

said to the air around her. 'I would never want to invade your privacy. And if there is anything that you don't want me to touch – just let me know, give me a sign.'

Penny breathed deeply and felt herself listening intensely to the ether, as if truly expecting Anna to communicate with her from the Great Beyond. But all she heard was silence.

'OK. I'm going to take that as you giving me your permission, Mum,' she smiled.

She looked around her and wondered where to begin. It's not as if there was a huge mess or a jumble of stuff to sort through – Elle had very easily located the business accounts and Anna had always been very organised and orderly when it came to administrative matters.

Sitting down at the desk, Penny placed both of her hands on the solid wood surface in front of her – she had so many vivid memories of her mother spending time at this desk at various times when she and Elle were growing up. Anna used to good- naturedly hunt them out of the door when she was 'doing the books'. Rubbing her fingertips on the surface, Penny pondered where to begin.

Seeing the desk drawers as the obvious first choice, Penny opened the top drawer to find pens, pencils, a stapler, tape, rubber bands, paper clips – typical office stuff. Closing that drawer and making her way through the rest, she was met with carefully labelled folders related to supplier invoices and utility bills. Penny couldn't help but smile. 'Oh, why wasn't I blessed with more of your organisational skills?' she whispered, taking out the files and placing them in a cardboard box she'd brought along with her for temporary storage purposes. Most of the drawers contained similar hotel or household related bits and pieces, but in the bottom drawer Penny found something different. She ran a hand over the spines of what she recognised as Harte family photo albums, reflecting on her own mess of photos taken over the years – in assorted boxes at her house or even worse, trapped digitally on her phone.

Penny pulled an album out at random – one from right in the middle – and sat back in the chair with it. Tucking an errant lock of fair hair behind one of her ears, she opened the book, immediately smiling at what she'd found.

This album was from around the time that Penny was seven or eight years old, which made Elle almost ten. Looking at the carefully displayed photos, she turned the page, and at once had her suspicions confirmed.

'Eight years old. The year of the Barbie birthday party,' she smiled, leaning closer to a picture that showed her resplendent in a pink dress, pink patent leather shoes, pink and white striped tights and to top it all off, a crown made of sequins and plastic jewels. Her eight-year-old self proudly displayed what she remembered to be one of her favourite gifts that year – a Barbie Dream House. The pile of plastic was nearly as tall as her. She wondered what had ever happened to it. Most likely lost to the place where all bits and pieces of childhood went when outgrown.

Turning her attention back to the photo, Penny couldn't

help but giggle. While she posed proudly next to the plastic monstrosity, Elle stood next to her looking unimpressed – no doubt disgusted by a birthday party gone way too girly for her more sophisticated ten-year-old standards.

She turned her attention to the next photo in the album. In it, she was sitting in Anna's lap, obviously exhausted from the day's festivities, because her eyes were half closed and her mouth gaped open. Not the most attractive picture of her, but interesting just the same.

Indeed, it wasn't that she was so interested in looking at herself, but rather what the rest of the family were doing. Her mother had one arm curled around Penny, in the other hand she held a glass of what appeared to be white wine. Anna was laughing at something or someone off camera – her smile was wide and open, her eyes bright and she was obviously trying to hold her composure enough not to wake her daughter, or spill her wine. Penny's heart constricted with sorrow at this wonderful depiction of her mother exactly as she'd been in life: happy and full of fun.

And then there was her father.

Ned was in the corner of the frame, leaning against the railing of what Penny recognised as the deck that had been directly behind the family quarters of the hotel until about ten years ago, when it had rotted away beyond saving. In the picture, Ned, as always, appeared to be on the fringes of the party. He was wearing a blue collared polo shirt and a pair of khaki trousers – appropriate for an outdoor birthday party in late spring – the middle of May. However, it wasn't so much what he was wearing or what he was doing that caught Penny's attention, but the look on Ned's face as he watched his wife and daughters.

Her dad looked content – happy. His face looked joyful, relaxed, pleased to be involved or at least partaking in the moment. Penny pulled the picture album closer to her face, trying to get a better look. Yes, he looked once again as if he was on the fringes of the family, but this picture though, said something different. It showed that Ned had definitely been a willing observer that day – and seemed to have enjoyed himself. Or at least revelled in the opportunity to witness his wife and daughters enjoying themselves.

Putting the album aside (she would take this to her cottage for safekeeping) she reached further into the drawer, to see if there were any other albums.

But instead she found something else. This particular drawer was much deeper than the rest and contained multiple leather-clad notebooks. All of the spines were neatly labelled with numbers: dates actually, though not month/year-specific like the hotel account ledgers. She already had those and had gone over them last night with Elle in preparation for this morning's meeting. Penny picked up one of the notebooks and looking inside, was confronted by her mother's familiar neat script.

Journals, she realised. She had been aware that her mother kept a diary of events on occasion, but understood now that perhaps this had been much more than a one-off type of activity. Judging by the number of books in the drawer, it had been a dedicated hobby, something that Anna must have done regularly throughout her life.

Scanning through the dates listed on the spine of each book, Penny discovered that her mother had diaries going back at least forty years and more, to even before she and Ned had been married and bought the hotel. Pulling out some of the small books, Penny now saw that her original estimate of how many in total had been way off, she was probably looking at a couple of dozen volumes.

'You were busy, Mum,' Penny smiled, feeling as if she had struck gold in a sense. She recalled a worry expressed to Elle days before that all her mother's wonderful stories and vignettes about the hotel and family life were lost forever.

But if these diaries contained what Penny thought they did, it could be quite possible that all of those memories were still alive and well – safe on the pages of these books. The thought immediately comforted Penny but then something else dawned on her.

Was she right to consider violating her mother's privacy? After all, these were *her* diaries, her most private thoughts, desires, confessions probably. Was it really right to go ahead and read them?

Penny swallowed hard.

If she read this stuff, there was no going back, no matter what it said. It's not as if she could ask Anna for clarification on something that she didn't know about or didn't *want* to know about, Penny thought, swallowing a little.

Though knowing her mother, she decided that it was unlikely that Anna had any deep, dark, hidden secrets that could potentially change the way that her daughter viewed her. And if she had, then that was a risk that Penny was willing to take.

She opened the first book that came to hand – the most recently dated – and flipped through the pages, finding that the majority of it had not been written in. Finally, she spied some pages that contained Anna's careful handwriting. The last entry was only last Tuesday morning, and the moment that Penny laid her eyes on it, she felt a chill go up her spine.

The last one – the very last thing that Mum wrote, thought Penny. She swallowed hard as she began to take in the words and then realised that she couldn't do it. Not just yet at least. It felt too soon. She closed the little book and placed it back in the drawer.

Penny looked closer at the spines of the other, older-dated books, and chose one at random. '1981. I would have been three.'

She opened the book, grimacing slightly when the spine cracked and the pages crinkled under her fingers – it had obviously been some time since this diary had been opened and it had grown brittle with age. Flipping through the pages randomly, she stopped on an entry dated 'July 29, 1981'.

Penny immediately smiled when she saw what the entry was about – it had been one of her earliest memories as a little girl – and one that she was quite fond of.

Happy Wedding Day! Roused the girls from bed this morning with the encouragement of 'Get up, get up, it's time to go and see a princess!'

Today Lady Diana Spencer is marrying the Prince of Wales – and well, a Royal Wedding doesn't come around all that often now, does it? Of course, Ned says I shouldn't encourage the 'princess' stuff with Elle and Penny, says it's not good for little girls to believe in fairy tales and happy endings. And of course, he being the ray of sunshine that he usually is says it's likely that anything involving the Royal Family will end in disaster – his words not mine – but still, I can't help feel a bit wistful and excited – it's still a wedding! And there is a real princess involved! Of course he's right; not many little girls end up as princesses when all is said and done – but it's fun to imagine the romance of it. And the Royals always put on a good show, that's for sure. As I said, it's a good day.

Of course, regardless of Ned and his opinions on the Royals, Penny was thrilled by it, Elle, not as much, but of course our eldest has never shown the slightest interest in princesses, dolls or other such girlie things. Nine times out of ten she'd much rather play with Lego.

But despite this, even she was glued to the telly the moment Lady Diana emerged from the carriage in her gown. Penny then insisted on having me drape her in a sheet from one of the guest rooms that she deemed her own 'princess dress'. In my eyes, it was a bit more of a toga, but I suppose to a three-year-old it was quite glamorous. She paraded around in it for the best part of the day, and was even able to get her father to address her as 'Princess Penny'. I reserved comment on that – Ned looked enchanted by his offspring – royal intentions or not.

Oh how I would have loved to be in London to see the wedding – I mean, not see the actual wedding, but at least stand on the roadside and hope to catch a glimpse as the carriage passed by. I suppose I will have to wait until the next Royal Wedding, and by then maybe Penny can come along with me. Maybe she'll have a three-year-old that she will need some help minding – I like to think that maybe Penny will utter the same words to her future daughter that I did to her. 'Time to go and see a princess ...'

Feeling a tear slip down her cheek, Penny couldn't help but feel sad at the notion that Anna would never see her grandchildren. Not that either she or Elle seemed anywhere near providing any, but still ... Then another errant thought ran through her head.

Dad had been 'enchanted' by me she repeated, pleased, remembering the sheet she had worn in a royal fashion that day – designer wedding dress it had not been. Pondering this for a moment, she quickly turned her attention back to the diary, flipped to the next page and continued reading.

No, there is nothing to fear here, she thought with a smile. *It's just Mum.*

All of this stuff, the photos and diaries, Penny realised,

they weren't just her mother's belongings and not just her story – but their history too. And this hotel was as much about the family's life as her mother's.

Taking another look at the photo album, Penny opened it again and flipped to the next page, then the one after. In every one the hotel was centre-stage, not just a backdrop to family life, but an active part of it.

Penny checked the time on her watch, realising that it was now almost eleven a.m. Elle would back soon from her meeting with Doug Grant.

Penny hoped against hope that the verdict was a good one. They simply couldn't lose the hotel, this vital part of the Harte family unit – and quite possibly, she realised sadly, the only thing that would keep the remaining disparate parts of that family together.

Chapter 10

Rob took Elle to his house on the outskirts of town. It was further up the coast a bit, where the shoreline got rocky and rough. He lived on a small half-acre with wild fruit trees and room for his Labrador dogs to roam. He kept chickens too and had taught the dogs to be so gentle that they barely looked at them. The chickens, so to speak, ruled the roost.

His house was small, but neat and tidy. Elle had never been there before, of course, and now she was surprised at how sparse it was. There was a single bookcase, the barest necessities of furniture, no TV and a single painting on the wall. Very simple.

'I know,' said Rob, sensing what she was thinking. 'It's a bit spartan looking. I don't spend a lot of time here.'

Elle wondered where he did spend his time, but didn't ask. It was odd, the situation she found herself in, but at the same time it felt comfortable, like she had been here a thousand times.

Rob showed her to the bathroom. 'Why don't you clean up?' he said. 'There's still some blood under your nose.'

Putting her hand to her face, she felt it now, where she hadn't before, flakes of dried blood on her upper lip and chin. She felt embarrassed, suddenly; she must look a fright.

She was shivering, with shock she supposed, and Rob gave her a shirt to put on over her stained dress. One of the dogs tried to follow her into the bathroom and they both laughed. 'No, you don't, boss,' he said. In the bathroom, finally Elle was alone again. She washed her face with warm water and studied herself in the mirror for a moment. She was calmer now, but still not ready to go home and face Ned and Penny. How had it all gone so wrong, so fast? Just yesterday they'd all sat around the table and laid out plans for the future, and now those plans were in ruins. She was partly to blame, for letting them hope in the first place, and for losing her temper at the bank manager.

If she hadn't, perhaps something could still be salvaged, but now it was beyond repair. Elle would be lucky if she was ever allowed to go through the bank's doors again, not that she wanted to. She would have to go home and break the news sometime, but not yet.

Going back outside, she sat in Rob's bay window and watched the sea break itself against the rocks. It wasn't a cold day, but she was wrapped in a blanket as well as Rob's shirt. She felt chilled through from the shock of the morning.

'So,' said Rob, bringing her a cup of hot tea. 'What happened?'

'Well, to cut a long story short, I pretty much lost the lot today – my temper, the loan, and the hotel.'

He shook his head. 'I'm sure it didn't happen exactly like that.'

'It may as well have. That man, he was so awful. It was like he didn't care at all, like he'd already made up his mind before I came through the door but just wanted the pleasure of saying it. And I just couldn't stop myself. I started to shout at him, like a madwoman. I've never felt so humiliated.'

Rob nodded. 'I've heard he's a smooth-talking, small-minded git.'

Elle laughed. 'That's pretty much what I called him.'

'I wish I could have been there, Elle. I can't believe you were escorted out of the bank.'

'Well, probably better that you weren't there, to be honest. You wouldn't like me when I'm angry,' she joked, raising a small smile. 'But it's all over now,' she added, any humour darting away just as quickly. 'The only thing to do now is go back and tell the others what's happened. They'll be devastated. And just when things were starting to come together, too. Dad was starting to take notice of what day it was and Penny was gaining some confidence.'

She shook her head. 'It's weird, the hotel has been part of our lives for so long, I never really knew how much I was comforted by the thought of it just being here, part of the family, if you like. The thought of it being run by someone else just sends me spinning.'

'I get it. Sometimes you don't really know what you've got

until it's gone,' Rob said gently, and Elle knew that he was talking about more than the hotel. She looked at him, not sure what to say. 'I . . .'

'Let's not talk about it now, Elle. I don't think you need this day to get any more intense.'

It was true. But to be fair, she didn't think there would ever be a time when she and Rob were ready to talk about what happened between them.

'Can I just ask one thing?' she said to him.

'What's that?'

'How come you never got married?'

'I don't think it's really fair of you to ask that question, Elle. Why didn't *you* get married?' He sighed. 'You know how it is. Penny does, certainly.' He chuckled. 'She and I are forever bending the ear off one another about our relationship woes. Though I think your poor sister has had more bad luck than me. Ah, you try your best with people but you just never really find anyone who's right, I suppose, anyone who's worth it, I mean. And time goes on, and you've been ambling along on your own so long you don't know how another person would even fit into your life at this stage. It got so I'd tell myself: not everyone needs to be in a relationship.'

'Exactly,' Elle nodded vociferously, sounding like they'd just discovered they shared the same birthday. 'That's how I feel, too. Not everyone needs to find that "special someone" and get married and live happily ever after, and all that. Maybe some people are just meant to be alone.'

He shrugged. 'Well, if you feel so happy about it, Elle, maybe you truly are better off alone.'

They stared at each other for a minute, realising that each had hurt the other. Elle opened her mouth to speak, but he cut her off.

'Come on, I'll take you home.'

They drove back towards the hotel in silence. Rob wanted to say something, anything, but it felt like Elle had built another wall of ice up around herself.

At the hotel, she got out and closed the door, saying only: 'I'll have your shirt cleaned and back before I leave.'

And that was it. He might never see her again. Had he waited so many years for this, only to ruin it in a matter of seconds? Don't be stupid, he told himself. There was nothing to ruin. She said it herself: she doesn't want love.

The road back felt longer than it ever had before and Rob's house was not the welcoming beacon it usually was. It felt lacking, somehow, now that she had been there.

Penny was facing a problem – namely that once she'd started reading her mother's diaries, she couldn't stop. She found herself immediately entranced by this more private side of Anna, one that of course she'd known had existed, but something that had only ever been present within her peripheral vision. Each entry she read provided more insight into a woman that she knew so well – but one that perhaps she hadn't known completely.

But another thing that Penny was beginning to find fascinating was Anna's uniquely intimate insight into her father and who Ned was as a person.

February 12, 1987

Getting ready to celebrate Ned's birthday. Of course, he doesn't know it. I'm not even sure if he keeps track of his birthdays any more, but I do. This is a milestone birthday though for him. Forty years old. Are we both old enough to be forty? It seems crazy to think that Ned has four decades behind him – as will I shortly – and I hope we have another four decades ahead of us.

The girls are very excited with the party planning – Penny in particular is a little girl who loves a good celebration, no matter what the cause. I do wish that Ned would encourage her a bit more though; he doesn't seem to realise that she's not the same as Elle, and somehow is a little bit needier.

I realise, of course, that for him these big occasions always seems like a struggle up until the day, and then he has a good time – even if begrudgingly. And regardless of his gruff exterior, I always feel especially pleased when he comes to me and notes something special or interesting that Elle or Penny did. For instance, just the other day he approached me as Elle was finishing her homework – she was out of earshot and didn't hear what he had said. He said, 'What level is she now reading at? A bit ahead of things, isn't she?' And I agreed with him and told him that though only eleven she was reading at the level of a four-teen-year-old, that's what her teacher had told me.

'And she likes to draw too, doesn't she?' he com-mented. I told him that yes, she loved that perhaps most of all, and joked that maybe we have a future artist on our hands. It's nice to see how proud he is of her.

Penny smiled at this, but it was to her merely another example of how Elle was yet again the favourite in Ned's eyes. She couldn't ever remember her father seeming the least bit interested in her school work – it was always her mother who attended parent–teacher meetings, helped with home-work. Feeling a little unsettled about what Anna had written about her being 'needy', Penny put down that journal and picked up another, opening it randomly.

June 30, 1987

It seems as if the sun is shining on our family as of late. Penny's school dance night is coming up. She has a solo, which is thrilling – she prances about on stage quite well, it seems. But for the first time, Ned has actually volun-teered to come along to the school with me. I can't help but giggle a bit at the reason, after all, Ned has never shown a particular interest in dancing or leotards. But it's because his prodigy of a daughter decided to pick a Beatles tune for her solo: Twist and Shout. I think she is quite good at dancing to it. I would venture to think she might even inspire Ned to get up and dance himself on the night. Wouldn't that be a sight to behold …

Penny stopped reading for a moment and laughed at the memory – that dance display in particular had been quite memorable. She did recall that her number had brought the majority of the school hall to their feet, and she had the fuzzy recollection of her father standing up, next to Anna. No, he wasn't dancing to 'shake it up, baby', or anything like that, but he was indeed clapping and singing along.

'How had I forgotten about that?' Penny asked herself, thinking of the moment where she had looked down from the stage and seen both of her parents stand up and cheer. She found it so difficult to connect with Ned sometimes that such memories were golden, and she ran her hand over the diaries, grateful for this rare and precious insight into her childhood.

But right at that moment, the door to the office opened, and Ned himself stepped tentatively in, looking around the room with a somewhat stricken look on his face, as if he was afraid of Anna's ghost jumping out and yelling, Boo!

'What's so funny?' he asked gruffly.

Penny's smile faded and she quickly snapped the diary shut, unable to escape the feeling that she had been caught doing something she wasn't supposed to.

'Nothing,' she said evasively. 'Just remembering something nice.'

Ned scowled, as if the idea of laughing in this 'Temple of Anna' was something wholly inappropriate at such a time. Looking again around the room, he grunted, 'Doesn't look like you've got too much done.'

Penny hurriedly closed the drawers, hiding the diaries from sight. She'd come back and clear them all out later. 'Just making sure I don't throw out anything important,' she replied. She indicated the box of photo albums. 'OK if I take those home with me?'

Ned shrugged as if he couldn't care less what she did with such precious family mementos and this irritated Penny afresh. But before she could say anything, her father spoke again.

'The car just pulled up. Elle's back with the verdict.'

Chapter 11

Elle stood outside the hotel and watched the windows gleaming. She had never truly known how much she cared about the place, and now that it was being pulled from her reach, she did.

She wondered if her realisation about Rob was the same, but it had taken longer, and was possibly more devastating. How could she have thought that they could be friends or work together on this? Or maybe, she told herself savagely, maybe, like an idiot, you thought that something might happen between the two of you. That old feelings might flare up. Well, he'd made it quite clear that would never happen. Hadn't he just said himself that she was completely unlovable?

Now, trying to pull herself together, she prepared to tell her father and sister the bad news.

'It's almost lunchtime. Where have you been?' exclaimed Penny from the doorway. 'And what happened to your nose? It's all swollen.'

'I crashed in to someone in the street,' said Elle. 'It's a long story.'

Penny looked around out front. 'Where's the car? I hope you didn't forget to bring the cats,' she said when Elle didn't reply straight away.

'There was no point,' said Elle. 'You'd just have to take them home again.'

Her sister looked at her blankly.

'We didn't get the loan, Penny,' Elle said, seeing her father watch impassively from the hallway. 'It's all over.'

She looked from Penny whose eyes were brimming with tears to her father who appeared to have had the wind knocked out of him. 'I'm so sorry, I did everything I could. I stayed up most of the night making a business plan and outlining the best course of action and—'

'But we have been banking there forever!' Penny cried. 'That has to count for something.'

Elle studied her hands, wishing that she was somewhere, anywhere else except for here right now. When the silence became too deafening, she looked at Ned. Both were staring at her as if they were willing her to say something else, anything.

Her poor sister collapsed into a chair silently, crying.

'Penny, I know this is hard.' Elle reached out to grasp her sister's hand as her own voice broke. 'I am just so sorry.'

'It's not your fault, Elle. I know you tried – and you were the best person to go to the bank – I just can't believe that this is happening. I can't believe that we are truly going to have to sell this place. When we made all of those plans –

and then with Rob coming out here to give us the estimate and especially after yesterday, I just felt so positive that everything would work out. That we would be able to *make* it work. For Mum.'

As Penny said the words, Elle felt a mix of emotions. Relief in that she and Ned seemed to truly understand the position they were in and that they would have to sell the property, as well as resignation of the fact that they had no other choices. Finally, there was sadness – about so many things, the fact that they were letting go of their mother's legacy, brokering the place that contained their history and all their family memories. And the worst part?

For the first time in her life, Elle felt that she had let her beloved mother down.

The hotel was a gloomy place that night, the shadows longer and the creaking louder. The walls seemed to shudder in knowledge of their own demise. There were no stars visible from the windows, and Elle thought it fitting as there was no room for joy here tonight.

Penny was in her room, still crying, and Elle hadn't seen Ned either since she told them the news. They had retreated into their shells again, letting the hotel shelter and comfort them while it still could.

She felt that she would never sleep. The events of the day, the throbbing in her nose, Rob's harsh words spinning around and around in her head; it all kept her wide awake and wretched.

She wished for Anna. Her mum was the only one who could fix this, who had enough fight to do so. She would have told Doug Grant what was what and where to go. No one messed with Anna's beloved hotel.

But in her heart, Elle knew that maybe even her mother couldn't stop this. It was too late, and she must have known before she died what a terrible position the hotel was in. She must have been carrying so much stress, bearing a heavy burden perhaps to the point that it had all eventually been too much for her.

Elle finally did slip into a troubled sleep, tossing and turning to the sound of the eaves of the decrepit roof moaning overhead and her own bad dreams. Before dawn, she slept properly at last, and woke up to find Penny on the end of her bed once again.

'Have you come to help me pack?' she asked, with a weak smile.

'You're not going anywhere,' Penny replied, looking determined. 'I've been thinking all night, and there must be a way to do this. I don't know what it is, but we'll figure it out somehow.'

'I don't think so, Penny. I've been thinking too, thinking that Mum would have found a way, but I just don't see how.'

'I found something yesterday, amongst Mum's things. Her diaries.' This was revealed with no small measure of guilt, and Elle instinctively knew that her sister didn't simply find Anna's diaries, but had been reading them too.

'Oh?'

'There are dozens of them, some going back to even before our childhood. And there's lots about the early days of the hotel and how much she loved it, right from the beginning.'

'Penny, I know Mum loved this place – we all did, but I think now it's time for us to say goodbye—'

'Please, Elle,' her sister begged. 'Just stay a few more days. Give it a chance. We'll work something out, I'm sure of it.'

Elle sighed. She didn't think there was much to work out, other than put the hotel up for sale, and see about finalising the business for good, but she had already extended her work leave until the beginning of next week anyway. 'One more week, then. But that's all.'

'Great.' Penny grinned and jumped off the bed. 'We really should start brainstorming straight away, but I'm going to let you get dressed first.'

'Cheers.'

Her sister turned back in the doorway. 'Oh, and you didn't tell me it was Rob you bumped into on the street yesterday. He rang up this morning asking after you and your nose. Very concerned.'

With a cheeky grin and before Elle could answer, Penny shut the door behind her. Elle could hear her chuckling in the hall, her little sister's optimism once again blinding her to reality. If only you knew the truth, Elle thought. There's nothing to laugh at in this sad mess.

Nothing at all.

*

Penny was disappointed by yesterday's turn of events in more ways than one. Mostly because of the hotel, of course, and what it meant to her: the thought of restoring it to the place it had once been had filled her with hope, as though it was that easy to restore everything to an earlier, better time.

The other reason she was so disappointed was because she had felt that doing this would bring her and Elle closer again, back to something resembling their former intimacy. In all honesty she missed her sister, and had been missing her for years. How to put this into words, though? She was scared that Elle would soon dismiss her outright, citing phone calls, emails and Christmas visits as signs that their relationship was fine.

And it was fine, if that was all you required. But she wanted to know Elle again, truly know her, and missed the feeling of having someone to tell everything to.

The truth was, she was a little bit afraid of her, too. Afraid that Elle's years in a big city had hardened her depths, and that she would have no interest in Penny's confidences, or find them petty and provincial. If Elle went back to London now, Penny knew for sure that she would see less and less of her. Her sister would be sucked back into the addictive and all-consuming rhythms of the city, and without Anna here to lure her back, would soon forget all about life in Mulberry Bay.

So something had to be done. Penny knew that a miracle of epic proportions was needed to get what she wanted: winning the lottery, a large donation from a kindly benefactor. She sighed. Those things were as likely to happen as the new bank manager magically changing his mind and granting them the loan.

She would never tell Elle this, but she had rung the bank herself that morning and asked to speak to Doug Grant just in case there was something to be done. Grant wouldn't take Penny's call, which was hardly surprising, and one of his underlings had made it emphatically clear that there was no chance of a loan. The man, Tom Collins who lived locally, wasn't entirely without sympathy, though. 'It's a shame, you've got a great place up there,' he said. 'We celebrated my father's 90th birthday there in the tea rooms. But Mr Grant can be fearfully unaccommodating when it comes to these things.'

Unaccommodating isn't the word, Penny thought now as she mixed pancakes for breakfast. Ned was nowhere to be found once more, and there were no guests today, but Penny felt that if she and Elle were to come up with a miracle idea to save the place, they definitely couldn't do it on empty stomachs.

Just as the first spoonful of batter sizzled in the pan, Elle appeared. There was a faint bruise appearing across her nose and under both eyes that Penny hadn't noticed in the shadows of the bedroom earlier.

'Oh Elle,' she gasped. 'You look like you've been in a bar fight.'

'I feel that way too,' Elle said, putting a hand to her face. 'But I'm starving, too. Unnaturally hungry actually.'

'Well that's a good sign, at least,' Penny smiled. 'I just

hope you're not too concussed to think of some wonderful solutions this morning.'

Elle smiled back. 'Something tells me you wouldn't allow that to happen.'

Rob was having a hard time staying away from the Bay Hotel.

He couldn't even use the excuse of checking up on Elle, since he'd stupidly rung that morning. On the phone, Penny the eternal optimist, had seemed determined to make something out of a bad situation, and come up with some kind of solution to keep things going, but Rob couldn't imagine what that solution could be.

Elle had painted a pretty grim picture of the hotel's prospects the day before. Notwithstanding the renovation loan, the day-to-day financials were in pretty bad shape and the Hartes were heavily in debt to the bank already.

It sounded like the only thing to do was to shut the gates and let the estate agent hang the 'For Sale' sign. It was an image that made Rob sick to his heart. The place was like a second home to him and occupied a huge place in the history and community of the Bay, but it was more than that.

It symbolised Elle for him too, its ever-present silhouette on the landscape somehow linked with the knowledge that she was out in the world, doing something wondrous, and he liked to think of that. He would rather see it torn down than in other hands. It belonged in the Harte family, Elle's family.

He supposed it was only a matter of time before she

packed up and returned to London. He felt that there had been some deep misunderstanding between them yesterday, that they had both expressed themselves wrongly.

He hadn't lied to Elle when he'd told her that he'd never been able to find anyone that was worth it – what he'd truly meant was that he'd never found anyone beside *her* that was worth it. He didn't know if he could say what he felt to her now without making a complete idiot of himself, though, so perhaps it was best to stay away. He suspected that Penny knew how he felt, of course, but she wouldn't say anything. She was a solid friend through and through.

He arrived at Ryan's Antiques and Restorations on Main Street and entered the shadowy store. He had told a couple he was doing some work for up the coast that he would look for some Victorian era ceiling moulds for them. If anyone had them around here, Wally Ryan would. He and Rob were about the same age and had gone to school together, and Wally had inherited the place a few years back from Arthur, his father.

He'd always liked the Ryans' store; the general air of dis-array made it feel like a shop out of the 1880s, where anything could be found if only you had the patience to look for it. There were newer pieces towards the front, beautiful dressers and mirrors, vases, urns, coat racks, jewel-green goblets. At the back, older random pieces from different eras were coated in a fine layer of dust. Rob ran his hand across a writing bureau to reveal the fine dark wood beneath.

'I don't need you doing my housework for me, mate,' said

Wally, appearing magically from nowhere, like the wizard he resembled, with his overgrown beard, long grey hair and large bulbous nose. Though like Rob, Wally was only in his mid-thirties, his hair had greyed prematurely, and he had long grown into the look.

'Looks like you need someone to do it,' Rob laughed. 'As usual, I don't have a clue where to start looking for what I want.'

'It's all up here,' said Wally, tapping a long, bony finger to his temple. 'That's the trick you see, you have to talk to me in order to get what you want.'

'Your dad trained you well all right.' Rob told him what he was after, and they spent a pleasant half hour going through the shop's treasures. Despite Wally's insistence, his mental map of the shop was a little less clear than he made out.

Finally he found something. 'Is this along the lines of what you're looking for?'

'Maybe,' said Rob. 'This couple have got particular tastes. I'll take it and show it to them and see how it goes.'

He and Wally had an easy-going arrangement whereby Rob took what he needed and paid for it later if it was to the client's liking. It was one of the benefits of working in a small town; everyone knew and trusted everyone else. Except Doug Grant of course, he reflected wryly.

'How's the work at Bay Hotel coming?' Wally asked.

'All over before it began, I'm afraid,' Rob told him. 'Times have been hard and the bank won't extend any more finance. Looks like they might have to sell.'

'If it comes to that, it'll be a bloody shame,' said Wally. 'Apart from the likelihood of some fancy developers erecting an eyesore on the beach front, that place has been the beating heart of this town since I can remember. I've been to the best knees-ups of my life at that place.'

'Don't I know it. But it looks like bad news all around. Only a miracle could save it now.'

Rob left his friend shaking his head and grumbling in the cool, shadowy confines of the shop, and stepped back out into the modern age. He had a few errands to tick off the list this morning.

But all day long, he was asked about the Bay Hotel. From his coffee order at Pebbles Café, to buying paints from the hardware shop, or steaks for his dinner at the butcher's, he had to break the news again and again: the hotel would have no choice but to close, for good. He wasn't even sure it was his news to tell, but he couldn't lie to people.

He was met by disbelief, disappointment, and downright despondency. He didn't say that the new bank manager was responsible, but people could read between the lines, and they were angry about it.

The Bay Hotel belonged to all of them in a way. It was the site of their most treasured memories. Rob was regaled with tales of proposals, weddings, courtships, birthdays, graduations, celebrations for the sake of celebration, until he was ready to burst with other people's memories.

His own recollections were of a somewhat more intimate kind: long hours spent with Elle in the garden, lounging under the huge eucalyptus trees, telling her things he hadn't told anyone, then or since. And then later, joking with Anna over the bar, giving Penny brotherly advice, teasing her. He had taken his place in the family, and while it pained him to hear occasional news of Elle, he also had to admit to himself that this was one of the reasons he kept coming back there.

But one thing was obvious: everyone in Mulberry Bay cared about the fate of the hotel. They had let it sit there for years, safe in the knowledge that it would always be there, perched up there on the hill, in the shadow of the sugarloaf, watching over the town like a sentinel. The idea of it being taken away had got people fired up. The town wouldn't be the same without it, they all said.

Their passion for the place had started an idea flickering at the edges of Rob's brain. This thought, though still vague, was enough to get him driving towards the hotel later that afternoon, sure that if he talked it over with Elle and Penny, something might take hold.

Chapter 12

Elle and Penny had been doing some thinking of their own for most of the morning, but it had resulted in no such revelations. They had a big list, written by Penny, of positives about the hotel that could be exploited somehow: its prime location, the history and romance of the place, its way of making you feel you had gone back to a more glamorous time, the many moments that had been celebrated between its walls.

'We don't really advertise weddings enough,' Penny said. 'People here know about us, of course, but we could be reaching out to couples in Dublin. It's a unique location.'

'That's true,' said Elle. 'But it's going to take more than a couple of weddings to get us back on our feet, Penny. Besides, I don't think it would go down well if the ceiling fell in during someone's precious nuptials. It would kind of spoil the moment, wouldn't it?'

'What if we offered something like part-ownership, the way they do abroad sometimes?' Penny pondered.

Elle made a face. 'Fine for somewhere warm like Spain or France but who's going to want to time-share a cold, wet rock in the North Atlantic? No, what we need is cold, hard cash, that's the long and the short of it, I'm afraid.'

They made a full list of possible money-making ideas. On it Penny wrote:

Ask a different bank for money? Under which, Elle had written: Rob a bank.

'We're not really getting anywhere, are we?' Penny sighed.

'Not really. I'm sorry but there's just no way around it, Penny. We need to bring more business in to pay off the debt, yet we can't do that until the place is up to standard. And we need more money to bring the place up to standard.'

'Well, let's not give up just yet. Let's have some lunch, take a walk and then come back to it all with a clear head.'

Elle sighed in the face of her sister's relentless optimism. She couldn't see that it would make any difference, but she had promised to try. And Penny was right, all this thinking was indeed hungry work.

When Rob arrived at the hotel, Ned informed him that he had seen the girls walk off down the beach some time ago.

'How are you keeping, Ned?' asked Rob, aware that he had barely seen him since the funeral, and also that Ned Harte would likely not be inclined to share his feelings. He was a good man, a little bit on the unusual side with his strange humming mannerism, and odd obsession with Lennon & McCartney music, but that was one of the things

Rob liked about him. The world had too much sameness in it sometimes, too many people talking nonsense about nothing. When Ned did speak, (or hum) it was usually worth listening.

'Grand,' he said, before humming an instantly recognisable Beatles number, *She's Leaving Home*. Rob immediately interpreted this as Ned suggesting that Elle would be on her way again soon.

He didn't want to share his glimmer of an idea with him just yet. He couldn't stand to get the man's hopes up if it all came to nothing. 'It's a terrible shame.'

'Yes,' said Ned, looking stricken. 'I can't help but think if only I'd paid a bit more attention, been a bit more involved ...'

'It's not your fault, Ned. I know what Anna was like. A whirlwind. If you had tried to help she would have said you were getting in the way, poking your nose where it shouldn't be.'

'I know, I know,' the older man sighed. 'It's just, you always think of these things when it's too late, don't you?'

You certainly do, thought Rob, having an intimate acquaintance himself with hindsight and its pitfalls.

Elle and Penny weren't exactly getting much work done down on the beach. In fact, prompted by an excess of energy, Elle was running in and out of the tiny waves, the bottom of her dress soaked and clinging to her legs.

'Come on!' she called back to her sister. 'The water's actually OK.'

Penny tentatively came up to the water's edge, then backed off with a shriek when Elle began to kick water at her, then gave herself up to the silliness. Rob arrived to see the two sisters fully clothed, waist deep in water, trying to dunk the other under the waves.

He watched for a minute then yelled: 'Am I in time to stop a murder?'

The looks on the girl's faces were priceless when they saw him.

'Crikey,' Penny giggled. 'What were we at, playing like a couple of toddlers? I think the past few days have gone to my head.'

Elle was a little shame-faced, then puzzled as Rob watched her emerge from the sea, his face solemn. Did he disapprove, she wondered? But he had always been a great one for fun and joking about. And then she realised, the deep seriousness of his gaze, the slight flicker of want: it was the look she had seen on seventeen-year-old Rob, grown into the plain desire of a man. She looked away quickly. What would he see on her face, if she could still read him after all these years?

'Well, I've had quite a day,' he told them, quickly back to normal, and proceeded to tell them about his errands all over town, and exactly what everyone had said when he told them about the fate of the hotel.

'But we know how people feel about the hotel, Rob,' said Penny. 'That's exactly why we're trying to save it.'

'Yes, but have you thought that people's feelings about the hotel could be the very thing that *could* save it? I mean, this town takes care of its own – that's what we do. We live here on the coast and we're used to weathering all kinds of storms, no matter if they come in from the sea, or if they brew somewhere else.' He smiled. 'Like your dad himself might say, sometimes you need a little help from your friends.'

Some of the stories Rob had gleaned from the townspeople were astonishing, and incredibly heart-warming.

There was Wally Ryan's dad, Arthur of Ryan's Antiques and Restorations, who had been to some rollicking 'knees-ups' in the hotel as he described them to Rob when he bumped into him on Main Street not long after chatting to Wally.

He had seen the very best days of the ballroom, when people came from miles around to dance and hear the best show-bands in the region. He had danced there with his wife May, until she died fifteen years back. 'And of course myself and the boys played our best sets up there, back in the day,' he added fondly, reminding Rob that Arthur used to play in a band with some of the other locals, Johnny Chips being one of them, from what he could recall.

Vivian, who ran The Grain Store Bakery, had celebrated the fifth birthday of her granddaughter in the hotel's gardens. She and her granddaughter, who was now nineteen, still remembered how wonderful that day was. 'It was autumn and the trees were strung with yellow lanterns that looked like giant flowers, a long table was covered in fairy cakes, jelly and ice-cream, red lemonade. Oh,' she gasped breathlessly to Rob, clutching her chest as she remembered, 'it was everything a little girl could dream of.'

Elle's old friend Hazel had been married to her husband Glenn at the hotel, before they settled down to the business of running The Orchard Garden Centre and Karen of The Wonder Room Accessories had met her future husband at Hazel's wedding. Inspired by the Gatsbyesque drama of the evening, the beauty of the sugarloaf in the distance and the feeling of joy and magic that the night had held, they had locked eyes during the ceremony and that, as Karen put it, was that.

Joe, the town's general mechanic and handyman, had gone to the hotel almost religiously every Sunday to partake of Anna's generous helpings of Sunday roast, but also to chat with her about the goings-on in the town, and to confide in her about how he missed his wife, Cora. 'Anna's passing has made a big enough hole in my week,' he told Rob gruffly, 'but the hotel not being there any more is simply unthinkable.'

Even Rob's own mother, Grace Callahan, had fond memories of the hotel, 'before it went to scrap' as she acidly put it. She had taken Rob and his sister to the annual Easter picnic that had been held in the hotel's heyday, an event of sack-races, egg-in-the-spoon, treasure hunts for children and adults alike. Elle recalled that those days had always ended in a big picnic in the gardens, Anna handing out hot meat sandwiches to one and all.

One thing was clear: the hotel was irreplaceable to Mulberry Bay and its people.

Also obvious – to Elle in particular – was that Anna's hand had been behind each and every one of these events, working subtle magic, guaranteeing that each occasion would be remembered and treasured. It was one thing to hope that the town might be behind them in their quest to save the Bay Hotel, but quite another to think that she or Penny would be able to live up to such a legacy, and continue Anna's work with the same dedication and expertise.

'It's just such a huge ask,' she said to the others later that night, over dinner.

Penny had prepared cannelloni and Elle had braved the depths of the cellar to procure what Ned told them was a special bottle of wine. Hard work, since he couldn't remember the year or vintage, or even where it came from. In the end, she had closed her eyes and chosen one at random.

'Well, nothing worthwhile is easy,' said Penny. 'That's what Mum always said when I was struggling with something.'

Elle was familiar with the maxim too. 'Yes, but I'm not sure exactly what we're hoping for here. Are we asking people for money? For labour? How do we turn all of this goodwill into something tangible?'

'I think you're asking people for whatever they can offer to help get you over this rocky patch,' said Rob. 'In return, they get the security of knowing this place will always be here whenever they need it. And if things go to plan, then the whole town will get the extra tourism boost a thriving hotel will provide.'

'It's not just that, though,' Elle argued. 'Let's say it all goes to plan, and we get some contributions of money or labour or whatever to help to keep us afloat in the short term. Let's suppose that we fix up the rooms, give the place a lick of paint and with the best intentions and a heavy marketing push, somehow manage to secure an unprecedented number of bookings for the summer season. Can the hotel handle that? Can *we* handle that?' She looked at Penny, and took a sip of her wine. She actually thought it had turned slightly, but never mind. 'Mum was a natural at this. *She's* what made this place so special. I'm not sure about you, Penny, but I know I don't have the talents that Mum possessed. I'm not good with people, I don't have a mind for community, I can't envision the perfect evening for someone and make it happen with a snap of my fingers.' To say nothing of the fact that she had a life in London that she needed to get back to, soon. Her boss was being very good about her absence thus far (possibly because she rarely took days off or used her annual holiday entitlements) but there were some crucial projects in the pipeline that would soon require her undivided attention. She needed to get all of this sorted and soon.

Rob started to laugh. 'First of all, Elle, I think you sell yourself short. If I didn't know you better, I would think you were fishing for compliments. But the truth is, and I'm sure Penny and your dad would agree with me, Anna wasn't exactly a natural at this either. She would tell you that herself if she was still here: there was a lot of trial and error before she became the expert she was; there is in every business.'

'That's true enough.' Ned sat forward. He looked around at them all, and they could tell he was gearing up to tell them a story. He so very rarely spoke at length, that there was an air of expectancy around the table. Penny had turned the lights in the dining room very low, and put candles on the table. The whole room seemed alive with the past, almost like the shadows of those who had dined and celebrated there were moving around the room.

'When we first bought this place, Elle was just a wee thing, and Penny was just rounding to her mother's belly. Well,' said Ned, 'you should have seen us. A pair of green-horns if ever you saw them. Anna was up and down ladders sweeping cobwebs out of corners, painting walls, or else she was on her hands and knees scrubbing the floor. When I expressed concern, she told me: 'I'm just trying to get this baby accustomed to hard work.' My job from the start was the gardens. I'd take Elle out there with me, sit her in the dirt and weeds, and plant and water until my back almost broke. The building was still in good condition then, but the garden was a jungle. Worse than it is now.'

He pushed his glasses back on his nose and looked at Elle. 'You ate your fair share of dirt, I can tell you. I could only pray it would make you strong, which thank goodness, it did. Now where was I? Oh yes, we got everything to rights, and then the guests started to arrive in droves. We were driven half mad. Penny arrived in the middle of it all, but

Anna just kept on going. She was so tired she was mixing up bookings, putting salt in the desserts, disaster. One day she turned a whole washing line of white sheets bright pink. But it didn't matter. There was something about the place, even then, and about a year after we took over, she was so good at what she did, it was like she was born to it. Even guests who had experienced the early days came back again and again, because even when Anna was making mistakes, she had a trick of making people warm to her.'

There was silence around the table as they took it in. None of them could remember ever hearing Ned say half this much. 'So,' he said, 'this certainly is a business that can be learned. You girls both have your own talents, and I'm not going to just sit back and watch the days go by any more. I need to keep myself busy. I'll try to be the backbone of this place, if Penny might consider being its eyes, ears and mouth. And Elle, you do the talking.'

Touched by her father's words, Penny's eyes glistened as she spoke. 'We'll do our very best.'

After dinner, Penny said that she and Ned would clean up and asked if Elle could bring Rob up to the attic to check if there was anything saleable in there amongst the old stored furniture. It would be a start.

'What are you playing at?' Ned asked when they were alone in the kitchen.

'What do you mean?' Penny was all innocence, but then she smiled. 'Ah, just seeing if we can't bring about two miracles for the price of one.'

She could feel that if Elle let loose just a little bit, then perhaps something wonderful could happen for her while she was here. Then at least if the hotel didn't work out, there would be a silver lining, of sorts.

Chapter 13

Elle had always been a tiny bit afraid of the attic, though she would never in a million years admit it.

She supposed it was entirely fitting that a property as old and grand as this should have an attic that matched. Creaky, shadowy, full of old junk from the hotel down the years, much of it from previous owners, and probably bats nesting in the eaves, watching for any visitors with baleful, glowing eyes. Elle hated bats and the thought of their frail and thin wings brushing against her gave her the shivers.

Rob chuckled on the shadowy stair behind her. 'You know there was an old rumour going around about this place at one stage? That it was haunted.'

She frowned, but a sudden shiver ran up her spine and she couldn't be sure if it was because of the possibility Rob had suggested, or the mere proximity of his presence in these dark quarters. 'I never heard anything of the sort.'

'I'm serious. The story goes that a jilted fiancé of the first owner haunts the place. The story has probably been responsible for a few bookings over the years. You know some people are desperate to see a ghost.'

'I think I would have noticed a ghost hanging around for my whole childhood,' she countered.

'I didn't say it was true.' She felt him shrug as they climbed the narrow stairs up to the attic door. 'I just said there was a rumour.'

Now Elle imagined ghosts swooping like birds from the corners of the attic. Stop being an idiot, she told herself. You'll give yourself nightmares.

The attic smelt old as all attics do: of books not opened for years, mouldy wood, and a musty damp smell from the leak in the roof. Rob picked up a feather and held it out to her. 'I think you've got a few visitors.'

'I think a few things worse than birds, probably.'

Elle turned on the light and the bulb flickered uncertainly, then gave out a weak and watery light. It made it slightly easier to see things, but also made them a bit spookier somehow. You couldn't be exactly sure what each thing was. Was that a coat stand with a sheet over it, or was it a tall man, hiding in the corner? Did the ancient wardrobe in the corner just creak open a little, or was it just her imagination?

'You start at one end, I'll do the other,' she said briskly, hoping to overcome her fear by being extra practical. She sometimes tried this trick when she had to speak in front of the other more senior architects at the firm, or present a particularly audacious modern piece of design. She would simply be even sharper, cutting away any room for doubt or nervousness. She would pretend she wasn't able to feel things like that. She would build a barrier between herself and any distracting emotions.

They worked in silence for a while and Elle wished she was less conscious of Rob's presence. She could hear him working, sometimes humming snatches of tunes under his breath, like Ned did.

It had felt so natural to have him at the table tonight. Paradoxically, the very ordinariness and comfort his presence provided made her feel awkward all over again. What was that look he gave her earlier today at the beach? Did it really indicate what she thought, that he still had feelings for her? It had been so many years.

But of course she shouldn't take anything for granted. Elle couldn't tell if she was still angry at him for what he had said yesterday about her being unlovable, or if he was still angry with her for suggesting the same to him. It was true that when they were young she had often known what he was thinking. But he would open up, and then shut himself away again, as though scared by what he had revealed to her.

Elle couldn't blame him, she sometimes felt that way herself.

She started to think of the story her dad had told at dinner. It was nice to get a glimpse of the past from his eyes. Everything she knew about the hotel's early days, or indeed her own early days of childhood, had been told to her by

Anna, who spoke in general terms and often missed out the details that really gave a story life.

Elle was sorting through a box of old bronze ornaments, quite hideous really, but perhaps worth something, when she was confronted by a heart-stopping sight. Someone's face, pale and bruised, was sitting heavily in her hands. She screamed and threw the object away before she realised that she had been holding a mirror. Rob was by her side in seconds, his hands on her arms.

'What is it?' he asked, concerned. 'What happened?'

'Nothing,' said Elle, shakily. 'It was stupid, I picked up a mirror and saw my own face. I didn't realise ... I was thinking about your ... ghost story.'

He laughed gently. 'Oh Elle, I'm sorry. It was just a story.'

They looked at the shards of the broken mirror, glinting on the floor.

'Seven years' bad luck,' she said.

'Actually the saying is seven years' bad luck in *love*,' Rob corrected, his voice softening. 'But I don't think ...' He gave her a tender look that she recognised instantly but hadn't seen in almost two decades, 'that you need to worry about that.' Without warning, he gathered her gently into his arms and kissed her. Elle felt her hands tingle, the blood rushing straight to her heart, which was beating like a drum.

'Your poor nose,' he said then, as though he had just noticed the bruises. 'Your poor, poor nose.' He began to kiss her nose, then her cheeks, and then her forehead. He held her like he was holding something infinitely precious.

Stunned by the unexpectedness of it all, and at how familiar and natural it seemed, Elle felt herself respond, and the job at hand was temporarily abandoned.

Penny returned to her mother's office after dinner, the pull of Anna's story irresistible, especially after what Ned had revealed about the early days of the hotel.

Pulling more of the diaries out of the bottom drawer, she began making neat stacks in groups of five years, starting from the very beginning. When completed, she found that she had approximated the length of time that her mother had been keeping a diary – about forty years.

'That was a lot of writing Mum,' she said in admiration, recalling her own inability to keep a diary for more than a week before getting distracted and abandoning the endeavour completely.

Consulting the spines of the books, she found the very first one and picked it up with eager hands. The first entry was dated March 10, 1975 and it was clear what this entry was about.

I've never kept a diary before – but I feel that now is the time. Don't ask me why, I just feel events occurring that I need to keep track of. I hate to say for 'longevity's sake' but I suppose that is a part of it.

Anyway, I met someone. His name is Ned.

I feel so foolish and very much like a schoolgirl starting a diary just because I met a fella. But I can't escape the idea that this one happens to be special. But he isn't at all like some of the guys I know from town – I suppose that is why I like him. Of course, I have no idea what the future holds, if it holds anything really – but I have a feeling. Just call it a hunch.

So what's he like?

Well, he is a bit quiet – a bit introverted, private, pretty much my exact opposite truth be told, but you know what they say about opposites ...

Penny chuckled at her mother's description of her father being her exact opposite. Complete understatement of the millennium. But when Anna went on to describe Ned for the apparent gentleman he was – opening car doors, kissing her hand, taking her to the cinema, the whole shebang, Penny felt herself feeling somewhat envious. Her dad was obviously besotted with her mother, much like Rob was besotted with Elle, and she felt herself ever so slightly jealous of both of them – she couldn't remember the last time a man had kissed her hand – or treated her like something precious. In fact, that had never happened. In her love-life, she was always the one doing the chasing or making the effort. Forgetting her own thoughts for the moment, Penny read on.

June 1, 1975

So the 'M' word was mentioned today. And not by me. It was Ned who asked if I had ever thought of it. Marriage, that is. He kind of caught me unawares, truth be told. After all, we have only been going out for a couple of months.

But I would be lying if I said that I had never thought about it. Especially recently as things have been going so well. So, I told him the truth. That I had thought about marriage and it was something that interested me – something that I saw in my future. Something that I wanted in my future.

He nodded and smiled – and then, being Ned, started humming a song, together with lyrics about arms that longed to hold me and keep me by his side. Of course, I have come to understand by now the meaning of this little tic of his – Ned seems to find it easiest to express emotion via music lyrics, and this particular insight is from the Beatles song *From Me to You*. I think it's lovely and find it full of promise. So I think this might be it. I think he'll ask me soon. Either himself or in the words of Lennon/McCartney. Either way is grand with me.

Penny read the last paragraph again. It was the first time that her mother had openly acknowledged Ned's curious penchant for quoting Beatles' lyrics. And she put up with that willingly even back then? Penny asked herself, scratching her head.

To her mind, it was easily the most frustrating thing about her dad. Everyone knew of course that both Elle and Penny had been named for famous Beatles songs but she didn't realise that her mother had been so complicit.

But it appeared that Anna didn't only put up with it – she also seemed to find it endearing – *cute* even.

She continued reading. *A bit like modern day poetry*, her mother gushed in another entry, and Penny's eyes glistened, captivated and moved all at once by this insight into the early days of her parents' romance.

As the hours passed, the years did too and as she read through her mother's diaries Penny felt as if she was pulling back individual layers of an onion, peeling away at time.

She read the continuing journey of her parents' courtship, experiencing Anna's emotion and excitement come alive and spring off the page, and even found herself with tears in her eyes as she read through her mother's interpretation of her father proposing – complete with getting down on one knee and expressing his love for her (with what else – a song lyric) on the strand.

And next Penny was reading about their wedding day and the way her dad's voice caught and broke when he toasted his new wife at their reception right here at the hotel. Penny had known that her parents had frequented the hotel as local patrons before they bought it, but had some-how forgotten that they were married here. Ned and Anna's first dance as a married couple was right here in the ball-room to *Let it Be*.

Her mother had also dedicated one entry at considerable length, to the wedding gift she had given to Ned – and how excited he had been when presented with it. Her dad, excited? That was a new one on Penny. Apparently, Anna had procured an autographed vinyl LP of a first edition Beatles record from 1964. She described it as a 'VJ 45' that contained the songs *Anna* and *Ask Me Why*. Apparently, the record was quite rare – and when Penny read the price that Anna had saved up, and eventually paid for the vinyl, very valuable, too.

'It will go perfectly in his collection,' Anna had reflected.

'Weird,' said Penny, reading the passage again. Collection … what collection? She wondered what it meant – a collection of Beatles memorabilia perhaps? But Ned didn't have such a collection, certainly not here at the house and she couldn't imagine something like that being stuffed away in the attic somewhere, as it would be something her father would be obsessive about, and she was sure she would have heard of it. He played music, yes, but mostly on the hotel CD player. There was certainly no turntable that she was aware of.

She pondered this for a moment and read on in the diary, but nothing else was detailed about the wedding present or the 'collection' – the next entry simply outlined a weekend trip to Dublin that Anna and Ned had taken for their honeymoon.

Wondering if she should ask her father about it, she quickly decided against it, as this would mean she'd have to reveal she was reading Anna's diaries. She didn't want to admit this; it seemed like something that was off-limits somehow.

And Penny wanted to keep the diaries and this precious insight into her mother's life to herself for the moment. As it was, they represented an outlet to her mother, a comfort of sorts, and for her at least, helped fill up the huge void Anna had left in all of their lives.

Much later that night, when everyone was in bed and the hotel was silent, Ned went into the ballroom and switched on the chandelier. He couldn't say why he felt like being in that room in particular, but he was still having trouble sleeping, and he'd been wandering through the rooms each night, reliving the memories associated with each one.

Of course, most of his memories contained Anna, which was painful to him, but he didn't want to forget the little moments they had shared over the years.

In the majority of his memories were images of her working here at the hotel: on top of a ladder, polishing a side-board, laughing with guests, stuffing a turkey. Just ordinary old domestic moments that most couples had. He hadn't known at the time that he would come to treasure those seemingly everyday moments like jewels.

The ballroom had once been the gleaming diamond of the hotel. Its high vaulted ceiling, huge chandelier and gilded wallpaper had all spoken to the beauty and mystique of another time. Now the floor was scarred by sharp stiletto heels, the wallpaper faded and ripped in places, the chandelier dim and dusty.

It was no surprise that it was so worn: it had seen its fair share of celebrations. He remembered a wedding when Anna had been persuaded away from her work and out onto the dance floor. He could still see her skirt flaring, her skin like gold under the light.

There were memories of the girls, too, from the days when they made their hotel their playground. Elle and Penny playing ladies and gentlemen, dancing with their dolls beneath the chandelier. Elle, having somehow found her way onto the roof, waving down at her frantic parents below. The girls having a midnight feast in the kitchen, taking advantage of how soundly Anna slept.

He wondered about what Rob Callahan had suggested earlier. It was great that the town was behind them, but realistically what could anyone do to save it? No, Ned had to seriously consider his options. What could he do, at his age? It had been so long since he'd done anything else but mosey around this place, while Anna kept everything going.

Ned left the ballroom and turned out the light, his heart heavy with regret that he hadn't done more. Perhaps if he'd paid more attention, understood more about the financial side of things, he could have helped.

But now it was too late; his Anna, the centre of his universe, the very axis around which the family circled was gone.

Ned wasn't sure about the hotel, but he felt that if he could just keep the rest of the family together, everything would be OK.

Chapter 14

The following morning, the hotel shone beneath the crisp springtime sun. Wispy white clouds floated behind it, threaded through the endless blue sky. It seemed to stand just a tiny bit straighter this morning, with an aura of hope almost, as though there was just a tiny suggestion that something good might be about to happen.

When Elle woke around eight a.m., her first thought was not of the hotel but of Rob. Had it really happened? Had he really kissed her last night? And she had kissed him back ...

She couldn't tell how she really felt about that now. She probed at the memory of the night before, as though it might give some clue. Certainly, she had felt completely at peace in his arms, and being honest, she hadn't felt like that in a long, long time. Perhaps this more than anything was the proof she needed that her relationship with Sebastian wasn't meant to be. In truth, she'd barely thought of her ex these past few days. But where was all of this headed with Rob? This morning she felt a fresh layer of anxiety settle over the events of the night before. She didn't want for them to become involved again while she was here, only to have their relationship come to a halt when she returned to London. She'd already just come out of a messy situation, so she would have to put a stop to everything *now* before it went too far and began to interfere with what they were trying to do with the hotel.

There was more at stake here than just her feelings. It was her family's livelihood, her father and sister's happiness. And she couldn't risk hurting Rob or herself again for the sake of a short fling.

Elle got up and greeted the day with the feeling that she had made a difficult, but ultimately sensible decision.

'Good morning!' Penny greeted smilingly when Elle went downstairs for breakfast.

'You're very chirpy this morning.'

'I just feel a renewed sense of optimism after our chat last night. And speaking of last night,' her sister added, eyeing Elle, 'Rob seemed quite distracted when he left. Did you two find any great treasures in the attic?'

Elle looked at her sternly. 'Penny, you may think that you're being smart, but it's pretty obvious what you're playing it. And you should also know that it's a very, very bad idea. Nothing good will come of Rob and me getting together. We've been through it once and that was enough. What happened last night was a moment of weakness and will just have to be written off as a mistake. It's not what I want, in any case and I'm going home soon, after all.'

Penny's disappointment was palpable. 'Oh Elle. I just wish you would let yourself relax a little bit and go with the flow. I think you could be so happy if you did.'

'Maybe you should concentrate on your own happiness, instead of worrying about other people's. You're like a meddling old woman. Now, if it's all right with you, I'm going for a walk.' Elle hadn't meant the words to come out so sharply and regretted them the moment she spoke. Penny's face was a study in shock, then hurt.

'I'm sorry. I didn't mean to interfere . . .'

'It's OK,' she replied, stiffly. 'We've just got more important things to worry about at the moment and I think it's best for everyone if we concentrate on the task in hand.'

When Elle returned from a walk on the beach after breakfast to try and clear her mind, she was surprised to see scaffolding set up on the front of the hotel.

She was even more surprised to see Ned and Penny balanced on the long plank between the two scaffolds. They both had electric sanders buzzing away at the exterior. Elle could see the long cords snaking through an open window.

'What are you doing?' she yelled, during a break in the noise. 'This place is as big as the Coliseum. It will take ages.'

'Even the Coliseum started somewhere,' Penny called down, then emphatically switched her sander back on.

Elle went back into the house feeling yet again as though she had been left out of something.

'It's strange that Rob didn't stick around today,' Penny commented at lunchtime. 'He just helped us set up the scaffold and then left. He didn't want to stay, even when I told him we were having chicken salad for lunch.'

'I think it's roast chicken that he's especially partial to,' Elle said. 'Anyway, it could be that Rob's getting a little bit tired of running around after us. He does have his own business to look after, you know.'

'No, I don't think that's it,' Penny said eyeing her. 'I don't think that's it at all. Anyway, he'll be back tomorrow. He said he wants to get started on the roof.'

'I suppose I should finish getting rid of the stuff in the attic, then.'

'Oh no, I'll do that. You'll want to be getting out and about in the town, talking to people and asking for help with the hotel.'

'What?' Elle was absolutely shocked. 'You can't expect me to do that! Look what happened last time you sent me to talk to someone in the town. Besides, I haven't lived here for years. It's you that everyone knows and likes.'

'It's not really something I'm good at, though,' her sister pointed out. 'Not to mention that they all just see me as Penny from the tourist office, and I can't see them taking me seriously as a business person. You're the one with a way with words, Elle. You're used to pitching things for your work, aren't you?' She waved her hand in the air vaguely as though one of Elle's presentations was hanging in the space between them.

'Ah I really, really don't want to do this.' Elle looked at Ned who was sitting quietly at the table. Of course, it was no use at all appealing to him, and he would be the very last one in this family you could expect to do the talking. Unless they wanted the fate of the hotel to rest on whatever random Beatles lyrics her father chose to communicate the urgency of the matter. He duly kept his head down, stoically munching on a piece of bread as though that was of the utmost importance.

'You said you would help,' Penny challenged haughtily. 'In fact, you promised. Now you're saying you won't? In that case, you might as well slink off home to London.'

The word 'home' cut Elle to the core, the implication being that the Bay Hotel was no longer her home. Well, she had as much emotional claim to it as Penny did, she thought angrily.

'Fine then, I'll do it. But first I'll need to think about what I'm supposed to say.' she said, sounding a lot more confident than she felt. It was true what she'd said about messing things up completely the last time the hotel's fate rested in her hands.

Elle sighed, taking Penny's advice about pitching and tried to think of it like a work project. Taken like that, the task didn't seem quite so momentous.

Second time lucky?

*

148

Penny did some more sanding after lunch. It was nicer being up there later in the evening when it was cooler, a glorious sunset starting to develop behind her. The sun was sinking like a drop of molten gold and she imagined fancifully that it would make a huge sizzling sound when it disappeared beneath the water.

She found she liked the physical side of the work as well. There was some satisfaction in watching the old flaky paint disappear, leaving a new canvas underneath for them to work with. She knew it would be a huge job, but she didn't want to just sit idly with her thoughts or Anna's diaries all day long, now that there were no more guests or wouldn't be until what little maintenance work they could afford was complete.

As she worked, Elle took up a substantial amount of her thoughts.

She felt that her sister was making a huge mistake. Rob still cared about her, any fool could see that. And Elle would be a worse fool if she threw that away.

Penny knew that it was partly her own bad relationship experiences that made her so keen for her sister to be happy. She had fallen in love so many times, with locals mostly and the odd tourist over the years, but none of those relationships – if you could even call them that – had ever lasted beyond the early stages. Rob had tried to set her up a few times with his mates and even a couple of lads from his work crew, to no avail.

It was part of the reason Penny didn't want to go and

speak to the town's business people. She just didn't have enough confidence in herself, and thought her tongue would stiffen like concrete if she had to persuade a single one of them to help the hotel. Elle, who was used to this kind of thing, had to do it; it was their only chance.

When her arms got tired, Penny turned and sat and watched the sun go down. She felt that if she could have this view every night for the rest of her life, perhaps it might not matter if she always watched it alone.

That night Elle had another restless slumber, thinking of the unpleasant day ahead of her tomorrow. She would have to clear the air with Rob for starters, before things got too awkward. Obviously he felt the embrace the other night was a mistake, too, since he'd been in such a hurry to get away after dropping off the scaffolding today. He hadn't wanted to face her either.

She felt oddly disappointed, despite her own decision earlier that morning not to pursue it. Well, it was never nice to be rejected.

Then there was the awful task Penny had set her: asking the town business community for help. Elle could hardly think of anything she wanted to do less. The problem was, she had left this town so long ago, and she knew they would all be judging her, coming back and grovelling now. They would automatically think that she had failed in her life in the city, suffered some big disappointment or something, seeing as she was back now begging for charity. Well, she would set them straight on that score from the outset. And she was darned if she was seeing a single person without buying a suit. She would get one tomorrow morning at Handbags and Gladrags after she talked to Rob.

There was a scratching at her door. 'For a place that promises rest and relaxation and a break from the world,' she muttered, echoing their vision for the hotel, 'I'm certainly getting nothing of the sort.'

She opened the door and Penny's cats rushed in, twin streaks of black and white. 'Why don't you go and sleep in your owner's room?' she asked them, but the pair of felines simply curled up in the middle of Elle's bed, and stared at her placidly as they had for the last two nights since their arrival.

Chapter 15

When Rob pulled up at the hotel early the next morning, loaded up with materials to get started on the roof repairs, Elle was waiting for him.

His dogs leapt out from the back of his truck and rushed at Elle like she was an old friend, licked her hand, and then deciding she wasn't so interesting after all, tore off through the gardens and down towards the beach.

'That was Gruff and Kaiser,' he said. 'I don't think you were properly introduced last time.'

Elle was wiping doggy drool onto the legs of her jeans. 'Pleasure's all mine.'

He chuckled. 'Don't worry, they'll be back when they want attention.'

She studied him. He didn't seem to feel awkward or unsure about the other night. He was easy in himself, swinging his tools off the back of the truck and she couldn't help but admire his lean, strong body.

'I thought we could go for a quick walk this morning,' she said. 'You know, talk things over.'

His face was suddenly serious. 'I'm glad you mentioned it. I hoped we would be able to talk. I didn't get the chance to see you yesterday as I only popped up with the sanding stuff for Penny.'

Elle nodded, unsure how to feel. He certainly wasn't giving much away.

As they made their way down to the beach towards the dogs, Rob spoke again: 'You know, it's stupid, but I was sort of afraid to see you yesterday. I felt like a teenager again, my heart going like mad. Scared of seeing you, scared of not. I almost ran out of the place. I think Penny was a little offended.'

'Don't worry about that,' Elle said, then took a deep breath. 'But Rob, maybe your instinct wasn't wrong. Perhaps we shouldn't see each other, in that way. I've just come out of a ... situation recently and in fact,' she said, gaining confidence now the words were out, 'I think we should keep our relationship strictly friendly from now on, for the sake of the work we're doing here at the hotel.'

If she had been looking at Rob's face, it might have told her something for a second, before he rearranged his features into a kind of pleasant mask. But Elle was looking out to sea, scared that if she looked at him, something inside her would snap and break, like dry grass underfoot.

'Yes, you're right,' he agreed. 'I was thinking along the same lines. There's so much at play, we don't want any additional complications on our hands. Best to keep things on the straight and narrow.'

'Exactly,' Elle said, wondering why her voice sounded so shaky and uncertain. 'So, we're agreed, then?'

'Absolutely,' said Rob.

'Shake on it.' Elle held her hand out, feeling a little like an idiot. Rob took it gently in his own. They shook hands and didn't meet each others' eyes for the remainder of the walk, even when the dogs frolicked in the sand, and urged them to do the same.

Eventually they made their way back towards the hotel in silence and it felt ten times longer than it should have. Elle was relieved to get back and ready to attack the second unpleasant, but necessary task of the day.

'I could order in something,' Mona from Handbags and Gladrags was saying. 'One of my suppliers does beautiful Italian trouser suits. But we don't have anything like that in stock at the moment.'

'I need one today,' Elle said, looking around the store's pitiful selection of professional workwear. As usual, it was all floaty silks and wispy linens and nothing whatsoever that would work for a serious business meeting. Things were going from bad to worse.

'We just don't get much call for suits around here,' said Mona 'People don't dress so conservatively. It is a beach town after all. Most people just like to look neat.'

'Isn't there anywhere else?' Elle asked, a little irritated by the woman's airy-fairy approach. Just because it was a beach town didn't mean that everyone should dress like beach bums.

'You'd probably have to go into Wexford. But wait just a minute, I'll pop out back and have a quick look.'

Elle supposed she was being too picky but she refused to approach any of the town's businesspeople in the same old clothes she'd been wearing since she got here. She only had her funeral garb, which was hardly suitable, or a collection of casual dresses and shirts, and a couple of pairs of jeans. No, for this she needed to look sharp and in control. Mona or indeed Penny who suggested she borrow one of her gypsy skirts, didn't understand that in business, appearances were important.

'Well,' said Mona. 'I've got these ...' She sounded unsure, and Elle could see why when she laid eyes on the suits. One was a horrible old-fashioned polyester trouser suit, embellished on the lapels and sleeves, perfect for an Elvis impersonator maybe, but not exactly suited to her present purposes. The other offering was a mid-length linen skirt and matching jacket in a sort of pale tan, almost beige colour.

'Let me try that one,' said Elle.

She put the suit on and stepped out of the fitting room to show Mona.

'Well, it fits anyway,' the boutique owner murmured, evidently trying to make the best of a bad situation.

'I'll take it.'

'Really?' Though Elle could see why Mona was surprised. The suit might fit, but that was about the only thing recommending it. The linen looked a little wrinkled and untidy and the colour completely washed her out. Against it, Elle's freckles stood out as if someone had drawn them on with crayon. But a bad suit was better than no suit, she reckoned, showing an uncharacteristic lapse in judgement.

Mona charged her well below what the suit was worth. *I know desperation when I see it*, she thought to herself as Elle left the shop. She shook her head. If only she hadn't been in such a hurry, she could have ordered in something beautiful.

As it was, that outfit made Elle Harte look a fright.

Work continued apace at the hotel. Ned and Penny were sanding the outside, and Rob was clearing out the attic so that he could get to the roof.

Penny wasn't surprised by the fury with which he worked. She had some idea of what had happened on the beach that morning, and an even better idea as to how it made him feel. By mid-morning, he was stripped to the waist, gleaming with sweat, his face strained from lifting so much of the ancient furniture down the stairs.

'Maybe I should give him a hand with some of that stuff,' Ned suggested. 'It's a big job.'

'Don't you dare,' Penny warned. 'I don't need to be worried about the both of you.' Her heart ached for Rob though. He was such a good person. She knew he would continue to break his back for the hotel, despite his pain over Elle. It was just who he was.

She sighed so loudly that Ned gave her a strange look. 'What's wrong?' he asked. 'You almost blew the building over with that one.'

'I'm just wishing that things would work out the way they're supposed to,' she said.

At midday, Penny was startled to see Rob standing at the bottom of the ladder, trying to get her attention. 'What is it?' she yelled, switching off the sander and lifting up her safety glasses.

'There's a guest here,' said Rob. 'Says he's got a reservation.'

What? But that was impossible; she had cancelled what little reservations there were for the next few weeks. 'Oh, he's probably just selling something,' she said, climbing down the ladder. 'Couldn't you put him off?'

Rob shrugged. 'He was pretty adamant that he was supposed to be here,' he said.

Standing at reception was a tall man with floppy brown hair and thick glasses. He looked to be in his late thirties but was wearing a tweed coat, patched at the elbows, making him seem a lot older.

'Yes?' Penny said with some impatience. 'Can I help you?'

'Well,' he replied, looking uncertainly around the abandoned reception area. 'I'd like to check in please. My reservation is for two weeks, starting from the 11th. Today,

157

in fact.' He laughed nervously, evidently disconcerted by this rather unwelcoming first impression.

'No,' Penny muttered, 'That can't be right. I cancelled all the bookings; we're renovating.'

'I never received any cancellation,' he said, looking stricken. 'This can't be happening. I've come from Sussex in England.'

Penny flushed with shame. What a mess. Surely this surpassed any early mistakes her mother had ever made. 'I'm so sorry,' she said, meaning it. 'I must have missed you when I sent out the emails. But it's impossible for you to stay here at the moment. We're repairing the roof and repainting. There are other hotels in Wexford, the closest town over. I'll ring a couple and see if they have any vacancies.'

'But I had my heart set on this place,' he insisted. 'My parents stayed here years ago and raved about it. I'm writing a novel, you see, set in a seaside town just like this one.'

'Well in that case, you'd be even more uncomfortable. As I said, we're renovating. There'll be lots of noise.'

'Oh that's fine, really' said the Englishman, brightening. 'I go into my own little world when I'm working. A brass band couldn't distract me. And I'll be no trouble at all. I'll be in my room mostly, or on the beach. I'll wash my own things and I'll eat what you eat and when you do. I'm not at all fussy.'

Penny found him impossible to put off and a little charming, so just like that, the Bay Hotel had a single guest.

His name was Colin Forbes and as he'd told Penny, he was a novelist, intent on finding inspiration while at their hotel. Certainly plenty of drama around here at the moment, she thought, showing Colin to a quiet and drip-free room at the back of the hotel. Just don't expect the obligatory happily ever after.

Chapter 16

That afternoon, Elle's first meeting in Mulberry Bay was with Jim and Della Cleary, who ran the builders providers. It's where Rob got all his materials from and he'd insisted that they would be only too happy to help.

Elle refused the coffee and biscuits the wife had set out, thinking that it might seem a bit unprofessional to be munching on biscuits while outlining a business proposal. Della had looked askance at Elle's suit when she greeted her. Della herself was wearing overalls, but that was basically a work suit when you were in the hardware business.

'Well, I won't waste your time,' Elle began quickly, just as Jim had opened his mouth to talk about the weather. 'Our proposal is quite simple. You support our cause by donating some resources to the Bay Hotel or providing some at a discounted price. Then in return, when the hotel starts making a profit you are considered an investor, and will thus see a financial gain.' Her words came out like bullets, Elle knew, but she felt extremely ill at ease.

Jim and Della looked at each other doubtfully. Elle hated how married people always thought their 'secret' communications weren't completely visible when it was usually painfully obvious what they were thinking.

'It's not exactly what we discussed with Rob ...' said Jim slowly and Della shook her head in unison.

'It could turn out to be quite lucrative, I assure you,' Elle insisted.

'Yes, but it's not very ...' Della didn't finish her sentence and the three sat there uncomfortably, unsure what to say.

'Fine,' Elle said, standing up. 'I won't take up any more of your time. Thank you for seeing me anyway.'

And before Della or Jim could say another word, Elle had shown herself out of the warehouse.

The next two visits, to The Grain Store Bakery and Pebbles Café, proved to be much the same, as was Elle's pitch to Luca at Scoops Ice creams and Johnny's Fish & Chips shop. People seemed to be confused as to what she was proposing, or disliked something about the idea itself.

She couldn't work out what was wrong with them. 'I don't know,' said Luca, Johnny's handsome Italian brother, standing in his cheery little ice cream shop near the beach. 'Something about it just doesn't sound right to me.' Though he did offer Elle a scoop of pistachio ice-cream, her favourite.

Next on the list was Ryan's Antiques and Restorations. Her old schoolmate Wally was away, so Elle went through her pitch with his father, by now feeling like she was reading from a script, without hope.

Arthur had started shaking his head almost as soon as she walked through the door. So much for everyone crying out to help them!

'Girlie,' he said as Elle walked away, 'Come back and see us when you can sit down and chat like a civil person.'

Elle was enraged. She had been perfectly civil, and she hated being called 'girlie'. That man had always been a bit nuts anyway.

Last stop was Hazel and Glenn at the Orchard Garden Centre. The plan was to ask them to donate some plants and expertise so that the hotel's gardens could be reimagined. Elle had a vision for a paradise to exist behind the property overlooking the sea. A real oasis amongst the eucalyptus trees, where you could find lots of private little nooks to sit in and read or dream.

She sighed as she pulled up the long driveway past the apple and pear trees. At least her old friend would be a friendly face.

'Welcome, welcome! Let us show you around, and then we can have a good natter,' said Hazel effusively.

'Oh no,' said Elle. 'I don't want to take up too much of your time. I can see from here how beautiful everything is.'

'OK,' said Hazel, looking a little crestfallen. 'Come and meet Glenn then.'

Her old friend's husband was a handsome, muscular man with a huge grin. He was carrying little Alex on his shoulders.

'It's fantastic to finally meet you, Elle,' he said. 'Hazel's told me lots about the mischief the two of you used to get into growing up around here. She's looking forward to a proper catch-up.'

Elle smiled politely. 'We'll have to keep that for another time. I'm here to talk business today, I'm afraid.' She chuckled lightly, but even to herself she sounded fake and a little condescending. She just didn't want to ask more of people than they could give, especially when she knew how busy they must be.

She spoke to Glenn and Hazel out on the porch outside the old farmhouse. When she had finished, there was a long silence.

'I suppose we were thinking of something a little …' Glenn too, struggled to find the word he was looking for.

'Friendlier?' said Hazel, folding her arms.

'I don't know what you mean,' Elle said frowning. 'I thought it was a very fair proposition.'

'Well if you don't get it, Elle, then obviously you've changed even more than I could have dreamed.' With that, Hazel stormed back into the house and Glenn followed her, looking concerned.

Slightly perplexed, Elle was left to walk back to the old Cortina and begin the drive back to the Bay Hotel.

Once again, she had completely and utterly failed.

Penny, Ned, Rob and the new guest, Colin, were sitting out in the sun. It had been a hard day's work, for three of them anyway, and they were enjoying crisps and a bottle of red lemonade. Colin had just wanted to 'get to know them all'. Surprisingly, he was actually quite funny.

Rob's dogs were stretched out at his feet, begging for tit-bits.

'This really is a charming place,' said Colin. 'I hope you're not going to change it too much.'

'Not too much,' Penny told him. 'Just enough to drag it into the "modern era" as my sister says.'

'Just as long as it retains its original charm, though,' said Colin. 'You don't see places like this very often any more. My parents have very fond memories of their time here. Of course, they may have just been glad to have been on holiday without me and my sister.'

They all laughed and then heard the sound of the Cortina roaring up the drive.

'She's coming fast,' Ned commented.

'Hopefully she just can't wait to tell us all the news,' said Penny. She hadn't realised how anxious she was, but her heart was racing and her palms sweating. She was sure that Elle would have great reports of the entire community want-ing to help out and get behind them.

When Elle appeared on the lawn, her dad, Penny, Rob and some random stranger looked at her as if she was an alien.

'Oh, Elle,' Penny gasped. 'That suit.'

'It's awful,' Ned agreed. 'Makes you look a bit mental.'

'I'm quite aware,' Elle spat, 'of how putrid the suit is.'

'Well,' Penny queried hopefully, 'Putrid suit aside, did everything go well?'

'No, everything did not go well,' Elle raged. 'In fact, it was a disaster. Every single person in town looked at me just like you're looking at me now, as if I'm some kind of impostor. No one seemed to have the faintest idea about what I was asking. So much for banding together to help out, Rob. They refused to understand.' She ran a hand through her hair. 'You can forget about it. Forget about this hotel, Mum's legacy being the heart of this town. It means nothing to them. I'm sorry, I tried – I really tried, but it's all ruined.' They heard her voice crack on the last sentence and then she rushed inside.

Elle never let people see her cry if she could help it.

'Well if you ask me,' said Colin into the silence that followed. 'I'd say that suit was her first mistake.'

Penny walked Rob to his car. 'I don't know what we'll do now,' she said despondently. 'I'm all out of ideas.'

'It's so strange that everyone would turn her down flat like that,' he said, shaking his head in confusion. 'I know for a fact that Jim and Della wanted to help, Wally and Arthur too. And Luca was talking about how he owed so much to Anna for letting him use the hotel's freezer last summer when his broke down.' He scratched his head. 'I can't believe it could've been just talk.'

'I suppose it's easy for people to wring their hands and say how terrible it is, but then when presented with a chance to change things they get cold feet.'

Rob looked grim. 'I just wish I could do more.'

'You've done more than enough,' said Penny. 'We wouldn't have got this far without you. I know how hard it's been for you too with Elle ...' she trailed off.

'Yes. Maybe I should have learnt something the first time round.'

'Perhaps all's not completely lost. I know that she can be—'

He cut her off. 'Thanks Penny, but I think it's best if I go back to living my life the way I know how. Of course I'll still help out with the roof and the painting and any other way I can, but I just can't be around your sister too much. It's time to move on.' He shook his head. 'I should have told myself that years ago.'

Penny watched Rob drive away, and thought about how powerless she was to stop any of these things happening: her mum dying, Rob getting hurt, losing the hotel. Knowing she was powerless didn't make her feel any better about any of it, though.

That night Ned went up to the top floor and knocked on Elle's door. He hoped he had given her sufficient time to calm down.

'Come in,' she said.

When he entered, he wasn't surprised to see her suitcase was open on the bed and she was folding her clothes into it.

'Don't try to stop me with some random Beatles quote,' she said. 'I've made up my mind. I've done nothing but mess things up since I got here.'

'That's not true. You've been a real comfort to your sister.'

'A comfort! I've managed to sabotage the only two chances of saving the hotel. I've said awful things to Penny, and even more awful things to Rob. I might as well have come and set fire to the place for all the good I've done.'

Ned said nothing, just waited patiently. Sometimes Anna would get herself worked up like this and need to just talk herself out. He thought maybe this was what his eldest needed, too.

'I just don't understand it,' she said. 'I went and talked to those people in good faith based on what Rob had said about them wanting to help us. And every single one of them seemed to be offended by my very presence. What did I ever do to them? Yes, I moved away from town, but is that some kind of crime? Now I'm trying to do something useful for the place and they throw it back in my face.'

'They don't hate you, Elle. And they certainly don't hold it against you that you left the Bay.'

'You're wrong, Dad,' she said. 'I know you and Penny like to think the best of everyone, but they just didn't want to hear it. I tried to take up as little of their time as possible, and the proposal couldn't have been clearer, but they didn't want to hear a word.'

She continued to roll up socks and fold jeans and place them determinedly into her case. 'I don't see what else we could have offered them, really. It's the best return we could give in the circumstances.'

'I don't know if it's about "returns",' her father said quietly.

'The people of this town wanted to help because they loved your mother, they love the hotel and they wanted to help merely out of the goodness of their hearts. But it seems like you might have reduced all that into a business transaction. Here deals are done over tea and cake, or a bottle of wine and a good dinner. Thinking of it now, I'll bet you didn't exchange one nicety with those people. Not a single word about their families or the weather?'

Elle didn't answer so Ned knew he was right. 'Ah it's not money people wanted to be rewarded by Elle,' he said. 'It's the fact of the hotel, standing where it's always been.'

'Well, that's not going to happen now,' she replied tightly. 'And I think that the sensible thing for everyone, ourselves included, would be to come to terms with it.'

Chapter 17

After Rob left, Colin went into town for dinner, and the other members of her family once again went their separate ways. So Penny had no one to turn to for comfort but her mother. Or rather her mother's diaries. She'd moved them all into her old bedroom by now, and was able to read at her leisure and without fear of being discovered by Elle or her father.

The particular volume she was reading covered the days leading up to Elle's birth, and in this entry her sister was just about to be born.

May 14, 1976

I think the time is near – and while I have never done this before, I'm fairly sure that labour has started. Amazingly, I have this incredible sense of calm about it all. As if I understand my body knows what to do and how things are supposed to go and I'm not nervous, just excited. I can't wait to meet him or her. Imagine me with a baby?

Of course, Ned is a different story. He's tuned tight as a fiddle. Keeps running around the place, double, triple and quadruple-checking my hospital bag, making sure I have everything. He stocked up on film for the camera (he has made four trips to the chemist alone to buy more in case they run out) and in between every errand he runs, he comes in to check on me, and he has also been putting on records from his collection – what he insists are the baby's preferred songs. Seems baby is a big fan of *Yellow Submarine*, and *A Hard Day's Night*. In any case, I have no doubt that this baby will be a Beatles aficionado the minute it's born. If it comes out with dark hair, a bowl cut and a grey suit, I won't be surprised in the least …

There it was, mentioned again. Ned's collection.

Penny's mouth broke into a smile at the idea that her father played Beatles music in preparation for Elle's birth. Did he have her name in mind at that point then? Likely. She'd often wondered how he'd managed to talk her mother round to naming them both after Beatles songs. While Eleanor had quickly been shortened (she couldn't remember anyone but school teachers calling her sister by her full name), and Elle wasn't enamoured of her birth name, Penny's original moniker had been retained. As it happened Penny liked both her name and the song that inspired it. It could have been worse; at least neither of their names had resulted from a song about LSD. She continued reading.

OK yes, no denying it now. It's time. Ned insists I stop writing now. He wants to meet his son or daughter. I don't think I have ever seen him so nervous. So, I'm signing off now. When I write again, I'm going to be a mother – imagine! And my darling husband is going to be the dad he has wanted to be for so long now.

Penny raised her eyebrows at these words. 'The dad he has wanted to be for so long now?' That was interesting.

The next entry was dated two days later. And Elle had indeed been born.

May 16, 1976

I would like to introduce you to Eleanor Anna Harte. My beautiful baby was born last night, on May 15, 1976 at 8:39 in the evening. I am over the moon and Ned I don't think has ever been more in love. And he got his wish too, Eleanor. I stuck to my guns on not having her middle name 'Rigby' though I'm not sure even Ned would go that far. Needless to say, I really think that he was born to be a father. He was a complete star throughout the labour and when little Eleanor was finally born, he cried as much as I did. I am so excited to have my little family. It's all I have ever wished for and knowing that I have this wonderful husband who is so committed to sharing this journey of parenthood with me makes my heart so incredibly happy.

Pausing, Penny ran her hands over the words that her mother had written. The emotion and the love practically sprang off the page. Suddenly struck by the magnitude of what she had just read, she felt herself choking back a sob. Ned had wanted to be a father. He was just as thrilled about Elle's arrival as Anna was. She knew, of course, that Ned and Elle had always shared a bond, a relationship very different to her own father/daughter experience. She'd often put this down to the two of them sharing certain traits, or that it was simply that some offspring shared a closer bond with a certain parent. She and Anna had been incredibly close, which was one of the reasons Penny was reluctant to leave the Bay like Elle had, but she'd just never managed to connect with Ned in the same way, nor communicate with the ease he and Elle seemed to. She'd noticed him come out of his shell so much more since Elle's return; instead of retreating away to quieter parts of the house like he did when it was just him and Penny, these days he was involved in everything and could almost be described as chatty.

So was it just her then, Penny wondered, her heart tightening, that her dad was ambivalent about?

The following morning, Elle arrived downstairs with her suitcase.

'What are you doing?' asked Penny aghast.

'Going back to London, of course. There's no point me sticking around here any more, Penny. I have to get back. I need to get back to my real life.'

'Oh, so we're just a fantasy, are we?'

'Don't be silly. You know that's not what I meant. But I have things to do. I can't stay here forever. What's the point?'

'I can't believe it,' Penny gasped, shaking her head. 'Just when we need you most, you're leaving? You promised you would help us get back on our feet. You can be so selfish sometimes. Rob is right, you know; he should have written you off years ago.'

Elle was too shocked to reply, and there was no point, because Penny had already left the room. Had Rob really said that? She didn't believe he could be so harsh. But then again, didn't he have a right to be?

It was just another sign that her time here was over.

She sighed. If Penny didn't want to say a proper goodbye, that was her decision. They would just have to make amends by phone, or email or whatever.

It wasn't ideal, but when had her relationship with Penny been ideal? Not since she was fourteen years old, probably.

Ned drove Elle back to the airport. As they pulled away, he began humming a tune she recognised as *Octopus Garden*, some lyrics about hiding away from a storm.

She looked up at the sky. 'Does that mean there's an actual storm on the way or you trying to be metaphorical?'

Ned said nothing.

'Oh Dad, I'll be back soon enough,' said Elle. 'I'll come and help when you move, maybe?'

She experienced her arrival of the weeks before almost in reverse. There was the hotel in the rear-view mirror as if shrinking to the size of a dollhouse. The main street could have been any street at all, nothing charming or special about it.

The people, the shops and the buildings, and then the sea itself became smaller and smaller, before they gradually disappeared to nothing in the distance. It was as if they never mattered at all.

Elle wished it were that easy. She wished it didn't feel like the hotel, the town and the sea didn't have a grip on her heart, trying to pull her back.

Trying to get her disappointment at Elle's swift departure out of her head, Penny took Colin into town that evening to see a band play at the The Sugar Loaf Pub. She had since dubbed him the 'English invader' and he quite took to the nickname.

'I do love it around here,' he told her in his charming cut-glass accent. 'The town is so quaint and lively and I've never seen such a stunning stretch of coastline. It's an absolute shame that you're going to lose the hotel.'

'Oh, I'm sick of talking about it,' said Penny, meaning it. She wondered if Elle would ever come back, or if she and Ned would have to travel to London to meet up in the future. Some awkward reunion in the restaurant of a hotel, nothing to look forward to but a cramped shower and a hard bed afterwards. She guessed that if she and Elle hadn't been able to become close again, like real sisters after all this, then they probably never would.

She and Colin watched the band play, an old-style show-band that you couldn't help but tap your toes to.

'Let's dance,' he suggested.

'Oh, I couldn't, I'm awful,' said Penny. It had been a long time since those dance classes in her school days and as much as she loved it, she'd never kept it up. It wasn't as if there were many opportunities for dancing in a small town like this anymore. 'Can you dance?' she asked Colin.

'Didn't you know, my dear? English schoolboys are taught to dance on pain of death. I learnt to dance the fox-trot with a broom for a partner.'

She laughed. 'Ah, I'm too clumsy, I'd probably be all over your feet.'

'After the experience of dancing with an inanimate object, you could sever my toes and it would still be a pleasant evening for me,' said Colin. He had a way of expressing himself that made her laugh. She couldn't really tell if he was joking or not. You would think that writers would be more serious. She was even starting to think his ridiculous university professor coat actually suited him.

As she gradually overcame her hesitation and she and Colin jived very badly on the floor in front of everyone, she couldn't help but think this was the kind of band that would have played at the hotel, once upon a time. She idly remembered that Arthur Ryan from the antiques shop and a few of his old cronies used to play there now and again, Arthur on trumpet and Johnny Chips on the guitar, she mused. But there was little appetite for such a group now and she imagined their instruments had long since been retired. It was a shame really.

She and Elle had liked to sneak out of bed and sit on the staircase and watch people go in and out of the ballroom when the hotel used to host ballroom dancing sessions on Sunday nights. She had dreamed that one day she would be one of the women in the sparkling dresses, spinning and whirling. The sisters had tried to learn the steps from watching the movements of the revellers in the ballroom, but they moved too fast.

In the end, like Penny's dance lessons, it had all just become a forgotten dream.

But Colin danced so well and directed Penny so gently that her rhythm and movement gradually started coming back to her.

'This is so much fun!' she laughed, boogieing unashamedly, and Colin grinned. She was enjoying just kicking back, letting loose as if she hadn't a care in the world. It had been a long time since she'd done so.

She caught sight of Rob sitting at a table near the back of the pub, talking with a young woman with short dark hair. He caught her eye and mimed shock. He had never seen her dance around the place like that. Penny wondered who the girl was; she hadn't seen her before. A tourist, probably. Rob was always a great man for tourists. The impermanence of it suited him, she guessed. No real chance of a lasting relationship. Thinking of Elle's departure, her heart ached for him yet again. She couldn't imagine that her sister had said goodbye to him when she'd barely done so to Penny.

For the rest of the evening, Penny was able to push all thoughts of the hotel out of her mind. She hadn't had so much fun in – well, since she was a child, probably. She looked back over the years and saw that she had always been worrying about something, her father, leaving her parents behind, whether she'd ever find someone to love her for who she was. But what was the point of that? Things were going to happen as they were meant to. Maybe it wasn't always what you hoped for, but that's how life went.

But when the night was ending, and Penny and Colin drove back home, the mere sight of the hotel filled her with sadness once more.

It looked like it was gently sagging in regret, as if the building itself knew their short-lived renewed hopes had sadly come to nothing.

Chapter 18

The storm her father had hinted at actually hit when Elle was about fifteen minutes from landing at Heathrow. And when it hit, it seemed like it was going to sweep the plane clean out of the sky. With each shudder of the aircraft's interior, passengers gasped and moaned. There was no relief to be had from the flight attendants, as they were safely strapped into their seats. Elle had the sudden realisation that airplanes weren't altogether as sturdy as they looked, and it didn't seem all that unlikely that this one could be torn open like a packet of crackers.

She didn't want to think of all the things that she would regret if she died now. She didn't want to think about her family, the Bay Hotel, or especially about Rob. Using her tried and trusted technique for blocking out all unnecessary emotion, and returning to equilibrium, Elle breathed and ignored her way through the rocky landing. If you had met her disembarking on the runway and asked about it, she would have shrugged and said: 'It wasn't too bad, really.'

Back in Clapham, she opened the door to her flat for the first time in almost two weeks. It was almost exactly as she had left it. There was a towel draped over the back of the couch, the coffee pot was sitting on the countertop, filled with the coffee she had neglected to drink before she left.

The only difference was that Sebastian had in the interim moved the last of his stuff out. He'd left nothing behind, not even a goodbye note. She hadn't told him about her mother's death so it wasn't as if she'd expected tea and sympathy, but still. Though Elle guessed this said much about the quality of their relationship in the first place. If he could disappear from her life so easily, barely leaving a trace, and she could remain so unaffected by his absence, then clearly the whole thing wasn't worth much in the first place.

She went and opened the curtains and looked down at the humming, heaving and glittering high street below.

Somehow in those two weeks, something had become painfully clear – she had lived in London for all these years, yet it still wasn't truly 'home'.

Back in Mulberry Bay, work began in earnest on clearing out the hotel.

A 'For Sale' sign had been erected out front by Paddy Corbett, the local overzealous real-estate agent, who had been hoping to get his hands on the property for years. He had investors 'lining up to knock the place down and put apartments on it,' he'd told Penny gleefully, wrongly assuming that the youngest Harte girl would be only too delighted to get the old place out of her hair.

Penny and Colin had watched him from the window and chuckled while he hammered it in: it was pointing straight at the sea. 'Well, if any seagulls want to buy a hotel, they're in luck,' Colin pointed out. They had scoffed at the time to try and make Penny feel a bit better, but that was really the end of any light-heartedness.

Ned had once again withdrawn from everything and mostly stayed in his room playing music, or wandered through the garden. Penny spent her days reading Anna's diaries and going through the rest of her mother's belongings, as well as sorting out bits and pieces around the hotel.

Most of the furniture could be sold with the place, but there were a few things that she wanted to keep. Anna's bedroom mirror, for instance, a full length wooden-framed, vintage piece which she now knew, thanks to the diaries, was given to her by her parents on her wedding day. It was a very flattering mirror and Penny thought it might look nice in her own little cottage. She didn't think Elle would mind, and if she did, tough. She should have been here to do this too.

Penny hadn't heard from Elle since she left and she didn't think Ned had either. It had been a week almost, and not a word. She supposed that Elle was angry at what Penny had said to her on the last morning. She felt a stab of guilt for mentioning Rob. And what she'd said about Elle being selfish hadn't exactly been true either. It wasn't fair to blame her sister for anything, really.

She had wanted other things from life and she had gone out and got them. It wasn't her fault that Penny had decided to stay behind. She just wished Elle could accommodate both her dreams and her family. But was that even possible? she wondered. After all, she had chosen family, or at least had chosen to put aside her dreams and make a life for herself here in the Bay. It was nowhere near as glamorous as her sister's of course (in truth it wasn't in the least glamorous at all) but it was a simple life and Penny believed herself to be a simple, straightforward person. She'd never wanted or expected anything other than the basic things, good times with friends and family, an enjoyable but undemanding job, someone to love and perhaps someday a family of her own. She figured she'd achieved at least two of those things so there was really nothing to complain about. Penny guessed that Elle wondered if she'd felt resentful over the fact that she had left, but she could honestly say that wasn't the case, though she did occasionally envy how her sister could so easily extricate herself from family responsibilities. Penny could never do that; even if she wanted to. One of her greatest joys was spending time with her mother here at the hotel and she wouldn't have swapped that for the world. Tears came to her eyes. She just wished she'd opened her eyes a little more to what was really happening with the business, perhaps then her mum wouldn't have ... But no, she couldn't go there, couldn't torture herself with the notion that she might have been able to prevent anything. Anna was a little like herself she knew, always wanted to look on the bright side on things. Maybe her mum never truly did understand the magnitude of the problems here. Either way, Penny didn't think she could possibly have figured it out either; she'd never possessed Elle's analytical mind – her incisive ability to see beneath the surface, and ferret out the truth, emotions aside. It was yet another marked difference between the sisters' personalities. While Penny continued hunting for things to save, she figured she might as well keep an eye out for her dad's mysterious record collection, the elusive Beatles vinyls so often mentioned in her mother's diaries. There was no turntable in the hotel, so it was likely that her parents had stored any records away somewhere in the meantime. And since there was going to be so much upheaval when they moved, she didn't want to run the risk of them getting lost.

She decided to focus firstly on the entertainment centre in the family living room where they kept all of their CDs, tapes and other various assorted formats for playing music (Penny had bought her music-mad father an iPod years ago but she didn't think he had ever used it). But no joy there: Ned had lots of CDs certainly, mostly all sixties and seventies music, but definitely no vinyl.

If what she had been reading was to be believed, then the collection would be considerable, several boxes of vinyls maybe, so they would have to be stored somewhere that could afford that kind of space. Remembering that Rob had cleaned out the attic and stored everything in the ballroom, she went in there and started lifting the lids to various old wooden and cardboard storage chests – looking for anything that might contain records. But after looking through several boxes, mostly containing old junk from the hotel down through the years, once again she came up short.

She shrugged, guessing she would just have to ask her father about them. Perhaps the collection was so valuable, to him at least, that he kept them under his bed, or knowing Ned and his beloved Beatles, Penny thought, sighing, quite possibly under his pillow.

Rob had turned up halfway through the week. 'I'm going to finish that roof,' he said. 'It'll take thousands off any sale price, the way it is now.'

And over the following days he worked with that same intensity as always, while his dogs scampered and teased the cats below. Sometimes in the evenings that woman she had seen him with in the bar picked him up. Penny didn't ask him about her but she knew that Rob would tell her if he wanted to.

How confusing everything had become lately.

Colin the English Invader interrupted Penny's thoughts as she cleared out the cupboards in the kitchen. 'Quite a marvellous day for a picnic, don't you think?'

'Well yes, go ahead then.'

'I was rather hoping you'd come along.'

Penny sighed. Lately he was forever asking her to go here,

there and everywhere with him. It was a strange situation because while he was supposed to be a guest, this was far from a normal hotel situation. And the truth was, she had sort of stopped thinking of Colin as an invader, and started to believe he was actually a godsend.

He was so easy to talk to and very relaxing to be around. With him there were no expectations, no awkward emotional stuff to tiptoe around. Penny didn't know how he was getting on with his novel because he seemed to spend an awful lot of time just hanging around the hotel and the gardens, staring into the distance. Still, she supposed that was just what novelists did.

'But I've got so much to do ...'

'I've actually already packed it. All you have to do is walk with me a bit, sit yourself down on a blanket on the beach, partake of these delicious morsels and then if you wish, you can come back here and continue to work your fingers to the bone. But you do look as though you need a break.'

It was true. Penny was emotionally and physically exhausted. 'Dead on her feet' as her mother might have said.

They set off down the beach for the picnic, followed hopefully by Rob's dogs. They didn't go too far, just far enough for Penny to feel like she was no longer working. She sat down, ate a ham sandwich and a slice of fudge cake, and then listening to Colin talk about somewhere he had travelled to, promptly fell asleep in the sun.

Almost an hour later she sat up bleary-eyed. 'Ah, you

shouldn't have let me sleep!' she complained, more than a little embarrassed.

'I saw no harm in it,' Colin said. 'Your unpleasant tasks will still be there when you get back. And you looked like a sun-kissed goddess, lying there like that. I didn't want to upset the vision.'

She blushed. Only he could say a ridiculous thing like that and not appear entirely ridiculous himself.

They walked back up the beach towards the hotel in companionable silence. 'How's your novel going?' she asked.

'Not well, I'm afraid. The truth is, I'm finding life here rather too interesting to concentrate. To say nothing of the fact that I haven't yet hit on a decent plot idea.'

Penny laughed. 'I'd say you're one of the few that find life around here *interesting*,' she commented. 'Charming, maybe. Picturesque, certainly. But interesting? I don't so.'

'I think you would be surprised to hear exactly how interesting I find you and your life, Penny,' he said, in a way that made her blush afresh.

She went off into an almost incoherent babble. 'Well here we are – oh there's Rob and his friend, and I really shouldn't keep you any more from your work.'

And with that, Penny rushed off, leaving Colin standing there with the picnic basket looking surprised, but not altogether concerned.

'Hey Penny,' said Rob, as she approached. 'I've made quite good progress, but that leak is bigger than I thought. It's going to take me a few more days. Just pray that we don't get rain in the meantime. That tarp won't hold off anything but a light shower.'

'OK, thanks.' Penny looked up at the roof to see a blue tarp rippling over a large slate-free patch. It was as if the old hotel had been bandaged up, losing a fair bit of dignity in the process.

'Oh. This is Celeste,' he said, motioning to the smiling girl with him.

Rob gave no other clues to how they'd met or what their relationship might be, and Celeste just kept smiling, so Penny assumed that he was doing his best to forget about Elle and that the newcomer was part of the remedy.

Well he'd get no judgement from her.

Chapter 19

Penny picked up the diary that she had been reading the day before, finding where she had left off. Anna had been a diligent writer, and had been good about detailing the events of family life – especially as a new mother. She found this particularly interesting considering she had heard from many of her friends with children that it was hard to do anything else with a newborn except take care of the baby and try to work in a shower a couple of times a week.

Apparently her mother had been a natural at parenthood, Penny thought, once again feeling a pang as she realised that if she ever had a child, her mother wouldn't be around to help her find her way. She felt tears prick at her eyes before her subconscious reminded her that she hadn't yet managed to find a boyfriend or a husband so there was no need to get ahead of herself. Her thoughts automatically segued to Colin's strange comment the day before, and she quickly put it out of her mind and turned her attention back to reading.

Penny continued through the entries for about an hour, reading with relative ease until she felt her eyelids begin to droop. Yawning and scratching her head as she worked to finish the latest entry – at this point her parents had not long bought the hotel – she guessed that this was a good time to put it aside and get some sleep.

However, just as she was about to close the book, she came upon a passage that immediately began with a different tone than the others. Anna's nervous energy was apparent in her writing – it practically jumped off the page – and Penny felt herself become alert as she read.

November 17, 1977

Feeling a little at a loss over what to do. One day everything is fine, the next, our world has spun on its axis. Of course, this puts a major spanner in the works, particularly with the hotel. If I am being honest, (and there is no point at this stage in not being honest) we haven't been as good with our finances as we could have been. Yes, we bought the hotel and yes, we have also been spending some money on furnishing and renovating the place – but we haven't been saving like we should have been, and another mouth to feed is really going to impact on everything.

I'm an idiot – I should have paid more attention, taken more care. But I hadn't truly considered how another baby so soon after we'd started our hotel venture would throw everything off-balance ...

Penny's heart dropped. She'd always known deep down that she'd been unplanned and this confirmed her suspicions. *A major spanner in the works . . .*

She tried her hardest not to be hurt by what she was reading; it wasn't as if her mother sounded disappointed by the news or was rejecting it, but there was no doubt that at that point in her parents' life she was an unwelcome surprise.

Was that why Ned had always been so aloof towards her? Because until Penny's appearance all had been going well with just the three of them – him, Anna and little Elle? And then her arrival threw all of their great plans for the hotel into chaos. Then Penny looked to the next paragraph in the passage and felt goosebumps make their way down her arms.

Ned had a suggestion on how to deal with it. And I don't like this at all. He's suggested that he sell his first editions. He said he could easily get a good price for them, and that the extra money would help keep us afloat for a while – pay for someone to take over the running of the hotel immediately after the baby comes, and ensure that the new arrival doesn't disrupt things too much.

She felt all of the air rush from her lungs. Her dad wanted to sell the record collection? she thought, feeling frantic as she read and re-read the last paragraph. 'Oh Dad no, please say you didn't . . .' he skimmed the rest of what her mother had written – she was mostly just agonising over the idea of

Ned selling his beloved collection to accommodate her, but there was nothing definite and she felt herself start to relax.

That is, until she got to the next entry. Dated three days later.

Well, it's done. He sold the lot. Every single record. And he was stoic through it all. But I feel broken-hearted because I know this has been hard on him – and I'm afraid we rushed into so much without thinking it all through. Yes, I know it's just records. But Ned has been saving up for and collecting these for years throughout his youth, and long before we were married. His first editions were his most prized possessions – and I can see the disappointment in his eyes. It might sound silly, but I believe there is a piece of his soul attached to those records, and of course the songs are so much more than mere songs to Ned – and to me now too. They are poetry, and they have been the backdrop, the soundtrack and chorus to his life – and mine – since I met him. They have been lullabies to Elle since before she was born.

And now I feel like our family has lost something, an heirloom of sorts. I know that he did this to take care of his family – to provide for Elle and me and now the new baby, but I can't deny that I believe something terrible happened today. Something beautiful was sold for the sake of mere utility and practicality.

What's worse is that when he came home this evening, I looked at my poor husband and I saw an expression on his face that I had never seen before – like a light had turned off inside him. It made my heart hurt. Something about his face had changed and it worries me – quite a lot, if I am being honest. A light, a passion almost, that I had been used to seeing in Ned's eyes was no longer there. I hope it comes back.

The passage ended, just like that, and Penny put a hand to her face realising that she was crying.

'Dad sold the albums for me. Sold them because of *me*,' she whispered, swallowing hard as the reality of the situation hit her like a truck. 'And something died in him. Something changed.'

Penny looked away from the diary and thought about the words that she had just read. The way he is … withdrawn and quiet, it was her fault, she realised. The collection, the songs, the family all knew that certain songs had always been Ned's preferred way to communicate his feelings. But she'd had no idea that the music had truly meant that much to him.

No, her rational mind answered. It wasn't your fault. The timing was just wrong. They'd just bought the hotel and there was no more money …

But nonetheless the incident had changed her father. The momentousness of the situation had changed him, made him retreat into himself somehow. He had given up something that meant so much to him, just to accommodate her arrival.

And Penny couldn't deny that regardless of how illogical it sounded, she felt responsible.

Selling his Beatles collection had been a defining moment in Ned's life. Penny guessed that a day didn't pass that he didn't think of it. She knew he regretted it – losing that collection, for Penny's sake or indeed the sake of the hotel.

And not only had he since lost Anna, but now he was about to lose the hotel too. Straight off, she remembered his words when after the funeral she and Elle first discussed selling the hotel. '*We already sacrificed enough to keep it.*'

Then suddenly, Penny had a thought. She might not be able to save the hotel or bring back her mother, but there was nothing to stop her from getting her father's collection back, was there?

And right then, with a renewed understanding and a fresh sense of purpose, Penny knew that she would move heaven and earth to do so.

'First edition Beatles albums?' Colin was intrigued. 'Your father definitely made a pretty penny back in the day selling those – obviously enough to help your family get by while they got the hotel off the ground, but Penny, I don't think you understand – those albums today would be worth a fortune. You would have to spend a lot of money to get them back. Which, given your family's current predicament, you obviously don't have.'

Penny felt some dread creep up on her – she couldn't deny that she hadn't really considered the money factor when it came to the search. She had a vague sense that yes, she might have to spend something on getting the albums back – but just how much, she wasn't sure.

'Do you really think it will be *that* expensive?' she asked, trying to keep the worry out of her voice. Colin seemed to be somewhat of an expert on the subject. He certainly knew more than she did in any case.

'It depends. Some of them yes ... and especially if you want first editions in mint condition. I'd imagine you should be able to find some at reasonably decent prices – and there are ways of trying to control the price, too.'

Penny's ears perked up at this. 'How so?'

'My dear. Let me tell you about this wonderful new invention called the *internet*—'

Rolling her eyes, Penny cut him off. 'Yes, very smart.'

Colin continued on. 'Anyway, I think you could probably start online, eBay to begin with of course, and then there are lots of other websites run by collectors and music dealers specialising in vinyl. The only thing you have to worry about in that regard is the quality, naturally enough. Won't be much use to your father if he is unable to play them, or if someone has been using them as tea coasters for the past thirty-odd years.' He thought for a moment. 'I also have some contacts in Sussex – namely a friend of a friend who owns a record store in London. He might be a resource for you, especially on the rarer ones. You said your mother had some trouble tracking down the one she gave your dad as a wedding present? Well if she had trouble finding *Anna* back in the seventies, I'm willing to bet that particular record is even more rare today ...'

'Well, thanks.' Now Penny wondered if she'd bitten off way more than she could chew. 'No one ever said anything about a collection of records, or about Dad selling it to hold onto the hotel. I never knew for sure that I was unplanned or that they'd had money troubles back then – it feels weird to discover these things so long after the fact. I just wonder why he or my mum never told us these things.'

'She probably didn't want you to feel bad for your father or guilty or anything like that, I'm guessing,' Colin offered. 'Anyway, I am sure there's always lots going on in any marriage that just isn't always meant for kids to know. I've been there myself in a way. My sister and I.'

'How so?' Penny enquired, truly curious.

Colin cleared his throat and locked eyes with Penny – feeling a little put on the spot.

'Well, it was when I was about sixteen I think. My sister, Tricia, she's three years older, was poking around in the attic of our house in Sussex and came across some old photo albums. Pictures taken before either of us were born, pictures from early on in my parents' marriage. In any case, she was looking around and found some pictures and what not of my mother, and she was pregnant. But interestingly, the picture was dated three years before she was born. It seems that my mother had fallen pregnant shortly after she and my dad were married, and they were delighted. Even more so when they found out they were having twins.' He looked unusually pensive. 'But when she was about five months or thereabouts, from what she told us later, she miscarried and lost the babies.'

Penny drew in her breath. 'Oh no.'

'She'd never told us up to then. I suppose she thought that if we'd known about that pregnancy, these siblings that we had never known about, that we might think or believe that we were a backup or some kind of consolation prize. She didn't want us to feel second-best. So she and my father never told us about it. It was their secret.'

Penny looked at him. 'And did you? Feel like a plan B of sorts?'

Colin shook his head. 'Absolutely not. Of course it's a little odd to think about the possibility of my having other older brothers or sisters, but it's not something I dwell on.' He looked at Penny. 'Just as you shouldn't dwell on your father's kind sacrifice.'

'I know. But I really would like to try and get them back for him; it feels right, especially now, when it seems we're going to lose the hotel after all. But I wonder now if it might be a huge undertaking ...'

'Never fear, Penny, I will help you,' Colin assured her, looking considerably more enthused than she felt. 'A project like this is exactly the kind of thing I've been wanting to get my teeth into.'

Chapter 20

Elle had been home over a week and hadn't heard a word from her family. She wasn't too surprised. Penny was obviously still angry with her, perhaps not without reason, and her father had more or less said straight out that her own coldness had brought about the failure with the townspeople.

She thought about it. She didn't think of herself as a cold person, but knew that she could sometimes come across that way when she felt uncomfortable.

But as she thought back over her time in Mulberry Bay, she realised that she had behaved quite standoffish a lot of the time, through awkwardness, or simply through not wanting to get anyone's hopes up.

Whenever there had been a small success that Penny took pride in, she had poured cold water over it. Whenever she herself had felt hope or comfort, she had told herself that it wasn't real, that it was distracting her from getting back to her normal life. How long had she not been listening to herself?

She thought back to her first few years away from home, at college in Dublin. She had adored city life back then, she was sure of that, loved how getting up each day was like getting up to a starter pistol, how every little thing was vitally urgent and important. And then later, when she graduated and moved to London to work, she had loved being successful, her buildings getting noticed and her name being mentioned. The late nights, all the different people from all walks of life, the string of exciting, more sophisticated boyfriends, the accents, the bright and ludicrous fashions: she had loved it all.

But then somewhere along the line, it had all started to get a bit commonplace. And the easier it all was, the more stale it became. Lately Elle was coming to the conclusion that she was no longer exhilarated by the rush; she was tiring of it. She felt jaded by the pointlessness of her fleeting romances.

Often she needed to really gear herself up before walking out the door. She knew her work was good, and she enjoyed it still, but could have done with a change of a scenery, a new challenge perhaps. There were various things that had been telling her this over the years, but she hadn't been listening.

Well, it was too late now.

Or was it?

She could think about going back to Ireland and making a new life, a different life, she supposed, but the one she really wanted was gone. How long had she been ignoring thoughts of Rob, too? Writing their relationship off as just nostalgia, when really her mind was trying to tell her something different.

How ridiculous, to just realise it now, Elle thought, her heart sinking. More ridiculous still, that she'd had a second chance and squandered it again.

She was supposed to be working on a new project now for the firm. It wasn't very exciting, just a functional office block outside of Central London and the owners were very locked down about what they wanted. No frills, nothing too audacious. Elle could have done this kind of work in her sleep.

Well, she *should* have been able to do this kind of work in her sleep. But something seemed to be preventing her. Every time she sat down at her work table, pencil in hand, she felt an unbearable tiredness wash over her. The pencil felt as heavy as a block of wood and her hands as clumsy as large mallets. It was frustrating, particularly since she had missed a lot of time over the last week or two and had quite a fast-approaching deadline.

She took a break, and made herself cheese on toast. She looked at her laptop, dead on the table. She could just fire off a quick email to Penny, try and explain things a bit better. But no, emailing didn't feel right. She didn't exactly know what would be right, but that wasn't it. Besides, it was probably better to wait until she knew what she wanted to say.

She went back to her work desk and sat down with great determination. She would do this. She had to make it happen. If she could just pick up her pencil and begin, if she could just lose herself in her work as always, then perhaps she could begin to reclaim her life here. Maybe, bit by bit, she could stop feeling like a complete failure and be more like her old self. Sure of things. Not full of silly regrets.

Not dreaming uselessly of the past.

Elle began slowly, like someone drawing for the very first time. Just a few rough lines on paper, it doesn't matter if they aren't straight, she told herself as she always did when she hit a block. You can fix it up later.

Bit by bit, something began to take shape underneath her hands. She didn't stop to examine it too closely, but let her hands do the work as though they were something apart from her. As though they were sleepwalkers.

A room began to take shape. A conference room? No, something else. The ceiling was high and vaulted, individual blocks of wood forming a delicate ribcage. It was supremely detailed. She drew in a long wooden floor, dark and smooth. At one end of the room there was a raised platform. The walls were ornately patterned, and even though she was working in charcoal, she could tell that in reality it would be gold leaf that caught the light of the hanging chandelier in the middle of the room.

The chandelier itself was a masterpiece, each tiny bulb, each hanging jewel exquisitely formed. It was the beating heart of the room.

If Elle recognised what she was drawing, she gave no sign, outward or inward. She was very practised at keeping her thoughts from herself, and if sometimes that talent worked against her, in this case it was leading her towards something special, something magnificent.

People began to fill the room. People in fine garb: tailored suits and long dressed that made a seductive sound when their wearers moved. If Elle had had some coloured pencils handy, she would have drawn them in the boldest colours that came to hand. But never mind. It lived for her anyway, in her head.

She filled the stage with instruments: a double bass, the fine wood shining warmly. A drum kit. A guitar. A trumpet. But where were the musicians? Oh, that must be them, gathered next to a table that seemed to be for refreshments. And on the stage she drew a woman, who seemed to be speaking to them all. She seemed to be acknowledging something, asking for something.

Elle went to bed without looking at her sketch, or thinking about it. She fell into a deep and dreamless sleep, her first in many days.

Penny clicked the 'Buy It Now' button and found herself the proud owner of a first edition *Let It Be* album. And it had really not been that expensive at all.

'Not as bad as I originally thought,' she said, as she grinned at Colin who sat next to her, his eyes on the screen. She pretended that she didn't see him raise an eyebrow. 'One down ... '

'And rather a lot to go,' he finished. 'Penny, you do realise that you were lucky with that one. You aren't going to find them all so easily or indeed so cheaply.'

Penny wouldn't exactly call a hundred and fifty euros 'cheap', but it wasn't as if she had to access her entire savings nest-egg to pay for it. Just a little.

'That's not what I meant. It just seems like there is loads of old vinyl for sale online. I just need to take the time to find what I want.'

Colin had arrived down for dinner to find Penny in her mother's office, deep in the middle of an internet search for the albums on her list. Realising that she was dangerously close to buying several that were definitely *not* first editions, and had other red flags, to boot, he had pulled her back from the edge of making some disastrous choices.

'Yes, Penny, everyone sells their rubbish on eBay, it's like one great car boot sale – but that doesn't mean you have to buy it. Think about it this way; pretend these albums are first edition novels or say um … silk scarves,' he said, casting a glance at the jaunty scarf she had around her neck. 'Would you walk into any establishment and plop down good money on anything that had the markings of being mass-produced?'

She frowned. 'No, of course not. I only buy hand-made. Most of mine come from The Wonder Room in town.'

'Exactly. Or what about a pair of shoes that looked like someone had already worn them? That stink of foot cheese?'

Cringing, Penny shook her head. 'Disgusting.'

Colin smiled and sat back in the seat alongside her, crossing his hands over his chest. 'So, that's how you have to think about these albums. Because I can tell you that if your dear old dad was a collector at one point – that is how he thought about those vinyls when he was tracking them down and buying them. To him they were like exquisite hand-made accessories.'

Penny nodded as the point hit home – she hadn't thought of it like that.

'I understand. I had no idea you were so knowledgeable about this stuff, though.'

Colin ran a hand through his shaggy hair that was by now badly in need of a trim. 'I'm a novelist my dear – research is my forte. So let's review what we have already learned,' he said, returning his attention to Penny's computer screen. 'You begin your search by looking for mint condition, first edition Beatles albums. Then you need to verify that it is a UK pressing. The record has to come with the glossy jacket. No gatefold covers. Shrink-wrap or the words 'never played' are another bonus. Avoid anything that says that it was made for jukeboxes. Those are easy to spot by the great big holes in the centre. And if the listing mentions anything about "original stickers" that's good too . . .'

Penny nodded, taking it all in. It was as if she was navigating a strange land and Colin was her compass.

When Elle looked at her sketch the next morning, it took her a while to remember when she had done it. She almost felt that it hadn't been drawn by her own hand. It was almost spooky. But she couldn't deny that it was accurate.

Looking at it closely, a tiny idea began to creep into her mind. Little by little, this idea grew larger and larger, until it was all she could think about.

Later, arriving at work, she walked straight into her manager's office and sat down for a very long and frank conversation. He was disappointed but resigned and eventually agreed to Elle's request for a further period of leave. Until the end of the summer, they decided. She was a dedicated worker, and an asset to the company. This was the first time she'd asked for anything and she was relieved her boss had recognised that. Because she didn't know quite what she'd have done if he hadn't. She wasn't quite ready to give up city life, but one thing was clear, she needed time out.

In any case, there was no time to waste. What had to be done couldn't be done here, and what if the worst had happened in the period she had been away? What if the hotel had already been sold? The image occurred to her for a second, as strong as if she had been standing in front of it: her family home, its grand windows shuttered and blinded, a padlock on the front door, weeds growing up the walls. But no, if it had been sold, Penny would surely have told her that much at least.

Back at her flat, Elle packed a bag, once again not paying close attention to the contents, put her picture into a poster tube, and for the second time in as many weeks, prepared to return home to Mulberry Bay.

Chapter 21

The following day, scrolling through her email on her phone, Penny came upon a message that both excited her and filled her stomach with anxiety.

'OK. Cross another one off the list, I just won the auction,' she said to herself, as she extracted the list of albums she had been keeping in her handbag, while trying to keep pace with Colin, who walked beside her on the street with purpose in his step.

'Which one?' he enquired without slowing down.

'*Sergeant Pepper's*,' Penny answered, trying to make a note on her list while walking. 'Can we just stop for a minute?'

Colin immediately halted and turned around, noticing that Penny had stopped a few paces back, using a nearby letterbox as a makeshift desk. He strolled over to her and peered over her shoulder as she made notes.

Whistling, he raised his eyebrows. 'Goodness. Five hundred for that one?'

Penny finished logging the price she had paid on eBay for the popular first edition album, trying to quell the anxiety in her stomach. 'Yes. I've decided I don't like auctions. At least when they have other bidders. I would have been able to save a fortune if that someone else hadn't stepped in during the last hour and jacked up the price.' The fact that a new bidder had snuck in unexpectedly just before bidding closed had totally discombobulated her. It wasn't good for the heart.

'Well that's the internet for you,' Colin replied. 'Trolls everywhere.'

'Well, I wish they would stay under their respective bridges then. OK, so take a look,' She offered the list to Colin. 'I think we're making real progress.'

He took the paper from Penny and looked down at her handwriting.

Please Please Me
With the Beatles
Beatlemania! With the Beatles
Introducing . . . the Beatles
~~*Meet the Beatles!*~~
Twist and Shout
The Beatles' Second Album
~~*The Beatles' Long Tall Sally*~~
A Hard Day's Night
Something New
Beatles for Sale

~~*Beatles '65*~~

Beatles VI

Help!

Anna (Go to Him) **Single**

Rubber Soul

Yesterday and Today

Revolver

~~*Sgt. Pepper's Lonely Hearts Club Band*~~

Magical Mystery Tour

The Beatles

Yellow Submarine

Abbey Road

Let It Be

'You know they had singles other than the *Anna* record, of course? Even so, it's actually a rather extensive list.'

Penny took back the paper. 'Yes, I know, but that's also the only single that I know my dad had for sure. And when I checked the list of Beatles singles online – well, it's just way too much to focus on, so I decided to concentrate on just the albums for the moment.' Obviously she had no idea what Ned's original collection consisted of, but her mother had mentioned 'albums' quite a bit in the diaries, and from her limited knowledge, these did seem rarer and more prized while singles (with the exception of *Anna*) seemed much easier to come by.

'Indeed. A shame you can't just download each of these on iTunes. Would be so much easier, but I suspect that's rather missing the point.'

'Exactly.' Penny put the list back in her handbag. 'I think it would be best if I just focus on the full-length albums. If I start getting into the extended play albums and the live recordings and all of that, well, I could easily be at this for the rest of my life. And I would also be broke. Besides, I'm guessing that I don't have to worry about anything that was released after 1977 – that's when my dad sold his collection after all.'

Colin nodded. 'Good theory. Now let's see what this gentleman has for us today.'

Having placed some phone calls to record stores around Dublin, Colin had a lead on a first edition *Yellow Submarine* album at a place in the city and he and Penny had travelled up there first thing that morning.

Penny walked quickly next to him on the street. 'What did he sound like on the phone? Do you think he might give us a discount?'

Colin chuckled. 'I doubt it. These people can be somewhat reclusive – socially introverted usually. Sorry to disappoint – but he is connected. That's why I felt it was worth our visiting in person.'

Penny shuddered. 'I feel like I am dealing with the mob.'

Coming to a stop in front of a store that looked decidedly vintage, Colin looked up, double-checking the address he had on his notebook.

'This is it. And for the record, yes, you are rather dealing with the mob – just on a somewhat geekier level. And where the mob has guns – this group has turntables.'

*

Rick Carter loved records – and he loved vinyl more than he loved anything else. This was a statement he heard often, both by his subconscious and voiced by his friends – or the people who might be his friends if he was into that sort of thing. It was also an accusation that was delivered at least once per day by his mother – whose back bedroom he had been living in since he dropped out of college twenty years before.

But he knew his mother just didn't get it. He couldn't remember her being passionate about anything – except maybe *EastEnders* – and that rubbish certainly didn't count. Albums were a living thing – and vinyl was his passion. This store that he had successfully opened (much to his mother's chagrin) with the money left to him by his father when he died was his life. Moreover, he appreciated when other people came to him – searching for some lost piece of music history – because he knew he could help them. For a price, of course.

Rick was searching through a section of his back room where he kept his rare and collectible albums. The English guy on the phone had been adamant that the version of *Yellow Submarine* he was looking for had to be a first edition UK pressing – and Rick had assured him that he could deliver.

Quickly finding what he was looking for – and holding the LP gingerly, Rick couldn't help but snigger. Judging by the sound of his voice on the phone, the guy was a toff whom Rick would have never pegged for a Beatles fan. Still, it took all sorts.

He was snapped to attention by the bell over the front door of the shop. Smiling, he picked up the record and made his way through to the front. His first customer of the day. Crossing the threshold to the counter – he saw that this customer was in fact a toff. And he had a girl with him too. A pretty one.

Rick put on a thin smile when the guy introduced himself. 'Yep. I have the record you called about.' At this statement, he realised that Colin's facial expression remained neutral – but the girl's didn't. She showed immediate excitement.

OK, she's the shopper. Stay cool, man, he thought, looking at her scarf that looked unusual and expensive. *Brown Thomas prices,* he reminded himself.

'Hello there, thanks for seeing us. This is the album in question?' Colin asked as Rick headed behind the counter and laid the record out in front of him.

'Yes. Still in shrink wrap, as you can see. Mint condition.' Rick looked from the guy to the girl next to him, who was looking towards her companion, clearly hoping for direction.

A vinyl virgin, Rick thought. The toff, on the other hand, seemed not to be.

He gave a small nod and returned his attention to Rick. 'This is my friend, Penny Harte. She's looking to buy a gift for her father.'

Penny was already nodding, eager to contribute to the conversation. 'Yes. I'm trying to track down an entire catalogue of first edition Beatles albums. My dad had a collection – he ended up selling them all in 1978 and ... ow!'

The guy had elbowed her – and not too subtly either. Rick

209

struggled hard to suppress his grin. Dealing with collectible records was much like a high stakes poker game. You didn't say too much, you didn't give away too much information – it was like showing all of your cards. And Rick knew right then and there that the toff was trying to control just how much his pretty friend was looking to shell out on this record – especially if she was trying to buy an entire first edition catalogue. *That* was a pricey endeavour. Pity his Fab Four first edition inventory extended to only one.

Rick looked at the exchange that was currently happening between the toff and the girl called Penny. Apparently, she was receiving loud and clear the silent message her companion was broadcasting. Namely, let him do the talking.

Too late for that, Rick thought satisfactorily.

'OK,' he continued. 'If you are looking for a first edition *Yellow Submarine*, this is your copy. Take a look.' He pushed the album across the counter to where Penny stood, but it was the toff who picked it up instead. He lifted it up to his eyes and started to study the shrink wrap.

'This is the original wrapping?' he asked sceptically, as if he knew his stuff.

Rick nodded, happy to play along. 'It is.'

'And where did you get it?'

'At a record show, a couple of years ago. After my dad passed away, it was one of the first collectibles I bought to stock my back room. Just in case a collector came calling.'

Penny nodded sympathetically. 'I'm so sorry for your loss. My mum died only a couple of weeks ago. It's hard, isn't it?'

Rick considered the girl standing on the other side of the counter. Was she really trying to strike up a conversation with him? He narrowed his eyes. Pretty women always had an ulterior motive.

'Yeah. But we weren't that close,' he said, shutting her down. She wasn't going to get some sob story out of him. 'Anyway. What do you think of the album?'

The toff considered Rick and then handed the album to Penny. 'It looks good, but I am not sure if the shrink wrap is original,' he said.

'Yes it is original,' Rick interrupted annoyed.

'Of course, I'm just saying that it doesn't look exactly the way it should, it's a bit loose around the edges there – you see? It's easy enough to find a machine that can rewrap vinyl. But you do have to have an eye for these things,' he added with a nonchalant shrug that made Rick's blood boil.

What are you saying, mate? That I don't know original when I see it?

Rick opened his mouth to speak, to defend his knowledge and more importantly his honour, but the other guy ignored him and continued talking to the girl.

'But it is indeed a UK pressing. That's what we are looking for.'

Penny nodded and took the record from him. 'He played *Yellow Submarine* to me and Elle – when Mum was pregnant with us. I read it in her diary. He really wanted us to love the Beatles as much as he did – so he played their music for us.' She chuckled nostalgically and Rick felt a lull of boredom overcome him – it was the same feeling he had whenever anyone started talking about their family, kids, the holiday they took last year. None of that mattered – it was the fuzzy background noise on a 45 to him – he simply wished they would get on to what mattered, namely the music. The records. The vinyl. The cost.

'So what do you think?' he interrupted.

Penny smiled kindly at him and started to open her mouth to speak, but the guy beat her to it. 'How much?' he asked dryly.

'Two grand,' Rick answered with conviction, causing Penny to go immediately white.

But the toff didn't hesitate. 'Absolutely not.' He took the record from Penny's hands and pushed it across the display case, giving it back to Rick.

'That's a fair price,' stated Rick, trying to get the thought out of his head that this was the first enquiry he'd had since sinking a considerable amount of money into the record when he himself first bought it.

'No it is not,' said the guy nonplussed. 'I know all about this one. Because I did my research before getting here. Now, I would tell Penny to buy this if this had been pressed by Odeon, and not EMI, which we both know was a subsidiary of the label back in the 1960s.'

Rick swallowed hard. The guy *had* done his research.

'What would make this album worth two thousand euros is if this record had been one of the limited number of export copies pressed for distribution in Portugal, where Odeon had a distribution centre. And we would know that if the record had an Odeon sticker on the back of the sleeve that covered the Apple logo, but this doesn't. So this was pressed in the UK, which indicates it was by EMI and not the company's subsidiary. This brings down the price significantly.' Rick saw Penny exhale with some relief, but with further questions on her face. 'Don't worry, it's still a first edition,' her companion reassured her. 'It's just not a member of the very rare pool of Odeon pressings. Your father probably wouldn't have had that in his original collection in any case.'

Penny nodded with understanding. 'So what's fair?'

'Five hundred tops,' her companion answered, looking Rick square in the face.

He must be joking. Five hundred? No way!

'Not a chance. Fifteen hundred,' he countered.

'Too high. Six.'

Narrowing his eyes, Rick felt a surge of adrenaline. If the guy wanted a bidding war, that's what he would give him.

'Fourteen.'

'Seven.'

'Twelve.'

'Eight hundred.'

Beginning to feel angry, Rick shouted, 'But that's what I bought it for!' Immediately, he knew that he had said too much, because the other guy smiled widely. Rick had just figuratively shown the entire table what he held in his hand.

He witnessed a smile that passed in between the two across the counter, and wondered if it was too early in the day for a drink – or at the very least a drag of the joint he had in his pocket.

'Nine hundred then,' Penny offered diplomatically.

Rick considered her counter-offer – it would be a small profit – and it would also turn that record into liquid funding for the store. Not a huge return on his investment, but a return just the same.

But what about his dignity? he thought. Rick wondered if he could get another fifty out of her?

'Nine fifty,' he said. 'Final offer.'

The toff provided him a small smile and a knowing look, as if he understood what he was doing, and that he would allow him gracefully to finalise the deal even though he had said way too much, too soon.

Game, set and match.

Chapter 22

When Elle's plane landed at Dublin airport this time she didn't take a taxi south to the coast. Instead she hired a car, and on arrival at Mulberry Bay, instead of heading up the hill towards the hotel, she headed straight to the Orchard Garden Centre.

She had reparations to make.

Little Alex was the first to greet her when she got out of the car.

'Have you come to buy a flower?' he asked.

'No,' said Elle, 'I haven't, I'm afraid.'

'Have you come to buy a tree?'

'No, not a tree either.'

'Well, in that case,' the six-year-old said, with the world-weary sigh of an old man, 'you'd better come with me.'

Hazel was surprised to see Elle Harte. Surprised was putting it mildly.

Upon hearing that Elle had left town, she felt somewhat guilty, supposing her outburst may have had something to do with it. She thought that they would probably never see Elle again, and here she was on Hazel's front step looking for all the world like she had ridden a horse here.

'Elle!' she cried. 'What in the world? You look like a wild woman. What are you doing here?'

'For starters,' her old friend replied, 'I come in peace. Secondly, let's have a proper catch-up in our old stomping ground. Third, I need your help, because everyone in this town thinks I'm some kind of imbecile, and I don't quite know how to win them over.'

Hazel was exactly the dose of fresh air and practicality that Elle needed. She hadn't changed much at all since their school days, and still looked upon most things with a wry and accurate eye. However she was also deeply sympathetic and not given to holding a grudge.

'When I think of how you looked in that suit,' she said, 'coming in here like you'd never clapped eyes on me before and that we hadn't spent most of our teenage years smoking in that corner. It would be funny if it weren't so serious.'

'I'm so sorry. I didn't have the faintest idea what I was doing,' said Elle. 'It was one of the most awful days of my life. I just fell back on the facts, hard and simple. I must have come across like such a cold fish.'

'I do think your idea is a good one, though,' said Hazel. 'And Glenn and I are more than happy to help out. Have been all along, actually,' she said with a twinkle. 'But there's the matter of everyone else. Not to mention ...'

'Doug Grant,' finished Elle.

'I'm afraid so,' said Hazel. 'Unfortunately the bank manager is the one you need most, and the person least likely to be won over.'

'Well, I'll have to see if I can dig out that store of charm I keep locked down deep,' Elle sighed.

'It might take more than charm, though. That man speaks in money, thinks in money and if you cut him open, he would probably bleed money.'

'Unfortunately that's the very thing that I don't have,' said Elle, sighing afresh.

'Don't lose heart too soon,' said Hazel. 'It's your Shakespearean flaw. The hardest bit is over. You're back. You've got the plan. Now all you have to do is make it happen.'

'Do you mind telling me what you think you are doing?' Colin enquired.

Penny raised her eyes from the computer screen and shrugged. 'What do you mean?' she asked. 'I'm just … checking my email.'

'No,' Colin said, shaking his head. 'I'm talking about this advertisement, on a site called Done Deal. I just found it. And I know it's yours.'

Plastering an innocent expression on her face, Penny decided to play it cool. 'I don't know what you are talking about.'

But Colin didn't budge. 'Are you looking to get abducted? Do you have a death wish? No one puts an ad on a public trading site that not only includes an email address, but also a phone number, proclaiming they are "willing to meet in order to negotiate". Honestly Penny, I thought you were cleverer than that.'

She narrowed her eyes and shot daggers at him. There was no sense in denying that it was her ad on the Irish trading site and that she had posted it – just that morning, in fact. But she was curious to know how Colin had come to know about it so quickly.

'How did you find it so fast?'

He shrugged. 'No mystery. I've set up an alert – any time the phrase 'first edition Beatles album' gets mentioned or posted about online, Google lets me know. There was an alert waiting for me when I got out of the shower just now – your ad. Now, don't argue with me, Penny. Take it down. Please. You could be putting yourself in all kinds of harm.'

Penny was already shaking her head. 'I'm not going to take it down. I've sold plenty of bits and bobs from the hotel on Done Deal over the years. And I don't have to respond if someone replies. I am a pretty good judge of character you know – and it's not as if I included my address. I'm not stupid, just desperate.'

Colin sat down, and put his head in his hands. 'Goodness Penny, you are way too trusting. Please promise me that you won't go and meet anyone on your own.'

She smiled. 'That's no problem – you can go with me. In fact, I already had someone get in touch. A guy in Galway says he has a first edition *Beatles for Sale* album, so I'm going to drive down there on Saturday. I think it's sort of fitting. *Beatles for Sale* – funny, isn't it?'

Colin groaned. 'Well, that was fast, worryingly so. But Penny, I can't go with you, I'll be homeward bound by then.'

Her face fell. He was going home – already? Yes, his two-week stay was nearly over, and of course with the hotel closing it wasn't as though he would stick around forever, but they'd been becoming so close and were really starting to make progress …

Of course, she knew that her little project wasn't the only thing he had going on in his life. For one thing, he was supposed to be writing a novel.

'Don't worry, I have every intention of returning as soon as possible,' he added then. 'But I've had an idea for my story …'

'Of course,' she mumbled, trying to put her disappointment aside and concentrate on the task in hand. A sudden knot the size of a tennis ball had appeared in her stomach. She swallowed hard, willing herself not to get too affected by this. He was leaving, like so many others …

Penny turned back to her computer, determined not to let her disappointment distract her from the task in hand. She would try and take a leaf out of Elle's book and try to remain unmoved.

But there was no doubt that if Colin couldn't go to the meeting with her, a crimp was placed in her plans. First, she couldn't guarantee the album's authenticity, and secondly, as he pointed out, she certainly couldn't go and meet a complete stranger on her own.

'So, I need to go back to Sussex and put some things in order before I return.'

'You're coming back?' Penny didn't want to sound too hopeful.

He chuckled. 'Yes. And I know what I'm going to write about now. This. Your quest.' He indicated the list displayed on Penny's PC. 'The very notion has been burning a hole in my brain since you first mentioned it. I want to discuss it with my publisher and as I said, I need to make arrangements to stay a little longer.'

Suddenly everything looked so much brighter. Penny didn't want to ask him what would happen if the hotel sold, where would he stay – she was just a little taken aback by how relieved she felt upon realising she would see him again.

'So you'll have to cancel the meeting until I get back,' he continued.

'But I can't wait ...'

'Or you'll need to get someone else to go with you. What about Rob?'

'He's already going out of his way to fix up the roof for us, I couldn't ask him to drive all the way to Galway with me.'

'Then that leaves the obvious, doesn't it?'

She looked at him, confused.

'Ned. Tell him what's at hand. And if you insist on going to meet this stranger, there's surely no better person than your father to go along with you.'

Chapter 23

When Elle took her leave of Hazel she felt at least a little more confident that she hadn't returned to the town in vain. If nothing else, she had repaired her friendship with her childhood friend.

Elle tried to explain how she'd become so caught up in college life when she'd first moved away that gradually her visits home had lessened and lessened. And when she went to London, the already tenuous connections were reduced even further. It wasn't that she'd intentionally abandoned their friendship, or ignored her wedding, but—

'Life gets in the way,' Hazel said smiling. 'Of course, I understand that and I don't blame you. I did the very same thing myself when I went to Waterford. College life always undermines old friendships, and if I hadn't met Glenn and moved back here, I'm sure I would've been the very same.'

And Hazel hadn't thought her idea was bad either, not at all. She had tweaked it here and there, and given Elle a few useful tips. But looming over the whole thing was Doug Grant, who had taken on the proportions of a villain in Elle's mind.

When she thought of him now, it was almost like a caricature: a top hat perched on his slick head, his long, pale fingers gripping at a cane, cash stuffed into his pockets. Don't be stupid, she told herself sternly. He's just a man, and like any other he must have a weak spot. He must have a heart too, though she couldn't quite be sure where he had it hidden.

She took the coast road up to the hotel, and looked around with new appreciation for the beauty of her surroundings. She decided that the place had hooked her, that her eyes could never tire of gazing upon the bay's serene beauty.

Over the years in London she had got used to staring at the grey grid of the city streets and the endless rush of people, but it took something from you, watching the endless movement and the drive to be somewhere else. Whereas the more tranquil vistas of the small coastal town replenished you, gave something back that you hadn't known you were missing. Here, there was only the lazy glide and swoop of the seagulls to watch, small groups of tourists ambling down to the beach and the never-ending in and out motion of the waves.

The hotel too, was part of this calm, and now as much a part of the coastal landscape as if it had grown there, organically created – the walls growing slowly like a tree, the carpets creeping slowly across the floors like moss.

As she made her way up the driveway towards the building, determinedly averting her gaze from the *For Sale* sign, Elle knew this notion was silly, knew that it had in fact been built by a rich man as a gift for his betrothed, the perfect token for his lovely bride-to-be. Maybe that was part of it, though, that the house had been created in a spirit of love, and everything that had happened there since, aspired to the same ideal. What she was doing now was born of love: love for her father and sister, love for the hotel itself and the town it sat in, love for ...

There was Rob, on top of the roof. She could see the back of his shirt was wet with sweat from this distance. What was he doing, working like that in the midday sun? He would kill himself up there.

She pulled up around the side of the building, and he turned at the sound of her car door slamming. He shaded his eyes and looked down at her, and Elle could not think of a single thing to do except raise her hand in greeting. His arms stayed by his side, a hammer dangling from one hand. They seemed to stand there a long time, just saying nothing, before he turned away and continued with his work.

He hadn't acknowledged her at all. Well, she shouldn't be surprised. From what Penny had said, it seemed that Rob was finished with her completely, even with her friendship. She didn't know what she had expected from Rob, but it wasn't such an open declaration of hostility. She had never known him to be like that before.

Elle entered the shadowy doorway, hoping for a warmer reception from everyone else. Even though she still thought the entrance hall needed gutting, she was glad to see it. She ran her hand over the smooth wood of the reception desk, calming herself.

Penny, alerted by the ding of the bell on the front door, ran from the ballroom where she was sorting through bits and pieces, to find her sister standing by the reception desk as though she herself were a guest wanting to sign in.

She couldn't even find words of exclamation, an unusual occurrence for her.

'I've come back,' said Elle simply. 'And I've got an idea.'

Rob was pushing himself to the limit. Every night when he got home, his body burned with the day's effort. Each day, he worked until his lungs were ready to pop like balloons. Ned, who in the beginning had been humming bars from *Fixing a Hole* whenever Rob rolled up in the mornings, had lately turned to *A Hard Day's Night*. Rob supposed he was working like a dog, almost like a man possessed, which he thought was good description for how he felt. He *was* working to rid himself of something, something that had haunted him for years. But no matter how hard he worked, no matter how exhausted he was when he fell into bed at night, he still woke in the grey dawn light to think of what he had wanted, and what he had lost.

Now Rob wondered if he was dreaming. Had he worked himself into such a state that he was hallucinating? But no, there was the green rental car, sitting placidly below, as though it had not delivered a huge shock ten minutes before.

He hadn't been able to react, so strong was his surprise. Elle's appearance had sent a wave of feeling over him, the kind he had been trying to avoid since she left. He felt confused, sad, and angry. Angry at himself for being unable to forget her, angry at her for being the thing that he couldn't forget. He was afraid that if he moved at all, he would step right off the roof.

So he worked on, the sea moving endlessly behind him. He wished he could borrow some of its constancy and sameness. What had happened to his life since Elle came back into it? He had, over the years, fashioned a life that he was content with, like a sculptor slowly, carefully, chipping away at a block of marble until something was revealed beneath it. His life was simple, and it was this simplicity that he needed and sought refuge in. He had his work, his dogs, his friends and for a long time he had believed this was enough. His association with the Harte family had been painful at first, but had become necessary to him. He had been able to go long stretches without thinking of Elle, but when thoughts of her did creep up they were painful and all-consuming. He thought of these jags of memory as a kind of illness he had to get through, a seasonal bout of the flu.

But since her return to the town for Anna's funeral, it had seemed that there was no way through his thoughts of her. No way under, over or around. A maddening riddle.

And now she was back. It almost felt like pouring salt water over the wound. At whatever cost, he had to keep his feelings to himself.

Whatever reason she was back in Mulberry Bay, it had nothing to do with him, he was sure. Rob would just keep working, keep living his life, and stay as far away from Elle as he could.

Later, in her room, Elle reflected on how lame and powerless her words to Penny had sounded: *'I've got an idea.'*

All of them had had ideas aplenty over the last few weeks and nothing had come of them. What made this one any different? Did she really think she could pull this off?

Penny, for her part, had seemed almost too numb to react. Her questions had been comically distracted. 'Did you forget something?' she had asked. 'Has something terrible happened?'

Something terrible will happen if we don't do something, Elle had thought, but didn't say anything.

When she looked into the mirror in her room, she could see why Penny might have wondered. She did indeed look as though she had been through some harrowing ordeal. Her face seemed thinner, more heavily lined, her freckles stark against the pallor of her skin. The bruising on her nose from her encounter with Rob's chest was starting to fade, but the yellowish tinge around her eyes made her look even more ghastly.

Elle had never been one to worry unduly about her looks. She accepted them for what they were and went about her business. Of course, she had the odd twinges of worry about her ageing face and whether her tawny hair would soon fade to bronze, then grey, but now, looking at herself, she wondered if things were truly taking a turn for the worse. Perhaps she would get old all at once, overnight almost, and previous acquaintances would hardly recognise her on the street. She didn't have any of Anna and Penny's firm plumpness that somehow ironed out, or altogether resisted the invasions of age.

She turned away with a sigh. It wasn't worth worrying about now. She had more pressing matters on her mind, such as how to achieve the thing that she had come back to do. It was one thing to see it in dream form almost, completely another to drag it into reality. She didn't want to see her vision compromised, changed, cheapened. She was like this with the execution of her buildings too. It had to be right, otherwise it wasn't worth it. If it couldn't be the way she envisioned, then it would be a failure.

Could she count on Penny for help? She hoped that the vagueness her sister had shown when she encountered her in reception was just shock. It would need to be all hands on deck if she was going to pull this off.

She headed for bed, too tired to even think about dinner. To her surprise, she was happy to find the cats already there, as though they had sought out the one in the house who was the most in need of comfort.

She steadfastly refused to think of Rob, though she could still hear the swing and thud of his hammer as she drifted to sleep, and later in her dreams.

Chapter 24

First thing the following morning, Penny was beating a rug mercilessly.

Colin, still in his pyjamas, had come out onto the lawn and was watching her with a solemn expression. 'Oh dear,' he said, 'I'm afraid you will beat that rug to pieces if you're not careful. Are you out of sorts?'

'Yes,' she said. 'Yes, I am "out of sorts".' She continued to beat the rug, though it had long since ceased to emit exhausted puffs of dust.

'And would this have anything to do with your sister's reappearance in the hotel yesterday?'

'It's just so typical,' Penny huffed. 'Blowing hot and cold. One minute, she couldn't wait to get away, the next she's back with some far-flung idea to save the world! Or the hotel at least.'

'Fascinating. What's her idea?'

'I don't know,' Penny admitted. 'But I don't need to, either. It's far too late for ideas. We've moved on.'

'Well,' said Colin, 'I don't pretend any great knowledge of this place. After all, I've only been here a couple of weeks, hardly a lifetime. But I've said before that I think this place is special and worth saving. And if your sister has an idea that might help, however late in the day, I think it's worth exploring. Quite apart from the other affections I have developed here, I have become quite attached to this place.'

Penny didn't answer and eventually Colin wandered away in the direction of the kitchen. She kept beating the rug for a full five minutes before she stopped to consider what he had said. Could he be right? And what were these 'other affections' he mentioned?

For the next half-hour, Penny was distracted, abandoning every task she put her hand to. She was having a tug-of-war argument with herself. Should she allow herself hope in the matter of the hotel once more? Or was it better to be stoical about it, as Elle herself had been before she left?

And even more stoical about the fact that Colin would be leaving soon. She was surprised by how much the notion saddened her. She'd enjoyed their recent adventures in tracking down the records, and especially enjoyed having someone to bounce ideas off and to give advice on whether or not she was doing the right thing, as well as having someone, other than immediate family, concerned about her safety or indeed her whereabouts.

She supposed that at least one good thing had come out of her sister's return, though; she could now ask Elle to come with her to Galway on Saturday to meet that guy. She just hoped Elle would understand her reasoning and her desire to restore Ned's collection. Though she would probably think she was mad. Much like Colin did, despite his kindness in helping her so far. Though of course Penny now knew that this had more to do with finding inspiration for his novel than any true desire to help. Which also disappointed her more than she was willing to admit.

Deep down Penny knew that in a way, replacing Ned's collection had supplanted her worries and fears about the hotel, and had given her something to concentrate on since Elle left and all hope seemed lost.

She didn't know if she could allow herself to hope again. For the hotel or ... anything else.

And she wasn't sure if her quest was futile either, and if she was just wasting her time running around and spending a small fortune trying to restore Ned's prized possession. Thinking about it, it was over thirty years ago since he'd given it up, so there was also the chance that her dad had forgotten all about the records and couldn't give a hoot about them now.

Penny sighed, her mind a mass of confusion. If only there was a fortune-teller in town, she would almost be tempted to go and ask a few questions.

At breakfast, Ned was more than surprised to see his eldest daughter walk into the kitchen.

'Elle,' he said. 'What on earth are you doing here?'

'I'm not exactly sure,' she replied, shakily. 'Well no, that's not true. I've come to give things another shot with trying to save the hotel. I know it's almost too late. But while there's still even the tiniest amount of hope, I need to do this.'

'Well, I'm glad you want to help. But I just don't see what else is to be done. I don't want you to set yourself up for another disappointment.' He shook his head. 'I know we put too much on you last time. We asked too much, and it was all our responsibility. You shouldn't feel like all of this is down to you.'

'I don't,' she said. 'I've had an idea, a bit of a revelation, really, but it's not just that.' She took a deep breath. 'When I got back to London, it was as if nothing fit there any more. My whole life seemed … out of sorts. It was exactly the same, but I felt so constrained suddenly. Sounds melodramatic, I know, but I felt as if the life was being sucked out of me.'

Ned nodded. He had never lived in a city, but any visits even as far as Dublin had felt a little bit like this. He felt completely out of place with all these polished people who seemed completely unafraid of saying whatever came into their heads.

'So, I came back, for a little while at least. I took some time off, a leave of absence until the end of the summer. I'm not sure if there's a place for me here, but I'm pretty sure it's where I want to be just now.'

'This is your home. And for as long as it remains our house,' said Ned, 'there will be a place for you. But now, let's get these puddings on the griddle. Our guest has a wicked appetite for black pudding.'

'Guest? What guest?' Elle had not had time to become acquainted with Colin before she left for London. She had been vaguely aware of a tall, lanky, stranger with the others that day when she had returned from her failed expedition in town, but she had been too upset to wonder who he was or what he was doing there.

A guest? How on earth had that happened when Penny had supposedly cancelled all bookings? And especially given the hotel was up for sale.

'Yes,' said Ned. 'English Colin. He's made himself quite a fixture around the place over the last couple of weeks. I hate to think how much harder things would have been for Penny if he hadn't shown up when he did. He's been a real distraction for her.'

'Really ...' said Elle, raising her eyebrows, but nothing more was said on the subject as the man himself appeared. Elle found his appearance amusing, to say the least. He was wearing a pair of blue and white striped pyjamas, with a pair of open-toed slippers on his feet, and to top it off, a paisley dressing-gown loosely tied about his thin waist. Elle thought he had the air of an escaped mental patient, but a friendly one all the same. He shook her hand enthusiastically.

'The prodigal sister returns,' he exclaimed. 'So pleased to meet you properly at last. Don't mind me, I prefer to be rather casual over breakfast, but I will be sure to don proper attire for the rest of the day.'

Penny entered the kitchen then and completed the group. Elle was a bit taken aback at how raucous breakfast was that morning. So different from the solemn gatherings of just a couple of weeks before. Penny was practically glowing in Colin's company and they were both laughing and teasing each other. Which was interesting ...

Still it was all a bit unnerving – as if the hotel wasn't about to be sold out from underneath their feet. Had they completely forgotten what dire straits they were in? Apparently so.

By the time breakfast was over, she felt quite left out. Again. She would have been almost angry if Penny hadn't turned to her and said: 'Why don't we go for a walk along the beach, Elle, and you can tell me about this idea of yours?'

Then she looked at Colin and Elle saw some kind of private communication pass between them. What on earth ...?

'I need to talk to you about something else anyway,' she said. 'And we can all discuss what to do about the hotel later.' Penny smiled at her sister. 'For the moment, I'm just glad to have you back.'

It was another beautiful spring day, everything in perpetual motion, a light brisk wind in the air. The surface of the sand eddied around Elle and Penny like a golden stream.

Elle was reeling by the time her sister finished outlining her story about their father's albums, and how Penny was now like a crazy woman, trying to track down and replace the entire catalogue.

'Are you serious?' she said, when Penny finally paused for breath. 'As if we didn't have enough to think about.'

'Didn't you hear what I said? Dad gave up all of those albums for me, for us! Our family. You know it must've been a huge sacrifice for him, especially with how he is about music.'

'I know what you're saying but I just can't ...' She just couldn't get her head around the notion that Penny seriously believed she could get an entire first edition Beatles collection back. It could take months, years even. If at all.

Once again her sister was setting herself up for disappointment. This couldn't work.

And yet ...

Wasn't the same sentiment part of Elle's reason for returning? Wasn't she, too, trying to restore something, something that would help heal the fractures that had developed in this family? So if this was so important to Penny, (and she had to admit it tugged at her heart too, to imagine their dad giving up his beloved collection for their sake) maybe she should get on board and help her out.

She guessed she had a better sense than Penny of the value of such things, and certainly had more means, and from what Penny had told her about the cost of her most recent purchase, it seemed as though her meagre budget would be used up in no time. So Elle would go with her to meet this guy on Saturday, and like Colin sensibly pointed out, ensure that he wasn't an axe-murderer for a start.

Penny took a piece of paper out of her pocket and handed it to her. 'This is what I've got so far.'

Elle read through the list of records, surprised at how

much progress her sister had made in such a short space of time.

'You'll help me?' Penny asked hopefully.

'I might be nuts, but yes, I'll help. What's another impossible task in the scheme of things?'

They began to turn back towards the hotel. It looked disappointed and shabby, made more so by the blue tarp Rob had hauled over the gaping roof. Maybe it wouldn't stay disappointed for long, if only Elle could bring her plan to fruition.

As they walked, she began outlining that plan to Penny, her hands moving in great arcs and then drawing in for finer, more precise movements. Her sister nodded and smiled, occasionally interjecting with thoughts of her own.

By the time they reached the hotel, Penny too was in agreement that this was the last chance they had of saving the hotel, and knew they had to put all they had into it.

It was make or break time.

And her little sister was right about something too, Elle realised. If her plan didn't work and the hotel was fated to certain doom, at least they would have done something positive in hunting down Ned's old collection. If she and Penny couldn't save their mother's legacy, then they owed it to their dad to take a decent shot at restoring his.

Chapter 25

'So how will we recognise this guy?' Elle asked the following Saturday as she and Penny emerged onto Eyre Square.

She had driven the rental car to Galway that morning, leaving Ned in the hotel with only Rob on the roof for company, as Colin had checked out and returned to England the day before.

Penny wondered if he'd been serious about coming back and writing a novel about all that was happening. Or if he was serious about coming back at all. She'd bid him a polite goodbye yesterday, afraid to say too much for fear he would see something more on her face.

She'd done it again of course; fallen head over heels with someone who surely saw her as little more than a brief distraction, someone to pass the time with while in town. Same old story.

And while he was still insistent she should tell Ned, and let her dad participate in the quest, Penny didn't want to get

Ned's hopes up about this, not until she was further down the line. Ideally she wanted to one day just walk up to her father and present him with the entire collection, but as Elle pointed out, this could realistically take years.

In any case, first things first, and she and Elle were here to meet the prospect from the Done Deal site. She just hoped the journey this far north was worth the effort.

'Hmm,' she said, looking around to get her bearings. 'I'm not sure. The guy just said his name was Paul and that he would be at the JFK memorial and that I would know him when I see him. The memorial is this way,' she pointed toward their destination.

Elle raised her eyebrows. 'He actually said that? That you would know him when you see him?'

Penny nodded. Keeping pace with her, her sister shook her head in some disbelief. 'And that doesn't seem a bit odd to you? A red flag even?' she questioned. 'Some stranger asking to meet in person and telling you that you will simply know him when you see him? Colin was right – you really did need someone to come here with you. You're way too trusting, Penny.'

Chuckling at the suggestion that she didn't know how to take care of herself, Penny waved a hand, dismissing Elle's comments. 'You've been living in the big city too long. It's not that odd at all actually. Plenty of people meet strangers in public. And you don't always have to give a detailed description of what you are wearing or what you look like to draw someone to you. There is an actual Law of Attraction you know, in that people who are looking for each other can usually spot the person in question – crowded place or not. Besides, I'm sure we will recognise him; he's likely to be carrying a record, isn't he?'

Admittedly, she had a point, Elle thought. But she was glad that she had come here with her all the same. One could never be too sure, after all and that so-called 'Law of Attraction' had the capability of attracting crazies, too.

The pair walked brusquely toward the centre of the square, where the John F. Kennedy Memorial stood. Reaching the base of the bronze artwork, Penny cast an eye about, looking for the 'Paul' they were to meet. Elle wondered if Penny's notion about the 'Law of Attraction' would prove true or if they would be left standing here, looking around.

'Do you see anyone holding an album?' Penny asked, looking at her watch. 'It's twelve noon on the dot now. Right on time.'

She looked around the mass of people who were congregated in the square – this area in itself was a popular meeting place, and a busy traffic junction.

Checking her watch again, Elle shifted her weight from one foot to the other. 'I hope this guy hurries, I'm cold.' The weather up here in the West was always considerably colder than the South East, and she longed for the sunny skies they'd left in Mulberry Bay first thing that morning.

However, as she thought about her next words, Penny was distracted by a busker on the other side of the square singing a song she recognised. It was *Eight Days A Week*.

'What the ...' Elle muttered, as a man carrying a guitar

and wearing a 1960s-style grey suit strolled toward the pair. He sported a bowl hair cut – just like the original 'Paul'. The man was now standing directly in front of Penny and Elle delivering his serenade seemingly for them alone. However, a small crowd was gathering to watch the performance and Elle suddenly realised just what was happening.

'This is hilarious,' Penny laughed. 'What are the chances?'

Elle snorted. 'Penny, all of these songs. They are off the album we're looking for, *Beatles for Sale*.

Recognition suddenly dawned on Penny's face. 'Do you mean that *this* is *Paul*?'

Elle rolled her eyes – she was clearly not finding the humour in the situation. 'Yup. An impersonator. A *Paul McCartney* impersonator. Colin was right. This is just internet craziness.' She looked at the singer in front of her, who was clearly delighted with himself and the show he was putting on. 'Are you Paul?' she yelled, trying to raise her voice above the hoots and cheers of the crowd around them.

The singer smiled and took a hand away from his guitar. '*Sir* Paul, that is. And you must be Penny. I hear you are interested in authentic Beatles music – well that's me. In the flesh. Doesn't get much more authentic than this.' And he continued singing – on to the song *Rock and Roll Music* – apparently, he was going to cover the entire *Beatles For Sale* album.

'For crying out loud,' muttered Elle. 'Law of Attraction all right.' She looked at Penny. 'Come on. This guy doesn't have an album to sell.'

'What?' Penny was crestfallen. 'But how do you know?'

'Because dear sister, I understand a crazy when I see one. This guy was having you on.'

'What? But I can't believe he would do that. We drove over three hours to get here ...'

Elle pulled a five euro note out of her purse and dropped it into the hat which had magically appeared at Paul the impersonator's feet, then turned with Penny to push through the crowd, which had now swelled three deep around the impromptu performer.

Making their way away from the sculpture, Penny heard a round of clapping behind her – the busker had just finished one song and was on to the next. Two young men, who were heading toward where 'Paul' was singing passed them by chatting away about what was happening. Elle heard, 'This guy is great. He usually performs in front of Classic Records on Shop Street – I wonder what brought him over here?'

Penny, who had heard the same, stopped in her tracks. 'Did you hear that? They said that our Paul impersonator made his way over from a record store in Shop Street. Maybe it's worth a look.'

Elle looked dubious. 'I'm sure it's easy enough to find. I suppose we could take a look – we might as well do something while we're here. But on one condition,' she said, holding out her little finger.

'What's that?' Penny enquired, wide-eyed at this unexpected resurrection of their old childhood ritual.

'No more internet meet-ups. Promise?'

Chuckling aloud, her little sister held up a finger in return, sealing the vow.

'A great haul!' Penny grinned happily an hour or so later. She waved the shopping bag from Classic Records in front of her, satisfaction rippling through her body. 'Paul McCartney impersonator or not, I'm glad that little change in plans paid off.'

The pair had been successful in not only finding the record shop and getting the attention of the owner, but also in snagging an invitation to the back room to peruse through some of the rarer albums.

In all, they had been able to acquire three more on their list: *Beatles for Sale*, *Rubber Soul* and *Something New*. All were first editions, and based on Colin's checklist they were confident that all were definitely authentic, and the shop's owner had assured them of a full money-back guarantee if found otherwise.

'So how is your list looking now?' Elle asked, happy to see Penny with such a bright smile on her face.

'Ah, I nearly forgot. I think that might be the best part – crossing more of these off the list.' She extracted from her handbag the piece of paper that she was now carrying with her everywhere.

Please Please Me
With the Beatles
Beatlemania! With the Beatles

Melissa Hill

Introducing ... the Beatles
~~Meet the Beatles!~~
Twist and Shout
The Beatles' Second Album
~~The Beatles' Long Tall Sally~~
A Hard Day's Night
~~Something New~~
~~Beatles for Sale~~
~~Beatles '65~~
Beatles VI
Help!
Anna (Go to Him) **Single**
~~Rubber Soul~~
Yesterday and Today
Revolver
~~Sgt. Pepper's Lonely Hearts Club Band~~
Magical Mystery Tour
The Beatles
~~Yellow Submarine~~
Abbey Road
Let It Be

Wow, Elle thought in wonderment, realising just how much Penny had achieved in such a short space of time. Perhaps there was hope after all.

Chapter 26

Later that evening, when she and Penny returned from Galway, Elle wandered through the rooms of the hotel, assessing the magnitude of what she was considering.

The adrenaline rush of her sudden return was gradually faltering, and in the cold light of day she was now beginning to have second thoughts.

Was it even possible? Could the hotel be tidied up in time? Of course, the main question was the roof. They couldn't have people turning up here with it looking like that; everyone would think the whole place was about to collapse.

She didn't particularly relish the thought of asking Rob about it either. Since their unsettling, wordless encounter on her arrival a couple of days before, she had avoided him. It wasn't hard. He was on the roof from dawn till dusk, and the only way Elle knew he was there was the regular sound of his hammer and his dogs on the grounds begging for affection. Still, if she wanted to put her plan into action, she needed to find out how progress was going.

Now, she waited down below the ladder when she knew he was due to finish. She wondered how he was getting home, because his truck was nowhere to be seen. One of his building crew had it probably.

Rob made his way down the ladder slowly and carefully. When he got to the bottom and turned to her, she took one look at his face and knew he was bone tired. His face seemed caved in somehow, as though he had lost weight since she last saw him. There were bags of sleeplessness under his eyes, and his eyes themselves were dull and shot through with red.

He didn't say anything, just raised his eyebrows in question. It was almost as though he couldn't bring himself to speak, or was too tired to.

'I'm not sure if anyone's told you,' she began a little nervously, 'but I've come back. Obviously.' She chuckled but her voice wavered. 'I've had another idea for saving the hotel. One last ditch attempt.' He still said nothing, his eyes burning a hole into her own, so she finished up shortly: 'I was just wondering when the roof might be ready?'

When Rob did speak, at last, it seemed to cost him something. His shoulders drooped a little lower. 'Next week,' he said, his voice listless. 'As long as the rain holds off.'

'Next week? That's good. And it won't rain, not if I have anything to do with it.'

But he didn't smile, he just continued to stare at her dumbly. Elle decided he must truly despise her if he couldn't bring himself to have a civil conversation with her. Well, that was just another thing she would have to live with.

His truck pulled up the driveway then, driven by a young attractive woman with short dark hair who looked to be about Penny's age.

'Hello,' she greeted as she got out. The dogs rushed to meet her. Whoever she was, they must know her well, Elle thought, wondering why she cared.

Rob began to load his things onto the back of the truck.

'Hi,' she said, greeting the woman. 'I'm Elle. I live here.'

'Oh, Penny's sister. Lovely to meet you. I'm Celeste,' she replied. She looked shyly at Rob. 'A friend of Rob's.'

Ah, so this was it, thought Elle. He had found someone else and he didn't want her back in town, ruining things. Well, he needn't worry, she would stay well away.

Elle couldn't help studying Celeste as they chatted briefly about nothing, and wondered why Penny hadn't mentioned that Rob had met someone. She supposed her sister didn't want to open up any old wounds. Or she simply didn't think that Elle would care, given that the last time she was home she'd tried to make it perfectly clear to everyone – including Rob – that she didn't.

Was she a local or a tourist? Elle wondered, thinking that whoever Celeste was, she was very striking, with delicately drawn features, big blue eyes and dark curling lashes. She hated to admit it, but she could almost see a similarity to herself in the younger girl's face, something to do with her sharp chin, and the stubbornness that was evident in her eyes. She was quick to smile and Elle guessed that she couldn't know that she herself had a history with Rob.

Well, she wouldn't be the one to tell her. She wasn't going to make trouble. That was for kids.

Elle waved Rob and Celeste off like they were old friends, and then went back inside to continue her appraisal of the rooms.

Rob had asked Celeste to drive home; he didn't think he could trust his hands at the wheel. Elle had been so normal with him back there, so unaffected. He felt like his own feelings shone through him, like his skin was paper-thin. She must see it in his eyes.

'Was that the girl?' Celeste asked, with an annoying hint of pity in her voice.

'Yes,' he said. 'That was the girl.'

As Elle moved through the hotel, she realised she had memories that existed in each room, which now seemed to appear like ghosts.

How long had she had these stored away?

There she was with Penny, hiding underneath the lace table cloths in the tea rooms. They liked to peek out at the pretty clothes the guests wore back then: pastel twin sets, or brightly coloured shift dresses. Always with little hats, delicate watches and jewels.

Elle remembered coveting one pair of shoes in particular, a low-heeled emerald green pair of heels with diamante on the heel. She supposed they had been quite glamorous for the time. She had never been able to find a pair like it.

Back in the eighties, afternoon tea at the Bay Hotel was always an occasion to dress up for, and no matter what people believed about small towns back then, the women of Mulberry Bay had beautiful clothes and knew how to wear them.

Elle vividly remembered what went onto the platters. The first layer had been a selection of savoury treats: prawn and cucumber sandwiches, feta and onion tarts, little crackers with grapes and blue cheese. All miniature sized, so you could pop them into your mouth without spoiling your lipstick. Then a layer of scones, with cream and jam, little chocolate cheesecake morsels, a tiny aromatic slice of currant brack.

On the top, finely iced fairy cakes, in the kind of pastel hues little girls adored. Every once in a while, Anna had allowed her and Penny to dress up, put on pearls and one of her hats, and sit in the tea room like those ladies. She would wait on them and pretend they were very important guests.

The tea room itself was still delicately beautiful, though a little dated here and there. It wouldn't take much work to turn it into the enchanted bower that Elle remembered from the old days. But it wasn't the tea room that was to be the centrepiece of her plan.

The dining room, too, was still a beautiful old space. It couldn't quite fade into shabbiness, having the eternal beauty of that sea view. This room, the setting of so many celebrations, would still have a part to play, but it still wasn't the main attraction. Though with a little bit of work here and there it would do quite nicely.

Then the ballroom.

Such a gorgeous room, but probably the least well kept at this stage. When times got harder, Anna and Ned had put what little money there was into the upkeep of the rooms that were most essential day to day: the bedrooms, bathrooms, kitchen and dining room.

The ballroom truly was the jewel in the hotel's crown, but sadly used less and less over the years. As a result, it looked like a bit of a state and had become a dumping ground for unwanted furniture, and supplies. The wooden floor was scarred, the wallpaper marked and ripped. That would be a challenge.

Unbidden Elle had a sudden image of her and Rob, dancing in the middle of the floor here, arms around each other, moving to an invisible band.

Had this happened?

Of course. It all came back to her with a rush. It was the night before she was due to leave for college and he had put candles all over the ballroom, so that it was like their own magical cave. Shadows had moved round the edges, but it was only the two of them who were real, who really existed. They had whispered the loveliest things, and in the image before her, Elle could still see Rob's lips move, his face softened by the promises he was making.

She had made promises, too. At that time, caught in the moment, she had sworn she would come back for him, that their love would draw her back home as surely as a magnet. It took her a moment, and then Elle realised with a stab of grief, that it had indeed drawn her back.

It had just taken almost twenty years to do so.

Chapter 27

The next morning dawned bright and blue once again. Everything seemed to be blessed by the sun, which would grow to full heat by midday. But for the moment, the leaves on the trees stood out in vivid greenness, as though each one was clearly visible, shivering in the light breeze.

Penny felt thoroughly discombobulated. And whatever she tried to focus her mind on she failed miserably.

Yes, she had secured one more album since the Galway trip, winning another auction on eBay. Not overly difficult, albeit somewhat expensive.

But as she pulled out her list and crossed the newly acquired album off – *Beatlemania*! – she had that feeling again that something was off, something wasn't right.

Please Please Me
With the Beatles

~~Beatlemania! With the Beatles~~
Introducing ... the Beatles
~~Meet the Beatles!~~
Twist and Shout
The Beatles' Second Album
~~The Beatles' Long Tall Sally~~
A Hard Day's Night
~~Something New~~
~~Beatles for Sale~~
~~Beatles '65~~
Beatles VI
Help!
Anna (Go to Him) **Single**
~~Rubber Soul~~
Yesterday and Today
Revolver
~~Sgt. Pepper's Lonely Hearts Club Band~~
Magical Mystery Tour
The Beatles
~~Yellow Submarine~~
Abbey Road
Let It Be

Pondering what she had acquired thus far, she waited for a sense of accomplishment to kick in, something along the lines of what she had felt on the way home from Galway when she was crossing off records with Elle's help.

But she didn't feel the same.

Something was missing. *Colin* was missing. She hadn't heard anything since he left on Friday afternoon and she had no idea when if ever he was coming back.

And for the first time in days, Penny felt very alone.

Elle laid things out for everyone in the dining room. This is where her talent for organisation came in handy. If there had been resistance before, now Penny and Ned were nodding enthusiastically. She had infected them with her vigour.

She left them both with tasks for the day, as she went off down town on her own. She wanted to ask for help, but she knew she needed to do this by herself. It was part an exercise in getting her self-respect back, part proving to everyone else that she could do it.

Before she left, Penny asked, 'Shouldn't we tell Rob about this? After all, he has helped us from the start, he should be a part of this too.'

'I've already talked to Rob,' said Elle, which wasn't exactly a lie. 'He'll be putting all his energies into the roof. It needs to be finished in time.'

Penny nodded uncertainly. She felt that something was being left unsaid.

'Did you meet Celeste?' she probed.

'Yes, I did.' Elle smiled blandly. 'She seems like a lovely girl.

She wasn't going to make the same mistake as last time. The beige suit hung limply in the wardrobe. Elle felt like taking a pair of scissors to the thing. If only she had listened to Mona from the boutique. A blind man could have told her that it was exactly the wrong choice. She shook her head. She must have been mad.

This time, Elle wore something she could be completely herself in. A pair of purple skinny trousers and a jade green silk tank top. She slipped on a pair of golden braided sandals. There. Not exactly business-like, but she felt comfortable.

She didn't feel like she was an impostor, or an actress on stage, wearing someone else's borrowed clothes. As she set off towards Main Street you couldn't tell to look at her, but she was even more nervous than last time. If they didn't warm to her now, when she was being herself, it meant that the problem lay with her somehow. That there was something in her personality that just wasn't right. Elle hoped, as she drove, that wouldn't be the case.

From the roof, Rob watched her leave. You couldn't miss her, her hair stood out like a bloom beneath the sun. He couldn't help admiring her. She had left the town under such a cloud, and now here she was, striding out into the day in her vibrant, beautiful clothing, looking like she could do anything.

He wasn't exactly sure what she was up to, but he thought that she had guts for trying. He felt in his heart that it was too late for the hotel, though it tore him up to admit it. All he could do now was finish this infernal roof.

*

Penny thought she was seeing things. She'd just finished getting dressed after breakfast and had come back into the kitchen to find none other than Colin sitting at the table with Ned.

He was wearing a loose cream linen suit and a panama hat and looked for all the world like he'd never left.

'You're back!' she spluttered redundantly, her heart soaring.

'Indeed.'

'Already?'

Ned got up from the table. 'I'm going for a walk,' he said, shuffling out of the kitchen and leaving Penny and Colin alone.

'So how did it go ... with your publisher?' she asked, willing her delight not to show all over her face.

'Oh he loved the idea, but never mind that. I take it you haven't yet told Ned about our adventure, since he didn't mention anything ...'

'Not yet.' She told him all about Galway and how she'd persuaded Elle to go with her.

'I dare say that's sensible. Especially when considering the mammoth task we have ahead. But I think I can help with that.' He took something out of a satchel that was resting on the kitchen chair beside him.

'What's that?

Colin handed her a folder. 'Just a smidgen of progress. You can't depend on eBay forever you know.'

Opening the folder, Penny found a document that she

recognised as a copy of her list, but with handwritten notations alongside each item – names, addresses, phone numbers.

'What is this?' she enquired, intrigued. 'These are obviously all the ones that I haven't been able to find yet.'

Colin nodded. 'Exactly. My publisher happens to know a couple of chaps in Edinburgh – collectible record dealers. I gave them a call and they were able to track down some of the rarer ones on your list – the ones you aren't going to find online because people who own those albums probably aren't looking to sell them.'

Penny was flabbergasted. 'You did all of this ... for me?' Then feeling stupid, she remembered that of course any novelist worth his or her salt would conduct extensive research on a topic they were writing about. 'I mean, for my project,' she added quickly.

'Indeed.'

Penny considered the list. The addresses were scattered all over the UK but with a few in Ireland. 'So what am I supposed to do?'

Colin smiled knowingly and took the list from her. 'If I was a corporate sort, I might refer to it as "cold calling".'

'You mean, contact all of these people one by one and try to convince them to sell?' OK, so it was a long shot, but at least it was something. She looked at him, unable to believe that he'd made this much progress in such a short time. He had a contact for all of the records on her list except *Twist and Shout* and the *Anna* single.

'Thank you,' she said. 'I don't know how you managed it but …'

He followed her gaze to the list, all business and Penny knew that she was right about this being simply part of his creative endeavours. '*Twist and Shout* is proving to be an exceptionally difficult one, hard to find any edition that hasn't been used as a frisbee for forty years. And *Anna*, well, same situation.'

He stuffed his hands in his pocket. 'That one might be a bit more tricky, since it's a single, and rarer. But I'll keep looking.' Eyes twinkling, he looked at Penny and rubbed his hands together. 'So, my dear girl … when do we begin?'

Elle began, once again, with Della and Jim at the builders providers.

'I've come to make amends,' she said to their puzzled faces.

'What for?' said Della. 'It's really us who should be … I felt that we weren't exactly helpful last time, but I couldn't make myself clear.'

'You shouldn't have had to,' said Elle with a nervous smile. 'I was out of touch with the way things are done. In London I suppose it's all rush, rush, and straight to the point, trying to get everything underway as quickly as possible. I didn't want to take up any of your time, knowing how busy you are, and I realised too late how rude that made me seem.'

Soon enough they were chatting easily, and it was a pleasant conversation for Elle. Della and Jim were old friends of

Anna and Ned's, and had many memories of watching the sun go down over the bay from the dining room, having spent a night talking and laughing with Elle's parents.

'She was such a gem, your mother,' said Della tearfully. 'Always ready with a joke. She teased your father something terrible for being so quiet. A less patient man would have been driven up the wall. But I actually think Ned enjoyed it.'

'We want to help in any way we can,' said Jim. 'We've had less and less time to get up to the hotel the past few years, what with the business and our grandchildren, but the thought of it going is just awful. Anything we can do ...'

'Well,' Elle said. 'There's a few things, and luckily, they're all very simple. Tell me, do you own a good pair of dancing shoes?'

When she left the warehouse an hour later, Della and Jim had been brought into the secret.

Elle smiled. Things were starting to come together.

Chapter 28

She spent the entire day reversing the other terrible day she had spent two weeks before. If the people of the town had considered the eldest Harte girl to be cold and patronising before, now they thought that she was charming, sincere and intelligent, to boot. They could see why young Rob Callahan had lost his head over her. It wasn't mentioned, but they all felt sorry over the situation.

Elle had even managed to pop back into Mona's to look for a decent dress. They shared a joke over the suit. 'I felt terrible letting you walk out the door with it. I seemed to see it happen in slow motion.'

The morning had gone well, no doubt about it. Elle felt more in control than she had in weeks. She had offers of materials and promises of help all over the place. It was the first piece of the puzzle, so to speak.

The problem with this plan, she reflected, was that each bit of it depended on another. If one piece was missing, the whole thing would be a failure. She needed the support of her family and the town, as well as for the hotel to show some semblance of grandeur, for the initial part of the plan to be a success. After this came the especially hard challenge: facing Doug Grant once more to try to convince him to give them a loan. Her stomach quaked at the thought, but she told herself not to worry about that until it was absolutely necessary.

She made her last call of the day just as the sun was beginning to touch the water. Ryan's Antiques and Restorations was still open and Arthur was on duty. He often stayed until late in the evenings, pottering about in the back of the shop. He no longer had a great deal to go home for, and was only too happy to let his son Wally off to spend time with his young family.

'Ah, it's you again, is it? You'd better come in quick so you can rush back out again.'

'I'm so sorry about last time, Mr Ryan,' she said. 'Believe it or not, I was trying to be polite.'

'I've often noticed that people from cities have a funny way of being polite,' he remarked. 'A very funny way.'

'I should have known better, though,' Elle said. 'I might have lived away for a long time, but I'm still a Bay girl through and through. It's just a pity it's taken me this long to realise it.'

It wasn't that hard to win Arthur over in the end. He had an eye for a pretty face and he truly wanted to help save the hotel. It occurred to him that if this girl and her scatty sister were running the place, there was no reason he couldn't go up there the odd night and have a bit of a chat. Stave off his loneliness a bit. He was used to it, but listening to his own thoughts did get very boring.

Besides, he thought as he saw Elle off, a bit of a get-together was exactly what this town needed.

The next day, Elle stayed back at the hotel and helped with the more physically demanding tasks.

Penny moved down the end of the ballroom to begin sanding from one end. Elle started from the other. It was a big job but they both felt the satisfaction of seeing the scars and dents being ground out of the floor.

'Well, I'm glad to see you muck in,' said Penny. 'After yesterday, I thought you were going to leave us with all the hard work while you went off and had coffee with half the town.'

Elle wasn't bothered by her grumpiness. She had a pretty good idea of what was getting to her sister. She was falling for English Colin, but didn't want to make a fool of herself by admitting anything. Elle was torn between letting things take their natural course, or giving things a helping hand. She remembered how Penny had meddled with her and Rob when she first arrived. That hadn't had a happy ending, but it was patently obvious that Colin and Penny were nuts about each other.

What Rob and Elle had ... well, it wasn't hard to see that it had meant nothing. He had someone else already.

And try as she might, she couldn't dislike Celeste. She had

no reason to, of course. But often it felt as though she should, as though the other girl had something that was rightly hers. But Rob wasn't hers and hadn't been for a long time. She had given him up freely.

Elle laughed at Penny. 'Never fear, little sister,' she said. 'I am determined to get this precisely right. I will be here every waking hour from now on. But I need a favour,' she added and Penny looked at her. 'I need you to get Dad out of the way for the next couple of days.'

'But how can I do that? What on earth would possibly make him want to leave?' Elle watched Penny's face as she came to the same realisation.

It was time to tell Ned about the albums.

Chapter 29

Penny sat in the passenger seat of Ned's Cortina, while her father drove. She could feel her nerves kick into gear the closer and closer that they got to their destination. She had been somewhat successful in tuning out her father and Colin from the backseat, who were currently in a battle of wits and mini-war of words over how good/bad the Beatles were.

Ned had reacted predictably to Penny's announcement that she was trying to track down and restore his old music collection.

'I had almost forgotten about that,' he'd said, but Penny had seen the way his face changed when she'd mentioned it.

'Lovely.' She put her hand on her hips. 'So I should just sell back the ten or so I've already found then, should I?'

'That many?' For once in her life, Penny felt she'd truly got her father's attention and seeing his face light up as he looked through the records she'd already procured, was a heady feeling.

And then, out of nowhere Ned began humming a Beatles tune that Penny recognised instantly, but hadn't heard her father use in many, many years.

In fact, the awareness of that song in particular instantly sent her right back to her childhood, to those lazy summer days she and Elle had spent running around outside from dawn to dusk.

She remembered Ned putting it on in the background, while Anna hung sheets on the washing line or sat in the garden reading a book, smiling at her daughters as they frolicked happily in the summer sunshine. He hadn't played on vinyl obviously, but on tape perhaps? Penny's heart soared as right then, she recognised *Here Comes The Sun* as the soundtrack to those days, halcyon times in her family's past.

And now that he had some of his records back, Ned was humming it again.

Tears came to her eyes as she went to her father and enveloped him in a huge hug. She didn't care that he didn't go in for overt physical displays of affection; Penny recognised that this was precisely Ned's way of showing affection, appreciation even.

And it made her even more determined to push on and track down every last one of the remaining records.

But all morning Penny's mind was elsewhere – on a number of topics including, but not limited to, what to say to the man in County Meath they were visiting, to try to make him part with his *Revolver* album. Then she wondered what Elle had planned for the hotel while they were away, how much more money she would have to spend on her quest to reunite her dad with his albums, and finally, the way she was feeling about Colin's return. When presented all together in one never-ending stream of consciousness – the thoughts were a lot to deal with.

But all too soon she realised she had the opportunity to only focus on one thing, at least for a little while. They had arrived at their destination.

Pulling into a long driveway, Penny peered through the trees at the little cottage that was set back away from the main road. Looking around, she wondered how Colin had managed to track this person down.

'We're here,' she said, getting out. 'What was this guy's name again?'

'Joe Armstrong,' he confirmed. Ned also got out, gave Colin a warning glance and started heading toward the house.

'OK if Dad and I do this one ourselves?' she said, feeling a little mean for leaving him out, but she knew he would understand.

Colin nodded. 'Of course.'

Penny nervously approached the house. Now she appreciated a little what Elle must have been feeling when she was going around the town asking for help. But this was so much worse; this was engaging a complete stranger. Still, she couldn't back down, not with Ned standing right beside her.

Joe Armstrong looked at the two strangers standing on his doorstep. 'We're here to talk about a possible business transaction with you,' Penny began without preamble. 'We were told that you might be in possession of a first edition Beatles album, *Revolver*. And we hoped that you might be willing to sell it.'

Armstrong shook his head. 'I'm not interested in selling.'

Penny's heart sank. 'Please Mr Armstrong, could we possibly come inside?' she asked, a little taken aback by her own bravado. 'Just for a moment. If you still decide no, once you have heard what we have to say, then I understand.' She looked at him pleadingly. 'Please.'

Once inside, she and Ned were begrudgingly invited to sit down by their host.

'Now what is this all about?' Armstrong asked.

Penny tried smiling in an effort to warm the mood. 'First off, let me say thank you for having us. I appreciate that. I'm on a hunt of sorts, and it's been a long road.' Her voice shook a little. 'My mother recently passed away and upon sorting through some of her things, I found something out about my dad here that I never knew.'

Deciding that honesty was the best policy, Penny launched into the story about the records, explaining that her dad had a complete collection that he'd sold when she was a baby, telling Joe Armstrong that she had been successful in tracking down several on her list but she was now hitting a dry spell.

'So that is what brings me here. I was told that you might have a first edition *Revolver*. And well, if you were willing to part with it – we would be willing to pay well for it and make it worth your while.' Penny paused. 'Do you have a copy?'

The man thought for a moment and nodded. 'I do yes. And it's mint.' He looked at Ned. 'Look, I can appreciate what you did for your family. And I understand your situation. But this album is a collector's piece and it cost me a small fortune. You wasted your time coming here. I've no intention of selling it.'

Penny sighed, feeling defeat seep through her bones. This was a mistake; she should never have come, and certainly should never have brought Ned along with her, getting his hopes up. She was about to thank Joe for his time and leave, when suddenly her father spoke.

'*Revolver* was always a great favourite of mine,' he said softly. 'Eleanor Rigby is on that album.' He paused and smiled at Penny. 'Elle is named after that song, of course.'

Ned looked at the floor and a look of remembrance flooded his face before he laughed softly. 'Your mother gave in to me on that ... When your mother was carrying her, I probably played *Yellow Submarine* to her a thousand times. At least a thousand times ...' Ned's expression softened and she felt herself transfixed by her father's admissions. He stared at the floor and she knew at that moment, he was thinking of his wife, remembering her, remembering the soundtrack that painted their early life together.

'A true classic,' Joe said, piping up and finally speaking, this time with a softer tone in his voice. 'And I'm ... uh ... very sorry about your wife.'

Ned nodded, continuing to fix his gaze on the window.

'Yes,' he said, somewhat absently. 'In the beginning she could only name a handful of their songs. When we first met.'

Penny perked up, listening intently. 'Really? I never knew that.' She assumed that everyone growing up in the sixties was a rabid Beatles fan.

Ned looked down at his hands. 'But she got to like their music after a while, started to understand its poetry. I think that's what made me fall in love with her in the first place. Anna listened. Really listened.'

Swallowing hard, Penny willed her father to keep speaking.

'Did she have a favourite song?' she asked, almost forgetting that another person was in the room with them.

'Oh, she liked many. But she particularly loved *Love You To*. The mis-spelling tickled her.' He laughed lightly and Joe nodded in agreement, though Penny wasn't sure what he was referring to. Some kind of Beatles in-joke she supposed.

'And of course she loved *Anna*, her own song,' Ned said, once again looking out the window as if his wife herself might be standing on the other side, looking in. Penny felt tears prick at the back of her eyes.

'When did you lose her, your wife?' Joe asked kindly.

Ned looked at the other man; his face was blank, as if he couldn't recall how many days it had been without her.

'Nearly three weeks,' Penny offered in her father's stead. She heard Ned sigh heavily. 'Feels like three decades.'

Penny wanted at once to throw her arms around her father and embrace him. She had never seen this side of him, the emotional side that she craved.

'It's a hard thing, isn't it?' Joe asked. 'Maggie, my own wife, is three years gone this November. We were married for forty-two years. That woman was the love of my life, make no mistake.' The two men looked at each other and Ned gave a feeble nod. 'They make you whole, don't they?' Joe continued. 'The ones who just seem to fit – there were a few others in the early days, but never anyone like Maggie. I knew it too. She was once in a lifetime.' Joe had a wistful expression on his face, until he sobered and considered the other man in the room with him. 'I have memories of my Maggie that are just like yours. The little things I will remember until there isn't life in me, but when that happens, I'll be with her again. But until then, that's all I have. The memories. Things like that, I could never sell, never bear to part with anything that I associated with her, her life, our time together. But do you know something? Those memories don't have anything to do with that album. And apparently yours do – the songs especially. So if you still want *Revolver*, consider it yours.'

Chapter 30

Celeste, shy at first, had come in to the hotel the last couple of mornings to have a cup of coffee, at Elle's insistence. At first she was a bit reticent, but then she started to help with bits and pieces around the place.

'You don't need to help out, Celeste,' Elle told her. 'You've probably got far better things to do with your days.'

The younger girl laughed a little. 'I don't actually,' she said. 'I've mostly been hanging around Rob's house, bored senseless. Working is good. It helps me not think about … things.'

What these 'things' were, Celeste didn't say and Elle didn't press her for an answer. She had a fear of intimate revelations about Rob. It was one thing to be friendly to his new girlfriend, but quite another to talk about him with her. She was glad that Celeste only ever mentioned him in a passing, oblique way.

And it was also great to have another pair of hands. She

couldn't deny that with Penny and Ned gone, they were much needed.

Throughout the next day or so, various people came to the hotel to help. Hazel was there a lot, her infectious laugh ringing through the house. Wally and Arthur came to poke about in the furniture that Elle didn't want, and to see if restorations were possible with the pieces she wanted to keep.

Della and Jim came with painting and decoration supplies, and another day Mona came, bringing with her a wrapped package which she left with Elle, and departing with another package.

Colin, of course, had been eager from the start. He liked to be involved in things, and, Elle suspected, particularly liked to be involved in things that made Penny happy. He was an enthusiastic person and he put that same enthusiasm into emitting loud, tortured moans whenever he moved. He wasn't, he said, much given to physical labour and preferred sitting by the phone making arrangements with album collectors on Penny and Ned's behalf.

Molly, the cook, was having the time of her life catering for all of the extra people around the place. It was almost like old times, she said. Each morning began with bacon and egg sandwiches, hot coffee and lots of vigorous discussion about the day ahead. Lunch was a selection of breads from the Grain Store, cold meats, cheeses and spread, washed down with some apple cider donated by SunBurst Organics.

Dinner in the evenings was whatever else Elle could get her hands on locally: pork chops, lamb for a stew or shepherd's pie, all donated by Kevin the butcher. One evening Johnny Chips raised a huge cheer by arriving with a big brown bag full of fresh cod and chips, and tubs of chocolate chip ice-cream for dessert from his brother Luca.

It all added to a general feeling of festivity about the place.

There was one person who was not involved in these feverish preparations. Rob spent all of his time on the roof, watching people come and go at the hotel.

He wondered exactly what was going on, and asked Celeste, but she said she didn't know what was happening. A big event of some kind, obviously. But beyond that, she hadn't a clue. It seemed that Elle was the only one who truly knew what was going to happen.

Celeste had tried to talk to him about Elle, telling him how great she thought she was. He didn't need her singing Elle's praises. She nagged him too, about how much he was working. She was right, he was close to breaking point. But it wasn't for much longer. If he could just do what Elle wanted and get the roof done in time for whatever she was planning, then he wouldn't have to be here every day, watching her come and go, listening to her laugh.

It made him work even harder, though he hadn't thought it was possible.

He didn't know what he would do next. Ask Celeste if she wanted to go away for a bit maybe. He had never wanted to leave the town before, but then, he had never felt this despairing before.

Something had to give, Rob knew that much.

'Another one checked off!' cheered Penny happily as she and Ned left the home of Paudie Kelly in County Tipperary, whose son Jack had been the owner of a first edition *Abbey Road*. Feeling eager to continue the search after their early success with *Revolver*, she and Ned had got straight back in the car the next day.

Colin had stayed behind at the hotel, correctly sensing that this more personal part of the search was something Penny and Ned needed to do together.

In the interim he was working on the list of contacts, phoning ahead and paving the way for their approach to collectors who lived within travelling distance.

'Did you know that *Abbey Road* was the Beatles' last album?' Ned informed her, and she smiled at how animated he sounded. 'They were really on the way out by then – John Lennon had been breaking away from the rest of them. But Paul was determined to make this album great – to go out on a high note, before they ended everything.'

Penny shook her head that, no, she didn't know that.

Ned gave her a look, and for a moment she wondered if he was pondering how any child of his couldn't possibly *not* know when each Beatles album had been released, and in what order, or the drama behind the production. Sighing heavily, as if realising it was his job to in fact, instruct Penny on all of the music-related trivia she was obviously lacking, he spoke again. 'It was released on September 26th,' he said and her ears at once perked up – the date was familiar to her.

'That's your wedding anniversary,' she smiled. 'Was that planned? Did you and Mum mean to get married on that specific date? A coming together in answer to the band's parting?'

Ned chuckled softly and shook his head. 'No. That was the only day the hotel was free. And your mother was set on an autumn wedding. But I like your spin on it. Of course, the album was released in 1969, and we didn't marry for quite a few years after that. But I knew the date. And when she said, 'This is the only date the hotel is free, otherwise it is July or November,' well, I just knew that it was *our* date. So, we booked it.'

Penny smiled, delighted with this piece of trivia. 'I've seen the pictures, Dad, but what was it like? The day of your wedding, I mean? Were you nervous?'

She hoped that she wasn't pressing too much. She didn't want him to clam up again, which she knew he could do at a moment's notice.

But Ned didn't. 'No, I wasn't nervous. If it's right – and it was, your mum and I – you shouldn't be nervous.' Ned looked at his daughter and seemed to search her face with his eyes. 'When it's meant to be, it's like you are as light as a feather. Though of course I didn't know that before your mother came along. I'd never felt anything like that.

273

Sometimes it was like I was wearing concrete shoes.' Ned gave a small smile. 'That changed, though.'

Penny nodded, fully understanding what he was saying, even though she couldn't really relate; there had been a few men she had been quite mad about, but she didn't remember ever feeling light as a feather like her dad described.

And then suddenly, her mind was flooded with an image of Colin, and how it might feel for him to kiss her, and she felt a tremor rush through her body.

'You're vibrating,' Ned said, snapping her to attention.

'What?' she asked flushing, feeling as if her thoughts had just been broadcast.

'Your bag,' her dad said, clarifying. 'It's vibrating.'

It was Colin. He had a lead for another album owner. The man was in Kilkenny, not too far from where they were now, and if Penny and Ned could get there before teatime, the man was willing to talk to them.

Penny idly wondered what Colin was saying to those people to pave the way, but knew from experience that he could be quite charmingly persuasive. She also wondered how things were going at the hotel. It was obvious that her sister was making preparations for an event of some kind, but Elle was being maddeningly secretive. All she would say is that Penny getting Ned out of the house for a while would be an enormous help.

In truth, Penny didn't mind being away from all the commotion or away from the hotel full-stop. She was enjoying this time with her father, enjoying getting to know Ned a little better, as a person, outside of the usual domestic setting.

She wasn't too sure how to feel about Elle being around again. Might it be permanent this time? She wanted to fix her relationship with her sister, but it seemed easier said than done. She had seen her with Hazel over the past day or two and been jealous of their easy friendship and shared jokes. She knew that Elle had gone to Hazel for advice before she had turned up at home. Penny was a little hurt that she hadn't gone to her first. She must've been more upset at the way they had parted than she'd let on. Or else she just didn't trust Penny enough to 'get' what she was doing, thinking her too scatty and distracted.

'We are really narrowing down this list now,' she said to her father. In fact there were still about twelve records to go, and it would surely take much longer to track those down but Penny didn't think it mattered somehow. Ned was obviously enjoying the distraction and touched by the sentiment.

And that was more than enough for her.

She did wish though that out of all of the others, she could track down the *Anna* single for him. This was the one with the most sentimental value, named as it was after her mother, and of course given to him by Anna herself on their wedding day.

Ned was still holding the *Abbey Road* album in his hands, looking at the famous cover intently, almost possessively, Penny thought, as if someone was about to swoop in and take it away from him. He ran a finger across the iconic image of the Fab Four walking across the zebra crossing.

'Do you know about the controversy this album started?' he asked her.

'What? You mean the whole, play it backward on the turntable to hear the words "Paul is dead"?' Colin had told her all about the conspiracy theories surrounding the album, which were almost as famous as the record itself. 'Obviously he isn't.'

'Well, yes there was that. But there was other stuff too. Symbolism on the cover. This,' he pointed to the image of the four men crossing the street, 'is supposed to symbolise a funeral procession. Paul's funeral, in fact. Lennon is in the white suit, like a preacher – critics used to say that it was because he thought he was Jesus – but that wasn't it. Ringo, he's supposed to be the mourner, all dressed in black. And George here at the back, is supposed to be the grave-digger. Paul is the corpse. He's wearing an old suit and he's barefoot. Did you know they don't ask for shoes – at funeral homes?'

Penny's smiled faded and she swallowed hard – she had a funny feeling that her father might be talking from recent, more personal experience – and not about the album cover.

'Dad . . .'

'Paul is also out of step here with everyone else. And even though he is left-handed, he's holding the cigarette with his right hand. People said, when this album came out, that it was the coffin nail. There are other things too, a police van that was supposed to be a reference to the police who kept quiet about Paul's demise. And then you can trace a line from the Beetle here,' he pointed at the image again, ' to the three cars in front of it,' Ned traced his finger, drawing an invisible line through the right wheels of the cars, and right through Paul's head. 'The conspiracy theory went that this meant that Paul sustained a head injury – because of a car crash – and that's how he died.'

'You know that was just people who had too much time on their hands, the ones who came up with all of that,' Penny said, attempting to switch the focus, get his mind off all this death-related stuff. If she had known all of this 'hocus pocus' about this album, she would have insisted on going after it another time. Or maybe never.

But Ned seemed focused on pressing on, and providing Penny all of the grisly bits.

'It's not on this one,' Ned said, looking closely at the cover. 'But on the Australian version of the album, it looked like there was a bloodstain on the road too. There,' he pointed to the space just behind Ringo and John, 'like from a car accident. And on the back,' Ned flipped the album over, 'it was rumoured that if you turned the back cover and held it at a forty-five degree counter-clockwise angle, that an image of the Grim Reaper would appear. I never saw that, though.' He manoeuvred the disc around, as if trying to see if he could summon the anomaly.

Penny wished that he would stop. It was a bit creepy.

'OK, enough of that.'

'There's other stuff too,' Ned pressed on, looking at his

daughter as Penny tightened her hands on the steering wheel. 'The odd similarities. Car crashes. Head injuries. Mourners. A person running to get help …'

'OK Dad … it's unsettling. And none of it is true anyway. Paul McCartney is alive and well. So please stop.'

Ned looked up from the album and eyed his daughter critically. 'Stop what?' he demanded.

'What you are doing,' Penny said, refusing to meet his eyes. 'Don't ruin the music. You have happy memories associated with these albums, these songs. Don't spoil that for yourself. You don't have to make it so complicated.'

Ned paused for a moment to think about this. He looked back at the album cover, which he had been studying with increasing intensity and then transferred his gaze once again to Penny.

'No. You're wrong there, it's not all happy. Not every memory. That's impossible, Penny. In any relationship, no matter if it's with your spouse, a friend, a child, anyone. It's impossible to be happy all the time. You know that, don't you?'

Penny focused her attention hard, on the world that was flashing by on the other side of the car's windscreen. 'Of course I know that,' she whispered, feeling inexplicably sheepish.

Did she though? she wondered privately. She knew she wasn't good at handling conflict. She preferred a simple life, for things to be on the straight and narrow, needed to know exactly where she stood, what to expect and when. She knew this was partly the reason she'd never left Mulberry Bay. Never went out and took on the big bad world like Elle had.

As if in reply to her silent musings, Ned began to hum a tune again – Penny just didn't know from which song. 'It can be hard, you know. When you don't like dealing with the downs as well as the ups. And your mum and I had those too. Plenty of them.'

Penny was listening intently. While it seemed like Ned was rambling like this, just thinking aloud, lately she felt as if it wasn't just idle chatter.

'The good with the bad?' Penny offered, hoping to provide his thoughts some direction.

'Yes. I suppose. I hate that, though, too. I never like to be too far up or too far down. Never have. I've always preferred to be on the level. Never too emotional. But your mother taught me that such was life. That was just the way things worked. Sometimes I was OK with it all. Sometimes I wasn't. The messy stuff. Arguments. Happiness. Crying. Drama. You have to be there for it all. Sometimes I was. Other times, I didn't get it right.'

Penny took her eyes off the road and looked at her dad sitting next to her.

'I think I understand what you are saying,' she said softly. She knew that Ned was trying to explain something to her – a lesson of sorts. And she was also detecting something else. A note of apology perhaps?

'Do you?' Ned asked, and she nodded in the affirmative. Seemingly satisfied, he looked out the window and patted the album with his other hand, as if making sure it was still there.

'That's good, Penny,' he added quietly. 'Because I think you and I both know that I have never been very good with words.'

Chapter 31

Piece by piece, Elle's vision began to take place. She was assured by Hazel that the news was being spread throughout the town, so she didn't have to worry about that. People would come. In fact, if Hazel was to be believed, a buzz of great excitement had begun to spread amongst the whole community.

On Thursday night, when Penny and Ned returned from their travels, Elle gathered everyone into the dining room. 'I want to thank you for the last two days,' she said. 'You've worked so hard and it's time to let you in on the next phase of the plan. There's going to be a big celebration here on Saturday night. A party of the kind this place hasn't seen in ages.'

She paused to let this sink in.

'It's a special kind of celebration. Depending on how things go, it'll either signal the next phase in the life of the Bay Hotel, or it will be a spectacular farewell. Either way, it will be a night to remember.'

She stopped again and it was obvious she was figuring out how to say the next thing.

'As I said, you've all worked very hard. But for now, your work is over. For the next few days, I need you to stay out of the dining room and ballroom. Those two rooms are out of bounds,' she said with an enigmatic smile. 'I want what happens on Saturday night to be as much of a surprise for you as it is for everyone else. I want you to be dazzled. All I can say is, make sure you're looking your absolute best.'

As Elle was speaking to everyone that evening, Rob finally finished the roof. Temporary as the repairs might be, they were done, and it hadn't cost the family a thing. He had done it as the last gift he could give them.

He went home and stood for a long time under the shower, letting the hot water pummel his aching back. Celeste had told him there would be a party on Saturday night. Where was his suit? she wanted to know.

He told her he wasn't in the mood for any party but she wouldn't hear a word of it, had in fact accused him of being a grumpy old man. Eventually, he gave in. He was curious about whatever Elle was up to, he had to admit it.

All day Friday, Elle and Hazel worked their secret magic on the hotel. Vans came and went, delivering clinking crates and boxes of food. Baskets of flowers were whisked through the halls. Molly had been fully reinstated, as well as a crew of helpers donated from The SugarTree Restaurant. They were hard at work in the kitchen, preparing a menu to Elle's specifications.

Molly thought that some of the requirements were a little outlandish to say the least, but she would do her best. She hadn't worked for the Hartes on and off for twenty-five years without forming a pretty firm attachment to her job, and the hotel.

To her surprise, working with Elle wasn't as bad as she had feared. In fact, she seemed to know her way around the place as well as Anna had.

Wonders would never cease.

On Friday night, Elle and Hazel surveyed their work with pride. They clinked glasses and sat on the floor of the ballroom, which tomorrow night would be full of people.

'It's exactly as I imagined it,' she sighed to her friend.

'All that's left now is to sit back and enjoy it,' said Hazel.

'Speak for yourself. My most important work is yet to come.'

Hazel waved a hand. 'You've got nothing to worry about. People will be absolutely won over.'

'It's one person in particular I'm worried about,' said Elle.

'No use thinking about it,' said Hazel. 'Just concentrate on the next step.'

Elle supposed she was right. She could only deal with the things that were in her control. Everything else would have to be left up to fate.

*

Each occupant of the Bay Hotel slept well that night. Penny slept soundly, worn out from all her travels, and the sense that for the first time ever, she was starting to understand her father.

Ned slept soundly because he had renewed hope, his collection almost restored, and most importantly both of his daughters under the same roof once more.

Elle slept the slumber of someone well satisfied with their day. She didn't even wake up when Penny's cats again spread themselves out over her bed. Despite her deep sleep, she woke up early. Things were going well, yes. But there was still the nagging feeling at the back of her mind that certain things had been left unsaid between Rob and her.

It must only be she who felt that way, though. Rob had moved on, she told herself. He had ceased to care about her at all.

Chapter 32

The next day, a few storm clouds were obscuring the sun when Elle got up. 'Please don't rain, please don't rain,' she murmured all through breakfast.

'Would everything be ruined if it did?' Colin asked.

'Not exactly. But I want it to be perfect. Rain would just be a hindrance to that.'

Colin nodded. He understood the importance of making an impression.

Breakfast was a more solemn affair than usual. Elle felt that no one seemed quite as excited about tonight's party as they should be. Molly seemed positively nervous. She kept opening the oven doors and muttering about the meat drying out.

'I'm still not really sure about the main course ...' she confided nervously. 'It's a lot to live up to. The spuds in particular ...'

Elle smiled. 'It will be perfect. I have every faith in you,' she told her for the hundredth time.

That morning Elle had a few more errands to attend to, and then she had to get ready for the party. She knew it was important that she looked the part tonight of all nights.

After breakfast she made her way into town. Her stomach was aflutter with nerves. She felt almost the way she had the day Rob first asked her out. She needed to keep as calm as possible for tonight. She couldn't go getting stage fright now. Think of all the work everyone has put in, she told herself. Everyone needs this party.

She was outside Pebbles Café when she heard her name being called. She had popped in for a takeaway espresso to help cure her nerves. She didn't need to turn around to know who was saying her name, and the very voice sent a shudder up her spine.

'Hello, Ms Harte,' said Doug Grant, catching up to her. 'I'm glad I caught you. I was just about to come out to the hotel, but now I won't have to.'

Elle was mute. She didn't know what to say. Why was the bank manager being so friendly? He had a smug little smile on his face too, as though he was enjoying himself very much.

'The fact is,' he said, 'I've got some very good news for you. I have someone, an investor, who's very interested in the property. Very interested, taking into account the general dilapidation of the place. He's going to knock the whole thing down, start afresh with something modern. A fantastic idea, I thought. It will be wonderful for the town.'

He waited a moment, taking in her stricken face. 'What

on earth is wrong?' he said. 'I would have thought you would be delighted to have someone take the place off your hands.'

'The thing is,' she said, summoning reserves of strength she didn't know she had, 'I was hoping you could perhaps give us one last chance to keep the hotel. You might have heard about the party we are having tonight. I sent a personal invite to you at the bank and was hoping that you could come.'

'I'm afraid I have other plans tonight,' he said. 'Besides, my wife positively refuses to set foot in the place. She is afraid the whole thing will collapse like a pack of cards.'

'Please, Mr Grant,' said Elle, hating herself for her weakness but there was no choice; she needed to keep him on side. 'If you could just give us one more chance. We want to show the town what the hotel has to offer, show everyone how it can be if we could just get the finance to keep it going. If it doesn't work, we will sell, I promise. I know I behaved terribly when we met before, but I appeal to you for one more chance.'

There was nothing that Doug Grant enjoyed more than power. That was the thing that kept him going. He fed on it, the way a machine runs on fuel. If he gave Elle Harte one last chance to keep her pathetic hotel, he would have her under his power for just a tiny bit longer.

'You understand that it's a great risk I'm taking …' he told her as if he was seriously considering her proposal. 'But I will give you just one more chance, as I am a fair man.

Paddy will be bringing the interested party to the hotel first thing on Tuesday morning, though, so you should prepare your family.'

As he walked away, Elle finally let out the breath she had been holding. Had the little weasel really just given her one more chance? She could hardly believe it. Still, she drove back to the hotel feeling absolutely numb.

On the day of the only remaining chance to keep the hotel, the threat of it being ripped out from under them was closer than ever.

Penny stood in the centre of her room. She was supposed to be getting ready for tonight. She supposed she should have thought about what to wear days ago, at least then she might have been able to get something decent together. But she was too busy traipsing around the country with her father to even think about something like that. Now, she surveyed the contents of her wardrobe critically.

She had a lot of 'floaty' clothes. Light coloured V-neck dresses, things with frills around the sleeves, cute little button details. But nothing that was really fitting for a more formal event like tonight's, whatever it might turn out to be.

Well, she would just have to make do. She could entwine some of her mum's pearls in her hair and hope that had the desired effect.

She couldn't deny that she wanted this night to be special for more reasons than one. It was about the hotel, of course, but she couldn't let herself hope too much for that. It was better to see it as a grand farewell party, one that they couldn't afford to be giving, but why not? They had nothing more to lose.

Colin was leaving for good, first thing the following week. He'd done all he could to help her out with the records, and he couldn't stay indefinitely to write the novel, not when the hotel was either about to be sold, or renovated. He needed somewhere more permanent.

Penny didn't know how to tell him how much these past few weeks had meant to her, how *he* had added sparkle to her life. She hadn't known what a fun-loving person she could be until he arrived; she hadn't known that she craved laughter and hilarity at breakfast, lunch and dinner and a wonderfully easygoing approach to life in general. Colin brought a sense of elegance to things as well; he knew how things were meant to be done.

She supposed that she could simply tell him: 'Thank you'. But it didn't seem enough. It didn't feel as though she would ever be able to say how she really felt and she didn't want to make a fool of herself as usual. Perhaps after he left she could send him a letter.

There was a knock at her door. 'Penny?' she heard her dad call out softly.

'Come in,' she told him.

Ned opened the door and came in, holding a package. 'This was just dropped off for you,' he said.

'For me?' said Penny mystified.

Ned raised his hands, with a smile. 'Big mystery,' he said.

'Although something tells me you'd better open it before tonight.'

'Are you feeling all right about tonight Dad?' said Penny. 'It's just that we have no idea what Elle has in mind and I wouldn't want you to be getting your hopes up too much. I know that she's done so much, but I think it's probably a bit too late.'

'Well, as your mother used to say: Better late than never. You might do well, especially, Penny, to remember that.'

And then he left, closing the door gently behind him. Crikey, was everyone going to be so cryptic around here? It seemed Penny couldn't turn around without facing little hints, secrets and things left unsaid. She thought particularly of Colin. She felt that he had tried to talk to her about something for the last couple of days, but always ended by not saying anything at all, in a roundabout way. Ah, she was probably imagining it, reading too much into things as always. He'd probably guessed how she was feeling and as a result was becoming awkward around her. Terrified, more like.

She picked up the package. It was soft and had been hand delivered, there were no postmarks. So Ned must have known where it came from. Why was he being so secretive then? She sighed. Elle had infected them all.

She undid the twine that held the floppy package together. She tore a corner of the brown paper wrapping and immediately a satiny blue material slid out through the opening. Quickly, she unwrapped the rest.

It was a dress. And what a dress. Beautifully made of fine blue silk, overlaid with delicate lace and ribbon. Penny would never have picked out something like this for herself, but she reflected that sometimes other people knew better what you might look good in. Had Ned done this, she wondered suddenly, to thank her for helping restore his collection? It seemed impossible. Her dad wouldn't have the first clue as to sizing or materials and colour. She didn't think he had set foot in a clothes shop in his entire life.

Another knock. Honestly, you would think no one wanted her to get ready …

It was Elle. 'Do you like it?' she asked smiling.

Penny looked at her sister. 'You did this?'

'Of course. It was hard work, I had to smuggle one of your other dresses out so that Mona could get your size right.'

'I love it, Elle, it's perfect! I've never owned something this beautiful.'

'I wanted a light, delicate blue. Like the sky. I'm just glad you were out of the way these last few days so that I could organise it without you asking too many questions.' She sat down at the end of the bed. 'Not to mention distracted.'

'Oh Elle,' Penny admitted. 'I'm just so confused. You know what I'm talking about. I'm sure it's obvious to everyone except …'

Elle nodded amusedly. 'As plain as the nose on your face.'

'How can you be so flippant? I'm being tortured, here. What am I supposed to do? I don't want to look like a fool.'

'Penny.' Elle sighed. 'The only way that you could look a fool is if you decided to keep quiet and say nothing to him. I get the feeling he's probably tried to talk to you, but he's too polite. You're being too scatty, as usual. He's crazy about you. Everyone knows it.'

'What? Do you really think so?'

'Even Molly has been sighing while she's chopping onions in the kitchen, wondering when you're going to finally get together. I almost think she's got a bet on.'

'Now I feel like even more of an idiot.'

'Penny,' Elle put a hand on her arm. 'You're not an idiot and I really wish you would believe that. What you've done for Dad these last few days – actually what you've done for this family over the years is amazing. While I got to go out and spread my wings, follow my dream or whatever, you stayed here and held the fort – not just with the hotel but with Mum and Dad too. I don't think I've ever thanked you for that.'

Penny felt a lump in her throat. 'There's no need to thank me. I could never do what you did, go out there and set the world on fire. I wanted to stay here, you know that.'

'That doesn't mean I don't appreciate it, though. I suppose I never understood quite the level of dedication you had to this place, in more ways than one, but now I do. I'm not sure what's going to happen tonight, or afterwards, but if nothing else, I hope most of all that I can make you and Dad proud.'

Penny reached over and hugged her warmly.

'And as for Colin,' Elle said, pulling her close, 'I know you're afraid, but don't let him slip away too easily, either. Because then you'll really regret it.'

It occurred to Penny once Elle left that her sister had been talking from hard-won experience.

After going in to see Penny, Elle turned her attention to her own appearance. Once again, it was important, this time for completely different reasons. At least the bags under her eyes had finally disappeared, and she had managed to get a couple of good nights' sleep.

Her dress was simple. When Mona had suggested 'chartreuse' Elle had resisted emphatically. The very word sounded awful. But Mona had been right; the smoky green went perfectly with Elle's pale skin and vivid hair. The light material skimmed her body, the design round-necked with wide shoulder straps, and an open back. She didn't have to worry about it once she had it on. It made her feel confident without being fussy.

She piled her hair up on top of her head, a kind of graceful mess. She added a pair of amber earrings and that was it. A flick of mascara, a little concealer, some red lipstick and she was done. She almost wished that she was the kind of person who took hours over her appearance so that she would have something to do.

All that was left now was to wait.

Soon, people would start arriving and the night would take care of itself. She would be carried away with each stage of the event, unable to stop and think about anything until the next morning. She pushed away the thought of Doug Grant's potential buyer turning up with the estate agent on Tuesday. That could not be dealt with now.

Celeste and Rob were coming tonight, she knew. It would be the first time she would see them in public as a couple. That was something else she would have to get used to. If things worked out and she stayed in Mulberry Bay (though she hardly dared hope for that), then she would see them together all the time. She had to steel herself against it. When she had talked to Penny about regret, she was talking about the way she felt about Rob. What she felt now was so much stronger than feeling foolish, or humiliated. It was like being shipwrecked, and watching your last chance of salvation float away. She didn't want to see that happen to Penny.

Elle sat by her window until she saw the lights of the first car pull up to the hotel. The night had begun.

Chapter 33

From the very beginning, it was a night to remember. The hotel was lit up like a beacon, a signal to everyone that it was the only place to be in Mulberry Bay on that evening. Guests streamed across the lawn and up the stone steps to the hotel in a kaleidoscope of colour.

It was as though a large flock of exotic birds had landed on the grass, so loud was the excitement. There was a slight tension palpable in the air: everyone knew this was an important night. For the hotel, but also for the community. When was the last time so many from the town had joined together in pure celebration?

The hotel itself looked majestic. Elle had purposefully chosen this exact time of day for the arrival of the guests. It was dusky enough that any of the hotel's flaws or shabbier features were hidden by shadow, and by the orange glow of the setting sun glinting off each window, making the building appear to glow warmly.

Guests were ushered into the dining room to partake in pre-dinner snacks and drinks. Helpers from the SugarTree Restaurant glided smoothly between the groups, offering tall glasses of champagne. Though she hadn't approached him, surly Anthony had surprised Elle by very kindly offering to send up some of his waiting staff to help out on the night. On other trays appeared all the best-known classics of the hotel: tiny apple tarts, miniature fairy-cakes, bite-sized cucumber sandwiches. On this Elle had been adamant: the canapés were to be pure nostalgia, to be instantly recognisable as food people had eaten there in the past at some important point in their lives.

Rob watched people talking and laughing happily. The dining room looked perfect when it was filled with people, almost like something out of another era.

The long tables, set for dinner, had large bowls of water in the middle, filled with floating gerbera. Candelabras set around the place in various nooks and crannies gave a feel of the party existing in the past, as though they had all been transported to a celebration of the hotel when it was newly opened. The light flickered and made the detail in the paintings appear to move.

He saw Della and Jim being greeted by Elle, the three of them laughing and whispering about something.

Elle looked unbelievably beautiful tonight. She seemed to glow with an inner confidence, and the candlelight caught her flaming hair and made it shine. He had to turn away; he couldn't look at her. It hurt his eyes.

He wondered when the business part of the evening would begin. Surely there would be some kind of appeal to the people of the town for finance. Otherwise what was the point of all this?

Celeste had been like an over-excited child at the thought of a party. He supposed it was boring for her, being stuck with Rob all the time, when he wasn't exactly stimulating company. Well, hopefully she wouldn't be here too much longer. As soon as she got her life back on track, she could go back to Dublin. He could see her now, talking to English Colin. She had told him that there seemed to be something going on between him and Penny, an attraction that both of them were too shy to admit to. Rob had barely been able to process that. He didn't want to hear about love, think about love. He couldn't even listen to Celeste talk about her own relationship woes. She was the girlfriend of his oldest friend, and they were having problems. Rob didn't mind her hiding out here until it was worked out. He couldn't handle the analysis of every last moment too. He had done enough of that for himself.

He felt a pinch on his arm. It was Penny.

'You look beautiful,' he said, smiling at her.

'You and I know that beautiful is never a word that could describe me,' she said with a pleased laugh. 'Elle chose it for me. I think it suits me very well.'

'It does,' he agreed. 'And you do look beautiful, radiant actually.'

'I'm happy for you too ... about Celeste,' said Penny. 'Of

course I'd always hoped that you and Elle ...' she broke off at the sight of his face. 'But I want you to be happy regardless. Celeste is lovely.'

'Penny,' he said. 'You've got it completely wrong. Celeste is a good friend, nothing more. She's having a few troubles right now, things I can't go into. But that's all.'

'Oh, I'm sorry,' she said looking confused. 'I haven't been around much lately ... I just assumed. But in that case, couldn't you just give it one more try with Elle? I think this time, since she's come back, she's really starting to open up more, to soften a little.'

He looked at her sadly. Typical, ever optimistic Penny. 'It wouldn't matter if I gave it a million chances, your sister just doesn't want me, Penny. She never will. It's as simple as that.'

She watched him walk away and stand by the window, watching the last of the sunset.

'It's all going amazingly!' Hazel enthused to Elle, just before dinner. 'Everyone is having a ball. I haven't seen so many beautiful evening dresses collected in one place in a long time.'

'Yes, I think it's going well,' admitted Elle biting her lip. 'But the hardest bit is still to come.'

'You'll be fine,' her friend soothed.

'Something's happened, though,' said Elle, and she told Hazel of her run in with the bank manager that morning. 'It puts everything in jeopardy,' she said. 'How can I go ahead now, knowing that there is such a very good chance I won't be able to follow through?'

'You just go ahead as planned,' said Hazel, drawing herself up. She was wearing a bright red dress with a plunging neckline and deep red lipstick, and she looked very vampy. She told Elle she so very rarely dressed up she wanted to wear a colour that would make up for the denim dungarees she wore every day. 'You can't give up now, can't falter. There's still a chance.'

Molly's hard work with the dinner preparations had paid off. The guests sat at the long tables and ate a starter of salmon vol-au-vents with an apple and walnut salad. Each course was paired with a complementary wine, donated from The Grapevine wine store, just off Main Street. By using the extra help from the restaurant, the hotel proved that it could still cater to such a large crowd and big occasion, the plates appearing and being removed seamlessly. The other helpers, local teenage regulars from Pebbles Café, had been warned: No dawdling or messing and no idle chatter.

The arrival of the second course brought a collective chuckle from the guests: it was Anna's famous roast chicken, with a side of her colcannon, green beans and honey glazed carrots. Elle had been unsure how this course would be received, wondering if perhaps people might expect something that was more 'high cuisine'.

But it was perfect. It had been one of the things Anna was best known for, after all.

Dessert was decadent slivers of chocolate fudge cake, mini-chocolate and vanilla cheesecakes (Elle had tried her utmost to revive the famed recipe from her childhood) and a selection of fresh fruit from SunBurst Organics. Everything was petite so as not to overfill the guests for what was to come next.

At the end of dinner, Elle stood up and raised her glass. 'I would like to thank you all for coming,' she said. 'We are here tonight in the hope of saving the hotel, but most of all, we are also here to remember our wonderful mother. Anna would have loved an evening like this, and she especially would have enjoyed what is to follow.' She grinned. 'I hope you've all brought some energy, because you're going to need it!'

Chapter 34

Ned went into the kitchen and congratulated the kitchen staff on a job well done.

'Leave these dishes to the youngsters,' he said to Molly. 'You've earned yourself a rest.'

The older woman's eyes were shining. 'Anna would have been so proud,' she said. 'Wouldn't it have been brilliant if ...' Then she smiled, as if comforted by the thought that her old friend was indeed there in spirit.

They joined the parade of guests making their way to the ballroom. Ned himself had been exiled from the hotel for the last two days, so he didn't know what Elle had done with a lot of it. The ballroom couldn't be anything too drastic, not in two days. He knew that the floor had been sanded and polished though. He wondered if that meant an opportunity for dancing.

He didn't think he would ever forget the moment he first

stepped into the ballroom that night. Whatever he had imagined, it had been nothing like this.

The walls were adorned with greenery and blooms. Wisteria crept up along the walls as though it had been growing there for years. Great urns were overflowing with flowers, and delicate berry boughs were strung from the high ceiling.

The whole effect was of a wild wonderland, as though they had walked into the ballroom a hundred years from now to find it being taken back, bit by bit, by nature. It was beautiful, he thought, like something from those stories of woodland nymphs and fairies that Anna used to read to the girls when they were younger.

There were gasps of awe and wonder all around. Elle had truly transformed the place. Ned knew, with his accurate eye, that she had managed to do it without making any major changes either. Behind the startling array of flora, the wallpaper was still faded and ripped. But it didn't matter. It was perfect for this night.

The whole air was diffused with a pink glow, and Ned had thought that it was because of the emotion he himself was feeling lately, that everything seemed rose tinted.

But no, it was the chandelier. Elle had had it restrung with tiny pink crystals. She must have asked Pat from the jewellers to do it. It was magnificent. Each crystal shimmered in the air and made each person look radiant.

It was the kind of room in which special things could happen, Ned told himself. He teared up a little, thinking of how much Anna would have loved it. It was exactly the kind of thing she'd always pictured for this place, but because life got in the way, had sadly never managed to achieve.

When Rob entered the ballroom he thought he was seeing things. He couldn't believe all that Elle had done. He could hear Hazel telling someone about how hard it had been to work to her vision. 'In the end, she was right of course,' Hazel was saying. 'But it was bloody tough work!'

He immediately thought of Penny's original vision for the place when they were discussing renovations a few weeks before, '*Sparkle*'. Elle had got it in one.

It was almost too much for him; the people all talking at once, the exclamations of delight and surprise: he wanted to run from all the joviality. But he had to see this night through, had to support the family. He had come this far.

He watched as Elle took to the stage. No one else looking at her would have known she was nervous, but he did. He still knew what she was feeling, understood her little tells as easily as if they were his own. It was like reaching back through the years and knowing her as completely as he had then. Who would have thought that this was how it would all end up?

'Well,' Elle began, the strength of her voice betraying none of her nervousness. 'We've come to the crux of the evening. Don't worry, you'll all get to let off some steam with some dancing soon. Believe it or not, we've managed to get Old Time Magic here back together for a night to play up a storm for you.' There was a huge cheer as everyone turned to see old Arthur Ryan, with Johnny Chips and Tom the butcher gathered alongside the stage with instruments in hand. The trio used to play together back in the mid-eighties, when the hotel used to host ballroom dancing on Sunday nights. Wally had told Elle they met up in each others' houses a few times a years to play tunes together and he thought they'd be only too delighted to have an audience again.

Now, the men grinned happily to the applause, gunning to take the stage once again.

'But first, we're going to ask for your help,' Elle continued. 'I had disastrous results last time I asked you all for help,' – this raised a storm of laughter '– but I'm hoping tonight will be different. Of course, you know that we would never ask for anything without giving everyone something in return.'

Thus began the auction, Elle's grand plan to help save the hotel. It wasn't any old auction though, in that the things up for bidding weren't objects. They were services and resources from the Mulberry Bay community.

'First up is a weekend of landscaping from The Orchard Garden Centre.'

The auction went by in a flurry of activity. It was hard to keep track of who was winning, everyone seemed to be raising their hands all the time. Della and Jim offered building materials, Wally was doing restorations of old furniture. Mona was offering a dress or a suit, Karen offering beautiful accessories from The Wonder Room. There were cases of wine from the Grapevine, dinners at the SugarTree, ice-cream parties, jewellery-making lessons, coastal tours.

By far though, the most popular bidding item was the hotel itself. Elle was offering a full week's stay in the newly renovated hotel, a romantic dinner for two at a table overlooking the sea, full Irish breakfast on the terrace and afternoon tea before check-out.

The bidding for this reached a crescendo and Rob felt once again that he had to get away, that the noise and excitement was too much for him. It made him dizzy to look up at the dazzling chandelier, too. He didn't know what Elle's original vision for it had been, but he had known that she saw this room as the heart of the hotel, and he now agreed that it was exactly right. It was mesmerising.

As the bidding finished, the side doors were flung open to bring relief from the heat that had been building up inside. The garden was strung with fairy lights, leading all the way down to the edge of the path towards the beach.

As Elle thanked everyone once again, she was surprised to see Hazel hop up and take the stage.

'You all know me,' she said. 'And I know that everyone in this room, and in this town loves the hotel, and Ned, Elle and Penny. We want to keep them here. Tonight was about that certainly, but it won't be enough to save the hotel. The truth is, the bloody bank is what is keeping the Bay Hotel from returning to its days of glory. You've supported the hotel tonight just by showing up, but what we need from you now, well,' she smiled, 'we need you to be pests. We need you to rattle a few cages. More than anything, we need you to be vocal.'

A cheer went up around the room. Good old Hazel. She knew how to get a crowd excited. Rob knew that Elle would never have been able to ask for this kind of support.

The cooler night air flowed in from the sea and Rob felt somewhat revived. He would get through the night, at least.

Colin approached Penny. She was standing by the drinks table, talking to Mona and thanking her for the dress.

'May I have a dance?' he asked. The music had started and the local trio were playing a mix of upbeat fast numbers, interspersed with slower, more romantic tunes. Colin had waited until they played something slow.

Penny followed him onto the dance floor. He led her to the very centre and they moved slowly under the soft light of the chandelier.

'You look stunning tonight,' he told her. 'In fact, "stunning" seems like a poor word for it. I should be able to do better, considering.'

'Thank you,' she said, smiling simply. Unlike with Rob, she didn't want to pass off the compliment, considering who it was coming from. 'And thank you for all your help with the albums too. You don't know how much that means to me. I would never have been able to find so many in such a short space of time without your help.'

He shrugged. 'It was nothing, but I know how important it was to you and Ned. Happy to help.'

He held her closely, but lightly. He smelt vaguely citrusy. He had told her he had a personal scent mixed for him in London, and she had made fun of that, but he did smell delicious. She almost wanted to lean into his neck and inhale.

'Are you happy with tonight?' he asked.

'Very,' she said. 'It's wonderful to see the hotel sparkle again. And at the very least, it's a nice way to say goodbye, isn't it? But I do hope very much, that it will save us. I don't know what I'll do next otherwise.'

'Well, I've only been here a very short time but I feel the same. It's funny how quickly, if the mix of location and people is just right, that a place begins to feel like home. I want you to be happy Penny. I hope the hotel is saved for you.'

'I think that even if that happens though,' Penny said, her voice tentative, 'I couldn't be entirely happy, if ...'

Colin waited. He thought that surely she would say it, must say it. It needed to be from her. He couldn't risk making her feel any undue pressure while she was so vulnerable.

'If you were to leave,' she finished.

He was silent and Penny burned with embarrassment. How could she have been so foolish? He had been a charming friend, nothing else. Of course he was showing so much interest in her situation purely for material for his book, nothing else. If she could eat her words, one by bitter one, she would.

Finally, Colin spoke. Very casually, he said, 'Well, I've rather fallen in love with you, Penny, so I believe I'll stick around after all.'

Chapter 35

Elle watched Colin and her sister dancing. They seemed to have been speaking very seriously, but then she saw Colin spin Penny suddenly, and then dip her so that her fair hair swung almost to the floor. Her sister was laughing uproariously, in a way that reminded her very much of their mother.

People had been coming up to her all night to talk about Anna. She may have come across like a hearty, open person, but it turned out she had kept secrets as well as the hotel had, over the years.

Whenever people had found themselves in trouble, due to sickness, disagreements between loved ones, or just felt a bit down in the dumps, Anna had been there. She had made herself available, offering a sympathetic ear, as well as the shelter of the hotel.

One local woman told Elle. 'When my son went and got married without telling us, I felt as though I could never like his wife. I was awful to her and it was making me bitter and twisted inside. I'll never forget the talking-to Anna gave me. She told me straight: "Cop on to yourself, or you'll lose them both."'

There had been many more stories like it: stories where Anna smoothed the waters or stirred them up, whatever seemed to be best. Somehow, Elle always knew Anna would have had a better way of dealing with Doug Grant. She would have known how to butter the bank manager up, act as though she was playing into his hands. Instead, Elle had gone straight in and torn strips off him. At least she had learnt a thing or two from all of this, she reflected.

She knew the evening had been a great success. They had made an amazing amount of money from the bids, enough to cover the basic repairs and some interior decorating. People had been more than generous with their bids, realising that they could truly make a difference to this old sentinel of the community. She was grateful to Hazel for getting up and speaking, too. She couldn't have asked them, after all that, to speak up on the hotel's behalf.

She didn't know if people would or not though. It was a big thing, to stand up to a man who had control of your money. Grant seemed like the kind of man who would have no trouble holding a grudge, if it came to it.

Besides, after tonight, the hotel might just fade to the back of people's minds, the way it had before. People were good, but they couldn't always be counted on. Life went on at the end of the day and the community had their own businesses to worry about, their own families to look after.

So ultimately everything still hung in the balance. The best she could hope for was to make the essential repairs, work on a marketing plan to increase business in a major way when they reopened, and hope that this would be enough to get the bank back on side. Depending on what happened next, Elle was also considering selling her London flat to pay off the existing arrears and help the hotel start over with a blank slate.

It would be a blank slate for her too, of course, and she wasn't sure how to feel about that. Could she really give up everything she'd worked for after all of these years to come here and suddenly run a hotel? They all knew Penny wasn't up to the task and poor old Ned would likely be content for the rest of his days with his partly-restored record collection.

All of a sudden, Elle felt bone tired. She had put everything she had into this over the past few days, and she just couldn't imagine getting up tomorrow, and the day after, and the day after that, to keep pouring little bits of herself into the hotel. Maybe Penny had been right: perhaps tonight should be just a nice way to say goodbye.

Her eyes snagged on the sight of Rob, leaning against the side door, his back to the night. Why wasn't he dancing with Celeste? He had never been one to shy away from a celebration, loved talking to people, and usually cut a fine figure on the dance floor. She looked around the room and saw Celeste dancing with Wally. Though actually, from this vantage point it looked as though she was holding him up. But he looked happy, and had obviously enjoyed the free wine.

Rob, on the other hand, looked exhausted. He was gaunt, his skin pulled tight over his skull. His skin was tanned from the long hours he had spent outside on the roof. It came to Elle then that they had asked too much of Rob lately.

She had been so busy making sure that everything was right for tonight that she hadn't considered that it must have been almost impossible for him to get the roof done in time. But he had done it all the same, labouring away by himself while the rest of them laughed and had fun together, and Penny and Ned were racing around the country on their wild goose chase.

And Rob, who had been such a major factor in getting them this far, had been kept out of everything. Because of her, mostly, Elle knew. Because she couldn't stand to have him near, in case her face, her voice, everything about her gave her away.

Because it *was* like that. These days she wasn't lying to herself, and every nerve ending in her body seemed to move to the sound of his name. But it was too late. She wouldn't lie to herself on that score. He was with Celeste now and she wouldn't stand in the way of him being happy.

But she could at least reach out to him in the name of friendship.

She crossed the dance floor, moving in between all the dancing couples. There was her father, dancing with Molly. She hoped that he had had a good time and that the last few days had really brought him out of his shell. He certainly deserved it. People would be talking about the big party at the Bay Hotel for years.

She reached Rob and held out her hand. 'Dance?'

He said nothing, but took her hand and followed her onto the dance floor. They were so close that she could hear his breath moving in and out, short, halting breaths. He could probably feel her heart beat. They didn't really dance, but just moved slowly in each other's arms. There was no aware-ness of the music. It could have been a fast song, it could have been a ballad. It didn't matter. Elle knew in her heart that this was the last time she would be held by him and she closed her eyes, soaking it all in.

Rob remembered holding Elle another time, like this, in this very room. They had been alone then. He remembered the familiar way the rest of the world had seemed to recede when they were together. She had smelt the same then as she did now, a hint of vanilla rising from her skin, something sharper behind it. It was just her, so oddly familiar even after all this time.

He was also aware that this didn't mean anything, that it was just a peace offering of sorts, a way to say goodbye. Having her so close was almost dangerous, though. Rob felt as though he might burst at any moment. It was too much, having her so close, yet knowing that it was for the last time.

At the song's finish, he gently moved away from her and kissed her very lightly on her cheekbone. Then he left and waited outside for the party to finish and Celeste to come out.

Not a single word had passed between them.

Elle spent the rest of the night feeling as though she had been mortally wounded, and then was expected to carry on talking and laughing, as though the very life wasn't pouring out of her.

How Rob must despise her. He couldn't even talk to her. He had held her with the barest of touches, as though he couldn't stand to be near her. And that kiss ... it was his way of saying goodbye, she knew it. Goodbye, all the best and have a nice life.

She didn't know why she was so surprised. After all, he was with someone else now. He had made it perfectly clear that he wanted to be rid of Elle.

But still, a tiny part of her had truly believed that what she and Rob shared was special. That it had no equal. She had thought that if she could just be close to him one more time, then maybe he would realise it too.

She had been so, so wrong. All that was left for her now was the hotel. That, and maybe a couple of cats. Penny's did seem to have adopted her.

Elle comforted herself with the notion that at least she couldn't be altogether repellent.

Sometime after midnight, the guests began drifting away in pairs and groups. The rain had never made good on its promise, and instead a gibbous moon hung low and majestic in the sky. Elle remembered that she and Penny had always tried to see a face in the moon. Sometimes it looked friendly, sometimes not. Tonight it was giving nothing away.

She bade a personal farewell to every last guest. Penny was nowhere to be found and her dad had his feet up in the dining room, catching up on old times over a whiskey with Della and Jim. He seemed in especially good spirits tonight. Everyone had remarked that it was good for Ned to have his two daughters back under the same roof.

Hazel, having had one too many glasses of wine, was propped up by a grinning Glenn. 'We're not used to this kind of thing, any more,' he said. 'Your bad influence, Elle.'

'We did it, yay!' laughed his wife as they staggered down the drive. Her words seemed to bounce off the water and the low sky and come back to Elle in a kind of mocking taunt.

Emptied out of guests, the hotel felt haunted and lonely. Elle went through the rooms one by one, turning off the lights.

From the outside, the building appeared blind and abandoned once more. She thought back on the evening. It had been a fine occasion, all said and done. Now she just had to wait and hope that somewhere inside Doug Grant lay a beating heart that might be swayed in their favour.

Her heart quailed at the thought of tomorrow's clean-up. She didn't know if she had the heart for it.

The hotel was a bit like Cinderella, beautiful and regal for one night until the clock chimed midnight.

Chapter 36

The next day, the storm that had been threatening the day before hit with a vengeance. It seemed to have extra vigour from having held back a day.

'To think,' said Colin, over breakfast. 'I was supposed to have been on a plane today.'

'Will you get refunded for your tickets?' Ned asked. Such practical things were as always his first concern.

'Actually,' Colin muttered, reddening. 'I never quite ...'

'You never booked your ticket home at all, did you?' Elle challenged, teasingly.

'I always had a departure in mind,' he admitted shamefacedly. 'But it became clear the first time I left, that I wouldn't be leaving for a second time unless Penny wanted me to.'

'And I certainly didn't want you to,' a gooey-eyed Penny said.

'I just needed to introduce a little drama, to see if you actually wanted the benefit of my research skills, or me.'

They kissed and Elle smiled. If it was anyone else but her sister acting this goofily, she would have been sick. Penny was almost cross-eyed with happiness. Colin had declared that he was now a permanent fixture in Mulberry Bay, for as long as he was wanted. 'A writer can take his work anywhere,' he said airily. 'And of course we still have those remaining records to track down. The quest continues.'

'I think you two have done more than enough now,' Ned said quietly. 'I'm very happy with everything I've got so far.'

Penny's eyes shone afresh, realising that he wasn't just referring to the albums.

As it was, Elle was over the moon for her sister on both accounts. She guessed that recent events had helped her realise that Ned was Ned, and his behaviour towards her had absolutely nothing to do with any malice or preference. Elle could have told her that of course, but there were some things you needed to discover for yourself.

Last night, as he was leaving, old Arthur Ryan had whispered to Elle, 'Penny got her man, why are you letting yours go?'

Elle had shrugged. If it was a matter of not letting go, then she would have held on tight.

But you couldn't hold on to something that didn't want to be held.

The thought of cleaning up dismayed them all. Rain streaked the windows, making it almost impossible to see the wild waves in the distance breaking on the beach with relentless rhythm.

'It's got to be done,' said Penny, swiping the last of her rasher through tomato ketchup. Molly had treated the entire family to a big late-morning fry-up. 'We might as well start now.'

'At least we don't have to do the dishes,' Colin pointed out. That had been taken care of last night by the volunteers from the restaurant.

'Before we start,' Elle said, taking a deep breath, 'I have to tell you something. It's only going to make an unpleasant job even more unpleasant, but I'm afraid it has to be done. I didn't tell you before because I just wanted you to enjoy last night, but Doug Grant is bringing some buyers to the hotel on Tuesday. He said he would give us one last chance, and I think I was just desperate to believe him. But now I think he was probably just toying with me. He didn't turn up last night and I don't think he has any intention of listening to us at all.' Elle was trembling as she spoke. If they lost the hotel, they would have to give money back to anyone who had bid on related prizes.

But that was only the half of it. It was more the fact that she had been so sure of success, so sure that they really had a chance. She had got everyone in the community so heavily involved, and asked for so much help. Perhaps worst of all, she had given their little family hope again, when she Ned and Penny might have been better off saying goodbye to this stage in their lives and planning for the next.

Ned cleared his throat. They could all see how unhappy Elle was. He said: 'To my thinking, Elle, there's nothing more we can do at this stage. We've done our best, more than anyone could have asked, and without you and your extraordinary efforts and ideas, that wouldn't have been possible. I can't tell you what it did for me to see the hotel full of people again. I've never seen the place look so beautiful. It was like a dream. Your mother would have been so proud. If we have to leave, then that was the way to do it.'

'We have to wait now and just hope that people speak up for us,' said Penny. She went up and put her arms around her. 'Oh Elle,' she said. 'I wish I could give you some of my happiness,' which was a strange thing to say, but Elle understood.

She knew that her sister just wanted her to feel what she was feeling. This calmness, mixed with giddiness. The feeling of knowing that your life was full, that someone was waiting to hear whatever you had to say next, no matter how silly it might be. It was something – possibly the only thing – that Penny had wanted for all her life and she was thrilled for her.

'Might I suggest,' said Colin, sipping his tea, 'that we *don't* clean up the hotel, then? Might I suggest that it would be better for our … present purposes if it was left in its current disrepair? It's a pity that we can't cave the roof in again, but we'll just have to make do.'

He looked at the shocked faces around him. 'This has nothing to do with my dislike of manual labour, let me assure you.'

*

After they had made the (brilliantly strategic) decision to leave the hotel as it was, Elle found it surprisingly easy to slip into a state of almost childlike abandon. Suddenly there was nothing more to do, nothing more to plan and very little to think about other than what the next few days might bring.

Penny and Colin didn't mind if she tagged along with them. She suspected it was a case of: we've got the rest of our lives to be alone and happy together, why not spend some time with your poor lonely sister?

To Ned's delight, they went down into the town and got their hands on a turntable from Wally Ryan and played his new records in the ballroom. Colin taught a jive, how to waltz properly and more dangerously, the tango. Elle and Penny almost knocked each other unconscious with that one. Ned clapped along but refused to join them on the dance floor, but they all knew he'd never been a dancing man. Instead he seemed happy to watch his daughters being carefree, while he lost himself in the music, and whatever associated memories the songs inspired.

Very quickly, the ballroom started looking tatty again, the greenery beginning to brown and curl at the edges, the flowers wilting fast. It felt decadent in a way, to dance and have fun amongst the wreckage.

They watched old movies in the family lounge, curled up on the fat green and gold striped couches that Anna had loved. Colin made popcorn and they laughed their way through the old comedies while the house shivered and shuddered in the storm.

'If this keeps up,' said Ned on Monday night, 'the viewers may not be able to make it up tomorrow.'

'They'll make it up if that auctioneer has anything to do with it,' said Elle. 'Noah's flood itself couldn't keep them away.'

That night, even though she had spent a frivolously light-hearted weekend with her family, Elle felt strangely empty. No matter what anyone said, it was essential that they saved the hotel.

Their mother was everywhere in it, in the elegant furnishings, in the tiny little touches, like the towel arrangement that still sat at the bottom of every guest bed. She was in the library, with its selection of fat, spine-split paperbacks. She was in the bar, which she had always polished to high shine.

She was in the garden, amongst the tall eucalyptus trees that had been planted before her time, but had always been waiting for her. She was in the wild flowers that sprung up with abandon once she got too busy to weed them out.

Anna *was* the hotel. Her memorial wasn't some heavy gravestone in the plot beside the church; it was right here. The Bay Hotel was where she belonged.

And where I belong too, Elle realised.

'I like that you're so good to my sister, as well as my dad,' said Penny to Colin. They were still sitting up late, drinking hot cocoa after everyone else had gone to bed.

'Well, I liked Ned from the start, and I would be good to

Elle even if she was a weak-minded, mean-spirited witch, but I like your sister too. She's determined. I just wish her and that Rob fellow would get their act together.'

'How do you know about that?' Penny demanded, looking sideways at him.

'Oh, it's not hard to see,' he shrugged. 'They're absolutely mad about each other.'

'I don't think Elle is, though. She's turned him down twice. And Rob's too hurt to give things another go.'

'I don't think you can put much stock in that,' said Colin. 'The first time, they were both very young, from what I can gather. The second time, she was grieving for your mother. The third time could indeed be a charm.'

'I don't know. I wish you were right, but I just don't see it. It's funny,' she said. 'All my life I've been yearning to be close to my dad and reconnect with Elle, and I've been trying to think of so many different ways to make it happen, when all of a sudden it feels like it has. Obviously finding the albums and understanding why he let them go was a huge part of everything with Dad. And as regards Elle, I've spent all this time being jealous of her, and now I'm just not.'

'What were you jealous of her for?' Colin asked, curious.

'I don't really know. For going off and forgetting about me, I suppose. Going away and leaving us to deal with the hotel ourselves. Being Dad's favourite, hurting Rob. But none of those things were bad things, and she certainly didn't mean to hurt anyone. I don't know why I've spent so many years feeling upset, but I'm not any more.'

Colin looked thoughtful. 'Hmm, we've done so well with your dad, what's another quest in the scheme of things? Do you think there's some way we could get her and Rob together?'

'Don't even think about it,' Penny warned, meaning it. 'I've tried that before, with disastrous results.'

That night, when everyone was asleep, the sound of the storm buffeting their dreams, the wind began to push harder and harder. It was like it was possessed with some purpose, as though it wanted to see the hotel tumble into the sea.

It couldn't manage that. But every single occupant of the building was awoken by an almighty crack, a ripping that sounded like the sky itself tearing open.

The huge eucalyptus tree at the east side of the house, which was probably rotting in its core for years, had fallen over. It injured no one, but fell directly onto the side entrance, completely destroying the cloakroom.

Chapter 37

The next morning, which was fair and calm, the family surveyed the damage.

'It's completely ruined,' said Ned. 'That was a huge tree. We're just lucky it fell there, instead of on top of the main building. It could have killed someone.'

The heady smell of damp eucalyptus filled the air. 'Well, if we hold onto the hotel,' Penny pointed out, looking at Elle, 'there's your chance to renovate the entrance.'

Colin was nodding. 'I must say, unfortunate as it is, this just might increase your chances of being able to do just that. Hold onto the hotel I mean.'

Elle said nothing, just stared wide-eyed at the damage. Would there be any end to their troubles?

At 2 p.m. that afternoon, they heard the sound of cars approaching up the drive. They had all been waiting for it. Elle, Penny, Ned and Colin filed out to meet Paddy Corbett, the estate agent and the buyers. Who were accompanied by none other than Doug Grant.

What on earth was he doing here? Elle wondered. Unless … unless she realised, blood rushing to her brain, that Doug bloody Grant was an 'investor' in the new development himself!

'As you can see,' Ned pointed out to the estate agent, 'we had a bit of damage from that storm last night. It was lucky, but we were all unharmed.'

Paddy nodded and clasped his hands together. He seemed a bit vacant, possibly a bit nervous. Did he know that the community were against this sale? And perhaps worried about his own reputation amongst the townspeople? Either way, he needed to show the buyers around.

While they surveyed the property, Elle waited behind with Doug Grant.

'It's a pity you missed the party on Saturday; we raised a substantial amount of money,' she told him.

'Ah yes, I heard about that.'

'It's enough to pay off some of the existing debt and help make some basic renovations.' Although not any more, she thought, staring balefully at the fallen tree. 'Which makes us a much more stable candidate for additional finance.'

'Does it?' Doug replied airily. 'Seems that would be my decision to make, Ms Harte.'

'Will you consider it?' She might as well ask him straight out. 'You said you would give us another chance, and you have to also recognise that the entire community is behind us.'

'What I recognise is that there is currently a solid invest-ment opportunity here for the right buyer,' he told her curtly. 'In any case, this isn't the time or the place for such a dis-cussion. Come to my office tomorrow afternoon and we can talk further. I can only hope that there won't be a repeat per-formance of last time.'

'There won't,' Elle assured him, almost afraid to dare to dream.

'This time tomorrow, then.'

The truth was that Doug Grant was in a bit of a tight spot. If this investment consortium weren't interested, he would have to let the family have another go at the hotel. Hopefully, these people would buy. The hotel was a shack, the property market wasn't great in the area at the moment, and according to Paddy this was the only interest in the place there had been. Getting the place off the loan books wasn't going to happen in the short term, that was for sure, and his area manager had been on at him to bring under-per-forming business accounts back into the black.

There was another annoying factor too. For the past two days, he had been bombarded with emails and phone calls about the place and this family. Locals bleating into his ear about how much they loved the hotel and what it meant to them.

He'd found a selection of handwritten letters on his desk only that morning.

The Hotel on Mulberry Bay

Dear Mr Grant,
   I wonder if you have ever set foot in the Bay Hotel. I think, if you had, you would be less likely to see the town part with such an illustrious piece of community history, dating back from 1883, when the original owner built the property for his loved one. You may be intrigued by the interesting mix of architecture …'

This particular letter went on and on in what was, to Doug's mind, intolerable detail about the history of the place.

Mr Grant,
   It occurs to my wife Della and I that before this you have only worked in cities. Perhaps you do not know that one of the primary roles of a bank manager in a small town is to support the local business community. I'm afraid that in light of your treatment of the Bay Hotel, my wife and I will have no option but to move our business accounts, including all associated wages and staff accounts, to the Wexford branch.

Yesterday morning, he had been stopped in the street and subjected to complete strangers' 'fondest memories of the hotel', dreary nostalgias which he had little time for. Behind it all was the implication that people would leave the bank if it did not demonstrably support the business community.

He realised very quickly that it had been a mistake not to attend the party on Saturday night. He certainly hadn't experienced anything like this before.

In Dublin, he hadn't had to deal with people on such an ... intimate level, and he didn't particularly like it. He much preferred to view these people as the numbers on (or indeed in) their bank accounts, or the interest that gathered on their debts.

It was giving him a headache to think of all their endless stories about birthdays, romantic proposals, weddings, plain old family dinners. One man had brought his wedding photos in to show him, for goodness' sake.

When the investors appeared again, they looked grim. 'We'd hoped to keep the original structure as the common areas and add on to it,' Elle heard one of them say to Paddy, as they went back to their cars. 'People love that kind of thing, modern bedrooms and the old building to house reception and dining areas and such. But I'm afraid it is in a terrible state. If we decide to buy, then it will certainly be at a massively reduced price. But at the moment, we are still undecided.'

When Doug returned to his office that afternoon, he had a visitor. It was Maurice O'Rourke. Doug had no huge liking for his predecessor, in fact he had thought he was a bit of a soft touch. When he took over, he had immediately identified many ways in which the bank could be making more money.

'Having some trouble with the Harte place?' Maurice commented.

'As a matter of fact, yes.'

'I told you from the beginning, but you didn't want to listen. There's more to being branch manager in a small town than just moving cash around. It's about knowing people.'

'I'd prefer not to know people, thanks very much. I want to deal with their money, not their problems.'

'Sometimes it amounts to the same thing,' Maurice pointed out. 'And I'll tell you another thing, people in this community have long memories. They won't forget it, if you do the wrong thing by the Hartes. But I get the feeling that they've let you know that themselves.' He got up to leave. 'Don't be a fool about this one, Doug. It might come back to bite you.'

Doug thought for a long time after Maurice left. He sighed, realising he might just have painted himself into a corner.

On Wednesday morning, Rob drove Celeste to the airport.

'Thanks so much for letting me stay,' she said. 'I'm just sorry it took me and Dan so long to come round.'

'Not a problem,' said Rob. 'I don't think I could have a relationship like yours and Dan's, no offence. It just seems like a lot of drama.'

She shrugged. 'Ah, I think we like the drama. It might seem crazy, but when you find the one you really want, you're willing to go through a bit of grief for them.' Rob remained silent. 'You might think you've already had your fair share, Rob, but the hard part is actually being in the relationship.'

He looked at her. 'Celeste, I think I know what you're trying to do, but you don't know anything about what went on between me and Elle.'

'What went on between you isn't important now, that's in the past. What I can see is that you both genuinely care for each other. Don't let that slip away just because of pride. Hers or yours.'

Rob dropped her off at Departures and drove away. He was glad that she and Dan had worked things out (as usual) but the house would be pretty lonely without her. He had got used to having another person around.

This was his first day off in weeks and he meant to enjoy it. He would go back home, take the dogs down to the beach and throw sticks for them. The shore was bound to be a mess of driftwood, kicked up from last night's storm.

Approaching Mulberry Bay some forty minutes later, he drove through town and up along the coast road. Everything had the same dream-like quality that had been haunting him for days. When he moved his head, streaks of colour followed his movement, as though the thing he had just been looking at dismantled itself as soon as he looked away. He knew that he needed a break, needed some rest, but it hadn't been possible while he was fixing the hotel roof.

But now, he could enjoy the sunshine and try and rid himself of the events of the past few weeks. Was Celeste right? Should he try again with Elle? He wanted to. He had known since the first time she came back that he didn't want to let her go.

But it wasn't simply a matter of what he wanted. Elle had told him that she didn't think it was a good idea. But if they saved the hotel, wouldn't she be staying in Mulberry Bay? Wouldn't that perhaps give them time to slowly get to know each other again? They could rediscover each other without moving too fast.

He would think about it. He still thought that Elle simply wasn't interested in him, that she viewed their relationship as a thing best left in the past. It probably seemed trivial to her now, what they had shared. If she could write it off as meaningless, why couldn't he?

As Rob's car filled up with the warmth of the late spring day and he took the curves of the coast road in his practised and unthinking way, a slow miasma of sleepiness began to creep up on him, filling the car as surely as the temperatures.

His eyes felt so deliciously heavy, his body felt as though it was slowly and gently being lowered into a warm bath, his limbs becoming soaked and impossible to lift.

In the seconds before his car smashed through the barrier that separated the road from the sea, he felt as calm and untroubled as he had in weeks.

Chapter 38

Penny had sent Colin to Ryan's Antiques to check on the reparations to the hotel furniture, while she and Ned stayed behind to help with the deferred clean-up. There was no point in putting him through any more of the heavy lifting, she'd assured him wickedly.

Elle had dropped him off on her way to the bank, and after a nice cup of tea at Pebbles Café, and picking up some fresh bread from the Grain Store Bakery for lunch, he sauntered in to see Wally.

'Do you think there's any chance of the place being saved?' Wally asked, very taken with this mad Englishman who looked as though he was going to be a regular fixture about the place. He was a nice 'oul skin though, and Wally was pleased to see Penny Harte happy. While he admired her loyalty, his friend had always been too dedicated to her parents and the hotel, and it was about time she had a life of her own.

'I hope so. Goodness knows there's been enough adventure up there to last the family for a while.' Settling in for a long and easy chat, Colin took a seat in a dusty armchair and proceeded to tell Wally all about Ned's collection and Penny's quest to have it restored.

'Ah, I was wondering why ye wanted the record player the day *after* the party.' Wally commented. 'So Penny thought it might take his mind off losing Anna, or worrying about the hotel? Good idea.'

Colin shrugged. 'My guess is she just wanted to do something that allowed her to connect with him. Something that makes him happy. Now, I'm not saying that she is in need of his attention or craving approval or anything like that.' Colin thought this through and reconsidered his words. 'Actually, I think those albums are almost a physical embodiment of Anna's spirit.'

Wally raised an eyebrow. That was a bit heavy, even for a writer.

'And did they find them all, then? I can't imagine that would've been too easy.' Wally didn't deal in music memorabilia, though he knew his father had taken in a few boxes of old vinyl years ago. Junk mostly. It was still out back somewhere. He guessed Beatles originals would've been hard to come by.

'Unfortunately not. We tried every avenue available to us at this juncture but I suspect it might be a long-term prospect.'

'OK.' He had to laugh at the way the guy spoke. It was

sort of old-fashioned and nice in a way. In the business he was in, Wally appreciated old-fashioned. 'Well, there's a box of older vinyls out the back from my father's days – might be something in there that Ned might like. Tell him he can hang on to the turntable for as long as he likes; we don't get much call for those any more.'

'That would be wonderful, thank you. And if Ned doesn't like anything, perhaps I might. Anything from the twenties? Frank Miller perhaps? I love a good jive.'

Laughing, Wally went out back to find the box, leaving Colin to man the shop. They didn't get too many customers but he imagined a fella like him on the staff would be a bonus. If he was staying around the place, and the writing thing didn't work out for him, he might offer him a few hours.

It didn't take long to find the box. Like he'd said to Rob before, it was all in the head. Dusting the contents off a little, he lifted up the heavy box and brought it back up to the shop floor for Colin. As he did, something caught his eye.

'Well what are the chances?' Wally said chuckling. 'Is *A Hard Day's Night* on the list, by any chance?'

Colin sat up, felt a spark of excitement rush through him. 'As a matter of fact, yes.' Jumping up, he crossed the space to where Wally had set down the box.

'Well, I don't know much about music memorabilia, but I do know that ownership stickers affect value, though I'm not sure it matters ...'

'No, that wouldn't matter to Ned.' Colin turned the

record over to see what Wally was talking about. There was a small red sticker in the top right hand corner of the album. And on the sticker were two letters – likely initials, and a date.

Staring hard at the letters, Colin felt his heart start to beat faster.

Being back in Doug Grant's domain once again made Elle feel very nervous.

She was determined not to lose her cool again. That fateful day seemed as if it had occurred years ago. So much had happened since then, not just the events concerning her and Rob, or the hotel, or even the record collection and her sister and falling in love, but things had happened inside that had seemed to stretch out the days and turn them into a far longer period of time.

She was still in mourning for her mother, of course, still thinking of her each day when she woke up. It seemed easier to feel at peace with her grief here in Mulberry Bay, than it had been in London. Here, she could touch the things that Anna had touched and recognise her familiar smile in Penny's. She now had first-hand knowledge of how hard her mother had worked and what her daily routine had been like.

She had also come to terms with her love for the beach town, and her desire to stay there. She knew now that no matter what happened with the hotel, she would find some way to stay close to her family.

This time Doug had led her to a more formal office upstairs and had left her alone there while he went to get some papers. She looked around at its polished surfaces and dustless, tinted windows without envy. She had worked in many nice buildings, but she had acquired a taste for something else now.

He came back into the room and seemed to have lost some of his high-shine. Elle thought he actually looked quite tired. Gone was the man who had sat in front of her like an imperturbable, self-satisfied seal. Could he ... Elle wondered, with a spark of hope, be on the very edge of giving in?

'Well,' he said. 'You seem to have a lot of friends, Ms Harte.' He waved a handful of letters. 'Can you believe this? In the last few days I've received personal pleas from practically half the town. "Dear Mr Grant," he read, "I celebrated my 16th birthday at the Bay Hotel. The memories of that day are still dear to me ..." blah blah blah. "My late wife and I dined at the Bay Hotel under the excellent service of Ned and Anna Harte for many years ...", "I celebrated my grandmother's very last birthday at the Hotel, an occasion that is remembered with great fondness by all our family."' He threw the letters down in disgust. 'Who would have thought that people were so attached to a wreck? I've even received finger paintings from the local primary school, for goodness' sake.' He looked at Elle as though he expected her to sympathise with him. She was smiling inwardly.

'It would seem, in this case,' he said, 'you've got me

cornered. I have to give you a loan or risk losing half the town's business.'

Elle wasn't sure she had heard correctly. Was he toying with her? 'You're going to give us the loan?'

'I just said that, didn't I?' he muttered. 'If it were up to me, I wouldn't dream of it. But those investors were well and truly put off by the decrepit state of the place and who can blame them. If I didn't know better I would accuse you lot of knocking that tree down on purpose.'

'I'm so grateful to you, Mr Grant,' Elle gushed. 'I can't tell you how much this means to me and my family.'

'I don't need your gratitude, Ms Harte. I simply need you to make regular payments. You'll have to get the place smartened up quickly, reopened and get paying guests in. You can't be holding huge parties and asking for charity every time you have a bill to pay.' He pushed some papers across to her. 'You'll need to sign these. And then, if you would excuse me, I need to get some work done. I've spent the last two days reading ridiculous letters.'

Chapter 39

Penny could hardly believe her ears. Could it really be true? That her father's entire collection – his *true* collection, the first edition Beatles albums that had actually belonged to him – were simply sitting in Ryan's Antiques? That Arthur Ryan had been the 'dealer' who had facilitated her parents' cash infusion all those years ago when they were struggling with a new hotel, a young toddler and another baby on the way?

Colin told her that when he had seen the ownership stickers placed on the back cover of the albums with the initials 'NH' he had started to put things together. Realising too that not many people could possibly have those same initials, and feeling that the chances were just too slim that someone else in the town, or indeed the county, had sold an entire first edition Beatles catalogue to Arthur Ryan, was just too much of a coincidence for Colin. He knew at once that these records had to be Ned's.

Racing through the house to try and find her father, Penny felt elated that she would not only be responsible for restoring what he had lost, but also restoring the albums that had actually been his.

She simply could not *wait* to tell him.

She found him in the dining room, supposedly tidying up, but instead he seemed to be staring into space. He looked up when she walked in, and Penny felt breathless with anticipation.

'I need to ask you something. Back when you had your record collection, did you do anything to make it yours, per se? Was there anything on those to indicate that you were the owner? Like your name or anything?'

Ned looked at her with a confused expression on his face, as if he was trying to figure out where Penny was going with her inquiry. 'Do you mean, did I write my name on the albums?'

She nodded, her heart fluttering with the assurance that Colin was correct.

'No,' Ned answered matter-of-factly.

Waiting for him to explain further, Penny felt her stomach drop when she realised that there was nothing else to say. He hadn't written his name on his albums. And Penny realised that Colin must be wrong after all, that the albums Arthur and Wally had were not her dad's.

But then Ned spoke again. 'I would have never been so stupid as to write on a record, that is, I would have never been so stupid to write on a record *cover*. I would have never done that. There are betters ways to claim your property.'

Perking up, Penny tilted her head. 'How?' she encouraged.

Ned gave a small smile. 'Easy. I would have turned the album over and placed a small red sticker on the back top right-hand corner, and then I would have put my initials on it and the date I acquired it. That's what I would have done, Penny. And in fact, that's what I did do. With my albums.'

Penny's heart began to beat faster again. 'Oh Dad, that's fantastic news! Colin was right! Come on, grab your coat. We have to go down town.'

Looking taken aback by Penny's change in gears, not to mention her request to just get up and go, Ned frowned. 'What for?' he asked. 'And Elle has the car so we'd have to walk. Anyway why all the fuss, Penny? What's all this about?'

'Darn.' She'd forgotten about the car. But she knew she couldn't wait; she was too excited. She wanted to surprise Ned, but she supposed the only thing that was going to make him trek all the way down the coast road to Main Street was full disclosure.

'Would you want to go if I told you that we found your entire album collection?'

Ned looked puzzled. 'What? My collection?'

'Complete with little red initialled stickers,' she finished simply.

'Who found the collection? What's going on?' Ned pressed urgently. 'Where?'

'Colin found them down in Ryan's Antiques. Why didn't you tell me you'd sold them to Arthur?'

Ned appeared thoughtful for a moment before answering the question with gusto. 'I assumed he'd have sold them on years ago. He really held onto them ...' He was shaking his head. 'And he never said a word.'

Chances were Arthur had forgotten about them, as according to Colin it was Wally who'd located a box of 'old vinyl' out the back.

Arthur had been keeping it all out the back of the antiques shop – doing nothing with it for the thirty odd years. And then when Wally took over, he probably didn't appreciate what the records were, or understand the value of what they had.

'All of your records were still in Mulberry Bay, right in your backyard, since you sold them. Can you believe it?'

Ned closed his eyes as if he was saying a silent prayer. Penny wondered if he was thinking of Anna at that moment.

'Dad?' she asked. 'Are you OK?'

He nodded. 'I thought for years – wondered for years – where they all ended up. I thought that the entire collection must surely had been broken up and sold. Scattered to the wind. Lost to other people. Who would have thought—' His voice broke a little and he looked out the window.

'I can't believe it either,' Penny said delighted. 'I'm so happy. I'm so happy for *you*.'

Ned looked worried. 'But you spent so much money on

the ones we have so far. Not to mention wasted a lot of time.'

As always her dad was expert at stating the obvious, but Penny had already thought some of that through. They could sell the records acquired thus far – and if Elle was successful at the bank, the extra money would go towards the hotel. She wondered then, though, how much Wally Ryan would want for the collection – no doubt he would want to make a profit, so she guessed she still had some more cash to shell out in order to finish this quest. Still, it would be worth it, and maybe Wally might agree to a payment plan of sorts. She didn't think her friend would shaft them too much, especially seeing as he hadn't placed any value on them in the first place.

'Dad, don't worry about that. You and Mum took care of me my entire life, helped me if ever I was struggling, always made sure I had everything that I needed and wanted. And I appreciate that. And even though we now know the search was pointless, I think it taught me a lot about ... things. About you and Mum, about your relationship and about what you went through with this place,' she said earnestly. 'And I enjoyed our time on the road together. It made me feel ... closer to you.'

Somewhere in the distance a phone was ringing, and she cursed the timing, guessing it was Colin again, wondering why it was taking them so long to get there. Or perhaps Wally wanted to close up for an early lunch? Either way, Penny wasn't rushing anywhere, not when she and her father were sharing a moment.

Though Ned looked decidedly uncomfortable with so many regular displays of emotion these days so she decided to lighten the mood. 'Anyway I know you've always wanted Elle and me to learn about the Beatles, appreciate their songs – and maybe I do kind of like their music now,' she grinned. 'It was a soundtrack for you and Mum, wasn't it? And, I know for sure that it's your soundtrack.'

Ned considered her words and nodded. 'And yours too, Penny,' he said, approval of what she'd said thick in his voice. 'They're your songs as well.'

On her way home, Elle was in such a state of excitement that she could barely think straight. She couldn't wait to break the news to the others. More than anything, she couldn't wait to begin planning, to make all her ideas for the hotel come alive.

The experiment with the party had shown her how fulfilling it was to see each part of her vision come together, to be brought forth from a plain black and white sketch into something that could be touched.

She was aware, though, that Doug Grant was right about one thing. The hotel needed to re-open as soon as possible, something that was complicated by the other night's storm. Perhaps Rob ...? But no, they couldn't possibly ask him to do anything more for them. He was exhausted. And, she reflected with a slight ache, he would want to spend more time with Celeste.

They would just have to get in another builder. And it

would have to be all hands on deck for the next few weeks. She wanted the hotel open again within the month. She was gaining a reputation as a slave driver in her family, she knew. Elle smiled. Tough. Somebody had to make these things happen.

They would work from the original list of upgrades that she and Penny had prepared. At least now she would have no trouble convincing her sister that the entrance needed to be renovated.

She smiled to herself. She should be thankful for small blessings, at least.

Penny's heart sank as she heard the car pull up the driveway.

'Be brave,' Ned said to her. 'She will need you now.'

'Crack open the champagne!' Elle yelled as she ran into the dining room. 'The hotel is saved – we got the loan!'

Her father and Penny sat waiting for her, their faces so serious it was as though they were wearing masks.

'What's wrong?' she asked. A bolt of fear struck her. Had Doug Grant rung the hotel in the meantime to say that they couldn't have the loan after all? He wouldn't be so cruel. No one could …

'Elle,' Penny said, her voice breaking, 'It's Rob. He's had an accident. His truck went off the coast road this morning, and he's in the hospital. It's …' she began, and then paused to collect herself. Her voice was cracking at the edges. 'It's serious.'

*

The situation with Rob was very serious. He had broken ribs and punctured a lung but also had bad head injuries. They were keeping him in an induced coma at the nearby hospital until the swelling went down.

Anna had always loved Rob like a son, Ned reflected. She had cooked him meals, mended his clothes and told him off when he looked too tired.

But it was Ned who had talked to him, man to man, over the years, and watched Rob turn from a confused teenager into the great fellow he was today. He was proud of Rob, proud of his integrity, his dry humour, proud most of all that he was a good person through and through. He could have held a grudge against the whole family after Elle dropped him, but he had become closer to them than ever. Part of it was wanting to remain close to his last link with Elle, Ned knew, but also he genuinely loved the family.

All thoughts of his record collection were quickly abandoned. While he was delighted with the news earlier and appreciated what his youngest daughter had been doing for the last few weeks, in all honesty Ned felt a bit silly now. Yes, the music meant a lot to him, but his family meant so much more. That was the bit Penny didn't understand. He had given up those records, not in spite of his family, but because of them. And down through the years, Rob Callahan had in his own way, become part of that family too.

Ned honestly didn't think he could handle another loss, and he very much doubted that Elle could. How cruel it was to truly realise what you wanted and needed the same second that it was taken from you. For it had been written all over her face, when Penny told her: she loved him. Penny had delivered the news as gently as possible, but Elle had been bludgeoned with it.

To think there would be no more visits from Rob and his mad, energetic dogs. Something occurred to Ned just then, and though it was far past dark, he got into the car and drove.

They were in the backyard, confused that their master hadn't returned. They whimpered piteously when Ned arrived, wriggling their bodies in hope. 'I've got no good news for you, I'm afraid,' he told them. 'But I won't be leaving you here without any company.'

And with that, Rob's dogs were to become temporary residents of the Bay Hotel. At least, everyone hoped it would be temporary.

Chapter 40

The next few days were hellish for Elle. She moved from room to room with no purpose, lying down in different places as though she might find rest in one of them, since she couldn't in her own. All thoughts of the hotel and her success with the bank were torn away from her at once, as if they had never existed at all. But it was the walls of the hotel that contained her grief, and it was the hotel that cradled her as she tried to fall into a dream-wrecked impossible sleep in the evenings.

What she felt most of all was a crushing sense of guilt. If she hadn't been so desperate to have the roof fixed, if she hadn't needed it done in such a hurry, would this have happened? She *knew* that Rob had been exhausted, but she hadn't said anything because she had been avoiding him. How could she have been so blind? Rob had given the family all he had, and she hadn't thought about what it might be doing to him.

It was simply that he had always been like that, always willing to go the extra mile for you. It was the same instinct that had made him give Elle his jacket when she had forgotten

347

hers when they were young, which made him bring her snacks when she had been studying for exams. There had been a million little things like that. He always knew what you needed, what you were missing. When she met his mother and sister for the first time (Rob's father had died when he was a child) he had known how uncomfortable she was in the face of his mother's cold questioning. He had winked at Elle and made faces behind his mother's back, to put her at ease. Of course, it had the opposite effect of making her feel even more nervous, but that wasn't the point.

How had she forgotten these things? Moments where it had seemed that they were closer than anyone on earth. It was like he knew her even better than Penny, or her own mother. It was Rob that she had first told when she wanted to be an architect, and he had encouraged her, knowing deep down that he was encouraging her to go away and leave him.

She was so heart-sore that she didn't know how to get through another day. She would harden herself, tell herself that she needed to pull herself together and then it would overwhelm her again, paralysing her. And not to be able to go to him, to know that it was Celeste by his side, was unbearable. She dragged herself from room to room, the dogs following her, as forlorn and sad as she was.

The dogs were one comfort at least. The morning after Ned had picked them up, they had climbed onto her bed and nestled down beside her. The cats were ousted. Elle hadn't been separated from them since.

*

Penny knocked on her sister's door. For the past few days, she couldn't be quite sure where to find her, but there she was, curled up on the window seat, watching the sea breeze ripple through the garden below.

'Elle? Do you want to come down for some dinner?'

She shook her head. She wasn't hungry.

'You'll starve at this rate,' said Penny. 'Just a bite or two. It would make Dad so happy. I'll bring something up.'

Elle spoke as if she hadn't heard. 'Do you know what I keep thinking, Penny? It's the stupidest thing. I feel so sorry for Celeste, of course, but I'm also jealous of her. For being able to be with him, to see him. For having the right to feel as miserable as I do.'

Penny stared at her for a moment in complete confusion, then her hand flew to her mouth. 'Oh ... about Celeste, it's not what we thought. I forgot to tell you, on the night of the party. Celeste and Rob aren't together, they never were. She was just a friend. He was coming back from dropping her at the airport when it happened.'

Elle was silent. She looked to Penny as though she had been slapped, almost as bad as when she had given her the news about Rob the other day.

'So they were never ... all this time?'

Penny shook her head miserably. 'No, never. And I knew but I was just so caught up with everything else that I forgot about it. I'm so, so sorry, Elle.'

'It wouldn't have made a difference, anyway. I would still feel this horrible guilt, still feel that this is my fault. If I had never tried to save the hotel in the first place, if we had got someone else in to fix the roof ... there are a thousand "what ifs" going around in my head.'

'But Elle, you love him. I know you do.'

She raised her eyes to her sister. 'When has that ever done him any good? I've only hurt him Penny, again and again. Besides, even if I do, he doesn't love me any more. But it doesn't matter,' she said, rising from the window seat. 'I'm going to go and see him anyway.'

If Elle had thought that maybe the sound of her voice or the touch of her hand at the hospital would revive Rob, she was sadly mistaken. No matter what she had seen in movies or read in books, that kind of thing didn't happen in real life.

For starters, she wasn't even allowed into his room. They let her stand outside and look at him through the glass. He didn't look the same, she thought, but of course she wasn't close enough. He was covered in bandages and attached to a machine. She couldn't see the familiar curve of his lips, and the rough stubble that pushed its way through his skin. She couldn't see the dark curve of his eyelashes, the tender-looking bruises beneath his eyes. If she had seen any of this, perhaps it would have given her some hope. The bruising, the growing hair, all signs that his body was still alive, still pushing back.

But instead she left the hospital feeling worse than ever. He wasn't there any more; Elle knew it. Rob was gone.

*

'It's not doing her any good,' Penny said, a week later.

The news was still the same: there was no change to Rob's condition. However, Elle still went to the hospital every day, as though if she watched constantly, she would be sure to see some hopeful sign.

'Well, we can't stop her, can we?' Colin pointed out.

'We can't stop her, but we have to help her somehow,' said Penny. 'We have to face the fact that Rob might not ... get better.'

Ned looked grim. 'What do you suggest, then?' he asked, his voice muffled.

Penny sighed. 'We need to get started on the renovations,' she said. 'I know it sounds callous, but if we don't get guests coming in soon, the bank will withdraw the finance. If nothing else, it will be a distraction for Elle.'

There had been no mention of Ned's record collection since. To everyone it felt silly and frivolous, given what was going on with Rob, and Wally had assured Colin that of course he would hold onto the records in the meantime, until Ned was ready to come and get them.

It was decided that work would start on the hotel the very next day. Like it or not, it would be better for Elle to get back in her role as project manager.

The following day, Elle awoke to the sound of wood splintering. She went downstairs.

'What's going on?' she asked Penny, her face pale and tear-stained.

'They're removing the tree and tearing down the entrance,' said Penny, heart-sick at the wretched sight of her. 'So you'd better get your plans out.'

'Oh Penny, I just can't,' Elle moaned, sobbing. 'How could I?'

Penny went and put her arms around her sister. 'You have to,' she said. 'You just have to. I know it's hard. I know you're struggling. But if you don't snap out of this soon, you'll sink altogether. Rob wouldn't want to see you waste all this hard work, his work too. He would be so proud of you, Elle, just like Mum.'

Elle didn't say anything and Penny left her in the dining room. This wasn't going to be easy.

With Gruff and Kaiser curled at her feet, Elle grudgingly settled at a table in the dining room and pulled out a blank page. She already had some idea of what she wanted, of course, but she never fully realised a project before it was down on paper.

She admitted now that she had always envisioned working with Rob on the entrance and explaining to him exactly what was needed. He would get it immediately, of course. She had pictured them bending over her plan, him making suggestions here and there.

She pushed the image from her mind: it was impossible to think of now. Penny was right; she just had to concentrate on the task at hand. She had to concentrate on something ... anything but the sight of him in that hospital bed.

Tentatively at first, her heart still heavily entrenched in her stomach, Elle's wrist began to move over the paper, strong charcoal lines appearing where there had only been blankness before.

Soon she worked on like someone in a trance, and it was more healing to her than any nightmare-soaked sleep she had endured over the last few days. It was finally a reprieve from thoughts of Rob.

Chapter 41

Rob's eyelids flickered open. It was strange, but he thought he had felt something like silk brush across his face, the faintest scent of vanilla. But as he focused on his surroundings, his gaze rested on the unmistakably white ceiling and clinical surrounds of a hospital.

What the hell had happened? He tried to sit up, and was restrained at once by a blinding pain across his ribs and gentle hands pushed against his shoulders.

'It's all right, pet,' said a familiar voice. 'You're all right.'

His mother – what was she doing here? And why did she smell so like ...?

'Was somebody here?' he croaked, his mouth dry as the desert.

'I'm here, love, that's all that matters. And you gave us all a bit of a fright. Hold on, let me get a nurse—'

When the medical staff had carried out all their checks and given Rob some water, he struggled to comprehend what had happened.

He'd taken Celeste back to the airport, hadn't he? He was almost certain that was what he'd been doing before ...

'Is Celeste OK? Was she ...?' Rob understood that he'd been in an accident and for a horrible moment he couldn't remember if she was in the car with him when it happened.

'She's fine – lovely girl, too. But *that* one was just here,' Grace said grumpily and the way she said it, with so many years of built up dislike, left Rob absolutely certain that it had been Elle.

She had been here, to see him. He knew it.

'She's been over most days,' said his mother. 'I said to her: "You weren't that interested when he was in perfect health, were you?" but she kept on coming. Always did what she wanted, that one.'

Ah, yes, she did, Rob thought, smiling inwardly as he sank back onto the pillows. That was why he loved her. And why he'd woken up too.

'The doctors are saying that you were very lucky, you know. You could've been killed ...'

Rob could barely concentrate on what his mother was saying and he really couldn't care less. The thought that Elle had been here was all he could think about and it gave him a vague glimmer of hope.

But he wouldn't let it get to him just yet. She had probably been concerned about him, that's all.

Nothing more than that.

*

Elle was so absorbed in her work that she didn't even hear the phone ring. She had been working for some hours, even able to block out the whine and screech of the chainsaw outside.

She was roused by Penny's ungainly clattering through the hallway.

'He's awake!' her sister cried. 'He's going to be all right.'

The charcoal in Elle's hands was snapped in two, so tightly did she clench her hands. For a second she thought that she couldn't possibly believe it, and then relief flooded her. She didn't know that it was possible to feel like this, as though you had been given everything you asked for all at once.

'Thank God, thank God,' was all she could say.

'You'll be able to visit him in a couple of days,' Penny added, and she watched her sister's face change.

'A couple of days? If you think I'm waiting longer than ten minutes, Penny, you're absolutely mad.'

Elle Harte was back.

The following week was a hive of activity. Sometimes Elle wondered if they were doing so much work that the building wouldn't be able to stand it, would refuse to put up with all this cutting and moving and crashing. And for a time, it seemed that all they had truly done was make a mess that couldn't possibly be cleaned up.

What remained of the old entrance had been completely demolished and once again the hotel was bandaged with tarpaulin.

The carpets in all the common areas had been ripped up, leaving patchy, bald looking floors. The curtains had been taken down, and the floors re-covered in plastic as painting and fresh wall-papering commenced.

Ned, Penny and Colin helped wherever they could, which was mainly with jobs where no expertise was required. They carried timber for the builders (Rob's competition, but that couldn't be avoided), sanded floors and walls and helped Molly with the endless food that needed to be prepared.

Ned joked to Colin: 'I think you're building up a few muscles these days.'

Penny laughed out loud. 'Perhaps your days of being a writer are over and you can become a builder's apprentice instead.'

He looked horrified. 'I love you, my dear, but I don't think I could countenance that.'

These were happy days for Penny, now that the threat over Rob had receded and her relationship with her father had vastly improved.

She had visited Rob in hospital and told him about everything that had been happening since the night of the party.

'Lucky for me you're stuck in bed so I can bore you senseless,' she said. Though Rob wasn't quite as amazed as she was about Arthur holding onto Ned's collection.

'Arthur's no fool,' he told her. 'He would have understood exactly how much store your dad put in those records. He was obviously waiting for the time when Ned needed them back.'

But Penny realised now, it was she – not her father – who had truly needed them back. She was looking forward to going to Wally's with Ned one day to get them. But at the moment, the timing wasn't right.

She then continued to regale Rob with all the drama of her and Colin. 'I've always doubted that people in love were *really* in love, do you know what I mean? I thought that they couldn't possibly feel all that strongly. But now I know I was just waiting for the person who I could feel like that with.' She hugged herself, grinning delightedly.

Rob had to smile. 'I'm very happy for you, Penny. You deserve it.'

'Everyone is,' she said. 'Dad thought I'd be an old spinster forever. And Colin gets on so well with everyone around here too. I wish you could be as happy as me, Rob.'

She saw him grimace and apologised. 'I'm sorry, I said that without thinking as usual. I'm an eejit. I know that you would if you could be.'

'Did Elle really visit me while I was unconscious?' he asked hesitantly.

'Every day.'

'Then why hasn't she been in since? I hope my mother hasn't scared her off. Elle knows her bark is worse than her bite, and that never really bothered her.'

'Well, she's been busy with the hotel ...' Penny began haltingly, a little mystified by this herself. 'To be honest Rob, I don't honestly know. Elle is a mystery to me too. When you were unconscious, she couldn't be kept away. But now that she knows you're OK, I think she's embarrassed. You know how Elle is about showing her feelings.'

'Ah, it doesn't matter,' he said. 'I should've learned enough by now not to hope for anything from Elle.'

But the trouble was that Rob still hoped. That brief sense of her that he'd had in his dreams had been enough to open up a whole floodgate. He was desperate to go and see her, to clear the air between them once and for all. And he would if it wasn't for this damn hospital bed.

The days went slowly for him. He was used to being out in the open, to having his muscles strengthened through work, his limbs warmed by the sun.

He was the kind of person who knew that they couldn't be too far away from the sea either. It sustained him: its constant background lull had got into his blood, its moods inspiring his own. Stuck inside a place like this was torture, his mind going round and round like dogs at a racetrack. It was like his brain was a turntable stuck on one song, and that song was 'Elle' ...

He worried that some essential part of him was being leeched away during this separation from the outdoors. He could almost feel his muscles melting away and his complexion fading. He was happy to be alive of course, and so lucky, as everyone kept telling him, but he didn't want to get out of hospital and look like some sickly, weakened twin of his former self.

Taunting him too was the knowledge that work had

begun on the hotel. It was the best news he's had since he had been in hospital, that the family had got the loan. It didn't matter that he wasn't the one working on the renovations; what did matter is that they were happening at all. He just wished that he had heard it from Elle's lips. It was her victory. Everyone had helped, but Elle was the one who had made it happen, with her drive and brilliance. He couldn't help but think about her all the time in superlatives. If only she would come and see him and they could talk straight for once. He realised that since she got back to Mulberry Bay, they hadn't had one conversation in which they'd both said what they really felt. He imagined it would have to be like a child's game in which he would say something and then tell her, 'now you go', and back and forth like that until they had some understanding between them. Because there had been misunderstandings, he was sure of that.

Well, if Elle was going to play stubborn and keep away, Rob might just have to go to her.

Chapter 42

Still, as time went by, the hotel seemed to get worse, not better.

'I suppose it's always like this in the interim,' Colin pointed out, doubtfully. 'You always have to put up with a fair amount of discomfort when you renovate a place like this.'

It seemed like 'fair amount of discomfort' was putting it mildly. At times the electricity was off, meaning no hot water for showers. And one time, there was no water for an entire day.

'Are we going to throw another big party when the hotel opens?' Penny asked hopefully.

'Don't talk to me about parties,' Elle grunted. 'It's enough trying to make sure we've got carpets, let alone thinking about actual people walking around the rooms.'

'It'll be all right,' Penny encouraged. 'These things always turn out well in the end.'

There was a new lightness about Penny that Elle could attribute to both her relationship with Colin and her new-found understanding of Ned.

Where once her sister had been a bundle of anxiety, fizzing with nerves, she was now calmer, more sure of herself.

Of course, their father had had no idea of the effect that his apparent indifference had had on his youngest daughter but there was nothing that Elle or indeed Anna could do to change that. Penny had always been full of sensitive qualities: kindness, affection, altruism. And it was this sensitivity that had brought on her vulnerabilities where Ned was concerned, and perhaps made her so easily led when it came to men.

It was just that she hadn't realised all of that until now. Colin had brought out the best in her.

It was funny, Elle mused, how you could hear the same thing from other people again and again, and never truly believe it until one particular person says it in exactly the right way. She, Anna and even Ned in his own way had all told Penny her whole life how wonderful she was, but she didn't believe it, not until Colin had come along.

It was like how Elle had never believed she was beautiful until Rob told her she was. She'd never felt that way before.

So why not go and see him, if he makes you feel so good? said an annoying little voice in her head. 'Ah, shut up,' she muttered aloud. She had had enough about that subject from Penny, without having her own subconscious pitching in as well.

The truth was, Elle was afraid. Afraid to see him up close, to have him look at her and know absolutely what she was thinking. Because he would know she loved him; she couldn't hide it any longer. The words Penny had said, that he should have been rid of her years ago, still echoed in the depths of her mind.

She still felt guilty, as well. It didn't matter that he was recovering, it was her that had caused this to happen. Everyone said it: if Rob hadn't been working so hard, he never would have drifted off and lost control like that. They didn't blame her directly, but Elle felt that it was an unspoken thing.

She knew she was being a coward, and despised it in herself. But really, hadn't everyone been through enough in the last few weeks?

The day Hazel turned up with a truckload of plants and gardening implements was perfect weather for her and Elle to get stuck in to the garden.

'Usually, for a job like this, you'd need a few more people, at least. But we'll have to make do with what we've got.'

It was a case of 'making do' with almost everything, though. They were bleeding money. At every turn, there was some unexpected expense, something that hadn't been calculated for. Elle had hurriedly put her London flat up for sale so that she would have some cash to inject into the flagging funds.

Nevertheless, it was a hopeful time. Their vision for Anna's hotel was finally becoming a reality.

Ned and Colin helped with the garden as well, while Penny had taken a shine to hanging wallpaper. She said she found it very relaxing.

'I don't see why,' Colin said. 'It's absolute hell on the neck and shoulders. I'd much rather be out here, soaking up nature's bounty.'

Though 'nature's bounty' turned out to be harder work than any of them imagined. By the end of the first day, they were as tired as they'd ever been.

'My hands,' the English Invader moaned later that day. 'My poor writer's hands.' His hands were torn and red and Penny had to soak them in lavender water.

'I bet wallpapering doesn't seem so bad, now, does it?' she said smugly.

Bit by bit they all began to toughen up. Their bodies became stronger and they were able to work for long hours without paying for it the next day.

Despite her design background, Elle found she enjoyed the work in the garden more than any of the other parts of the renovation. She still loved watching her architectural vision come to life, but working in the garden took over her mind and let her stop thinking for a little while. Or, even if she couldn't stop entirely, it was a calmer, more productive kind of thinking.

She and Hazel spent time each morning discussing what should be worked on that day. Hazel took her work very seriously. She knew what Elle had in mind and wanted to make it a reality.

'It has to look as though it's been here for years,' she said. 'That's the effect that we want. It can't be new and neat and freshly dug over.'

So began a process of integrating parts of the old garden into Elle's vision. Where you were walking a newly laid cobblestone path, it was lined with wild flowers that had grown there for years. The small pond would be surrounded in long grasses. There were little tranquil bowers and benches to sit in, and walls covered in creeper that would make each guest feel that they had found their own private paradise.

Through it all there was to be a stream, cascading down dips and ending in a small pool. The sound of running water was to be heard all over the garden, and Elle wanted those who relaxed there to truly believe they were in some exotic, palace gardens. Tulips were planted in banks, and spiky aloe cropped up among the paths. Exotic-looking plants the people of the town had never seen before were procured by Hazel and Glenn, and the family were given strict instructions on how to care for them.

After his initial complaints, Colin found a lot to like about gardening. As his body grew used to the work, his mind became immersed in it. Once, he had barely given plants a thought, beyond how they could be plucked and put in a drab room. But he began to learn their intricacies, the way that water was a balm to one plant, an annoyance to another. He learned what variety of flowers to plant to lure birds other than seagulls into the garden.

'I've grown to quite like this business,' he told Penny at

the end of a long day. 'Before I came here I barely paid attention to things like that. I was so locked away in my mind, thinking that was how a writer should be. But I've found that the more I pay attention to the world around me, the more amazing things I see happening everywhere.'

Once Elle's plan had been carried out in its entirety, the garden looked truly beautiful. Beauty with an element of magic in it, the kind of place where you could lose yourself, even though you were only a few yards from the hotel building.

Hazel pointed out that it would only grow more and more beautiful over the years, the trees they had planted as young saplings becoming tall and stately, gaining a layer of moss over bark. They could tell guests with children that fairies lived there, and host lots of fairy-themed parties.

The real gift of the garden however, was that it would outlast the years of any who had been involved in its original planting. It would continue to grow and thrive and provide a haven for people for many, many years to come.

Elle had some inkling of this as she flicked on the outdoor lighting the night the garden was finally finished. The trees immediately lit up as though thousands of fireflies had alighted in their branches. Everyone else was quiet, as though in awe. She felt that more than anywhere else, the spirit of their mum truly resided here, in a place where Anna could still watch over her guests, listen to whispered secrets and see people enjoying the beauty of her wonderful hotel.

Perhaps that's why Elle had the sense that they had done

something that would outlast them all, and she believed that it was the jewel in the hotel's crown to date.

Colin agreed to take over the day-to-day maintenance of the garden. He was often in conversation with Elle about what needed to be done, what would look best where and so on. She had an inkling that sometimes he simply wanted to seek out a quiet spot to write or read, but she couldn't complain. She trusted that he would keep it beautifully, just as she trusted him with her beloved sister. These days he was part of the furniture, and would be central to the future of the hotel.

Chapter 43

With the garden finished, Penny decided that it was time for a celebration of sorts, or at least something to help keep spirits up and restore flagging limbs.

So she, Colin and Ned finally went down to Main Street and called at Ryan's Antiques.

Wally was smiling as they entered the shop. 'I have to say I had no idea why my father didn't sell these.' There was an uncomfortable moment as everyone could almost see the euro signs flashing in Wally's eyes. Clearly he'd done some research on the value of the collection in the meantime. He led them out to the box of records, which he'd dusted off out at the back and laid out in the interim.

Turning her attention to Ned, Penny felt tears spring to her eyes as she watched her father delicately pick up an album, flip it over and then give a small smile as he found the sticker with his initials on it that he had placed there so many years before.

He hummed a tune that she recognised as *Got a Hold on Me* from *With the Beatles* album. 'That one was a hit long before you were born,' he chuckled quietly. He ran his finger across the back cover of the album. 'Your mother bought this one for me. A birthday present. It was the first present she had given me after we started going steady. I marked the date here. See it?' He pointed to the sticker marked with the date Anna had given this record to him. He appeared lost in thought and Penny had no doubt that he was reliving a million memories right at that moment.

'Did you and Mum do something special for your birthday maybe?' Penny enquired further.

Finally, Ned shook his head. 'No, nothing too special. I wasn't one for going to dances and pubs and what not. And that wasn't our style either. She had made me dinner at her house. And we were listening to music ...' He closed his eyes, remembering.

'What were you listening to?'

Ned opened his eyes. '*Got to Get You Into My Life*. That was the song on the record player when Anna jumped up and said, "I have a surprise for you." Then, she was gone for a minute and when she came back she gave me this. Of course, I knew it was an album. From the shape alone, but it was covered in wrapping paper. The paper was red. And she had placed a little silver ribbon on it.' Ned paused and Penny knew that he wasn't trying to recall details; he had committed all of this to memory a long time ago – he was dealing with the naked emotion of the situation – those feelings that he was never sure what to do with.

Penny tried to think what her mother would do in a situation like this – to try to get her father talking. 'Were you surprised when you opened it?'

He nodded, still looking hard at the album itself, as if the item was a window to that day in the past.

'Oh yes. Very. Of course, Anna loved birthdays. She loved surprises. She loved doing things for others. She was always about making other people happy, as you know. I remember she was wearing a pair of red trousers. I joked that she had even tried to colour coordinate herself with the present.' He smiled. 'But there was more to that night. This was one of the things that she did that made me realise that I needed to marry her. That she was the right woman for me. The lengths that she went to, all the time, day in, day out, just to make me happy. She was one in a million your mother. Everyone needs that, I think,' Ned said, finally looking at his daughter. 'Someone who would do anything for you. Someone who just loves you more than anything in the world. Someone who would go to great lengths to see you happy, to make you happy. I'm glad you've found that, Penny,' Ned said glancing at Colin, before allowing his eyes to rest quickly on the teardrop on her cheek.

They began extracting the records one at a time, comparing the album title with what was on the list and checking each one off accordingly – or rather, Penny and Colin made an inventory of what was in the box while Ned lovingly examined each album as they handed it to him.

As they emptied the boxes and realised that they had gone through all the contents, Penny frowned. One record was missing.

Looking at the list that she had been working from and then at the empty boxes, she bit her lip. 'It looks like one isn't here.'

Ned looked at her with an anxious glance. 'Which one is missing?' he asked curiously.

'I thought they were all here,' Colin said airily, which caused Penny to look suspiciously at him. She didn't know why, but his voice had changed – it didn't sound normal.

'We're missing the *Anna* single,' she said. 'You didn't see it, did you?'

Ned began shuffling again through the records. 'I thought you said all of them were here?' he questioned gruffly, directing his attention to Colin. 'Where is that record? That's the most important.' His voice took on a frantic edge as he began looking through the box with renewed interest.

'I'm afraid that the one you are looking for has been sold,' called a voice from the hallway.

It was Arthur.

Penny turned as the very man her dad had sold the collection to so many years before entered the room. 'Sold?' she repeated frantically. 'But I thought ...'

Arthur smiled – a seemingly inappropriate response to the look of worry that had rushed onto Ned's face.

'That record ...' Ned said in a tone that Penny had never heard him use before. 'It was a present from Anna to me on our wedding day. Of all the ones in there that you could have sold ...'

Penny stepped forward, realising at once that her father was dangerously close to having an outburst of sorts over this new information. If today was any indication of just how emotionally tied Ned was to the collection, based on his reaction to one being missing, she knew just how much she had to find that record.

'Arthur, you said that the *Anna* single was the one that had been sold. I know it's been decades since you bought this collection, and maybe just as long since you sold this particular one; but do you remember who you sold it to? And if so, do you maybe have a way for me to contact the person? Was it a local?' She knew she was sounding desperate but she couldn't help it. They couldn't fail now.

Arthur's grin suddenly widened. 'I was thinking you might ask that.'

'As it happens, you're in luck.' Wally piped up. 'The buyer is local. And the man himself is here now, in fact.' He pointed at Colin. 'I'm sure you can work out a deal.'

Penny was mystified. 'What ... why would you ...?'

Colin was grinning as he held up the missing record. 'I couldn't resist one last bit of drama,' he said theatrically.

Then he handed Ned the record. 'The final piece in the puzzle, my dear man, congratulations.'

Penny wanted to kill him. 'Oh for goodness' sake ...'

But she was way too relieved to be annoyed. 'Is that really it?' she said, moving closer to Ned to take a closer look at the single. 'The one Mum gave you on your wedding day?'

Her father held the record carefully, as if afraid it might break, or worse, be snatched away from him again. 'I really never thought I would see this again,' he said quietly. 'I should never have parted with it in the first place.'

'It's yours now, Dad. It was always yours. And Mum will always be too.'

Ned ran a delicate hand over the front cover before flipping it over. Just like on the other albums, a small red sticker had been placed in the top right-hand corner. On it were the initials 'NH' along with a date. September 26th. Her parent's wedding anniversary.

Ned returned his eyes to his daughter's. 'Thank you, Penny. I've never thanked you properly. For doing this.'

She smiled. And she knew that she would do it all again – for her dad.

'And thank you too, Colin,' said Ned. He didn't express anything specific, but she got the distinct impression that he was thanking him for more than just his help in finding the collection.

Suddenly, Penny recalled something else about this particular record that had been written in her mother's diary. 'Oh, I remember Mum said something else, in her diary, about this one. She said it was signed. Is that true?'

Ned smiled. 'Yes. That's right. Look.' He pulled the record

from the sleeve and in the centre on the label, were four signatures.

John Lennon, Paul McCartney, George Harrison, Ringo Starr.

Examining the iconic names, Penny realised a new appreciation for the music – in a way, it had been responsible for bringing her parents together. Ned had been right: the songs were a form of poetry. They were modern sonnets – declarations of love. And ultimately, Penny also considered the thought that these records were also a catalyst for her own love story. The one she was just setting out on with Colin.

'That's wonderful, Dad,' Penny whispered over his shoulder.

'I know. Your mum was wonderful too,' Ned said.

From behind where they stood, Wally cleared his throat politely. 'If you all would like, you could play it. I have another turntable upstairs.'

'Would you like to play the record, Dad?' Penny asked, wondering if he might prefer to do so in private. But Ned nodded his head in affirmation as he continued to look at the record.

A moment later, Arthur's old record player had been brought down and plugged in. Wally took the record from Ned and placed it on the turntable, gently putting the needle down on the vinyl. There was a wonderful ceremony to it, Penny decided, and a kind of alchemy seeing the needle move over the spinning vinyl that you just didn't get with modern digital music. She'd gained a new appreciation for that over the last few weeks.

Again, as if by magic, the record crackled and spun to life. The bass guitar hummed heavily in the background, while the drums tapped out a slow beat.

As the song *Anna* played, Penny watched her father. He had gone from listening intently to the record, to suddenly investigating the inside of the sleeve. As he looked at whatever was inside the album cover, his expression changed, just for a moment, and a look of intense sadness crossed his face.

Oh no, was something wrong? Penny worried suddenly. *Had something been damaged?* Then, a different thought occurred to her. Maybe that wasn't a look of sadness. Was it reflection? Had he been thinking of a memory? Had the song made him recall something else about Anna, something long-forgotten?

But then Ned mumbled the words, *lyrics* from *Do You Want to Know a Secret*, and her heart sped up once more. Was there one final secret to be discovered?

'Can we play it again?' Ned asked politely as the song ended. Arthur obliged and moved the needle back to the beginning, starting the song over.

'Still sounds pretty good,' he commented. 'They really don't make them like this any more, Ned. Such a shame.'

'No they don't, and yes it does,' Ned replied simply, placing the record cover sleeve aside and giving his full attention to the music. 'Anna didn't know much about records when I first met her,' he explained, 'but she did her homework; she learned. For me, but I think she ended up enjoying it too. This was a great present.'

While her father's attention was elsewhere, Penny moved to pick up the record cover that Ned had just set down. She was curious to know what had caught his attention just then. What had her father been looking at a moment before?

And when she peered inside the sleeve her heart immediately sank. Oh no, someone ruined this, she thought. They wrote all over the inside of the cover! One of Arthur's customers maybe, or worse, could it maybe have been Wally as a child, scribbling on old stuff in the back of his father's shop?

She looked closer at the markings inside the cover – someone had definitely scrawled something – but then Penny's heart began to beat hard. She recognised that writing, and then recalled something her father had said the day Colin discovered the collection, and she had asked Ned about writing his name on an album to claim ownership. She thought of his words. '*I would have never been so stupid to write on an album. I mean, I would have never been so stupid to write on an album* cover.'

He would have never written *on* the album cover – and neither would her mother – Anna would have known how Ned felt about something like that. But Anna might have taken the opportunity to write a message to her soon-to-be-husband on their wedding day, *inside* the present that she was so excited to give him. Especially because she believed that he would never give it up, never be parted from it.

And when Penny read the handwriting inside the album sleeve, she realised that was exactly what her mother had done.

September 26, 1975

My Darling Ned:

I know you love this song – probably because you have a thing for a girl called Anna. But on this most special of days know that I cannot wait to wear your ring. I will never take it off from now until I draw my last breath. No matter what life throws at us, what challenges we encounter, I will love you. I am yours and you are mine. You are my soul mate, and I hope you know that you understand me, as much as I understand you. I cannot wait to begin our lives together – I know we have so much to be excited about. I promise I will love you forever and no matter what, I will always be part of you.

Your Anna

Swallowing hard as she looked over this private message that had been communicated between her parents, Penny felt tears well up in her eyes at the same moment that Colin sidled up next to her and put his arm around her waist.

She snuggled closer to him as the song continued to play. And she knew without a doubt that her mother was present right at that particular moment. She had been there through all of this – the search for the records, the ups and downs with the hotel – and would continue to be.

Chapter 44

The hotel had come through its disastrous, chaotic state and soon you could see faint outlines of what it might one day be.

'I've forgotten what it's like not to live in a construction zone,' said Penny to Elle. They were sitting down on the beach, avoiding the constant hammering which came with the renovation of the entrance hall.

'I know, I've almost grown accustomed to the constant noise. We'll probably get headaches from the silence when it's all over.'

'Everything seems to be falling into place. Dad has his collection back, Molly is back in the kitchen, Colin has the garden. Everyone's got a job.'

'Everyone except us, you mean?' Elle teased.

'Well, you're so busy with the renovation, but have you thought about what we're going to do afterwards? How we're going to run it day to day?'

'I suppose someone will have to deal with the bookings, management of the staff, things like that.'

Penny shook her head, understanding what she was getting at. 'I don't think so, Elle, I'm happy to help out like before but I don't think it's my thing ... Look what happened last time. I messed it up completely.'

'Yes, and it brought you Colin. I think that was the hand of fate, rather than a mistake, wasn't it?' said Elle.

Penny laughed. 'Maybe. You know, it's so funny, we haven't even had to talk about it; we just know that Colin is going to stay here and move into the cottage with me. Isn't that funny? So much is just automatically understood between us. I could have killed him when he tricked us at Wally's, though.'

Elle smiled. Colin and Penny had reached a stage in their relationship where everything they did and said was still very interesting to them. They needed to exclaim over it as though they had discovered a new continent.

'I suppose we'll all just muddle along for the moment,' she said. 'The important thing is, we don't want to be running a second-class establishment in such a beautiful building. Even all the renovations won't make it perfect.'

'It'll be fine,' said Penny. 'Look at the party. You pulled that off, didn't you?'

Elle wasn't convinced by Penny's optimism. This was something that had been worrying her for a while now. The hotel could be the most beautiful building to be found for miles, as it surely would be once it was done, but that wasn't everything, was it?

There was something else, something that their mother

had, and Elle wasn't sure that either she or Penny possessed that same quality. It was something like patience, but it was stronger than that. It allowed Anna to be constantly listening to the talk of others without it completely draining her. She was like a tree, bending and swaying in the wind, but never breaking. How did she do it? How did she clean and wait on tables and talk with people all day long, without it putting a sour smile of tiredness on her face?

Elle thought that maybe it might have something to do with her mother's own contentedness. She could listen to others all day, safe in the knowledge that happiness did exist: she had it, so they could too. She was able to dispense advice and comfort from a place of experience; she was no hypocrite. Could Elle ever aspire to the same thing, achieve the same mantle?

Because no matter what Penny said, she knew her family did expect that. Elle would be the face of the hotel, and the rest of them would be the puppeteers behind the scene. Because of them, clean towels would magically appear, beds freshly made, garden perfectly manicured, and roast lamb and tiramisu would wow the palates of guests. But Elle would be expected to be its heart, its Anna.

She had thought she would be happy when they got the hotel back. She could see it taking shape, see the day ahead when it would appear to her finished and perfect, just as she had imagined.

But her heart still chafed, restless. It wasn't that she

wanted to leave Mulberry Bay and return to London. She knew that she was finished with her life there, and while she felt that a move back home was the right decision, she worried that she couldn't hold a candle to Anna or the amazing things her mother used to do. She could still throw herself into the running of the hotel while the others helped out, though. She loved spending more time with Ned, and watching Penny and Colin fall deeper in love, as sickeningly annoying as they sometimes were.

But something was missing, Elle knew. She could carve out a new life for herself in Mulberry Bay, but somehow she knew that it wouldn't quite fit.

One day, when the hotel renovations were almost complete, a high breeze blew over the bay, bringing relief to the early summer-sun-soaked little town. It was to bring guests too, though that couldn't have been predicted in the morning when Elle, Penny and Colin sat in the dining room to think over plans to get new reservations for the hotel, and soon.

'Well, we will have to advertise in all the national papers, of course,' said Penny. 'Something like: "Famous Historic hotel returned to former splendour". Should we do a special deal?'

'No, no "twenty per cent off" offers or free dinners,' said Elle. 'From the very beginning, people have to see this place as being aspirational, as being truly special,' she said. 'We can't seem cheap, or desperate.'

'I hate to point it out,' Colin mumbled, 'but we are some-what desperate.'

'Yes, yes, I know that,' said Elle irritably. 'But I just feel like if we get off on the wrong foot then things will never be completely right again. It has to be perfect.'

'Don't put so much pressure on things, Elle,' said Penny. 'You'll stress yourself out. It will be fine.'

'Oy!' shouted one of the construction workers from the entrance. 'There's someone here.'

They went to the dining-room window and peered out, mystified as to who could be arriving now. Not a guest at this early stage?

A woman was getting out of a smart green Toyota rental. 'Good God,' said Colin. 'It's my sister.'

Rob could barely lie still. All day it seemed that energy ran through him like a current, but he wasn't allowed to expend any of it. If he wanted to go for a walk, his mother or sister accompanied him, a steadying hand at his back. He wasn't allowed to read for long periods of time because it gave him headaches. His mother had a habit of ushering visitors away as soon as they had settled into a chair, lest they 'tire' him out. He was hardly able to bring a spoon to his mouth with-out his mother or sister rushing to help him. All in all, it was putting him in a foul mood.

He had appealed to the hospital staff to let him go home, but his doctor was having none of it. 'Another week, at least,' he said. 'We want those ribs completely mended. Plus, I imagine you will still be getting spells of dizziness, as well as migraines for a fair while yet. You won't be able to drive.'

So he was stuck here, with nothing to do but sit by the window and watch the car park below. *That* was allowed.

Ned Harte visited him, and so did Penny, with the ever-cheerful Colin, but they avoided talking too much about Elle. All Penny would say is that she was still very busy with the hotel. So he was stuck here, with his thoughts.

Obviously she didn't want to see him. She was so wrapped up in the hotel she could think of nothing else.

Maybe the sight of him lying in a hospital bed had scared her off, made her think of what it would be like to have to look after him. Oh, why did he keep torturing himself? Rob had no idea what she was thinking, none at all.

Colin's sister, Tricia, was a photographer. It was an artistic family. She was as garrulous as Colin, but with a sharper edge. Penny found her intimidating, not least because she had admitted that she had 'come to look into Colin's situation' and see if he couldn't be persuaded back to England.

Everything about her was long and sharp: long thin arms with pointy elbows, a long nose, and long tapered fingers with sharply filed nails. 'I just can't believe she's Colin's sister,' said Penny to Elle. 'She's so different to him.'

But Elle was less concerned with that, and more concerned with making use of Tricia. A photographer could be just what they needed.

*

'There's no way I'm going back to England,' said Colin to Tricia at breakfast the next morning. 'Look at this earthly paradise I'm surrounded by.' The generous sweep of his arm was punctuated by the shrill appeal of a power drill.

Tricia seemed unconvinced, but she was used to her brother's stubbornness. If he wanted to stay here, it was really no concern of hers. She had really only come over at her parent's wishes, to inspect the woman he had got himself involved with. She would do, Tricia supposed.

Elle cut into their conversation: 'You're a writer,' she said to Colin, 'and you're a photographer,' she said to Tricia. 'We could use the services of both.'

And so Tricia was installed in the hotel until it was ready to be photographed. Elle wondered if it was worth it, to have her stalking around with her camera all the time, poking into everything, but at least it kept her from getting in Penny's hair too much.

She spent a lot of time in the garden, and Elle had to admit, she photographed it to beautiful effect. She shot it in the morning, in the full sun and at dusk, which seemed to suit it best. In a couple of photos, Elle herself could be seen, standing pale against the trunk of a tree. 'I didn't even know you were there,' she exclaimed to Tricia.

'That's what a photographer does, my dear. We're very sneaky.'

Elle was annoyed that she had been so unaware of the photo being taken. Once again, her mind had been overrun with thoughts of Rob; what he was doing, how he was feeling and so on. It was infuriating to her that she couldn't stop thinking about him.

One evening, when she was sitting out in the garden, her father sought her out. She could almost always be found out here when she wasn't in the house.

'Why don't you just go and see the lad?' he said. 'Stop being so stubborn.'

'Am I that obvious?'

Ned nodded. 'And what's the harm? There's no rush, you'll be around for a while, and so will he. Stop treating everything with such seriousness, Elle. Take a leaf out of their book,' he said, nodding towards the house where Penny and Colin could be heard screeching with laughter about something.

'What else do you want from me, Dad?' Elle asked, feeling hurt.

'I want to see *both* of my daughters happy,' he said, emphatically.

Chapter 45

Elle had arranged for a piece about the hotel to go in *Places and Spaces,* a magazine that focused on luxury Irish weekend retreats in traditional surroundings.

Rob's mother brought it to him in the hospital. 'I thought you might be interested in this,' she said. 'I must say, the place is looking far superior, from a distance, at least. Amazing what a lick of paint can do. It's a pity you almost had to break your back over it, though.'

Rob knew that far more than a lick of paint had gone into the renovating of the hotel, and it broke his heart that his crew hadn't been involved in it. It was evident in the pictures that accompanied the article that the Bay Hotel was simply stunning. How they had managed it without ruining the original pieces and the stateliness of the old building, Rob didn't know.

But it was time to find out. Enough of this waiting around. Elle would have to see him, whether she liked it or not.

He feigned tiredness, and when his mother left, he slipped out of the room, pretending he was going for a walk. He'd had his mother bring him some clothes for when he was finally discharged next week, which he now carried in a bundle under his arm. Rob's heart beat so loudly he was afraid someone would hear it. This was the most exciting thing he had done in weeks.

The feature piece that accompanied the photos on the press release for the Bay Hotel was a little unorthodox, and this was remarked upon by a few people. It wasn't exactly a story, but it wasn't exactly an article, either.

The Bay Hotel in Mulberry Bay was constructed in 1883 by John Winterson, as an engagement gift for his bride-to-be. The building has stood through the ravages of history, and experienced a slide into disrepair and was facing almost certain destruction, only to be lovingly revived and restored by the Harte family.

Many guests have spent nights between its hallowed walls, and the people of the local community all have stories about what the Bay Hotel has meant to them over the many years it has stood watch over the town and the sea, like a protector.

Each visitor has felt the magic and romance that exists in the hotel's very foundations. Built for love, and reared on it ever since, the hotel retains the original feeling of devotion in which it was created, all of those years ago.

As you stroll into the entrance, the air is splintered with rainbows of colour from the stained glass window above the front door. The old sash windows, lovingly restored by a local glazier, are your first clue that the space you are walking into is more than a hotel; it is a sanctuary.

Common areas are large and luxurious, suffering from none of the stinginess of space suffered by modern hotels. The dining room has long been a much-loved feature of the hotel and following its remodelling, can claim this title more than ever.

Lit by lanterns that sit in alcoves on the walls, the room is host to large parties, wedding feasts, birthdays, as well as more intimate affairs. Stretching the length of the room is a breath-taking view of the sea. If you didn't know better, you might think it was a ship you were dining from.

The grand ballroom, site of some of the town's most famous celebrations, is truly something to behold. The walls are painted as a forest, the ceilings dimming to a star-studded sky reflected in the magnificent locally cut crystal glass chandelier.

All of the hotel's twelve guest-rooms possess an enchanting view, be it the Irish sea, with its ever-changing moods of serenity and wind tossed drama, or the gardens, whose colours change with each season. Should you happen to glance into the gardens after dark, you could be forgiven for thinking it is the haunt of fairies and nymphs.

At the end of a long day, hiking on the magnificent

sugarloaf mountain, strolling along the coastline or partaking of the town's many local delights, there is no better option than to retreat to the Bay Hotel, order a bottle of locally sourced wine to your room, and sink into the claw-footed bath.

This hotel is special in so many ways, too many to do justice to on paper. The most magical thing about the place needs to be experienced in order to be truly understood.

It is the feeling that it exists almost out of the realm. Home to modern amenities, yes, but spend a day here and you will feel the troubles and banalities of everyday life recede.

The Harte family, including the recently departed beloved matriarch Anna, instinctively know what is required of a hotel: charm, relaxation, luxury and pleasant company.

'Hmm … I think you might have laid it on a little thick, Colin,' Elle said, when the first press article came out. 'We can't be certain that everyone will find the same kind of experience here. Plus, it's different from Mum's day. I'm not her.'

'Don't worry about it,' said Colin. 'We open tomorrow and we're almost fully booked, aren't we? You can learn on the job.'

Chapter 46

On the eve of the Bay Hotel's official reopening, everything was perfect.

The kitchen was stocked with local produce, and a fresh delivery of bread, seafood and fruit was due to arrive that morning. Molly had been working on the menu for weeks, and they had all been sampling her creations. Ned was advising on the best wines to go with them.

The beds were all made up with fine linen from Suds Laundry, and stocked with big fluffy towels and robes. All the products in the bathrooms, the scented soaps, shampoos and bath oils, had been obtained from local perfumery Ocean Breeze, and fresh flowers in the bedrooms picked from the hotel gardens.

The entrance was exactly as Elle had envisioned it: liberated from its former pokiness, the hallway now opened right in front of the staircase, giving guests on the way to reception a peek at the old-style grandeur that awaited them. The reception area itself was fitted with a big oak desk, which Arthur and Wally Ryan had gifted them.

They couldn't have asked for better weather: the July day dawned with high blue skies, light breezes and the smell of salt from the sea. The garden was awash with colour. Birds sung there all day and the stream running through it calmed all who walked through.

Except Elle. On the momentous evening when all her hard work was about to come to fruition, she was hit with an attack of nerves so bad that she was unable to confide in anyone about it.

It was too frightening to talk about, she thought. Her fears threatened to overwhelm her. She didn't even acknowledge the feeling as 'nerves', she would have thought that was too weak a word. Instead she thought of it as a foreboding, a premonition of everything going wrong.

Why had she even considered taking on Anna's role? Her mother was born to this kind of thing. She had an innate understanding of people, whereas when Elle looked back at her own track history with the community in general, she could have hung her head and cried.

First there was Rob – a thousand times over she had failed to tell him how she really felt, and a thousand times over she had caused hurtful misunderstandings. Then there was Doug Grant, and the people of the town who had found her manner cold and patronising. And her poor sister who had all her life believed herself to be inferior, and Elle hadn't bothered to convince her otherwise.

Why did she think she could do this? With a sudden cold clarity, Elle realised that she couldn't. Her job here was done. There was no way she could calmly greet guests tomorrow. She was more likely to scream in their faces. She had to go. For the sake of the hotel and everyone she loved, she should just leave.

She got into the car without thinking. Annoyingly, Kaiser and Gruff, Rob's dogs, who followed her everywhere these days, got in too.

'Well, if you're coming with me,' she said, 'there's no telling where we'll end up.' The dogs didn't seem to be particularly bothered. Instead they put their faces through the open windows, tongues out, while the wind made grins of their mouths.

If Elle had been thinking clearly, or thinking at all, she might have recognised herself to be somewhat ridiculous at that moment. Here she was, running from something she had put more work into than anything in her life, with no spare clothes, very little money, and only half a tank of petrol.

For someone who usually prided herself on being a logical person, reason and logic had fled.

All she knew was she couldn't possibly do what was expected of her.

'It's a pity your sister couldn't stay any longer,' said Penny to Colin.

'Is it? I can't say I mind too much myself. I love my

sister but she does poke her nose into everything. An awful lot.'

'Does she? I hadn't really noticed,' Penny replied. She guessed these kind of white lies were OK when it came to the matter of her beloved's family. When Colin had fallen in love with her, he had taken her family on board too. And Elle and Ned weren't exactly what you would call run of the mill.

'Don't feign innocence. I know she drove you mad too, poking into every last detail of your life. She even made a list of potentially suitable locations for the wedding, when I told her we would absolutely be having it here.'

There were a few moments of silence as Penny continued to fold towels. Colin was stretched out on the sofa, having just come in from the garden.

'Wedding?' she enquired. 'Is Tricia getting married?'

He tut-tutted. 'Our wedding, of course.'

Penny looked up. '*Our* wedding?' she gasped, wide-eyed. 'But we've never even talked about anything like ...'

'Haven't we?' Colin said, rising from the couch and slapping his palm to his forehead. 'Do you mean to say I haven't even asked you yet? That must be why I'm still carrying this around.'

And he pulled a small box from his overalls.

Penny and Colin spent the afternoon of their engagement delivering towels to the bedrooms and putting finishing touches in the common areas.

But, at the same time, they couldn't have been happier.

*

Elle drove along the coast road in a haze. She knew this was where Rob had had his accident and could see the temporary barrier that had been put up where he had crashed through the rails.

She didn't want to think about Rob, though. He went round and round in her head with no resolution. She now had two reasons for being guilty: one, for causing his accident in the first place, and two, for not going to see him when he woke up. She wasn't sure why. That day when he'd first regained consciousness she'd immediately thought that wild horses couldn't keep her away from the hospital but then something – she wasn't sure what – prevented her from going over there. It was much easier to be around him when he was still unconscious, when he didn't have the power to crush her heart. Penny had called her childish for not going but she had paid no attention. Why did she keep making the same mistakes over and over again?

From the back seat, the dogs began to let out a series of low, ecstatic whines and barks. At first Elle thought they might have seen a cat or a badger in the ditch at the side of the road, but ahead of her in the haze of the summer heat, she could see a man unsteadily walking along the road.

'Idiot,' she said aloud. 'You could be killed, walking on a road like this.' But that was tourists for you.

The dogs continued to make a commotion and Elle thought maybe the man was hurt or dangerous, and that was why they were making such a fuss. She gave the guy a wide berth as she drove past, not wanting to startle him.

Then seconds later, she slammed on the brakes.

When Rob heard the car stop in front of him, he thought it must be someone from the hospital, coming to bring him back.

The truth was, he could barely lift his head from his chest. After so many weeks in bed, he was weak and not used to walking long distances. He cursed himself for having left the hospital in the midday sun. He walked towards the car, ready to go quietly. It wasn't until he got almost to the door that he recognised Ned Harte's old banged-up Ford. But it wasn't Ned driving, it was Elle.

For a full five minutes after Rob got into the car, there was pandemonium. The dogs threw themselves at him, both wanting to fit in his lap at once. In seconds, his face was covered in dog slobber.

'I know you won't believe it,' he told Elle, once things were calm enough for her to drive, 'but I've missed this.'

'Oh, I believe it,' she said. 'They've kind of adopted me since you were in hospital. I've got pretty attached to these two.'

'Where are you going?'

'Where are *you* going?' she countered.

Rob shook his head. He felt somehow that maybe now wasn't the time for a declaration of love. Elle looked stretched tight, ready to break.

'If you must know,' she sighed, 'I'm running away from my responsibilities.'

He raised an eyebrow. 'Sounds desperate.'

'It is. You've got no idea. There's no way I can go through with tomorrow. I just can't do what everyone wants me to do.'

He didn't say anything to that either, though he knew unequivocally that she was wrong. 'Let's drive right down the coast,' he suggested. 'Away from everything. If I get spotted by someone from the hospital, they'll want to bring me straight back.'

'Do you mean you've escaped?' Elle looked aghast.

'That's right,' he said grinning. 'They'll think you're an accomplice, so you better keep driving.'

Chapter 47

They didn't talk much as she drove. Rob just stroked the dogs and watched Elle. It was a relief, after all this time of not seeing her, to be able to watch her freely.

Her long pale hands gripped the steering wheel, the veins like blue lines on a map underneath her skin. Her hair fell in front of her face and she brushed it away. He wished he could reach out and touch it, to confirm that was what he had felt against his face when he was unconscious.

Eventually, when Rob confessed he was feeling weak with hunger, they drove back towards town and stopped at the chipper for sustenance. Then they drove to a lookout over the beach, one of their old haunts.

'This is heaven,' said Rob, launching into his battered cod. 'The first real food I've had in weeks. Good old Johnny Chips.'

When they were finished eating they went down onto the strand for a walk. The water was rougher at this part of the beach than up at the hotel and the shore stonier, and they could feel drops against their cheeks when the waves slammed onto the rocks. The dogs ran ahead and then hurried back just as quickly, as if they were afraid to let Rob out of their sight again.

'I'm sorry I didn't come and visit you, Rob,' she said eventually.

'But you did.'

She blushed. 'But that was ... it was different. I should have come and apologised to you when you were awake. It didn't do any use while you were sleeping.'

'Apologise?'

'For the roof,' she said. 'For working you so hard. It was my fault that you crashed your car.'

He laughed. 'That's why you want to apologise?'

She nodded. 'I feel so awful. It was my insistence that the roof be finished on time and anyone could see that you were working yourself to death.'

'Forget about it,' he said. 'It wasn't your fault.'

He felt cheated. All along he had nursed some small hope that Elle had come to him because she realised she loved him, but it was nothing of the sort. She just felt guilty about something that wasn't her fault at all.

They walked along in silence and he felt that once again they were haunted by misunderstandings. He tried again: 'Why are you running away, Elle?'

'I just can't do it,' she said after a pause. 'I could save the hotel for us and I could renovate it, but I can't do what

Mum did. I've got no way with people and that's what visitors come for – from near or far. It won't matter if we serve the best food, have the most beautiful rooms, the prettiest garden. I can't be as constant and wonderful as she was.'

'Has anyone actually said to you that you need to be the new Anna?'

'No, but it's expected, isn't it? My mother is the one who made the hotel a success. Without that special essence she brought to it, there's no point.'

He smiled again, and shook his head. Elle was one of the smartest people he knew, but she could be so stupid sometimes. But his heart lightened. Despite her worries, it sounded like she was planning on sticking around.

'Elle, your mother was an incredible person. But she wasn't perfect,' he reassured her. 'Even she had days when she wanted to pack it all in. I know for sure that there were days when she felt just like you do, that she couldn't paste on one more smile. But, that's part of being in business. Sometimes you just have to pretend a bit. Anna told me that sometimes she would pretend so well that she would forget she was even doing it, and all of a sudden she would be enjoying herself.'

The dogs were walking beside them now and Rob tossed a stick into the water for them to argue over. Some low clouds had formed in the sky, looking almost as though they wanted to join with the sea.

He continued: 'The hotel doesn't need someone exactly like your mum for it to be a success. You've already proved that you can do it. You already won everyone in this town over. Della and Jim think I'm a fool for ...' He broke off and then began again. 'The hotel needs you, Elle. You're smart, you're strong, and you know intuitively what a place like that needs. You held it back from the brink. And I know that you don't believe it, but you're also warm and funny and a thousand other wonderful things. Don't you see that Anna would be so proud of you? You don't need to *be* her. You can learn from your mother, but trust yourself, Elle. You've got everything the hotel needs.'

She thought for a while. 'Well, whether what you say is true or not, I've got no choice really. I have to go back.' She shrugged. 'I didn't bring any clothes with me.'

She might have sounded flippant, but the truth was that what Rob had said did make Elle feel better. It was silly, how her heart had begun to flip slowly in her chest when he started talking. Did he really think those things about her?

'What *were* you doing?' she said suddenly. 'When I caught you on the coast road, where on earth were you going?'

He shrugged. 'I was just heading to the hotel. To tell you that I love you.'

She stared at him for a second and then broke into a slow smile.

And as Elle brought her hands to Rob's face, and his face moved down to kiss her mouth, suddenly everything became perfectly clear and there were no misunderstandings between them, no misunderstandings at all.

*

On the car journey back to the hotel, they finally got to have the discussion Rob had wanted.

'But you said I was cold ...'

'You never even looked at me on the roof ...'

'I thought you were in love with Celeste ...'

And so on, until their throats were dry from talking so much. The truth was, they both enjoyed it. It was a relief to each to know that the past couple of months had been a result of mix-ups and confusion.

They had cared about each other the whole time.

'It's silly, really, when you think about it. How much time we've wasted.'

Rob agreed that it was, but he was way too happy to wish that it had happened any other way.

It was lucky that Elle and Rob had had that conversation, because over the next few weeks there was no time for it. The hotel was so busy that they were run off their feet.

All the things that Elle had thought would be a success were: the new entrance and reception rooms, the mix of home cooked and locally sourced cuisine, the garden, the stunning views.

There were a few other things, as well. Ned decided to host a barbecue on the beach every Friday night for the rest of the summer, and guests and townspeople alike loved it. A bonfire could often be seen, and the sounds of Beatles music heard from the Bay Hotel on Friday nights.

Colin, who had since moved in with Penny, began to give

lessons on both writing and gardening, sometimes one directly after the other, to the bemusement of guests wanting to learn the art of the novel, when he appeared in his overalls.

There were picnics, garden parties, afternoon teas, birthdays and proposals. All of these things contributed to the feeling once again that the Bay Hotel was more than just a place, it was somewhere where people's dreams were made a reality, as though there was someone especially skilled at bringing fantasy to life between her walls.

Elle didn't have a minute to second-guess her skills as a hostess; she was just thrown right in. She worked so hard, and talked to people so much, that one day she was surprised to find that she was not only enjoying herself, but also, she was good at it. Just like Rob had said.

When the hotel was full, he was Elle's resident meeter and greeter. He didn't seem to mind the vagueness of his job description and outside of his own business commitments was happy being general handyman, helping out in the kitchen and garden now and then, or working behind the bar at the bigger occasions. He was especially good at that, apart from his tendency to get involved in long discussions.

Ned watched Rob with pride. If only he himself had been that way when he and Anna started the hotel. So involved. His favourite moments were when they would all gather late at night in the dining room and chat for a while.

If only Anna could see them now. It was her hotel that had done it, that had brought them all together and Ned would never stop being thankful for it. She was here, though, he knew, looking at the faces of their two beautiful daughters.

And as long as the Bay Hotel still stood, his beloved Anna would live on.

Epilogue

Two short months after its successful re-opening, the Bay Hotel held its first wedding.

Elle was used to big events by now, but this particular bride was very exacting.

'Are you quite sure that the cake will be here on time?'

'For the thousandth time, yes. Also the peonies have arrived and they look wonderful. Not too white, but exactly the right shade of off-white. The bridesmaid has had a practice run in her new shoes and didn't fall over, the food looks perfect and I'm fairly sure that the groom will show up.'

Penny laughed. 'I'm being a bit over the top, aren't I?'

'Well, brides who own their own wedding venue are allowed to be extra demanding,' Elle compromised, 'but just for one day. And you look beautiful by the way.' Despite herself, she was a little over-awed by her sister's big day. It seemed the perfect antidote to all the stress and heartbreak their family had been through over the past while, and signalled a new beginning of sorts.

Penny had chosen the dress with the widest skirt she could find, her reasoning being: 'Well, I'm only going to do this once, aren't I?' It was comprised of ten layers of tulle material, covered in vintage lace. She did look stunning, even if she couldn't sit, could only perch and had to have two people holding the skirt up when she walked across the grass.

'What about you and Rob?' asked Penny, as they were waiting for the guests to fill the rows of seats in the garden. They were looking down from Penny's bedroom window.

'We might get married one day. After we've fought about it, misunderstood what the other one was trying to say and then made up all over again.'

'And you're happy, Elle?'

'Happy as the moon,' said Elle, insensibly. It was more like something Penny would say, but it was exactly how she felt. A kind of happiness that came from knowing that everything had come together, as she had only dreamed it would.

No matter what trials this family had faced over the years, she, Penny and Ned always had each other, and they would always have the hotel.

Penny and Colin were married in the garden at sunset, right in front of the sea.

It was dusk, so the fairy lights sparkled and the sun lent its last rays of warmth to the guests before they made their way inside to the ballroom. It was a night to be remembered by everyone in Mulberry Bay as one of the most successful occasions ever held at the hotel. The speeches were hilarious, there was dancing and singing and good conversation.

Once more, the hotel's walls shook with music and its rooms were full of people who were happy, in love, or simply content with the way things had turned out.

The next morning Elle walked alone from the beach back to the hotel, thinking about how different the place looked from when she had first arrived home after her beloved mother's death.

Not just the physical renovations that had been made, but the whole feeling of the place. Before, the hotel had been reeling from loss and the sadness and hopelessness that had gathered there after her death.

Much like the Harte family.

But now, it seemed to hold itself up straighter, its windows twinkling like laughing eyes and saying: I knew it would all turn out perfectly in the end.

Just like Anna herself might have said.

Acknowledgements

Huge thanks as always to the following people:

Lots of love and thanks to my husband Kevin, and family and friends.

To my wonderful editor Jo Dickinson and the brilliant S&S team for working so hard on my behalf. To my fabulous agent Sheila Crowley and all at Curtis Brown who look after me so well.

To booksellers all over the world who give my books such terrific support, and who are always welcoming whenever I pop in for a visit – thanks again.

To bloggers and book reviewers for being so enthusiastic about spreading the word, much appreciated.

Finally, a special thanks to all who buy and read my books; I'm so very grateful. Thanks too for your lovely messages of support through Twitter and Facebook and my website. I love hearing from you so please do keep in touch.

I very much hope you enjoy visiting Mulberry Bay.